SCOT
FREE

Greg Moriarty

First published in 2022 by Greg Moriarty

www.gregmoriarty.com

Copyright © Greg Moriarty 2022

ISBN 978-0-9943133-1-7

Printed in Australia by Ligare
Cover design by BookSmith Design
Text design by eggplant communications

A catalogue record for this book is available from the National Library of Australia

This is a work of fiction. The author created the characters, businesses and events from his imagination. If any characters resemble real people, it is entirely coincidental.

To my mother,

Nuala

And to the other amazing women in my family,

Jacintha, Dympna, Nadine,
Hayley and Jo

In memory of Nabela

CONTENTS

CHARACTERS

Housefriends	Production team	Viewers
Bow	Adolpha	Christy
Jay	Alan	Eleanor
Myra	Everton	Frank
Nicky	Todd	Teddy
Patty		
Rosa		
Saoirse		
Sonny		
Taran		
Walt		

Part 1

Peep show

1

Fifteen years ago

Anita's friend raised a hand and whispered, 'Wait. Not yet.'

Anita released the straw from her mouth. It skirted the rim of the tumbler. 'What now?' she asked. 'We can't keep stopping and starting. They'll be here any minute.'

With a gloved hand, her friend pointed to the back of the unit. 'I'll have to leave that way. Your key?'

'Shit. I thought you checked. In the tray by the sink.' She nodded to the side. 'Hurry.'

Her friend dashed between the bed and the video camera on its tripod, frantic footsteps echoing through the ground-floor unit. Anita hardly heard them for the blood that was pounding in her ears. Beside the bed, her daughter lay asleep in a pram. If only she could kiss her one last time. Anita's body – with no movement below the chest – would not comply. The camera kept guard at the end of the bed, where the mirror once stood.

But that piece of furniture had vanished long ago. Anita sniffed the liquid. Odourless.

'Got it.' Her friend came back into the room, walking sideways to navigate the furniture.

'Now rewind the tape. I don't want anyone but me in the footage – I don't even want the police to know if it was a man or woman who helped me. Quick. Or you'll need to swallow some too.'

Her friend stopped the tape, rewound it, started recording again and pressed the pause button. A nod. 'We're good.'

Without warning, three knocks at the front door, metres away, thundered like a wrecking ball in Anita's ears. Her throat constricted so fast she gasped. Every rap on the door pounded against their secret pact, sending a ferocious crack through their plans and splintering each detailed step.

Thud, thud, thud.

'Miss Lessing! We're from the Health Inspectorate. We've notified the police.'

In a flash, the colour disappeared from Anita's face, as if a chalky shroud had settled on her. 'They're here.'

'Whoever is with you must let us in,' a second voice shouted. This caused Anita's friend to flinch, bumping the camera to face the wall.

'Fuck.'

'God, they're here,' Anita repeated. Her lips strained to reach the tumbler, a mile away on the overbed table.

'Wait.' Fingers shaking, her friend repositioned the camera and checked that Anita was visible in the viewfinder.

'They'll wake Liv. I want her asleep. She mustn't hear this.' Her voice trembled.

'That's why I wanted to leave her in the –'

'No.' Anita opened her mouth wide to take in air, making

her parched tongue drier. 'She'll be here when I go.'

'Bloody hell, Anita. You're such a –'

'Keep your voice down. None of this would be happening if her father had any balls. Where is he?'

Another knock at the door spurred her helper into action. Rewind. Stop. Record.

'Anita! … Miss Lessing!' The first voice, back again, became more insistent and the banging more violent. 'We know you're in there. You mustn't do this.'

'You have no authority to do this to yourself,' the second voice called.

'None, Miss Lessing. None,' the first voice agreed.

From the corner of her eye, Anita caught sight of her baby stirring in the pram and, after an age, she got the thumbs-up from her friend. Her attention zoomed in on the tumbler and the demolition at the front door seemed to lose its ferocity. All she had to do was put her lips to the straw and drink. She'd done that a million times. But with a mouth as dry as an outback riverbed, there was no guarantee the liquid would work its way past the rocks in her throat. She tried using her dry tongue to wet dry lips. No luck. Swallowing was ten times harder and yielded the same result.

She watched her friend's hand hover over the pause button, as they'd rehearsed, fingers counting down and pointing to her.

Anita nodded.

There was no going back. All her planning, her thinking, her doubting was behind her. She confronted the camera. A stranger would think her tone measured, certain. She hoped her words would be fingers jabbing the chest of her future audience.

'My name is Anita Lessing. Anita Laura Lessing. I'm of sound mind. No one is making me do this. I'm doing it myself. It's the one thing I can do, the one thing I can still do. This cup.

Cyanide. Where I got it is nobody's business.' Her eyes found her friend. 'I am doing what is best for my little girl. That's the main thing. She'll be adopted into a good family, like I was. I don't want to be sick anymore. No more. This hateful illness –'

Outside, the voices were now shrieks. Anita could make out some of the words, 'illegal' and 'punishment'. In her bed, Anita laughed her last laugh. A harsh law on suicide was as meaningless to her as the name of the stranger who would remove and analyse her tumbler.

'All the doctors tell me the same thing. Persistent and unrelenting. You go slowly. I don't want to go slowly.'

Her teeth found the straw as she breathed loudly, her nostrils flaring. Carefully, her lips closed over the straw and she exhaled through her nose. She drank, watching the clear liquid travel up the straw. With the cup drained, she grimaced from the bitter taste and spluttered as though she'd drunk a gallon of the stuff.

'Gaarrl.'

Hands over ears, her friend tiptoed off to anonymity.

A rocket of heat tore through Anita's organs, scorching her from the inside out. She coughed and choked and gasped and gulped. By the time the water in her eyes reached her cheeks, it burned like steam. Her head shot back and forward as she contained her howls. No further movement came from her and the next eight minutes of footage captured the crown of her head. For those few who got to play back the gruesome scene, it would look like someone had pressed pause.

With the commotion at the front door waning, the room was host only to the baby's coos and the whirr of the camera.

Part 2

Show business

2

Present day

In her modern, well-fitted office, Adolpha Martin bobbed in a fencer's crouch and her blade sliced an invisible opponent. 'I want good news from that mouth of yours.'

Her deputy producer, Alan Coldbreath, was perched on the sofa edge with a tablet in his lap. On the days Adolpha fenced inside, his breathing remained shallow. He joked to himself that deflated opponents didn't pop. Some days, she used him for target practice. Others, they were on the same team and she'd fight the air. Like today. 'All ten received their letters. Walt's physician, Doctor Ellis, wants to speak to you. He insists.'

'No.'

'Right. We also had an odd message from Superintendent Carlisle, head of Barton Correctional Centre. He says we can collect any prisoner, except Bow.'

Adolpha stopped moving.

'That is downright odd. What's so special about her?'

'Nothing. Maybe they're having an affair.' Alan held his breath, knowing Adolpha could tire of her air opponent any second and turn on him. She whipped her blade through the air and Alan stole a breathe-while-you-can lungful. 'Logistics are also wondering why the glassware order for the opening party keeps changing. They've had a request for a hundred glass flutes, but we agreed the order would revert to plastic. For some reason, they think we now want glass again. I'm pretty sure the confusion is on their end, so I'll call them to confirm we want plastic.'

Adolpha's arm lashed to the right. 'No.' The tip of her foil dug into Alan's chest. Her thrust was so intense the pain arrived not at the surface but under his skin.

Alan, the opponent.

He pictured the protective gear that should have encased him, heard the slap of straps, felt the comfort of compression.

'When the flutes arrive, our response will be as follows.' Her voice flooded with exaggerated denial. '"We did not order glass flutes. Giving the housefriends access to a potential weapon? At the launch? What lunacy. Oh well, it's too late now. Glass, it is. But we'll be lodging a complaint."'

'A hapless contestant then pockets a flute and things move on?'

'Exactly.' Instead of patting his back, she jiggled the blade at his heart.

Alan tapped the screen and spoke, which was a way of making his point seem minor. 'Can you keep me informed of these plans, please? It's not good if the team sees me in the dark on such things.'

'Your leadership issues stem not from my actions, but from your missing backbone. You're spineless.'

'If my backbone and I stood up to you, we'd clash too often and the show would come to a standstill.'

'You know what your problem is?'

'I have a foil at my heart, held there by an Olympian?'

Her mouth turned up, little lines disrupting the smooth skin. 'You're funny at times. And you know the correct fencing term. Bravo. You got hurt last time because you moved. See? Hold still and it's safe.' Withdrawing, she placed the blade in its makeshift stand, which was nothing more than a crude groove in her desk above which sat the guard and handle. She motioned for Alan to join her at the desk.

Team mates once more. His imaginary gear came off and he rubbed his chest.

'Your problem is you're weak,' she said. 'Your other problem is not seeing beyond your ski-jump nose.'

No amount of body armour would have saved him from that stab as the hit penetrated deep beneath the target area.

'Scot Free needs a spike in ratings,' she continued, unfazed, 'or we can forget next season. This time, we stay guarded and we manage everything. Our finale will go down in history as a defining moment in television under the Great Preservation. If we pull it off. And we will. It was an ingenious decision to host the launch party on opening night and in the house itself.'

'Absolutely. Your ideas are the best.'

'That alone will create a buzz. And we've invested too much in this season.' She leant back, ready to catch his reaction to the coming blow. 'I'm loath to dredge up the past, but seasons later, we still work under the shadow of season three.'

Alan played with his hair, which he treated like a security blanket. White patches at his temples and his salt-and-pepper stubble made him look older than forty-three, but a dollop of gel each morning gave his grey hair extra hold. He leaned over his screen to see his reflection and it soothed him.

Adolpha was still speaking. 'I know it's hard to face. You don't get to hear all the things I do. The board still uses that massacre against me when they threaten to shut us down. They grill me over why your head wasn't on the chopping block. "He approved Sergeant Major Blair," they say, "his name's on the paperwork." You lost them an entire season.'

'Must we?'

Adolpha laid a palm on the desk. 'I always support you. "He lives, eats and breathes this show," I say. I did you a huge favour.'

There was a pause. Alan scrolled through a screen that didn't need scrolling.

'I paid you back,' he said. As the words came out, he heard the weakness in his conciliatory tone.

'So you did. That's why this season's finale will seal the deal. Do this right and we've got three more seasons like that.' She lobbed a click of fingers his way.

'Yes, Adolpha.'

'Next. Tell me about Everton. He avoids me. He doesn't like me. But tell him he must keep me in the loop.'

'He's hard to locate. He's working around the clock, but it's going well apparently.'

'The single reason I keep that dickhead on is because of his technical skills. There are few people – very few men – I rely on, Alan. Unfortunately, Everton is one of them. I tolerate his rudeness, but he needs to watch it. You tell him that.'

On the desk, Alan placed a pile of colour photos, the ten housefriends for season six. Adolpha's fixed line rang.

'For goodness sake. What now?' She grabbed the phone. 'Yes? Doctor Ellis? Tell him to fuck off. Politely, please.'

Alan could hear her jaw grind behind red lips.

'Put him through then.' She covered the mouthpiece and

said, 'Walt's doctor, demanding we excuse him from the show.'

She removed her hand. Her voice was loud and fast. 'Adolpha Martin. Doctor, we are days from the launch. As you can guess, very busy.'

From the quilt of photos before her, she fished out the one of the doctor's patient. Walt's headshot gave little away, his bronzed, wrinkled skin concealing his poor health.

'I know he's on a kidney transplant waitlist.' Adolpha fell silent. 'He's first on the list? Wonderful news. But I am starting my show in five days with ten housefriends and it's too late to excuse any of them. Not one. If I scratch Walt, I'll have to remove his matching prisoner. Think ramifications, Doctor. As soon as you have a donor, call me and we'll send Walt home. But he will be at the opening.'

She pounded Walt's photo so hard the doctor would have heard through the phone. 'I need my ten starters. My viewers want ten.'

She ended the call.

'There's always one. Bring Walt in early. I don't trust that doctor. Now, what do we have here?' She spread out the glossy portraits. 'Lord, I'd forgotten how ugly they were this season. Don't attractive folk lose loved ones? After a long day at work, I'm in front of the screen, feet up, glass of vino and I've got to look at them?'

She snatched up a photo and brandished it at Alan. 'People will switch off.'

'We can get rid of him early.'

'Where's our star?' She fumbled around and took a photo in both hands. Her eyes were those of a curator studying the rarest of finds. 'Oh yes, oh yes. I can't wait.'

'What if it goes wrong?'

'If you screw up, I won't save you this time. Stay vigilant and make sure the clues are tighter than your arse.'

Alan clenched his butt cheeks.

He inhaled. 'We'll finalise the wording once we interview each of them. That's everything for now.' In his palm, he absently toyed with a dome paperweight housing a killer whale. Adolpha had returned with it from the Los Angeles Olympics instead of a medal.

With unblinking eyes, she addressed the subject of the photo. 'There's no way you're leaving my show alive. No. Way.'

She let the portrait slip to the desk. 'If this goes to plan, I'll die a happy woman.'

Alan put the heavy glass dome down.

'Like to smash someone's head in with that, would you? I'll have to keep a close watch on you.' She pushed the photos towards him. 'You've done well and you're not a complete screw-up after all. Let's leave it in the past, yeah? Don't kill me yet – we're more productive as a duo.' She tried drawing his gaze to the photo she had replaced on the desk, but he zipped his eyes away.

He stood up. 'I must get on.'

'Start collecting the lucky buggers. We've done so much preparation. You've gone above and beyond.'

Adolpha's deep laugh, bouncing low in her grubby throat, escorted Alan outside.

3

Christy sped around the unit gathering essentials. She tossed items onto the bed and watched Jay on the sofa in the middle of a video game. With the letter from the studio had come the daily rows. She packed a rucksack in the bedroom, argued and lost in the front room, then mumbled to herself and won in the hallway. Her black, burgundy-highlighted hair jiggled with her loud steps and her brown eyes glowed like a predator's.

'We have to run. We pack and we go. We hide for nine –' She imagined them camped at the edge of the Simpson Desert, where the yoga mat she was holding would come in handy for the delivery. There she was, counting chickens. But if damned chooks could have offspring, so could she.

'Nine days? I can't leave for –'

'Months,' she said, standing in the living room, her bum touching the screen. Baggy clothes on her small frame helped block Jay's view of the game.

'I can't leave. They'll find me.' Jay toppled sideways to see the screen.

She remembered the days when it was hard to stay annoyed with him, faced with his mousy two-day growth, dorky glasses and unkempt hair. Today was different. Not even his soft, innocent eyes could stop her getting worked up.

'Maybe the studio will find us. Maybe it won't. Maybe the police will stop us. Maybe they won't. Maybe we'll get through this' – she spaced her next words – 'maybe we won't.' She knew the message was too subtle for Jay to spot, obscured behind the video game, under the letter from the studio. For him to see something, it had to be in plain view. Like with his research job. On a slide, under a microscope.

'Anyway,' he said as he bumped his glasses up his nose, 'we're doing this for Harriet.'

Christy bristled at the 'that-was-that' in his tone and blocked his view again. Without shifting her heels, she threw the yoga mat into their bedroom. 'Who's "we"? You and your brother? Then send him.'

'My name's on the letter. What can I do?'

'Something useful. Stop playing video games, for a start. When we lost our second, and I wanted to try again, you told me not to get my hopes up.'

Jay sat upright.

Christy pointed at him. She hadn't finished and he needed to know. 'Yes, you said that to me within weeks of losing him.'

Him. Three miscarriages, each early in the first trimester before hospital scans had confirmed details, and she'd known the sex of all three. For sure, the first and third were girls, the second a boy.

'So, I'm telling you the same now.' She lowered her voice to mimic his. 'Don't get your hopes up. You'll only be disappointed because you won't get answers on that show. Forget revenge. You'll get yourself killed.'

'It's out of my hands. You know the consequences if we run.' Without leaving his seat, he made a clumsy attempt to reach for her, the game controller still in his grip. 'Besides, it's all about killing prisoners. The hunters rarely die. It's the criminals who get it in the neck.'

His calm words were no match for her punch. 'You're as good as dead. She's –'

'Christy, please. Harriet's only been gone weeks.'

'She got herself killed and now she's killed you.' Christy felt her rib cage relax. There. It was out.

Jay let the game controller tumble from his hand.

Christy continued. 'You need to hear this. Harriet was an addict. No, she didn't ask to be murdered, but now you're dragged into it. And don't make that face at me. You have responsibility here. To me. This weight you lug around for not being there the day she rang. Like travelling to Melbourne stopped you from saving her life. She died instantly. That's what the doctors said. You couldn't have saved her. You were hundreds of kilometres away in a lab.'

Jay held up a hand. 'Don't. I was fixing –'

'Her?'

'It. Fixing it. She was on the mend.'

'She died outside a shop in a random attack, probably drug-related. And you and your brother are trying to outdo each other in the caring stakes.' She could taste the resentment in her words. Of all her weapons that were hitting their target, a part of her wished she could withdraw those little knives. 'I've lost people too, remember. Your support is needed elsewhere. What do they tell passengers when a plane hits trouble? Fix your own mask before helping others.'

'I got called onto the show. I can't change that.'

'Notice anything?' she asked as she held her arms out to the sides. He looked her over and shrugged. 'It's time to focus on us. Not her, not the past. Us.'

'And that's where the money will come in handy. For us,' he said. 'Did you read the bit about prize money? It says millions.'

'Don't make this about money.' She took off into the spare room, the babies' room. She checked under the bed and in the cupboards. Nothing. She remembered to grab scissors from a drawer. To cut the cord. When she went back to the living room, Jay was on his feet, facing away and fiddling about by the shelves.

'Did you move the camping gear?' she asked. 'What are you doing?'

'Try the shed. But forget it. I can't run away.' He stepped back so she could see. 'There you go. A picture of Harriet and me. I don't think you've seen this one before. You can remember us when you watch the show.'

'I won't watch it.' She stood beside him, the closest they'd come to touching since getting out of bed. 'That was a photo of us you removed.'

'There are pictures of us everywhere.'

'It's not a decent one of her.'

'Yes, it is.' He placed the frame on the shelf and flicked the glass. 'That was us on Bondi Beach. In happier times, that's for sure.'

'I thought you looked happy enough in the one of us. We both did. I don't want a reminder of Harriet on the' – she caught Jay's side glance – 'a reminder she's no longer here.'

Jay pulled her to him. She took the longer route, resisting his tug for a second, then stopping against his torso. With the scissor blades facing away, she hugged him. Her fingers found the groove of his spine through his T-shirt.

'I hardly met her.' She exhaled loudly. 'When I see you take all this so calmly, my blood froths. Aren't you scared?'

He drew her to his chest and kissed her forehead. 'I'm terrified.' She heard the thuds of his heart and sensed her own. In a strange way, their shared thump-thump settled her. There was a chance she might still convince him to run.

'I want to share something with you,' he said.

'Oh?'

'It's to do with Harriet.'

Christy stifled a shriek. She felt herself expand in Jay's arms as she trapped the energy in her lungs. Damn it, she also had news. She'd vowed to share it with him once confirmation came from the hospital, but that blasted letter had arrived.

'There's something I want to tell you first and it's more important because it concerns us. I'm pregnant. Again.' Christy held still, and so did Jay.

'No, you're not.' He snorted a giggle. 'Nice try, Chris. Not even an invented pregnancy will save me from the show.'

Her cheeks caught fire before she could lift her head. She dug the handle end of the scissors into his lower back in a mock stabbing. Wriggling free from his grasp, she clomped to the bedroom doorway and hurled the scissors at the rucksack. She retraced her steps to the living room in time to catch Jay launching himself onto the sofa, like a teenager home from school.

'Start preparing lunch,' she said, heading to the garden. 'We're leaving after that.'

'Come back. I want to share my thing.'

She kicked the screen door open and cleared it, letting it slam shut behind her.

'You alright there? You've made your point,' Jay called from the sofa.

She almost flew down the path.

'A banging door gets your back up. But news that we're pregnant elicits a laugh.'

When she reached the shed at the back of the garden, she heard the doorbell. 'Get that. I'm out here doing the packing for two and the thinking for three.'

She skidded the shed door open, the cheap tin rattling in her grip.

'Christy!' Jay shouted from inside.

'What? Can't I step away for a minute?' From the unit, the clamour of furniture getting knocked around travelled to her. She abandoned her task and headed inside.

'Listen. I am indeed pregnant, even if you can't spot the loose clothes and the diet changes.' She arrived to an empty living room. Something was different about the place. The breeze. That draught only appeared on stifling nights when they slept with the front door open. 'Where are you? The reason I didn't tell you sooner is because I wanted to be sure. I couldn't bear to see that look –'

In the hall, she found the front door wide open. 'Jay?'

She rushed outside to catch a black van speeding off, but no sign of Jay. Her hands formed a futile megaphone to shout his name.

A window opened and a neighbour called down to her. 'They took him. Four of them. Was it to do with poor Harriet?'

Christy was shaking.

'Poor Harriet can go to hell!'

4

Bow sat in a chair near the door of Superintendent Carlisle's office. Hands on knees, she was an unobtrusive ball of baggy prison greens. She planted her gaze above Carlisle's bald head, where photographs of South Atlantic islands and seascapes adorned the walls. A bad energy sullied the room. Bow could hear the fizz of electricity shifting. Flies hurled themselves against the windows to escape.

Carlisle and his facility manager had recently argued or they were geared to start. The superintendent flipped the letter on his desk using his mobile phone, as though handling the sheet of paper would endorse its contents. In reality, few things in Barton Correctional Centre experienced Carlisle's touch. He tutted at his subordinate as if Paul had penned the letter. Ridges formed in Carlisle's brow, as defined as the folds in the page.

The echo of steel doors locking nearby stirred Carlisle from his silence.

'Bow, you remember the letter I mentioned? We've had a tip off.' He let her in on a secret. 'They're on their way.'

A yelp of delight shot up Bow's throat, nearly knocking her from the chair. She soldered her top teeth to the bottom row in time to trap it. Now the scene before her made sense, along with the pole that was Paul's spine and the creases in Carlisle's brow. She was witnessing the honesty that comes with controlled panic. Carlisle was fretting.

Her imagination went off leash. The office walls and perimeter of cabinets fell away and a view surged towards her. Miles of grass, trees, hills. Hills! She stood in the car park, where her limbs hung comfortably, liberated from the usual stiffness of arthritis. Her skin tingled under the sun until Carlisle's next words brought her back into the room.

'They're not taking her. What are my options? Go.'

'Sir, there are no options because the studio decides. She's our first contestant on the show and it won't look good if —'

'I know she's our first one, Paul. Don't tell me shit I already know. Explain to me how this program has so much bloody power.' Carlisle thumped the desk with a fist of sausage fingers.

'We could' – Paul paused – 'incapacitate her.'

'Have you got any idea what I will do to you if you lay a finger on her?'

A hushed profanity clipped the back of Bow's teeth. There were rumours of Carlisle threatening staff, but never in front of an inmate. She recognised the agony that took over Paul's expression. It was the unpleasantness of shame. Shame so deep it made a person hold their head everywhere but up.

'Right. Options,' Paul said. He looked at Bow mystified. He could have been hunting for proof that she truly could influence the tower of a boss filling the leather chair.

No way, he seemed to be saying.

Carlisle must have read Paul's expression, for he gestured to Bow with his phone. 'This woman is the reason three thousand inmates are calm, we can go about our jobs easily and Barton wins awards. Her horticultural skills mellow them. Understand?'

'Yet in all this time, not one visitor,' Paul almost whispered.

Carlisle tapped his mobile to his lower lip. 'What do I do if my star gardener dies on that show?'

'We'll get another. We can train someone,' Paul said.

'You've someone trustworthy in mind? Someone with the right know-how who'll keep their mouth shut?'

'Sir, with respect, the crops didn't die with the previous gardener.'

'They thrive with her.'

'We could send someone in her place. What with the closed courts, the relatives won't know any different.'

'We have someone who looks like her?'

Paul scanned the ceiling for names. 'Janice? She's the slow one. Blonde scraggly hair. Roughly the same size.'

Bow remembered one of the forty jobs she'd had on the outside. A factory worker monitoring products that trundled by on a conveyor belt, plucking inferior items from production. Paul's comment couldn't be allowed to sneak through. In her raspy voice, she spoke quietly but firmly. 'Janice is not slow. She is autistic. She is not in for murder.'

If Carlisle was surprised she'd trespassed on their conversation, he didn't let on.

Paul offered another name. 'Yates?'

'Yates? That one would let the cat –' Bow stopped.

'It sounds like you want to go on the show,' Carlisle said. He took on the tone of a parent wanting to dissuade a daughter – not a son – he was losing to independence. He could have said, 'If you move out of home, you'll break your mother's heart.'

'No, sir.' If these men would shut up for a second, they'd notice she wasn't clocking the letter. That's what 'couldn't care less' looked like.

'What are her chances of surviving?' Carlisle asked.

'Every season – almost every season – people survive. The show sends in ten people – five pairs. There's a convicted killer and a victim's relative.'

'I know that. We don't have time. What did I say about telling me –'

'Hear me out, sir. It's not a show about random killing. They can't attack just anyone. They're allowed to kill one person and there can only be four murders. If they kill the right person, they leave. Ten occupants are whittled down to eight to six to four to two. Rapidly.'

'Ten people, four murders. A sixty-per-cent chance of surviving. That's pretty good.' Having done the maths, Carlisle directed a rapid fire of encouraging nods at Bow. An oversized photo above his head stole her from the room. Tristan da Cunha, the remotest place on earth. Volcanic rock surrounded by formidable ocean.

Paul continued. 'Rules state the final two contestants cannot kill each other. That last prisoner goes free.'

'That cannot happen.' With one hand, Carlisle scrunched the letter into a ball and threw it at Paul. He caught it.

'She has to find the person sent to kill her,' said Paul. Their eyes went to Bow, the statue. 'Of course, the sooner the better because the longer she stays on the show, the bigger the drop in her sentence when she returns –'

Carlisle silenced him with a raised hand. 'You've got to act quickly, Bow. Understand? Get out as soon as you can. We'll honour whatever reduced sentence the show awards you. That's a promise.'

He dug a finger into his temple, then looked at Paul. 'We can't get her back if she wins?'

'New life. New name. New face. If they want it. They can even leave the country.'

Fireworks exploded under Bow's skin. A festival of sparks – blues, greens and reds.

'Scot Free has authority to let people cross international borders?' Carlisle groaned. 'Can't we give her a weapon?'

'They screen everyone.'

'That bloody studio. Can we find out who her hunter is?'

Paul shook his head. 'Hang on. They might reject her if she fails the drug testing. We could inject her with something. Something strong.'

'That will make me vulnerable,' Bow said, following it up with two short coughs. She couldn't overdo it. Sure, Carlisle was familiar enough with her smoker's cough, but he'd see through any attempt at weakness.

'She's right. Too risky.'

Paul said, 'You seem so keen to take part. Would you like to read the letter, Bow? Please read.'

He offered her the single sheet, its garish logo of a bleeding knife wound overshadowing the page. But it was the text itself that had most effect on her. Letters and words and paragraphs and reading. Bow froze. She noticed the sweaty palms and a chain response began. Her heart smashed at a speed that baggy prison garments couldn't conceal and the thumping turned her face red. Her red face made her palms leak more. Only her fingertips stayed touching her clothing – her way of reducing the tell-tale signs of sweaty hands. They'd be dried on the back of her knees later, once the audience was done looking.

'Enough,' Carlisle said.

'Silly me. I forgot. You don't know how. A complicating factor is the number of people you killed. We've got no way of knowing which relative of which victim will go on the show.'

'Enough, I said. You commented earlier about people surviving most seasons. Meaning what?'

'Season three. An army officer snapped one morning and killed the remaining contestants.'

'That rings a bell. Where is he now?'

'Dead. They electrocuted him live, shortly after his rampage ended.'

'In a chair?'

'No.' Paul chuckled. 'Poor sod, the first door handle he touched cooked him. Every inch of that place is rigged.'

Adrenaline shot though Bow. She brought her hands to her mouth and lifted her feet off the floor slightly. With her fingers at her nose, the dusty aroma of hemp filled her nostrils. She'd cultivated thousands of plants and smoked as many joints. Sniffing deeply brought on the tickle. Familiar. Intense. She went back to the calming image above Carlisle's head. Tristan da Cunha. A more tranquil island did not exist. Bow woke from her daydream to find Paul holding the office door open.

'Stop pretending to admire the photography and get to the greenhouse. You must leave everything in order. They'll be here soon.'

Bow clambered to her feet without looking at Carlisle.

'You'll just have to murder again, young lady,' Paul said. 'Not to worry. This time, there's only one person for you to kill.'

5

Myra batted flies away. She peered into the distance and blew hair off her weathered face. Any minute now. Ted from the pub acted as the communication centre of the town and if he said a black van with interstate plates was heading her way, then that's what would arrive. She told herself once more she was ready. Sure enough, the van came into view the minute it crossed the creek. Too far away for Myra to hear the engine, it shimmered in the afternoon heat. She hardly blinked watching it cut along the unsealed road that connected the farm to the highway.

Nearby, her teenage son serviced a tractor, having taken on the jobs his father had done before he left.

'Get inside,' she said. He mumbled a question but didn't move. 'Now. Underneath. Don't do anything silly.'

He scrambled away.

Raising a hedge of dust, the van stopped metres from her. The driver waved to her and opened his door a fraction. He would have known a weapon couldn't be too far off.

Myra latched the gate.

'We've come to take you to Sydney. My buddies are in the back. I'm getting out now.'

'Turn around and fuck off.' Without looking down, she reached for the rifle propped on the post and brought it to her chest. She trained the barrel and her fierce, steely eyes on his face.

'Don't do anything you'll regret. You know you can't stop this show. It's started.'

He stepped forward. Could he not see the gun? She found the lack of distress on his face unsettling. Beneath her T-shirt, she felt droplets of sweat slide down the curve of her back and she shivered.

'Leave, you hear me? Or I'll blow your head off.'

'Do you know what happens if we get hurt collecting contestants? There's the murder charge, of course. But that isn't the worst of it. Kate's killer goes free.' A shot of pain zapped air from Myra's lungs. He must have seen the rifle barrel lower. 'You didn't know that, did you? Yep, they walk.'

He nodded at the farmhouse and took another step. 'Anyone inside? We're not armed. We only carry weapons when we collect from prisons.'

He stopped a metre or so from the gate.

'Step back, arsehole.' Myra's mind was a flood of thoughts. Shuffling backwards would signal defeat and the men wouldn't get back to town if she took out the tyres and hopefully by now Adam was crouching in the windowless basement. She flicked the strand of hair off her face with a jolt of her head.

'You must miss Kate. How long ago was she killed?'

Slam! She shut off the pain.

'It's time.' He beckoned. 'Kate would want you to.'

'I'll be no good to you. There's no fight in me.'

He wagged his finger at the gun.

'I don't need revenge.' She tried with all her power to hold still, to not reveal the untruth. But her eye twitched once, only a fraction. Shit. His smile told her he caught her lie.

'Kate's killer will be with the others at the studio. You'll meet them. You'll have dinner with them, and when you discover who it is, you can snuff out their life, as they did your cherished daughter's.'

'Listen to what I tell you. I'm no good to you. Not anymore. I don't have the urge to —'

'You don't? That's a shame. Because I have a housefriend's outfit in the van. Someone must come back with us wearing it. Rules are rules. Where's Adam?'

'No.' Her voice climbed to a scream. She aimed and fired, and the driver's window smashed in. Smoke drifted in front of her face and she nudged sideways to see better. No flinching, no sweating, he walked to the van.

'You can take out the windows, but not the body work and not the wheels. If you hit the petrol tank, which is about here,' – his hand made circles on the bodywork – 'my men will go sky high, and they are not cheap.'

Myra heard the door on the far side of the van open, the men's footsteps scarpering. 'You're scaring my team. I've changed my mind. You're no good for the show. Bring me Adam.'

'He's not going with you. He's only a boy. Leave now.'

The man kicked the dusty ground and his tone became more aggressive. 'Kate's death needs to be avenged. But we need someone who can fight. If you've forgiven Kate's killer, you will die on that show. There's no point coming with us. Get me your son.'

Before Myra replied, the door of the house opened.

Adam stood with a rucksack on his back, like he was heading to a sleepover.

'Just you please, son. Leave the bag. We've got everything you need. You can change clothes on the way.'

'Back inside, Adam.' Myra lowered the weapon. 'I'll go.'

'No.' He kept his eyes on Adam. 'Look at this young man. Precisely what the show needs. You've raised a fighter.'

'Back off.' She lifted the rifle again. 'Adam, inside now.'

'I'll go, Mum.'

'Look at him. He's fit and he's willing to kill. That's priceless.'

Myra choked to catch her tears. She had one chance. One shot. Maximum disruption, minimum injury. She fired.

There was a clipped howl.

Clutching his thigh, Adam fell over. He gawked at his mother as the shock stole his breath. Blood seeped through his shorts and through his trembling fingers. In a flash, the Nikon in her mind clicked. Eggshell porch, bone-white boy, crimson patch. Seared and stored before she could look away.

'He's no good to you now,' Myra said, opening the gate and dropping the rifle.

Keeping a metre between them, the man ushered her to the van. 'We'll bring you back in no time. You will own this season, Myra. They're going to love you.'

'Call your uncle,' she said, without looking round at Adam. She placed her foot on the van's interior. 'No watching the show.'

6

The courtyard was teeming with prisoners. Basketballers made do with a soccer ball. A small gang lifted weights. Other men stood around in twos and threes. Smokes and murmurs and plans.

Taran sat in the shade at the wall, spindly legs extending out.

Even when seated, his remarkable height was obvious. Just as well, because there wasn't a soul nearby to lend perspective. His body ached, like after an assault. Although it hadn't happened yet, he lived as though that experience was around the next echoing corridor. Terrible nights, on edge when awake. His body seemed to have replaced oxygen and blood with cortisol and acid.

He tracked a lone cloud floating across the blue. Where other people might have seen an unrestrained puff of white, Taran thought it more trapped than he was. To live at the mercy of the winds was no existence.

From the gym area, the word 'forget' arrived on the stifling air. At least, that was how Taran interpreted it. Nice of the bodybuilders to encourage him to move on from his mistakes. Because when he wallowed, he could get so down or so worked up that he wanted to pass out. His last visitors had been two days ago. There was less tension and more conversation when they visited separately, but this week his parents and sister had arrived together. Demanding answers, interrupting each other. The pressure had magnified to head-bursting levels, affecting his vision and hearing. It sure made returning to his cell easier.

Oh, a spider.

Taran pounced. He lay prone and cupped his hands to make fortress walls. The creepy-crawly, the size of the clean nail on his little finger, had some climbing to do. It eventually reached the top of the skin cage and Taran shook it to the ground for another round of trap-and-escape. 'Come back here, fella. I won't hurt you.' The spider moved so fast that Taran had to wriggle along the ground to keep up. It darted over his fingers and skirted a section of scarred skin. A week ago, an inmate had knocked his hand against the oven wall and the welt was taking its time to go down. Taran filed it away mentally as an accident. No one treats a stranger that way on purpose.

'You won't judge me, will you?' he said to the spider. 'No, don't keep running off or I'll put on a magic show. I'll turn you into an insect.'

A silence engulfed the courtyard, like someone had wrenched down the volume. His skin prickled. His jaw hardened. He might look up to find thugs standing over him, set to teach him a lesson. Those words – all cliché and bluster – made him bellow. His laughter bounced off the walls. Teach him a lesson? Him? There wasn't a semester of schooling among the G-block inmates combined. Robbie, his previous cellmate, had thought James and Joyce were Taran's parents.

Taran lifted his gaze. At the other end of the courtyard, two good reasons not to smile were heading his way. With his hostage delicately trapped, he returned to the wall and dusted himself off with his free hand. The spider tickled his palm with the tiniest of movements. Taran wondered if oxygen would get through.

The guards stopped in unison three metres away. Then they spoke. One action at a time. One comment at a time. They aimed for a show of authority, but Taran twisted it into a sign of deference.

'Come on. Up you get.'

'You got visitors.'

'Again? I've got no news to share.'

'Up, Taran.'

'Not your family. Special visitors. Waiting at your cell.'

Taran's pulse kicked off and he nearly let go of the spider. People at his cell. That was strange: very-good strange or very-bad strange. He scanned the guards' faces for a clue. Nothing. Like a pair of empty billboards on the motorway.

'Up.'

'There's a good chap.'

Taran stood and a blast of heat bit into him. He stamped on the spot to loosen the grit from his trousers. He punched them clean using the knuckles of both hands and headed to the exit with the spider.

'Walk like a man and you'll fit in more.'

Taran's shoulders continued swinging.

'You're going to be on telly.'

Taran stopped. He felt his temperature tumble. Even his toes were icy. As cold as the shower block when the hot water packs it in. The fresh release of cortisol reached his tongue and he spat out metallic-tasting saliva.

'Keep moving.'

A violent shove from behind got him moving again. Taran squeezed his rigid fists tighter, felt the spider squish and cleaned his hand.

'Make friends, okay?'

'See you real soon.'

7

'They're here. Three fellas.' Elizabeth let the sheer curtain fall back and turned to Patty. In her clutches she bounced Señor Bones, her sister's mottled fox terrier. She made it look like he was celebrating Patty's departure with a cruel dance.

'You look splendid. Do us proud.' Elizabeth coughed. 'But why so much hairspray? No weapons, remember.'

'Give him to me,' Patty said.

'No. He has to get used to you being gone and you'll upset yourself if you cuddle him. I'll let them in.' At one notch below a skip, Elizabeth left the room.

'Have you come to take everything I own?' Patty said into her lapel, adjusting a brooch. If Elizabeth had heard, she would have popped her head around the corner and reminded Patty that she, too, had a share in the house.

Patty wore a brown suit and low heels, and crowning her outfit was thick, hoary hair. Her face needed little more than a dash of colour to the cheeks and lips as her eyes, fixed with natural sparkle, gave the impression she'd been made up professionally. Hers was a warm, inviting face, one that well hid how despondent she was. The asteroid spinning in her stomach was amassing carbon and ice. With heavy layer on heavy layer, it dragged her down. The letter. Elizabeth. The house. Señor Bones. When Patty imagined what her sister might get up to while she was not there, she had to steady herself against the furniture.

There were as many photos of the dog in the room as of Patty's late husband and son. Not casual pet shots. No lead-in-one-hand-mobile-phone-in-the-other amateur shadows. In each of the glossy snaps that hung from four walls, Señor Bones – who had come into Patty's life within days of her returning from a Spanish holiday – was posing. As was Patty.

Elizabeth led the men into the room. One of them carried a black suit bag bearing a red 'SF'. Another blocked the doorway. The third did all the talking. 'Patricia, we're here to take you in. You need to change into this. It's your size. Strict policy.'

'I'll go as I am.'

'Reporters will be waiting at the studio gates, and they can't know if we're transporting a hunter or a prisoner.'

'The cheek.' Her hand sought consolation in the silky coat of Señor Bones, but Elizabeth moved and Patty's reach fell short.

'It's not about you. It's the media. Don't keep the men waiting.'

'No earrings either. It was in the letter.'

'It was in the letter, he says.' Patty removed the gold pendants, an anniversary present from her son. She surveyed the room for where to store them, rubbing her bare earlobes. The jug on the bookshelf with the artificial pink heath would do.

Elizabeth extended her hand for the earrings. 'Hurry. They've got a schedule to follow.'

Patty elbowed her hand out of the way and deposited the jewellery in the jug. 'I'm keeping the brooch on.'

'No one enters the studio with any possessions. No exceptions,' the man said.

Patty's patience was running out, but she knew what she was up against. A subtle nod from Elizabeth gave her the okay. She held up two fingers and the suit bag with her made-to-measure travel wear was hooked over them. With leaden steps, she walked away. 'I understand not being allowed to take in my knitting, but this is absurd.'

Minutes later, she entered the front room in a cream suit and moccasins.

'Miami Vice. I like it,' Elizabeth said.

Patty marched over to her. 'Get up. You're not allowed to sit there. No one is. That was George's seat and you're the last person he'd want in it, I'll tell you that much. Why do you do this? Listen to me. While you're in my house, you feed him, you walk him, bin out, bin in, check the post. That's it. Change nothing. Touch nothing.'

Elizabeth spoke into the dog's ear. 'She's being mean to me, Bones.'

The dog showered her with licks so that Elizabeth battled to both smile and keep the dog's tongue out of her mouth. 'Look. Bones likes me.'

With one eye closed, she held still, giving Patty plenty of time to notice.

'That's not his name and you know it. I can appeal, can't I?' Patty asked.

'You can discuss that on the way,' Elizabeth said. 'Go.'

Patty went over to the man. 'I'm not able to chase people. Look at me. It's bad timing.' Her expression was as desperate as his was blank.

'Let's go,' he said.

Patty huffed and wriggled her shoulders to settle into the

new outfit. 'I can die in designer clothes, at least.' She leant in to Señor Bones and Elizabeth made a point of drawing away from Patty's stationary hair.

'No matter how much she annoys you, you mustn't nip her. Mummy loves you.' She squeezed her sister's elbow. 'Thanks, love. Keep the washing machine door open to dry the drum. I've filled the fridge with meals, and only one treat a day for him. If I come back and he's put on weight …'

8

Only one vehicle stood in the car park of remote Burranul Prison, and it was about to leave. A cover of sluggish cloud made the morning sultry, slowing the movements of the four people approaching the van. Three armed security guards had arrived an hour earlier. The driver traipsed around the front and got in, and the other men shadowed the female prisoner to the side door. One of the guards, whose height was in his favour but whose width was not, tapped a card on the security reader by the handle. The black door rolled open.

'Hands please, Nicola,' he said in a chummy tone. To remove her handcuffs, he crouched slightly. She raised her arms and turned away from his smile. The other guard merely watched her with steadfast eyes.

'It's Nicky,' she said.

At little over five feet, she was often the shortest person in any gathering. A puffed chest, spiked hair and abundant self-confidence bought her another couple of centimetres, but it was horizontal movement that made the difference. Nicky was a stepper. She rarely stood still, like she lived permanently on the edge of a dance floor. As she peered into the black leather interior, she shuffled from side to side.

In the back of the van two long seats faced each other, a metre apart. Nothing else. Tinted fixed windows darkened the interior even more. Where Nicky expected to see restraints, ordinary seatbelts hung idle. She got a hit of fresh citrus. Not at all like the overpowering smell of disinfectant that had coated her nostrils since she couldn't remember when. She caressed the seat that faced frontward. No surface in the prison was as smooth or as clean. She looked down at her new clothes, a foreign skin of a two-piece suit, and glanced at the men. Bewildering.

'No female prison guard to take me?'

'We're not prison guards. Get in,' Watchful said.

Anyone could see these men weren't prison guards. They were way too soft. She lifted her foot, now shod in a loose-fitting moccasin, and climbed up, ignoring the offer of a hand. The other moccasin stayed on the ground.

'Here you are, Nicky,' Chummy said. 'Get comfortable.'

As she sat down, the seat was so cool that she caught her breath. She slipped her fallen shoe back on, its canvas barely touching her skin. It was the kind of footwear that hampered running. Chummy and Watchful sat opposite her, their backs to the driver. She noticed the side door close automatically, or maybe the driver had pushed a button. Watchful reached for his seatbelt but didn't fasten it until Nicky buckled hers.

The sounds were hushed. Holsters and belts tinkling, seat leather shifting. That got drowned out as soon as the driver started the engine. Rock music blared from the radio and the four of them startled, making the van wobble. When the driver cut the music, Chummy turned to him.

'Jesus,' he said. His security card slipped from his pocket to the floor.

Nicky's pulse accelerated. She looked away so quickly she felt a muscle in her back tug. Clearing her throat, she covered the card with her foot and bounced her knees. So precious, so desired was the card that it felt thicker under her moccasin, like she was covering up a book. Blast her legs in the cream suit for standing out so much, as if a spotlight was trained on them.

Watchful scanned the interior. 'It's like solitary confinement on wheels.'

Nicky stared beyond him as the van moved off. Soon, up ahead, a thick steel gate opened to expel them from the prison grounds and they turned onto the highway. Too easy. Nicky's eyes glazed over and her heart knocked in her chest. 'Beautiful area,' she said. 'Ages since I saw this side of the wall.'

Both men looked out of the window briefly. She dragged her foot towards her, but the card didn't budge. Her foot slid out to cover it again. 'You're staring at me like you don't know how I got in here,' she said to Watchful.

'That's the brightest hair I've seen. I'm surprised they let you have dye in there.'

'It's natural.'

'What do you call that colour? Orange? Red?'

She wondered what would make him look away. 'As red as your dad's neck.'

It worked. A snuffled laugh came from the driver.

'Where are you taking me?' she asked. No answer. Nicky stepped her feet on the spot, bouncing her knees. Her right moccasin slipped off again. 'Dude, please.'

'To a television studio,' Chummy said. 'You're going to be famous. Sort of.'

'Famous for what?'

'For being hunted,' Watchful said.

She tensed her stomach muscles to steady her torso. Her lower body went to work. She scooped the card under her bare foot, her toes and sole affording it a better grip than the footwear. 'By an animal?'

'A human.'

'With a weapon? A gun?'

'Whatever they get their hands on.'

Her left foot curved to open the space between her arch and the moccasin material. 'On my own?'

'No.'

'Other women?'

'I saw women's names on the list,' Chummy said.

'List?'

'Ten of you.'

'How many are after me?'

She tilted the card so it leant against her shoe. One more flip and it would be safely inside.

'One.'

'Who is it?'

Watchful faced her. 'A relative of the person you slaughtered.'

The card fell flat.

'Fuck,' she said.

Nicky panted like an athlete. She needed a moment to catch her breath. It was tough work appearing relaxed while her legs laboured away. The arch of her left foot ached from the contortion. She was itching to lean forward and pick up the card. After a moment, her breathing settled enough for her to try again.

Watchful caught sight of her bouncing knees. 'Jeez, that's annoying. Sit still, would you? There's no need to walk to Sydney, you galah.'

'Small spaces,' she said.

'If this van gives you claustrophobia, wait till you see where we're going.'

'How do I survive?' she asked. Her edgy tone stemmed from the breathlessness.

'You kill that person.'

'Is that all?' She placed her hands on her knees, revealing eight letters tattooed at the bases of her fingers. H-A-R-D and C-E-L-L. Grubby ink on pasty skin. She twiddled her fingers.

'Dear me,' Watchful said. 'I've lost count of how many misspelled tattoos I've seen. If only you'd stayed in school.'

Nicky smiled at Chummy. 'I've lost count of how many people don't get subtle wordplay. They should've stayed in school.'

Watchful glared at her until she coughed in his direction. A silence filled the van. All three stared out watching the greenery speed past. Small patches of sky were poking through the grey clouds that kept the day dank and dense. Nicky waited until the road came straight. No point moving the card if the van had to navigate bends.

It was time for Operation Get-Card-In-Shoe to proceed.

'When it's over, do you take me back to Burranul in a van like this one?' she asked. Without looking at her, Chummy nodded.

'Or a hearse,' Watchful said.

She pressed down on one end of the card to angle it and managed to flip it up. That was step one. Next, she wedged it between her shod foot and her bare foot. Step two. If anything was going to knock the card over now, it was her damn pulse. Ferocious. 'Do they tell us which ones are the hunters?'

She raised the card horizontal with her toe but struggled to tuck it into the moccasin. Step thr – almost.

Chummy shook his head.

Nicky tutted at her unnecessary question. 'I'll know.'

Watchful gave her a puzzled look. 'How will you know?'

Hooking him with eye contact, she popped the card into her moccasin. Step three. In a second, the shoe was back on her foot. She exhaled loudly, like a confident smoker.

'I'm asking the questions.'

9

'I've raced tractors faster than this.'

They were doing eighty in an eighty zone about twenty kilometres from the Scot Free studios. Belt on, moccasins off, Sonny sat sideways to two security guards, his legs stretching along the seat. Sitting in that position shielded his scar from some attention. It was a ragged crescent that ran from the centre of his forehead through his left eyebrow, down the side of his eye, across his cheek, ending abruptly near his mouth. Despite the wound's age, it had managed to retain its redness.

Every minute or so, Sonny gave the seat a thump or rocked his chest in a wave. His body hummed. He recalled a similar feeling from decades earlier, off to see his favourite band in what he remembered as the world's largest stadium. Through the turnstiles, beer in his hand, music in his ears, ants in his runners, but the crowds moved so bloody slowly.

'Move it, driver.'

'Almost there, mate.'

The security guard opposite him checked his mobile. His colleague sat quietly beside him, arms folded.

Sonny looked through the heavy-tint window. Its airtight membrane bleached everything that passed by, the open country and bush aged and yellowed. Soon, the tree-lined motorway gave way to residential estates.

'I'm not one for cities, truth be told, but I'm looking forward to the break. Open spaces, me. I'll get back to a farming life one day, you know, living rough, away from it all.' He spoke with an index finger up his nose.

'Were you on the run?'

'Nah. Worked on the farm. Patrolled the lands. I got to chase off the duffers who stole livestock. On a good day, I'd catch the bastards and beat 'em up. That was one of the perks. I'd camp out and kill roos and rabbits to stay sane. Tell ya, that was living.'

'You killed one of the duffers?' the guard asked.

His colleague beside him shot him a look and signalled the button microphone above their heads that linked to the studio.

Almost imperceptibly, Sonny shook his head. The conversation vanished, as though tossed from the window onto the hard shoulder.

Later, the security guard smiled at Sonny. 'Not long now.'

'Thanks, mate. Tell you what, I did not expect the trip to be this much fun. It went crazy quick. Been great hanging with you fellas.' Despite the friendly tone, Sonny's tousled hair, stubble and disastrous teeth gave him a savage look. Not to mention the scar, which saw him sport a permanent scowl.

'Likewise. Good luck with the show. As I was saying, my wife loves it. She bets on who's matched with who. That's her favourite part, the huge prize money. I tell her she's got more chance of winning the lottery. She wants me to ask you lot some questions so she can win something. Each time, I tell her, "Stacy, the studio makes us sign an agreement not to ask questions."' He winked at Sonny.

'Stacy? Got a photo?'

The security guard cupped his hand over the mic. He leant forward, jiggling his eyebrows. His voice was saccharine and breathy. 'Go on. Who'd you kill?'

Sonny nodded. He shared a tale about a visit to a foreign beach. By the time he'd finished, the studio was directly ahead, a cluster of white buildings enclosed by a high metal fence. Reporters and cheering fans carried them through the checkpoint gates, which opened automatically. The van slowed to a roll as it covered the hundred metres or so to the building entrance, where three men stood waiting. As soon as the van stopped, the driver shot out and opened the side door. Only then did Sonny swing his legs off the seat.

'Always wait until the vehicle comes to a stop,' he said to the people outside as much as to the guards sitting opposite him.

Sonny sprang to the ground with his wrinkled outfit, flimsy moccasins and killer charm. He offered his hand to a grey-haired man in a suit who was flanked by two security guards.

'I'm Sonny. Who are you?'

Clutching a pack of cigarettes, the man tapped the tablet in his arm and directed his next words past Sonny. 'Housefriend Seven safely on the premises.'

'He's all yours, Alan,' the driver said.

Sonny spun round to address the guards he'd travelled with. He used both hands to give them a handshake. 'Promise me you'll watch the show.'

He poked a finger unnervingly close to the guard's face. 'Make sure Stacy votes for me.'

Once the van had taken the guards away, Sonny flashed his

blue eyes at Alan's cigarettes. 'Give us a smoke, buddy.'

Alan removed one from the pack, which he slipped back into his trouser pocket. He extended his arm, as did Sonny, and the cigarette passed between them. A reporter at the gates would later liken the interaction to that between God and Adam on the ceiling of the Sistine Chapel.

Sonny pretended to pat himself down. 'And a light? I left the matches back in my cell.'

An unsmiling guard lit the cigarette. Sonny smoked. He could see Alan glancing at his scar, so he swivelled around to take in his surroundings. Cheering supporters at the studio gates caught his attention and he waved back, lifting his heels. He turned to Alan.

'How about some food? I'm fucking starving.'

10

Alan faced the large screen in the darkened production suite and twirled a plastic letter opener. In the compact space, the video equipment seemed to huddle close, delivering soft-yet-crisp sound, as though invisible hands were cupping his ears. Twenty-four-seven stress was making his body throb. But it eased a tad as he stood re-watching a taped interview of yet another housefriend securely in his charge. She was being led through the legal formalities and checks the studio insisted on. Since arriving at the studio an hour ago, she hadn't whipped out a knife or lifted her clothing to reveal a bomb. Alan nodded to himself. No problems with the woman in the tape. A safe bet.

Sure, they did their research so the Scot Free team knew who was entering the show. Yet they never truly knew.

Todd, his assistant, paused the playback.

'What do I say if they ask a difficult question?' He was set to interview the next arrival later that day.

'Stop pressing pause and you'll find out. Stick to the script and bring it back to the documents they sign or the house rules. You'll have an earpiece, anyway.' Alan went to press the button to restart the tape.

'When do I get to do Scot's voice?' Todd asked.

'Not this season. You're good for face recognition tests and subliminals, but the voice privilege is only for senior staff.'

'Oh.' The solitary syllable chimed around them. 'Would you like to go on the show one day?'

'You will never get me in front of a camera. My place is undeniably behind it. Why, would you?' Alan stopped moving the letter opener, struck by the absurdity of his own question.

Todd became animated and raised his voice, making the suite appear to shrink. 'Oh dude. There's a question. Me and my mates always say we'd love to go in there, you know. But being this close to it brings home the terror.'

'I'm sure you and your mates are expendable. However, we set the bar high on other criteria. Like, are you watchable? Let's get back to this. Keep quiet.'

Behind them the door opened, letting in a shaft of brightness. Alan blinked away the sting, a ghoul's eyes scorched by the saintly light. Adolpha marched in holding a sheet of paper and took her place next to him.

'These are fine,' she said.

It was a list of clues they would drip-feed to the housefriends over the three weeks. Todd leant forward to take it, but Alan blocked him with the letter opener. Adolpha noticed the paused interview. 'Who's that?'

'The dangerous one,' Todd said. 'When they arrived to collect her, she shot her kid.'

Alan hit him with his plastic weapon. 'This is not her, dummy. You're referring to Myra, our farmer, who knows her way around guns. This woman here is the nurse, Saoirse, and she shouldn't go near firearms. Both white, middle-aged women. Both lost a daughter. But worlds apart by nature. Myra can look after herself, whereas Saoirse —' He pressed the pause button with the tip of the letter opener and a prayer-like silence fell over the three as the footage rolled again.

Saoirse was on her feet, flat against the wall, hands trapped behind her, with the interviewer sitting at a table next to a pile of papers. Her voice quavered so much that Alan thought at first something was wrong with the playback.

'I'm no good with secrets and anyone who knows me agrees,' she said. 'I talk. I'm Irish. I'm a talker. I married a talker. He's Greek. We're divorced now. Both of us talkers.'

Alan watched her blink constantly through bleary eyes, as if she was looking into a breeze. Each blink momentarily keeping the world at bay. Her face was pale and tormented, and the magnified image on the screen only heightened the trauma-taut wrinkles in her skin.

Next, the interviewer spoke. 'And that was how your daughter came to be in Greece?'

Saoirse darted over to him and sat down. Through the speakers, her voice came in gasps as though she were fighting for air.

'You're about her age. It's her younger brother's birthday in two weeks. He turns sixteen. You'll have to let me out for the party. I need to buy him a present. When your letter came telling me I had to be on the show, I hid it from my children. They still don't know where I am. My best friend has my phone and I made her promise to text them every day I'm in here. I told them I was going away. Which is for the best, isn't it?'

The interviewer tapped a cup of water with a pen. Saoirse examined its rim and peered inside. Only then did she take a drink. She stood up again, the camera recording each swift movement.

'She looks bossy and irritable,' Todd said.

'Wrong.' Alan pointed the letter opener at the screen. 'She can't concentrate because she's got a million things going on and can't process it all. And she's a parent. You don't know how to read the housefriends. That's why you won't voice Scot this season.'

Adolpha squinted and leant closer to the screen. 'I thought Saoirse was younger. How old is she? Mid-fifties?'

'Forty-five.'

'Oh, poor baby. It's taken a toll.'

They heard the interviewer asking Saoirse to remove her shoes.

'It's barefoot from now on. Studio policy.'

On tape, Saoirse paced the room. 'Is the place clean? Will the prisoners be clean? Can you tell them to shower?'

'They're usually pleased to have the facilities, and the house is brand spanking new,' the interviewer said.

Adolpha's eyes didn't leave the screen as the footage showed each of Saoirse's twitches. 'Is the aircon too cold in there? She's shivering.'

Alan shook his head. 'No, that's her.'

'Maybe we can give her a sedative,' Todd said.

'Shush.' Hands in fists, Adolpha knocked her knuckles in a deadened clap, her voice a whisper. 'She's perfect. Look. She's about to crack. She's got nothing.'

Saoirse now had both hands over her chest, seemingly coaxing her heart back into its cavity.

'Should she even be in here? On a show about murder?' Todd asked.

Adolpha glared at him. 'What?'

'Nothing.'

Alan turned to Todd with an angle of his head that conveyed a forceful *Would you shut up?*

'Scot Free is more than "a show about murder", kid,' Adolpha said. 'This woman represents the people, which includes your dumb family. Entirely devoid of security. This house is a metaphor for the dictatorship out there. We're so secure we're terrified. She's every adult who witnessed this country change under the Great Preservation. This wretch grew up with freedoms of speech, movement and association. The lot. Poor Saoirse couldn't be more scared. And when our viewers see her suffering, they'll feel it too.'

Alan's cheeks roasted. He looked away in case Adolpha felt the heat they had to be radiating.

'She might live,' Todd said.

Pressing into Alan, Adolpha reached beyond him and slapped Todd around the head. 'Twerp. She can't defend herself. She said as much not two minutes ago.'

The suite door swung open a second time and someone took a step inside. Alan caught the outline of a man with a scruffy beard, who instantly backed out and closed the door.

'Who was that?' Adolpha asked.

Alan pretended to be dazzled. 'I didn't see.'

'Everton!' Adolpha pulled out her mobile and dialled. Her diction was faultless. 'Hello, Everton. This is Adolpha. As you know, we are live in two days. Today is Wednesday and we have not spoken in a while.' She smiled as though he was in the room.

'I hope you are well and I look forward to seeing you soon. You have something to pass me. I am right, am I not? When you have a moment, please call me. You can ask one of your many colleagues where to find me. My contact details' – she raised her voice – 'have not changed in years.'

She hung up and yanked open the door. 'I'll find the arsehole myself.'

11

Rosa gorged on her reflection in the two-way mirror like it was breakfast. She swept up her frizzy hair, elbows high, and bunched it behind her head. A slight turn let her admire not only her tanned face, but her slender neck and jaw. She clamped her knees together. Her spine lifted. A couple of pouts and she was ready to speak again. Her voice, nasal and dramatic, gave her advanced English more power.

'Australian women would die for the lips like mine.'

Not only did she check herself, she also scanned her surroundings.

There were two chairs and a table facing the door. Todd was at one end of the table with a tablet and files. He was sweating so much that the pen in his shirt pocket had an outline. Rosa was next to him, with the camera over the door watching on.

'To answer your question, the only way to return to Brazil is by winning the show. If you leave the show before then, you go back to prison.'

'Don't remind me. I don't want to think of that place. Tell me how I win. To go home.'

Todd went over the general rules of the show, keeping his head down, reading notes.

'Look at me,' she said. He raised his gleaming head, damp hair at his temples, and she continued. 'Get this done and you'll look great.'

Rosa demonstrated the procedure on herself. She flattened the skin under each eye by drawing her fingers to the outer edge of both sockets. Todd instinctively opened his mouth to stretch his skin. 'Not much. Just a little tighten. Bit here, bit there. Don't overdo it.'

'This form for you to sign is the deed. If you die on the show, we are under no obligation ...'

Rosa watched his features move with each word he uttered.

'And this,' – she tapped the skin under her own jaw with the back of her hand – 'what's this called?'

Todd looked confused. Then he was taken aback. His hand came up and his cheeks reddened. 'Turkey neck?'

'That's right, turkey neck. *Obrigada*. Fix that and you'll feel amazing. I've helped so many people with the same procedure. It will show off the apple of Adam, make you more masculine.' She scraped the chair back and stood. 'See? I'm fifty and I look half my age.'

'What's so great about preserving skin?'

'Honey, look good on the outside, feel good on the inside. Trust me. You'll come out of surgery a different per–'

Every organ in Rosa's body seemed to shift one position to the left. She stiffened, but the wall of defence had risen too late. Todd flinched. Whoever was on the other side of the twoway probably did the same. She listened, but the room returned silence. How could a space crammed with that much discomfort and remorse remain so quiet?

'That was certainly true for one of your patients. They entered your clinic alive.'

Rosa's memory brought up difficult images. Each a punch in the gut. A botched procedure. A body that wouldn't wake. No matter how much she yelled. A forceful arrest. A trial that wouldn't end. No matter how much she bawled.

Head down, she resumed her seat next to Todd. This had to end. She looked up, hoping what showed on her face was something like a smile.

'It's all about feeling better in yourself.' She sat close and tapped his cheek. As she leaned back, she whipped the pen from his shirt pocket. 'Let's get this done.'

'Electronic signature,' Todd said.

She nodded, slipping the pen into her pocket and reaching for his tablet.

'Australians. Such hypocrites. You talk of sea and sun and beaches and the good life, but it's superficial. You eat at your desks and you worry your lives away. Laws, regulations and more laws. Do this, do that. Chasing your own home. Worse still. Homes. Plural. In my country, we're relaxed through and through, not only on the surface. You'll never be like us.'

Todd coughed and gathered his things. 'My pen, Rosa.'

She tutted, took it out and threw it into the corner.

'Take me to my room.'

12

Walt's prison was nothing more than the seat and chrome base he was sitting on and the footrest for his feet. In a small studio directly below where Rosa was giving Todd beauty tips, a camerawoman and her stylist were taping his promotional segment. His face was stiff from make-up that smelled of damp, dirty dog fur. Breathing anything but lightly made him want to vomit, and he could feel his poor nose cowering. He was reluctant to speak in case he spewed over the stylist.

It was obvious why they'd given him a stool and not a chair with a back. If he pulled away too much from the man who applied the touch-ups, he'd fall to the floor. He had to sit there and take it. And now his neck hurt from the stylist making him turn sideways and the camerawoman getting him to look ahead.

They knew all about him. So many questions. One after the other. His dead relative, his health problems, the pending kidney transplant. Tugging at him this way and that. But not with ropes. Like they'd scooped deep inside him and each taken an end of the longest, most delicate vein they could find to pull on for his attention. He was unravelling. Of the two, the camerawoman was furthest away from Walt. When she tugged on the vein, Walt imagined the floor splattered with blood.

'Over here,' the stylist said.

'No, face me,' the camerawoman said. 'We have to record that again.'

'Did I say something wrong?' Walt asked.

Up came a cotton pad to pat him dry, briefly blocking his view. 'Look this way, Walt,' the stylist said again.

'Face front, please,' the camerawoman said. 'Avoid mentioning your relative. We can edit it out later, but it's easier if you don't identify them.'

'Turn to me. Let's get rid of those beads of sweat. They are not your friend.' Walt could hardly feel the cotton make contact. It could have been down to the layers of make-up or the lightness of the man's touch.

Walt started to speak. 'I can't afford to –'

He stopped mid-sentence and shielded his face.

'Wow,' he said, almost to himself, his eyes glassing over. He knew not to touch his face. The stylist would gut him with the make-up brush if he even tried. He wanted to cover his ugly mouth, the mouth that usually came from crying. Chugging like a motor on a cold morning, his breathing came in gasps that were amplified around the studio.

'No tears. Don't you dare. Not until we're done.' The stylist wielded the cotton pad at him like it was a machete.

'I'm not crying.'

Wearing a look of indifference, the camerawoman peered from behind the camera. 'Let's get you ready to go again. Remember, this will be seen by millions of people. You have to give the right impression.'

She modelled a clenched-teeth grin by lifting the corners of her mouth with her index fingers. 'This is your chance for payback. Or maybe it's more about the money. What's the bigger motive for you? Money or revenge?'

'Turn to me,' the stylist said. 'How long have you been on the waiting list for a kidney?'

'Forever.' Walt tossed the word out like rubbish.

The stylist paused and seemed to weigh up the answer, deciding it made sense. 'Your generation always was more patient. Will you be okay with someone else's organ inside you?'

Walt saw his reflection in a mirror. A face too heavy to smile from the cement plastering his skin. His head and body appeared assembled from the flesh of two people. Above the neck, he sported a uniform, youthful, ruddy complexion. But the rest of him was a gaunt sixty-five-year-old frame of parchment skin. Blotchy and blanched. His oversized nose and sagging ears lent a rubbery look to a face that was topped with white hair cut to within millimetres of his skull.

'All set to start again? You can mention your nieces and nephew, but don't reveal your relationship with the parent.'

'Almost done.' *Dab, dab, dab.* 'How long does a kidney last?'

It seemed like the man was redoing the make-up as an excuse to pry. A tug on the vein. *Splat.*

From behind the camera, the woman got Walt's attention with a hand in the air. 'I'll ask you what you'll do with the prize money if you win. In the tens of millions. Can you imagine that now for me? Feel what it's like. All those zeros in your bank account, where the interest builds up quicker than you spend it.'

Before Walt could picture anything, before his insides could stir under the weight of the make-up, the next question came.

'Turn to me first. That's bad timing, isn't it?'

'That's an understatement. My life's at stake,' Walt said.

A loud gasp shot from the man. 'Damn.'

'What's up?' the camerawoman asked.

'Steak. He's reminded me. I forgot to defrost the steak. I've got friends coming over tonight too. I'll have to get something on the way home. Bugger.' He didn't so much as tug on Walt's bared vein as stand on it and dig in a heel. Walt tensed. If only the man handled him as delicately as he painted faces.

'It is not my day, what with my memory and your shiny skull.' He picked up a makeup brush.

'Face front, Walt. Bring one foot to the floor. It'll straighten your spine – that's it – and open you up. You want to connect with people. Give us a happy face.'

'If he wins first prize, he can buy several kidneys,' the makeup artist said. 'There you go. I saw your eyes flicker. You can't fool me. It's okay to smile.'

'Your brush went in my eye.'

'Face front, please Walt. Remember your nephew and nieces. You're doing this for the kids.'

Walt felt the man's brush tap his arm. 'You're not doing it for the kids. You're doing it for the kidneys.'

Tug.

Splat.

Part 3

Show time

13

Jay dug his toes into the lawn and gripped as many blades of grass as he could. His world was tumbling. He was a paper plane in a hurricane, a cloth in a washing machine. If only Christy could save him by leaning over and pressing pause. But this was no video game.

He scanned the scene like an Action Man doll. Only his eyes moved. All around, guests explored the location for four looming murders. An indoor living area to his right, a tended garden with flowerbeds where he stood, and a woodland to his left. Security guards patrolled the entrance to the party, a door in the garden wall that led to the studio and the outside world. Full-length glass windows comprised the entire external wall of the Scot Free house, looking down to its sunken interior, which heaved with socialites and sponsors.

This scene couldn't have been further from Jay's usual life. In the lab, he controlled the temperature of the specimens. He decided when the cell samples came out of the fridge. He chose which method of analysis the researchers would use. But at that moment, on the grass in the shade of the woodland's trees, the only thing he controlled was the tray of drinks he was balancing. He kept shifting it from hand to hand. Less from tired muscles, more from wanting to place something between him and the world, between him and the abyss.

Jay could hear the fans outside the studio. He imagined them crammed at the gates. Placards, costumes, air horns. Someone with a microphone was working up the crowd, sending their roars rolling towards him like ten-metre waves. If a distant horde could unsettle him that much, he could only imagine what the nine other occupants of the house might do. Chants of 'Scot!' cascaded around him, and he could make out the familiar promo – 'Four murders. Three weeks. Two jackpots. One killer goes scot free.'

A bolt of energy coursed through him. His toes latched onto the grass even more tightly. Flickering in the treetops caught his eye. Light beams at the front of the studio were catching the leaves. A fugitive could well have escaped. Jay's sense of unease grew.

But he had a goal. He'd done some planning. Take as much control as he could. Control the environment, control the conversation, control the outcome. He took a few deep breaths. Through the milling guests, he spotted a woman and a man chatting on a stone bench. They were dressed like him, fresh white T-shirts and form-fitting navy suits. Guessing they were also hunters, he swallowed and headed over to them.

The man saw Jay approaching and moved his foot from the bed of gardenias.

Jay read the name tags sewn into their suits and introduced himself. Patty laid a hand on his free arm, bringing him into the conversation. 'Walt thinks all these cameras around us are already recording. I'm not so sure.'

'Hard to say,' Jay said.

'I was telling Walt I had to leave my dog at home. It broke my heart. He could've played on the grass here. We'd all enjoy that, the viewers at home included.'

Disappearing sunlight revealed a yellow tinge to Walt's skin. He pointed behind Jay. 'What's back there?'

Jay could tell without looking that Walt was signalling to the woodland beyond the garden, with its three pathways between the hedgerows of lilly pilly trees. He dropped his gaze. A champagne flute was in the flowerbed, jutting out from under the leaves.

'How did that get there?' Jay picked the glass up. 'Not the tidiest bunch, are they?'

'I wondered where that had got to,' Walt said. He grabbed the flute and placed it on his own tray. 'Thank you, Jay. I can see you're going to be a big help around the place.'

Walt heaved himself to his feet with a grunt. 'Right. Back to it.'

Jay wondered what on earth he had said to make Walt walk away.

'There you are with your angelic face and fancy glasses, making enemies already,' Patty said. 'We must stick together.' She followed Walt into the house.

Jay watched her go as the abyss reappeared. Alone again. Well played, idiot. He turned to see another man dressed like him a few metres away. Gangly frame, soft face, slick hair. He held Jay's gaze for a few moments. Taran, his name tag read. He carried a tray of canapés, which a man and woman were dithering over.

Jay nodded a hello and spoke quietly. 'You're a hunter, right? Like me. We have to stick together.' Patty's words came in handy. 'You look like a hunter. Not a –'

He stopped. Saying the word 'killer' seemed sinful.

'I can't decide on the lobster or the pâté,' the man said to the woman. 'Excuse me. What's in the pâté? Duck or goose?'

Taran's face changed. 'Who gives a shit?'

Before the guests could choose, he swiped the tray away. 'Ungrateful sods,' he said, giving Jay his back and presenting the tray to other guests.

Jay went to touch Taran's arm, but loud swearing caught his attention.

'Fuck me. This is palatial!' A male voice behind him. Jay turned and watched the man climb three steps to the grass, wobble and right himself. His face was decorated with a scar curved like the east coast of Australia. 'Come 'ere if youse want some food,' the man shouted as he took in his surroundings. Jay saw his name tag. Sonny.

Jay followed Sonny's eyeline. There was nothing special about the garden. Frangipanis on both sides of the lawn, shiny rubber plants and rows of gardenias with their sweet fragrance. Pleasant enough, but a stretch to consider it regal.

Jay looked Sonny over. He was sure he had met his first murderer. Jay's thoughts went immediately to Harriet. But equally fast, he cast the memory of his dead sister from his mind. Merely thinking about her might splash her name across his face. If he was to survive, that name had to stay buried.

Jay woke from his thoughts to see Sonny shift his tray of food to one hand and step over to a couple of women. Sonny seemed to single one of them out. He rubbed her backside, causing her to yelp and lurch forward.

Jay swore. He rushed over to them and gave Sonny a hard shove. 'Watch your bloody hands.'

The woman righted herself with a tug of her suit jacket.

'This fool assaulted me.' Her flushed cheeks betrayed the quick recovery as a front.

'It's a nice butt, lady.'

'Now he's defending his actions. Good lord,' she said. 'We didn't bring you here to sexually assault people. You've been stealing drinks. How many have you had?'

'Calm your beans, lady. Couple of beers is all.'

'Alan, are you there? It's me, Adolpha.'

Jay looked behind him expecting to see the man she was talking to. But the three of them were alone now as everyone else had moved away. Jay caught sight of her earpiece. She was talking to someone in the studio. She didn't blink as she waited for a response in her ear.

'Let's look at Sonny leaving the show early. He mustn't be there for the grand finale. No prize for this one.'

She peered at him down her nose and held his gaze as she spoke into the earpiece. 'One more thing, Alan. I want him to lose his right hand. He only uses it to assault women. He has form there.'

Sonny swayed lightly, like a metronome with dying batteries. 'Who the fuck are you?'

'I'll tell you who I am,' she said. Her body came forward an inch, like she was about to share a secret. Jay found himself cocking an ear to make sure he heard it. She spoke to Sonny but her eyes moved between the two of them.

'I'm your executioner.'

14

Inside the Scot Free house, which wasn't actually a house but merely a decorated studio space, the chatter was deafening. With a living area contained within bare walls, glass doors and marble flooring, voices and words and echoes bounced from spot to spot in search of a resting place.

From the marble kitchen island, Bow surveyed the open area she would soon brave. A quilt of heads and champagne glasses stretched from the kitchen to the dining table and beyond to the sofas and beanbags. Beside the table, a set of steps led up to decking and a hot tub, and this was the only free space she could see. Even the hot tub accommodated a ring of visitors dotted around the tiled ledge. From there, guests headed into the garden, while those who'd been outdoors squeezed inside. It was aircon cool, but Bow was feeling the heat. She found the crowd suffocating.

This space was positively tiny compared to Barton Correctional Centre. Barton's greenhouse was bigger than this whole place. She had Superintendent Carlisle to thank for that investment. Today was her fifth day away from the place. Five days without pot and her arthritis was getting worse. Her pain switched between stiffness in a wrist or a finger to total discomfort. Walking barefooted on marble, although cooling, wasn't helping her joints. And while she should've been glad to escape the weight of prison clothes, she felt almost naked in the light, fitted outfit she now wore. No pot, no oversized prison-issue overalls to hide beneath. She shoved one hand up the arm of her jacket and splayed her fingers. Worth satisfying herself that it wasn't see-through. It sure felt like it. The heat of claustrophobia combined with the desire to shrink was making her queasy. She was unlikely to find a hiding spot in here. Her thumping heart would no doubt be a talking point for home viewers.

'What's your problem?' Myra filled the long-stem flutes on Bow's tray. She looked like she wanted to shake Bow until she confessed her crime. Every inch of her, intense. Nothing like the other contestants who had greeted Bow. 'I've been watching you and I –'

'Hurry up. I've got people waiting.' Bow nodded to a guest who was waving an empty glass metres away.

'I'm here for my child's killer. Are you a hunter or target?' Myra grabbed Bow's wrist. 'Tell me.'

Bow jumped at the contact. Bzzz! It was like leaning on one of the prison fences. She hadn't been touched in ages. Neither the Barton guards nor the inmates handled her that way. Maybe a fist bump on the way to collect dessert. 'Hands off.'

'Look at me.' Myra pulled Bow close.

Something kept Bow's eyes from quite meeting hers. It could have been Myra's powerful grip. It could have been her set jaw. It could have been Bow's own sense of self that didn't quite measure up. It made meeting Myra's gaze seem like raising counterweights on pulleys. Bow drew away.

'I know what you are,' Myra said.

Bow sought sanctuary in the crowd. Elbows in, she eased her way around with the tray of drinks, snippets of banter bumping into her.

'Visit the bedrooms. Four hundred thread. Egyptian. What was Adolpha thinking?'

'Where are the housefriends? I've not seen hide nor hair of them. It starts soon.'

'I couldn't survive one night. This place is a walk-in coffin.'

'Have you downloaded the app yet? Betting's about to open.'

'I know it's highly illegal, but I would kill myself if I had to –'

'If Adolpha even hears you mention suicide you can forget consulting for her.'

Bow stopped at the opposite end of the living area, far from Myra. She stood against the wall, which was the casing for the hot tub a metre or so above her. Nearby, a woman hovered. Dressed like Bow but looking overwhelmed. A head that can't sit still on its neck, eyes trying to flee their sockets. Bow recognised the type. Life's daily challenges presented as intractable hurdles. She went over and stopped on the woman's right, away from her name tag. That came from years of experience managing her illiteracy. No reading necessary.

'It's all too hard. I can't hold this and balance the drinks,' the woman said as she stepped closer to Bow. Splashes of wine on the tray confirmed her fears.

'Not long now. I'm Bow.'

'Try pronouncing my name.' She turned to show Bow her name tag. 'I bet you can't. It's Irish.'

Bow's mouth dried instantly, like she'd smoked ten joints.

She mumbled at the string of unfamiliar shapes, like talking in her sleep. 'I give up.'

'Saoirse. It's pronounced "sir-sha".'

Bow repeated it. 'That's a unique name.'

'I'm a nurse. Obviously I'm not a waitress. I'll tell you something. People are sickening. Someone took a glass, went to drink from it and put it back. And I've seen guests touch food then choose something else. Disgusting.' Her eyes bulged. She took a long breath. 'All I can think of is my son's birthday coming up.'

Another parent in the house. First Myra, now Saoirse. A memory rose and exploded in Bow's head. Limbs in the lift. Bodies. She forced the image down, like yesterday's mashed potato.

Saoirse read Bow's tag. 'How did you say your name again? Was it "bow" as in bow tie or "bow" as in take a bow?'

Bow forced a half-laugh. 'Watch me.' Holding her tray up, she approached the guests and stood feet together. There was a distinct curve under Bow's trousers where her legs separated at the knees, which Saoirse wouldn't miss. Bow retraced her steps.

'Bow tie it is,' Saoirse said. She took a step back to indicate the corridor behind her. 'What's along –'

Her bare heel squashed a man's foot in his boat shoe.

'Ouch.' The man pushed Saoirse so roughly that she lost her balance. A glass of wine toppled from her tray. It smashed on the marble tiles and splashed their feet.

'Watch your step, stupid woman. You just about broke my toes.' After checking his foot, the man gave her another unprovoked shove, causing more glasses to topple.

Saoirse saved them from falling. She balanced on the sides of her feet to avoid cutting them on the large shards. 'Sorry. I'm not a –'

From nowhere, Rosa and Nicky appeared. Rosa stooped down to clear up the debris.

'I got it. Don't come close. Watch the toes.' Her Brazilian accent stood out more with her raised voice.

Nicky pushed the man in boat shoes to the wall. 'Leave her alone.' Standing in the wine, shielding Saoirse, she brandished her tattooed knuckles: *HARD CELL*.

People close by stopped what they were doing and stared. Shock settled on the man's face like cement. These were undoubtedly the first tattooed fists he'd ever met, and female ones to boot. 'Tell your colleague to go back to waiting school.'

'She's in bare feet. She can't have done that much damage. When a woman apologises to you, you shut your fucking mouth and move on.'

'Where the hell did Adolpha get these animals from?' the man said to his friend.

Nicky was growling. Her fist backed up, ready to strike. 'Don't you ever –'

Bow stood between them and held Nicky's arm. 'Let's take a step back. Help Saoirse behind you, please.'

At Bow's side, Rosa stood from clearing the broken glass. She raised her hand and called to the security guards. 'A mop, please. It's still not safe here.'

There was a faint splashing sound above their heads, but no one seemed to notice over the drama.

Bow showed Rosa the button to activate the wall vacuum. A powerful humming sound started. Shards of glass shot across the marble, as did the wine, and vanished up the chute. Bow felt the draught on her toes.

Nicky and Saoirse took the stairs to the internal decking. Bow offered the man the last drink on her tray. She turned to switch off the wall vacuum and found herself the only housefriend in the area.

Rosa had already disappeared. As quickly as the glass up the chute.

*

Christy dug at the cushion. One she had swung at Jay a thousand times. If a comfortable spot on the old sofa still existed, she could no longer find it. She realised pregnancy would affect her posture, but so soon? Maybe not being able to settle was in her head. She cradled her mobile and Jay's. There was a recently updated voice message on his that she listened to at least once a day. His calming voice, confident words promising to return the call. As well as Jay's phone, she had his gym gear and pillowcase with her, which she sniffed intermittently. His clothing smells were like the scent of sex, his pillow a reminder of their intimacy, the phone message placing him that bit closer.

Now the television was her only company. A presenter was broadcasting live on the studio forecourt. 'Welcome to death's door. Let's go inside and meet the Scot Free Six household,' she said, as the image onscreen changed to the interior of the studio home.

Christy turned up the volume and hardly blinked. She'd been expecting an empty space but the house, with its marble surfaces and bright lights, was hosting a party. Waiters moved around serving the guests. She noticed Jay in the background, a tray in his hand.

'There.'

Speaking aloud in the unit only amplified her isolation. Why was Jay carrying drinks? A chime sounded through the house. Christy heard a hush settle on the guests and they began leaving with their drinks. Security guards collected the abandoned glasses.

Inside the studio home, the housefriends stood as though glued in their places. Jay's voice came through the television.

'It's only us left.'

15

Jay climbed the steps to the decking, where Nicky and Saoirse were peering out to the garden and Rosa was showing the hot tub more interest than it deserved. Her fingers trailed in the water. Jay would later recall the look on her face as someone up to no good. Outside, the fading light warped the trees into faceless giants, hunched and advancing. Jay's awareness returned to the interior, where Saoirse was thanking Nicky for defending her.

'Any time. That prick needed to learn some manners.' Nicky stood on tiptoe, balancing on Saoirse's arm. 'By the looks of it, that section of wood stretches a fair bit. I didn't explore it earlier. How about now?'

Even though Saoirse lowered her voice, Jay could still hear her. 'Not in the dark. Tomorrow. You'll come with me, though? I'm not going through there alone.'

Nicky spotted Jay looking at them. His hello-smile was shut down with a cold stare. He turned away, moving to the top of the stairs, surveying the open space. What stood out was how little furniture it had. There were three beanbags, two sofas – each with two cushions – and a rectangular dining table with bench seats. Everything else was fixed, including the overhead cameras and speakers. No free-standing kitchen appliances were visible and even the television controls were built into the sofas. Touch screens peppered the interior walls, which – along with the floors and surfaces – were bare marble. Not one hard thing to throw or smash on someone's head. No weapons. A modern, clean space. Not threatening at all. Yet Jay had to grip the railing. His rushing pulse knew better. Nothing could unnerve quite like hidden danger.

Below him, Patty and Walt were at the dining table and Taran sat alone on a sofa. Bow and Myra both stood, well apart from each other. Nine people waiting for something to happen. Only Sonny, the troublemaker, was absent, along one of the two corridors.

With her foot across the bench, eyes heavy, Patty addressed the group.

'How are the ten of us meant to sit here for meals? This whole place is tiny. Even with the guests gone, it doesn't seem bigger. I thought there'd be rooms and places. To hide.'

Nicky called out. 'Don't worry. It empties fast apparently.'

'Dear god,' Patty said.

Without warning the speaker system activated, making Jay's shoulders tense.

'Good evening, housefriends. This is Scot and we are live.' It was a sexless, electronic, near-human voice. Neither the spacing of the words nor the intonation matched the sentiment of the message. 'Welcome to your temporary home. Season six has begun. Please avoid swearing.'

Jay blew kisses and waved to the cameras with both hands. No way could Christy miss that display.

'You are five hunters and five targets. Do not reveal personal information to your housefriends. Do not assume to know the identity of your match, for the consequences could be disastrous. You will get free time and tasks to complete. That includes designing your exit suit. Beyond the garden lies a wood. To protect you from the fans, the perimeter is electrified and monitored. For now, make dinner, relax and good night.' Scot disappeared.

Jay hesitated. It was hard to know if the silence was a good or bad sign. With the host having contacted them directly, everything seemed more real. Immediate. Unavoidable.

Into that haze walked Sonny. He pointed behind him at the corridor he had explored. 'Hunting knife's locked under a dome back there. You won't get it open. If I can't force it, no one fucking can.' Without pause, he elbowed the floor-to-ceiling mirror next to him, adding in a needless *kiai!* typical of martial arts films. 'Thought so. It's not glass. Safe as houses, unfortunately.' He removed his jacket, threw it to the floor and paraded in the acrylic mirror. Standing side-on in his tight T-shirt accentuated his muscles.

Rosa stood up at the hot tub ledge and brushed past Jay to descend the steps. Her blood-red lips came to a pout. 'I'm going in. I need to cool off.'

Sonny's face beamed from the other side of the room. 'A lovely lady shouldn't be on her own. I'll join ya.'

'Fuck off,' she said, pointing at him, her arm as straight as a blade. She skipped up the other corridor, towards the bedrooms and showers.

'Awff,' Jay said. He looked away.

Nicky did the opposite.

'Bad enough getting a knockback, mate' – she pointed at the cameras and cackled – 'but on national telly? Jesus. Not the best start to your broadcasting debut.' Saoirse tried to discourage

Nicky by tapping her hand. Nicky ignored her. 'If you keep fucking up like that, this will be heaps of fun.'

'Shut the fuck up, Shorty,' Sonny said.

Jay got everyone's attention with one loud clap. 'Right, spaghetti bolognese? Who's going to help me with dinner?'

'Not me. Serving drinks was exhausting and my feet are killing.'

Bow moved to the kitchen and pushed on a cupboard door. It opened to show a walk-in larder. His steps almost silent, Jay hurried down the stairs and stood behind Bow, propping the door open. Three walls of shelves held tin after tin and tub after tub. Soup, sauce, diced veg, rice, pasta, cereal, bread. Everything they would need. Tea, coffee, juice, soft drink, alcohol.

Bow's mouth fell open. She picked up plastic tubs to her right and left at random. Mayonnaise, chickpeas, pine nuts. 'I see the food,' she said to herself.

Jay was nodding. Bow must have come from prison. 'Not used to seeing such a range of food?'

She squealed and dropped a tub of pine nuts, which hit the floor without spilling. She returned it to the shelf. Her smile gone, she strode towards him.

'Don't creep up on me. Out of my bloody way.'

As an apology he raised his hand, which she punched.

16

The minute Jay and Bow began preparing dinner, Saoirse shot to the kitchen. 'Stop. First wash your hands. All of you.'

Walt came up behind her, waving her off. 'Leave us alone. Do you really think you're going to police our hygiene?'

'When you cook, yes.'

'Isn't it enough we have cameras filming our every move?'

She retreated a couple of steps and raised her voice. 'Everyone, promise me you'll wash your hands before you prepare meals. I'm not asking much.'

Jay took liquid soap from a dispenser and kept the tap running for Walt, who only rinsed his fingers.

In her seat at the table, Myra spun round to Saoirse and spoke in a commanding voice. 'You. How do I say your name? Saoirse, is it? I don't want you behind me. Stand where I can see you. Either move into the kitchen, or sit with us.'

Nicky, who was also now seated, tapped the bench for Saoirse to sit next to her. Looking like she was about to burst into tears, Saoirse scuttled to the table.

Jay noticed that Taran hadn't budged from the sofa. Sitting alone, he seemed to be mulling something over. Jay pulled out handfuls of firm plastic cutlery from a drawer and asked him to set ten places. Taran obliged and appeared at one end of the table, where half the housefriends gathered. He sent harmless knives and forks sprawling over the surface, which Patty paired. In no time, the table was set.

Next, Taran fetched a plastic bottle of ginger beer and two stacks of tumblers in assorted colours. 'There's no cold beer. Only this.'

Sonny held his hand out. 'Give me one of those.'

Taran shook both stacks. 'Pick a colour.'

An expression of bewilderment came over Sonny, but it didn't deter Taran. 'Which colour?'

'I suspect Sonny's come from prison. He strikes me as someone who doesn't give a shit about kitchenware,' Patty said.

Taran found a camera overhead and clutched the tumblers to his chest. He glanced at Patty's name tag. 'They've spelt your name wrong. With that mouth, it should be Potty.'

As quick as anything, Patty replied. 'They've misspelt your name too. It's missing the "Z". Me Patty, you Tarzan.' She giggled to the others and pointedly looked him up and down, focusing attention on his spindly arms and legs.

Taran indicated Sonny's pecs and biceps. 'We can't all be bodybuilders.' His head lowered. 'Listen, all of you.' His voice came strong. 'I'm not meant to be here. I'm innocent. You must promise to leave me alone.'

There were tuts from Patty and Myra, and even over the sizzle of onions Walt's moaning was audible.

'I'm serious.' Taran gulped. 'I wouldn't hurt a fly. I worked in a bank. You'll be killing an innocent man, and nobody wants that on their conscience.'

He held up the towers of cups. 'You're each getting your own tumbler. That way, no arguments. Saoirse, you'll be pleased to know we aren't sharing cups. Use it, wash it, don't take anyone else's. No fights.'

He faced Sonny and reordered the cups into one stack to bring the dark blue tumbler to the top. 'Here. It matches your eyes. Myra, take this one. Purple. A bold colour, purple.' Orange was next. 'Nicky. For your blazing hair. And Saoirse, you take red. That cold exterior doesn't fool me. Inside, there's a fiery molten core.'

From where Jay stood in the kitchen he sensed Bow and Walt, like him, were making less noise to hear Taran's mundane explanations. There were oddly reassuring.

'Patty, look this way.' She opened her eyes and Taran plonked the light blue tumbler before her.

Slap, slap. Footsteps announced Rosa's return along the corridor and she slowed when she came into view. She had swapped her outfit for a bikini. Her hair was tied up and she carried a towel over one arm.

'Whoa,' Sonny said, eyes bulging, too busy leering to see Nicky shaking her head.

Rosa held up her hand and wagged it. 'Ladies, I got good news. Only we have the access to the women's showers. They're hand-operated. Thanks, Scot.'

Sonny beat his chest with one hand like an infatuated cartoon character. 'Can we kill the other men first?'

'Good idea,' Nicky said, pouring ginger beer.

At Jay's side, Bow was crumbling stock cubes into the frying pan. 'We're making dinner for ten here.'

Rosa climbed the stairs and reclaimed her spot on the hot tub ledge. 'I'll do it tomorrow night. I want now to relax.'

'Why the rush to get in the tub?' Patty asked.

'Brazilians love the water.'

Patty tutted. 'She's half-naked. It's not right.'

'Leave her. A woman's getting into water. That's all,' Nicky said.

All of them paused and watched Rosa. She eased her legs into the tub as though giving her audience time to admire her frame. She leant forward over her knees, watching her feet underwater. Then she stared at the cameras.

Taran continued handing out cups. 'Walt, take the white one, for your silvery-grey hair. What's left of it. Bow' – his voice took on a dramatic, breathless tone as he placed the green tumbler down – 'let's honour those haunting emeralds.' Only three cups remained with him. Yellow, brown and pink.

'Mine?' Jay said.

Taran approached Jay and looked him up and down. 'Go like this.' Taran pulled his lips back to reveal gleaming teeth and Jay indulged him. He left a tumbler on the island and returned to the dining table.

'Hey, my teeth aren't yellow,' Jay said.

'White, they are not.'

'Running around with no clothes,' Patty said about Rosa, who was still sitting on the hot tub ledge. 'Get under the water and stop showing off.'

'No thanks. I'll just sit here and relax.' Rosa removed the two bands from her hair, parked them on her arm and shook out her brown frizz.

Walt chimed in, stirring the meat sauce. 'Ignore her, Patty. It's all for the cameras. To win public votes.'

'Stop discussing her,' Nicky said, standing up.

Taran called to Rosa. 'I'll leave the brown one here for you. To match your hair. That leaves me with –'

'No,' Myra said. She prodded the place that Rosa would occupy.

'But –'

'Give her the pink one. Rosa means pink. Right, Rosa?'

'Okay, okay. Bloody hell. Pink it is for Rosa.' He shrugged. His way to confirm how little it bothered him not to get the pink tumbler. Nicky angled the soft drink bottle and Taran held the brown cup out, arm rigid. 'Which feature of mine does brown signify?'

'Poke out your tongue,' Patty said. 'You told us you used to work in a bank.' She agitated her drink and winked at him. 'Now everyone knows their cup colour. No fighting.'

'She shouldn't even be in a bikini' – Walt said from the kitchen – 'at her age.'

Sonny shook his head. 'Don't listen to him, Rosa. You've got –'

A scraping sound signalled Nicky had had enough. She pushed the table away with such force some of their drinks spilled. She raced over to Walt, a good twenty-five centimetres taller than her, and jabbed a finger to his face.

He was the second man in as many hours to get a visit from Nicky's tattooed knuckles.

'Who the fuck are you to decide who wears a bikini?'

'Or when,' chimed in Saoirse from her seat.

'It's a family show,' Walt said, knocking Nicky's finger away. 'We've been here less than an hour and she's already flaunting it.'

'You're hardly the picture of health yourself.'

Walt leant down. 'What the hell does that mean?'

With the intensifying argument a distraction, Rosa submerged herself.

'Who does this fucker think he is to decide when someone's flaunting it?' Nicky held his gaze and addressed them all.

'Anyone else got a problem with Rosa going in there so soon, you come to me.'

Jay separated the pair. 'Keep it friendly tonight, eh? How about we finish dinner?'

Nicky removed her jacket. 'He needs to leave her alone.'

Jay spoke to Walt. 'Can we leave Rosa be, please? We need to focus on dinner. Scot didn't restrict hot tub times.'

Walt pointed up at Rosa. 'She's out now. Hardly worth getting in. Told you. All for attention.' Rosa wrung her hair out and flattened it down one shoulder, the hair bands still on her forearm.

'It's got nothing to do with you, I said.' Nicky's fist came up to Walt's chest. 'I'll smash you one.'

'Everyone cool it,' Jay said. 'Dinner's ready. Right, Bow?'

Clutching the towel around her, Rosa stole down the stairs with Sonny eyeing her glistening calves and the pronounced curve of her rear under the white cotton.

'Rosa to the chair.' From nowhere, Scot's voice boomed through the house. Her face dropped. They all watched on, Nicky's fist still ready to strike.

Rosa shouted, 'I'm dripping!'

'Rosa to the chair.' Scot's command came louder.

17

By the time Rosa reached the door, the goosebumps on her arms looked like sharp blisters. Carefully, she looked over her shoulder along the corridor. She'd almost lost her balance on the polished marble and she could slip any moment. A trail of wet spots glistened in the low light. She had to be at the right room. Through the door she could see a white chair, the only furniture, in the middle of the room. She touched the luminous panel and the door retreated into the wall. A wave of cooler air made her shiver and her goosebumps stiffened into razors. She took one slow step inside, where the light was noticeably lower, and the door closed silently behind her. Facing a screen in the wall, the tufted leather chair was perched on a low platform. Soft downlights along the perimeter of the ceiling added a ghostly tinge to the scene.

Rosa inched to the chair. Her bum found the seat edge. 'Hello?' She stayed clutching the towel to her. 'I want to change into proper clothes. It's cold.'

Scot's voice seemed to come from the screen. 'Show everyone at home what you collected from under the water.'

'What?'

'Your right forearm.'

She raised it. 'Just damp hairbands.'

'Underneath, Rosa. We know what you have tied there.'

She tutted and rotated her forearm outwards. Wedged against her skin, secured by two hairbands, was the broken stem of a champagne flute.

'It smashed in the party. We have evidence.'

The screen lit up with a bird's-eye view of footage from the party, showing Rosa lobbing the glass into the elevated hot tub while Nicky argued with the abusive man.

'I wanted a weapon.' She held up the jagged glass and rotated it. Pink and silver flashes came to life and died. 'Clever, no?'

'It's against the rules.'

'No harm done.' She left the flute stem in the curved arm rest and stood.

'Keep it. You'll need it.' Onscreen, a large knife appeared. Then the camera panned away to reveal it lay on a bed.

Rosa's whole body jolted. A bolt of cold shot along her spine. 'Whose room is that?'

'We've armed your hunter. It's only fair.'

'No, it's not. That's enormous. I don't want the glass stem anymore.'

'Take it. You don't stand a chance without it.'

She stared at the flute fragment with its jagged ends. 'Have you told the person with the knife who I am yet?'

'And spoil the fun?'

'Give me something bigger, Scot. That knife's the length of my forearm.'

*

Superintendent Frank Carlisle was watching the show for one reason. Bow. There was a gardening magazine on his lap, crossword started, which he drummed with a biro. Head back, he gulped his beer and spied on Eleanor, his wife.

Her feet, in tattered purple slippers, rested on the coffee table. Beside her, heavy-on-the-gin, splash of tonic. She was absorbed in the television, with all ten housefriends at the dining table, elbows touching.

'Look at Rosa. Trying to eat spaghetti with one hand and hide her weapon. And with a plastic fork. She'll be there all night.' Across the bottom of the screen whizzed the gambling odds, grabbing Eleanor's attention. She was a sucker for a reality show. When she looked at Frank, he turned back to the screen.

'Just as well I upgraded to the premium package,' she said. 'You'll want that.'

His head leant closer, but he said nothing. After their three decades of evenings watching television, with him in the armchair and her on the sofa, a simple head tilt worked as clearly as language. Upgrade?

'You pay extra, you see the murders.'

Frank tutted. 'Revolting.'

He shook the creases from the magazine pages and went back to his crossword.

'Of course. When you film the executions at work, that's different.' She sipped her gin. He went to respond, but she spoke over him and pointed at the screen. 'Rosa has been told they've armed her hunter. Thank god I upgraded this morning. Pandemonium could break out any minute and we're ready for it.'

Frank spoke calmly.

'No. Nothing's happening tonight. Didn't you see where the knife was? On a bed. They can't access their rooms until bedtime.'

She stared at him knowingly. 'Look at you, doodling there with your green pen. That's the same colour as Bow's tumbler, Bow's green thumbs. Where would I be without you?'

'Exactly. I saw you. Watching the odds flash up. If you're going to throw money away betting on the winner, you'll need to pay more attention.'

*

Jay's bedroom door closed and the tension fell away from him like discarded clothes. Head bowed, eyes shut, he stood and he breathed. Air in, air out. He opened his eyes to inspect the cubicle, which he was locked in until morning. It was tiny.

A king-sized single bed and an opaque floor-to-ceiling partition cordoning off a combined toilet and sink. Drawers in the bed base gave the impression everything was compact, closed in, compressed.

He stretched his hands out and was only centimetres shy of touching the walls on both sides. Checking for air flow he raised his hand, but it picked up nothing. As if playing in reverse, the tension he'd seen settle on the floor rose and landed on his chest. His breathing became as shallow as his mouth was dry. The room danced before him. He blinked several times to give the walls a chance to behave. Small spaces had never made him feel like this. He sat on the bed. His body felt a hundred years old. Out there with the others might be safer.

He looked around, pleading for the room to offer a shred of comfort.

A monitor near the door displayed the house rules.

You can
kill your match only
enter one name in the weapon dome
share your clues

You canot
take your own life
intervene in attacks
collude

He walked to the other side of the partition. Above the toilet was a mirror and a shelf with toiletries. He splashed cold water on his face without looking himself in the eye. Something there could set him off and he wasn't ready for where it might lead.

He bared his teeth.

Taran was wrong. They weren't that stained. He'd seen yellower. As he brushed them, he realised he'd normally be bumping hips with Christy right about now. Cleaning his teeth had never felt so lonely. He rinsed his mouth.

Yet he wasn't alone. There was the camera. Gateway to over twenty million viewers. He'd seen enough reality TV shows to know what appealed.

He flashed his teeth, running his tongue across the top row. A contented shopper in a mouthwash ad.

Three steps and he reached the bed. He lay down, the house rules in his periphery.

Mentally, he made his own list. Relatives and prisoners. He threw everyone in the prisoner column and moved them across if he suspected otherwise.

Relatives	**Prisoners**
Me	Sonny
Patty	Nicky
Walt	Taran
Saoirse	Bow
	Myra
	Rosa

Some of it was guesswork. He had a gut feeling about Patty and Walt. Saoirse was too hygienic to have come from prison. Taran had kindly disclosed that he was a target, although an innocent one. And there was no way Bow had joined the show as a free person. Jay remembered how she had looked at the food in the larder. For Sonny and Nicky? Well, they just looked like criminals, if he was honest. Her tattoos, his scar. Jay was less sure about Myra and Rosa. Definitely wait and see for those two.

Down to six suspects. Not bad for the first night. Now to find out which one of those murdered Harriet.

18

In the corridor, it felt good to escape the tiny bedroom. Cold, hard marble was nipping at Jay's feet, but at least there was lots of it. Space was good. Space meant safety. Space meant oxygen. He tiptoed towards the light. Sounds and smells confirmed he wasn't the first one up. Coffee and sugar hung in the air, cupboard doors snapped shut. He turned the corner into the open area, where sunlight was interrogating every inch.

'Oh, it's you,' Myra said.

'What's that supposed to mean?' Jay shielded his eyes as much from the comment as the light bouncing off the surfaces.

'There's coffee. But it's lukewarm. The machine cuts out at high temperature.' She continued looking in cupboards.

Jay's eyes took a moment to adjust. Everything looked unfamiliar again. It must have been the orange tinge to the sofas, the decking, the kitchen island. He signalled the table. 'Did you do this?' Bread, cereal, jams, butter, sugar, juice and milk ran the length of its centre. 'What are you looking for?'

'This.' Myra held up an extension cord. 'We can make toast at the table. There'll be ten of us out here soon.'

Seconds later, the cord whipped across the marble all the way from a wall socket in the kitchen to the end of the table, where the toaster waited. Myra handed Jay his yellow cup and leant against the island, sipping her drink. He poured himself some coffee and sat down.

Soon the others trickled out, with only Walt missing. Jay knew he was up because his white tumbler of tea sat there unfinished on the island.

Myra circled the table handing out the cups, then returned to her spot in the kitchen. She pulled a slice of buttered toast apart as she watched the others.

Sonny sipped orange juice and glared at her. He ripped at his toast with broken teeth and chewed noisily. 'What's your problem?'

'Don't mind me. I'm making sure everyone eats,' Myra said.

'Bullshit. Feels like prison with you on duty.'

'I wouldn't know,' Saoirse said, stirring her tea. She squirmed and turned away. 'Please close your mouth when you eat, Sonny. Please.'

'Impossible. Need to breathe.'

Saoirse stood and carried her breakfast to the sofa, where Nicky joined her.

For Jay, the seconds of silence that arrived felt like minutes with these strangers. He had work to do, identities to uncover. Every moment counted. Fresh pieces of toast popped up, making him jump. He took one and joined the conversation. 'I also have no idea what prison's like.'

Sonny huffed. 'Tell me something I don't know, Goody-fucken-two-shoes. I can always tell who's been inside.'

'Rubbish,' Jay said.

'True. But you learn quick enough.' Sonny considered his

audience. Five seated at the table, Myra on her feet, Saoirse and Nicky on the sofa. He coated his next piece of toast with marmalade and stabbed the plastic knife back into the margarine. 'Take Tarzan here.' Taran pursed his lips. 'He's quiet. Last night, did you see the way he queued up to bring his plate to the sink? Tells me he's used to waiting in line.'

'Interesting,' Jay said.

Bow leant around Taran. 'If you're so perceptive, you should know what Jay's up to.'

She looked away and missed Jay's headshake of denial.

At that moment, Walt shuffled in from the right corridor. 'Someone's taken the knife.'

Patty shrieked. 'So soon?'

Gasps and mumbles and fidgeting travelled around the group.

'Good morning, housefriends.'

Like flowers to the sun, their heads turned to the speakers.

'Scot!'

A chorus of hollers enveloped Jay. Their waving arms not unlike cries for help. It was too early in the day to be that loud.

Scot explained they would later do tasks in pairs, and a stillness came over the table as they listened for the name of their partner. Scot's final pairing was Jay with Saoirse, who gave him a fleeting look from the sofa.

The speakers went dead.

'Who was first awake?' Rosa asked, eating with one arm in her lap.

'If you're wondering who set the breakfast table, it was Myra,' Jay said. 'We should start a roster.'

With her back to the group, Myra busied herself at the sink.

'I will do dinner tonight,' Rosa said.

'I'll help you,' Sonny said. 'We'll show 'em how well convicts cook.'

Rosa moved away. 'Arsehole.'

Jay imagined the two lists he'd drawn up the night before. Rosa was a target after all. Her name stayed in the right column. Myra's name shifted left.

Five relatives. Five prisoners.

*

Hours later, Jay and Saoirse went to collect vegetables, following Scot's instructions and taking the leftmost of three paths into the woodland. Beyond the garden, the wood stretched for several hundred metres. Its start was marked by neat rows of lilly pillies that ran perpendicular to the house. But they lost their shape further in and soon gave way to a small clearing where fruit, salad and vegetables flourished in clumps.

'Listen to that.' Jay stole a moment's rest in the shade and massaged his lower back.

Saoirse tossed her snow peas into a tub and stepped closer. 'Who's there?' She was breathless.

'Not who, what.'

'I only hear birds.'

'Exactly. Birds being birds. Beautiful.' He listened for each sound. A solo tweet, a drumbeat, a call – too many to count. Those very birds could once have landed in his garden. He closed his eyes. Home came easy. Hanging out the washing to a background of chirping, Christy nearby sipping a cocktail and reading.

'They're so –'

'If they make too much noise, good luck hearing someone creep up on us.' Jay opened his eyes.

Saoirse clutched more handfuls of snow peas. 'These'll need a good wash once inside.' She emptied her hands.

'I don't think it will be hygiene that gets –'

'Are you a killer?'

Jay exhaled. 'Not yet.'

He stepped past their tub of vegetables to another bush. From under its heart-shaped leaves, he picked a tomato and sniffed it, the sweetness catching him off guard. 'This section is unruly. They haven't maintained these tomato bushes. See how the suckers have taken over.'

'The what?'

'Offshoots on tomato plants. Suckers. To manage tomatoes properly, you're meant to get rid of the suckers.'

Saoirse blew her nose, tucked the tissue up her sleeve and glanced around her. 'Who did you lose?' Her thoughts seemed as jumbled as the surrounding overgrowth.

'Someone very close to me. Someone who –'

'I lost my daughter. Waking each day and remembering it is the worst. That split second when my brain says, "Hey, don't forget. She's gone!" and pain shoots through me. Every limb.' She joined Jay at the tomato bush, where she wrestled with the vine, pulling on two tomatoes. 'Argh. I can't do this. I can't stop shaking.'

Both tomatoes split open, their entrails reddening her fingers.

'Who's got it? Do you have the knife?'

Jay wiped Saoirse's hands clean and held her wrists. 'Breathe deeply. It will calm you. No, I don't have it.'

He recognised the flickering and insecurity in her eyes. Like Harriet, with her fretful glances and twitching limbs. Saoirse nodded that she was feeling better. 'Slow down and concentrate. Watch. Hands empty, grab one tomato at a time and twist. Don't pull.'

'You don't know what it's like to lose a child.'

'Erm, I –'

'And now this.' She waved her hand. 'It's a nightmare.'

'We'll look after you.'

Her gaze fell. 'That's a full-time role.'

Jay watched a tomato roll off the tub for the third time. 'This needs to go back to the house. Would you like to go?'

Saoirse look mortified. 'I'm not walking through there alone.'

She glanced around at the lilly pillies that formed a colossal green fortress.

'I think the others are busy. We're safe.'

'Come with me?'

Jay picked up the tub. 'Stay here. I'll be quick.'

He had only just taken a curve when Saoirse called out. Retracing his steps, he popped his head round a tree. 'What?'

'Don't tell anyone where I am,' she said. 'Come straight back, won't you?'

'Come with me.'

She shook her head and smoothed her hair to comfort herself. 'I'm safer here.'

*

Myra settled in the chair, hands on the armrests. A queen on a throne.

'Adam.' She coughed. Talking softly steadied her voice. 'He's recovering well from the wound?'

She wasn't worried about the nation discovering she'd shot her teenage son. Her concern was his health. And how long he would hold it over her. Had his rugby coach dropped him quicker than he'd dropped to the porch boards that day? What she wouldn't give to find out.

'You cannot receive outside news.' Scot groaned, almost itching to break the house rule. 'Walt needs your help in the kitchen.'

'With Kate gone and Adam's injury. And my husband —'

'You inflicted Adam's injury.'

'Please. He needs me.'

'You're here for Kate.'

She peered into a corner. 'Nineteen, she was. Sixty years with her stolen from me. I don't want to lose Adam.'

'Send him a message.'

Myra's face changed. Expectant eyes, a soft expression. 'He's not watching.' Her deep tone bounced around the room. 'Is he watching?' She took a breath and looked straight ahead at the screen.

'I told your sister every day how special she was, but she couldn't see it. We tried so hard – your father and I – to get her to see the beauty we saw spilling from her. God, how we tried. Her spirit filled the house. Yours, too.' She paused. 'Her high school science teacher put the idea of surgery into her head. Breast enlargement. He'd groomed her in her final year. He should be in here with me.'

'You and your husband were home when the police came.'

Myra closed her eyes. From her recollection, the last time the police had come to the farm had been to return a cow that had escaped. It had been found along the road into town. About thirteen years ago.

'I remember your father opening the front door and tripping back inside. Like he'd been punched. In walked the police.' She swiped the air with a hand. 'I hit the officer who approached me. The violence of denial.' Her glassy eyes opened. 'That was the last day your father spoke to me.' Her tone was matter-of-fact. 'I got blamed for capitulating. After all, I'd paid for the surgery. And Kate never woke from it.'

'That's two people you lost.'

Arms stiffened with retribution, Myra gripped the armrests, ready to rip them off and throw them at the screen. 'See you soon, love.'

She stood, the chair's raised platform affording her even more presence, and saw Walt standing in the doorway. 'How long have you been there? Scot, when did he come in?'

She marched over to him, her face close to his. 'That door was shut.'

'You hadn't locked it.'

19

On the right edge of the wood, the morning heat welcomed Patty and Nicky. At least the cool grass underfoot was soothing. Patty glanced over her shoulder as she rounded a hedge and watched the house disappear. If something were to happen, she wouldn't get to the others quickly. With the greenery too high to see over, by the time anyone found her it would be too late. She'd be dead. Despite the warmth, she shivered.

'Fruit's this way,' Nicky said, a tub swinging in her hand. 'Keep up. I won't bite.' Her orange hair stood out against the assorted shades of green.

Patty's attention went to a whirring sound overhead. Cameras on a cable. There was a momentary sense of relief at being tracked. But they weren't there for crime prevention. Patty kept her eye on one camera as she followed Nicky. She tripped on a bush root and rolled to the side, headbutting a low-hanging lemon.

In a second Nicky stood over her, offering her a rough palm.

'Those hands are normally threatening someone,' Patty said.

'You need to be more observant. Only wankers who don't know how to respect women.' She shook her hand impatiently at Patty. 'Or men who get in my way.'

'I'm heavier than I look, darl. You might get a face full of lemons too.' Patty held on with both hands and Nicky pulled her up with ease.

'Don't put yourself down like that. Or underestimate my strength.' Nicky squatted at a bush and rummaged through the leaves. 'Strawberries. There's cream in the fridge.' Nicky sniffed one and swallowed it. 'Mmm.'

'Keep doing that and we'll be out here all day.'

'Get cracking then.'

They worked quietly, filling a section of the tub. Each strawberry landed with a soft knock, the rhythm as fitful as Patty's pulse.

She watched Nicky out of the corner of her eye and went to speak. She closed her mouth without a word, then did it again.

'Say it, then,' Nicky said.

Patty's chin wobbled. 'I've come to die. I won't be leaving here.'

'And I thought you were the entertainment.'

'It's true. I've lost everything. My dog's out there. He's not used to being without me. When my husband –'

'Stop!' Nicky gave her arm a violent shake. 'I'll do whatever it takes to leave this place. Get it?'

Patty wasn't fazed by Nicky's tough eyes or tougher grip. She stood taller.

'My – relative – was taken. Doing what he loved doing. Preserving heritage.'

She returned Nicky's fierce look.

'I'm warning you.' Nicky's slow drawl came like a growl.

Patty now spoke to herself.

'I always thought his love of fast cars would bring him trouble. But he was nowhere near a road when he passed. Quite the opposite.'

Nicky released Patty's arm. Her eyes softened. 'Stubborn, aren't you?' They returned to their fruit picking, weaving around one another. 'Ooh, blueberries.' Nicky pulled the tub closer. 'This morning has been fruitful.'

'That's not funny,' Patty said. 'Is there a hidden meaning in that?'

*

Near the bedrooms, Taran and Sonny were in the poky, windowless room where each housefriend was to design their exit suit. All the furniture and fittings were fixed. A work surface, two floor-mounted chrome stools, a tablet in the wall and the obligatory ceiling camera. Cloth samples and a paper tape measure lay on the worktop. Once a housefriend killed their match, they had minutes to shower and change into the suit before the door in the garden opened for them to leave. They would be interviewed live, where the studio followed a strict no-blood policy.

Taran navigated the tablet with ease to find their instructions. Beside him, Sonny squatted down, examining the stool. He tried twisting the base with both hands. But it was so thick, he couldn't keep a firm grip.

'If you're hoping to use that chrome bar as a weapon, that suggests you don't have the knife,' Taran said.

'Correct.' Sonny sat on the stool and did full circles. He picked his nose so forcefully his scar wriggled like a worm.

Taran held his breath to stop himself gagging. He turned back to the screen. 'It says here we measure up today and choose a style. Then the studio does the sewing, and we come back for a final fitting.'

Over his shoulder, he saw Sonny stop moving and stare through the transparent door into the corridor. 'We need to find something that can hold your interest.' Sonny wriggled his eyebrows. 'Besides women.' Taran spun around to the worktop, spread out the cloth samples and surveyed them, one hand on his hip. 'Something … consensual.'

'It's years since I've been in a place where women outnumber men. There are six here.' Taran waited while Sonny counted out the right number of fingers to hold up. 'I want some action before I leave. Don't you?'

'If I'm honest, I'm too scared to think of that.'

'What's wrong with you? You saw Rosa last night. And Bow.'

Taran nodded. 'Bow's lovely, isn't she? She's easy to talk to.'

Sonny looked dumbfounded. 'Talk? Did she mention me?'

'We've only been here a day.' Taran's laughter earned him a wallop on the shoulder. 'Ouch! Go easy, please. I just want to get out of here.'

'Wake up. Three weeks around women, decent food and no screws pissing us off? Fucking luxury. I plan to enjoy it and stay as long as possible.'

'On your feet. Let's get on with this.' Taran moved the tape measure along Sonny's outstretched arm and entered a measurement on the tablet.

'Tell me about your job at the bank.'

'I don't have it anymore. Obviously.' Taran cleared his throat and glanced at the camera. 'Shall we talk about this some other time.'

'Shall we, fuck. Did you kill a robber?' Taran glared at him until Sonny slapped his chest. He thought he'd worked it out. 'No wait. You were the bank robber?'

'What I said last night was true. I haven't killed anyone. This ordeal has nothing to do with my job. I'm not a murderer. Nor have I stolen money from my employer.'

He fiddled with the tape measure.

'You've never stolen money from the bank?' Sonny held still, waiting for Taran to make eye contact.

'Quiet.' Taran stamped his foot. 'I need to concentrate.'

*

Alone, at the console, Adolpha was doing a stint of voicing Scot. On the screen ahead, Walt adjusted himself in the chair. His arms moved from the armrests to his lap and back again. When his fidgeting stopped, she activated the mic and greeted him.

'I want to go home. I'm dying.' He returned to the door. 'I need to be extra sure it's locked.' He peered through the transparent screen to check the corridor was empty.

Adolpha cut the microphone. 'For fuck's sake.'

Onscreen, Walt returned to the chair. Steadying himself with the armrest, he stepped up and took several movements to turn and sit. He fell back and paused, waiting for the rocking to stop, as someone might after landing on a pool float. 'I feel nauseous.'

'That's nerves,' Adolpha said in Scot's automated voice.

'Do I have news from Doctor Ellis?' Walt peered at the door.

'None. We've agreed to release you as soon as you have a donor.'

'I'm a lot frailer than I let on. They mustn't see me as weak. But it's all an act. I don't feel strong.' He repeated his diagnosis. 'I'm dying.'

'Technically, that's not accurate.' She paused to see Walt's response. He sat up straight. 'Our tests showed otherwise.'

'I'm not healthy. I'm at a disadvantage. Everyone else can defend themselves and attack their opponents, whereas I'll have extraordinary difficulty.' He stopped, lost in thought. 'Anyway,

I'm wasting my time even discussing it.'

'Bingo!' Adolpha shouted to herself.

Walt continued. 'I want to pass something on to my family.'

Adolpha tutted. 'Twerp. You can't use us as a messaging service.' Through the mic she answered. 'No.'

Walt spoke more loudly. His voice became clipped. 'I have to let them know what happened the day my brother died.'

Adolpha removed her hand from the mic button. 'Family secrets? Take all the time you need, Walter.' She pressed the mic. 'What do you wish to tell them?'

'No one knows what I'm about to share. I couldn't bring myself to tell Maisie. It would've been too …' His voice came through clearly, even with the waver. 'When Eric died, everyone knows we were talking while he was driving. But I've never shared the topic of our call. I knew that day I wasn't going to see him in person for a while, so I called to tell him.' Walt rubbed his face with both hands. 'How do I say this?'

'Get on with it!' Adolpha shouted at the screen, mic off. 'For someone who's dying, you're taking your bloody time. Why can't you be like Myra? At least she gets to the point.'

'I told Eric about needing a transplant. It must have distracted him, and that's what caused the accident. Of course, I'm not to blame for what came next.'

Adolpha hit the mic. 'He wasn't paying full attention and that was when –'

Walt closed his eyes. 'Yes, Scot. I've carried this a long time.'

Adolpha whistled. 'Timing is not your strength, buster. Maybe in the next life.' To Walt, she said, 'Please tell us you didn't hear him getting …' She stopped before verbalising the gruesome details. It worked.

Walt screwed up his face. Both hands whacked the armrests as he contained the emotion. 'I want my family to know this.

Please, Scot. I'm dying.'

'You had port last night after dinner.'

Walt frowned. 'To fit in. Everyone had some.'

'You could limit yourself to a small cup.'

'For god's sake.' Walt got up and left.

Adolpha pushed another button on the console. 'Todd, hold onto this. We won't air it yet.'

*

Bow and Rosa said nothing to each other, watching the hot tub empty. Bow could hear the water draining away. How freely it left. In seconds, it would clear the studio grounds to join the sea. After that, it might blend with the waters of the south Atlantic and never be seen again. Her thoughts returned to the seascapes in Superintendent Carlisle's office, as they often did. Her joints were getting stiffer by the day. Each movement of her wrists was like grinding bone.

With violent squelches, the last of the water left the tub. Rosa set her jacket on the ledge. She patted it as if comforting a pet and pointed at Bow.

'Don't touch my stuff.'

She put rubber gloves on, shoved a bag at Bow, climbed in the tub and began drying it. Every now and then, she clicked her fingers. A signal for Bow to lean in so she could discard the cloth.

Each time, Bow peered in the bag. She saw wet cloths, but they weren't dirty. 'Why are we emptying it? You're the only one who went in.'

Rosa mumbled as she dried the chrome jets. 'You heard Scot. We clean it.' A severe look settled on her face.

Bow stopped talking when Jay appeared from the garden. He went down the steps carrying a tub of fresh vegetables, which he emptied onto the kitchen island.

'Why did Scot call you to the chair last night?' Bow was whispering.

'Bloody questions.' Rosa stayed crouching in the tub and wiped the floor.

Rosa's irritation intrigued Bow, so she thought of more questions to bug her. 'What line of work are you in?'

'Australians. Always judging people by their job,' she huffed. 'Restoration.'

'Buildings?'

'Art. I make things beautiful again. You?' She almost spat the question at Bow.

There was no way Bow was going to divulge her prison job. Illegal cannabis harvester. 'Gardening. I also make things beautiful.' Gardening was her passion, so it wasn't a complete lie.

Rosa's big eyes drilled into Bow's. 'Good. No more questions. Understand?' She held the wet cloth to the light to inspect it.

'Have you lost something?' Bow asked. Rosa threw the cloth in the bag she held out and took another from the clean pile. 'What are you looking for?'

'My patience. It must be here somewhere. Oh shit, no. Gone.'

'I'm only being friendly.'

'I don't want friends. I won't be sticking around. And if I was, I wouldn't be friends with you.'

Bow's tongue found the inside of her cheek.

'You don't say much, but you're always watching.' Rosa brushed her hair from her face. 'Like a hawk.'

'Like most of us. Come on.'

'You move with caution. Like you're nervous. Or guilty.'

'Honey, that ain't nerves or guilt. That's inflammation. I've lived with arthritis all my life. Normally, I have something to relieve the pain.' Bow moved along the tiled ledge to collect Rosa's final used cloth.

Rosa lunged for her jacket. 'Don't touch that.'

'I heard you the first time.'

*

Empty tub in hand, Jay returned along the grass trail he had trod shortly before. He relished stepping from sun into shade. He could make out two people laughing. When the path straightened, he saw Saoirse first. Someone was feeding her a plump tomato. Orange hair, slight frame. Nicky. She batted Saoirse's hands away with her other arm. Her playmate was half-resisting, half-nipping at the gift. Saoirse's eyes, weary and wrinkled minutes earlier, were beckoning and charged.

'I swear it's clean,' Nicky said. 'Eat it.'

'Okay. One bite.'

Aware that he was intruding on a private game, Jay dropped the tub to alert them. Its thump was drowned out by the pair's playful cackles. He coughed. 'Glad you're feeling better.'

'We'll take over,' Nicky said, without turning around. 'Get lost.'

'Who were you with?' Jay asked.

'Patty. Over there.' Nicky used her head to indicate the far side of the wood. 'Ow, Saoirse! Bite the tomato, not my thumb.'

Saoirse spat out the contents of her mouth for laughing. The pair jostled some more, fell against the tomato bushes and slid to the ground, where their laughs turned to howls.

'I see.' Jay went looking for Patty.

20

If someone had peered through the window, they might have thought Christy had friends over. Dips, bags of corn chips, tissues, Jay's pillowcase, her phone and Jay's surrounded her. She tilted her head back to finish off another bag and saw the photo of Jay and Harriet. Smiling and tilting heads to one another. Christy slowed her chewing and licked each dusty finger. On the telly, the action was live outside the studio, crowds chanting. A presenter announced the housefriends would soon receive their first round of clues. Christy pressed mute and dialled the last number in her call history.

'My ultrasound is on Wednesday. My doctor brought the date forward and I thought I'd check it's still going ahead.'

'You called yesterday.' It was a sympathetic voice.

'I –'

'Is this your first? Mums-to-be are eager to see them on the screen.'

Christy glanced at the telly. No sign of Jay.

Keyboard sounds travelled down the line and Christy pictured the receptionist checking records. Christy's troubled history would emerge. Appointments booked, then cancelled. No postnatal entries. Repeated petering out from the hospital system. Then the typing stopped. Christy's throat swelled with a thousand words that banked up. Glued in the running-not-running of her nightmares. She broke free of her paralysis and answered an unspoken question.

'I'm fine, really. This will be my first ultrasound. I've never carried this far before and my doctor and I – well, we agreed bringing the date forward was best and the reason I'm ringing is to check it will definitely go ahead. I haven't been moved off the list, have I?'

'We won't do that to you. Your ultrasound will happen.'

'And if one of the sonographers calls in sick – because there's always something going around – can someone else do the ultrasound? Is it a big team? What if the equipment breaks? Do you have a back-up?'

'Miss Lau, we'll be here. This is the largest hospital in Sydney and we will look after you. See you on Wednesday at ten.'

'Should I phone again to confirm?' Christy imagined herself in bed, wires hooking her to the television and phone, her mobile screen beeping like a heart monitor. And if this receptionist didn't throw her some support, she might flatline.

'Would you like to call on Monday morning? I start at eight.'

21

Saturday evening saw the sky darken and a breeze pick up. But with no drop in the mercury, outside remained balmy. In the house, cool air circulated as each housefriend stood facing a screen, waiting for their clue.

Flanked by Myra and Sonny, Jay stood tall, jaw as angular as the house decor. The authorities had shared little about Harriet's death. A Friday night. Stabbed to death. She died before the medics got to her. Jay knew nothing of the motive. Yet the culprit was in the house. One of them seemed to obviously fit. Sonny. But perhaps everyone thought Sonny was their match.

Jay was as prepared as could be for what might happen next. He'd decided running up either corridor was pointless. Not only were there no heavy objects, there were no hiding places. If anyone came tearing towards him brandishing the knife, his only chance was to head outside.

A tone sounded through the house. He waved to the cameras and blew a kiss.

She was betrayed

Jay stared at the screen until it went blank, the three words coming like a slap. His throat tightened so much it burned. Harriet knew her killer. A friend or a colleague or a neighbour? He was itching to glance around and work out who the betrayer might be. Each prisoner in his suspect list needed a fresh looking-over.

On his left, Sonny stood with his palms flat against the wall, as though getting searched. Sounding like a child reading to a parent, he spoke his clue aloud. Although far from a confident reader, he had a buoyant tone, each word spaced and pronounced.

'A. Parent. Wants. To. Kill. You.' Jay heard Myra stifle a laugh. Sonny called out, giving his back to the wall. 'Clue's not fucking helpful, Scot. I could've guessed that.' There was a loud crack as he elbowed the monitor. He headed off.

Jay joined Myra on the sofa, where she indicated the space next to her. He'd never seen her so friendly towards him. A resolute look on her face, she waited for him to settle and leaned in.

'Two green bottles hanging on the wall.' Her whisper-singing was callous.

A chill clapped Jay's shoulders.

*

Bow had chosen a spot away from Myra near the kitchen, with Rosa on her left and Nicky and Saoirse to her right. With a mouth like a wasteland, she rinsed with soft drink and placed the cup by her foot. Next to the wall vacuum vent. Then she nudged it further away. She might need to bolt. No trip hazards.

Her body was reacting to the prospect of looking at jumbled shapes. She smudged away palm prints of sweat on the marble around the screen. She wasn't confident she could even pretend to read the clue. And with cameras and an entire country watching, her movements were stiffer than ever.

Luckily, beside her, Nicky was serving as a distraction. Arms up, she moved from foot to foot like a boxer. Sidestepping, she knocked Saoirse's hand from her mouth.

'Stop biting your nails.'

'I can't do this.' Saoirse's hushed words travelled to Bow.

Bow heard the tone and luminous shapes appeared on her screen. Holding her breath, she counted six of them before they vanished. She stayed still. Being the first one to abandon their spot might raise suspicion.

There was a scream. From the corner of her eye, Bow saw Saoirse cup her hands over her mouth. 'Aggy knew her killer.' Her comment made Nicky roar, as much to scare Saoirse into silence as to drown out the echoes of her revelation.

'Keep your voice down!'

Seconds later, Bow stepped away from the wall and almost bumped into Rosa, who was mumbling in Portuguese.

*

Patty tugged on her earlobe. She was thinking of Señor Bones. Elizabeth had probably won his amiable, naïve affections by now, all the while wearing her gold pendant earrings around her house.

Your target is illiterate

She covered the screen with both hands and whimpered. That wasn't her secret to know. Poor wretch. A life that saw them robbed of the joys of schooling. If not books and learning, what must they have grown up with? Patty's heart was heavy.

She peeped under her hands to check the clue had gone. With sluggish steps, she turned away.

She almost missed seeing Taran and Walt cross paths, shake hands and walk off. Hitchcockian spies in a busy station.

22

Rosa had a hard time cooking. Sonny was a hassle as much as a help. He used every chance to paw her hips and shoulders, her instructions seemingly more effective with touch. Elbowing him and swearing didn't stop him. There wasn't even time to pause and think about the clue. A woman was here for her, it had said.

She had her flute stem, held to her forearm by hair bands, to keep safe. On top of that, she came under Saoirse's gaze whenever Sonny touched the ingredients. If Saoirse stood up once more to check on hygiene, Rosa would scream. She tested the stew, which sat in a sunken hob, secure from anyone harbouring thoughts of scalding an assailant. Too bland.

Walt stood at the table. 'No extra salt!' Rosa swore in Portuguese and sprinkled some in.

'What about dessert?'

'Trifle. In the fridge,' Sonny said.

'Are you going to add salt to that too?'

'Knock it off, Grandad.'

'What's taking so long?'

'Almost ready. Have patience,' Rosa said.

'You try working with utensils on a fucking chain.' Sonny yanked a tethered chopping knife and strainer, making the metal cords screech.

'Stop fussing, Walt. Or Sonny will spit in our food,' Saoirse said.

Rosa and Sonny dished up the meal. Their pace quickened, like a team in the closing minutes of a cooking show challenge. Sonny served his next plate, his right hand moving down Rosa's back. She whacked his arm and went to step away. But they knocked each other, and the flute stem came free. It slipped from her long sleeve and smashed against the floor, the pieces scattering. 'Shit!'

Everyone stood for a better view, the sound of breaking glass clearly a surprise.

At Rosa's feet was no weapon, just bits of glass. Glass that wouldn't scare a child. She grabbed a piece the size of her thumb nail.

'Yaarrr!' A roar from the table.

Rosa knew who it was – the woman that Scot had armed. Looking up, she met Myra's savage glare.

Myra shot to the sofa. Her arm slipped under the frame, but Rosa didn't wait to see what appeared. Her heart thumped her into action. She sprinted past the table and flew up the stairs, leaving behind gasps as the others saw what Myra was chasing her with.

Outside, Rosa crossed the grass, taking the middle path into the woods, where the greenery enveloped her.

Damp soil muffled her footfalls and moist air clung to her, almost weighing her down.

She pressed herself against a tree and heard Myra shouting her name.

'It's no good hiding!'

Rosa shrank further against the bark. There was quiet. She strained to listen, but the only sound was her own breathing. She gripped the glass piece tighter. A mobile camera moved overhead.

'Let's get this done, Rosa.'

Myra's voice seemed further away. She must have passed her on another path. Rosa abandoned her hiding spot to return inside. Passing the housefriends, she took the corridor to the chair.

'A bowl of this will kill her,' Walt hollered.

At the transparent door, she checked behind her. Despite her gruff breathing, she confirmed the corridor was empty. She tiptoed inside. The door slid shut. When the automatic lighting came on, she thumped the panel, the blanket darkness startling her. A dim glow came from Scot's screen. Otherwise, the room was as dark as the woods.

'Scot.' She waited. 'Myra's after me.'

She sat in the chair curling her feet under her. If Myra looked through the door, she would remain unseen. She stretched her neck as she whispered. 'Please don't turn on the lights. And don't speak. You're too loud.' She brought a finger to her lips in hopes the cameras recorded in the dark. 'Are you there?'

'Yes,' Scot said, in a loud whisper, mimicking her. 'Hey, Rosa?'

'What?'

'Did you lock the door as you came in?'

'Fuck.' She peered around the seat. With such low visibility, the corridor appeared empty. 'You do it.'

There was no response.

Rosa listened for sound, besides her pounding heart.

A faint noise. Maybe the whirr of a camera.

'Scot? Is she outside?'

Rosa swallowed hard.

'Is she – in here?' She heard breathing.

A hand shot over the seat and grabbed her in a terrific grip, forcing her head against the leather. A second hand crossed in front of her and the glint of moving steel stole what little breath Rosa had left. Myra pulled Rosa's head back and up.

With all her strength, Rosa ripped at Myra's forearm with her clump of glass. Myra made no sound as Rosa opened the skin.

Without cutting straight away, as though time was on her side, Myra brought the blade to Rosa's neck. Her grip on Rosa's head extended her throat and further exposed the skin. Rosa gurgled and struggled, but it was no use. She ditched the clump of glass and tried in vain to tear Myra's arms away. Rosa felt Myra walk the blade up her neck, as though she knew the best place to slice. The first cut was swift and deep. Every drop of blood seemed to rush to her swelling throat to evacuate her body.

Myra's hand was back in striking position in no time and the second gash had Rosa slump to the floor.

Part 4

Show case

23

Sleepy-eyed and breathless, Jay reached the weapon room, having dashed there, heels off the floor. Through the door, he saw that Bow had beaten him to it, blocking his view of the weapon unit. He entered. Bow stepped aside, revealing a steel mallet under the thick glass dome. Before he said anything, she left.

The oblong unit that housed the weapon, waist-high and centrally secured, unlocked if a housefriend entered the correct name into a panel. Prying the dome open was useless. Jay tried. Its rim sat beneath the surface, which prevented him from getting a strong hold on the glass.

How the mallet gleamed. Made from continuous stainless steel, it had a long handle and a cylindrical head. A flat face and a textured one, for a chef to tenderise a cut of steak, juicy and bloody.

Absently, Jay rubbed his head.

Out in the corridor, he peered into the room with the chair.

It was empty and seemingly cleaned of all traces of the previous night's horrors. The image that would stay with him was how differently Myra had returned from the corridor compared to how she'd crept along it. Stooping, brushing the wall, clutching the knife. A minute later, she'd strode past them, head high, straight to the showers to wash off death and leave.

Breakfast was underway. Second morning and again the scrawny python ran from the wall socket to the toaster. At the table, Patty, Taran, Walt and Sonny occupied a corner each. Bow stood buttering toast at one end, and Nicky and Saoirse were outside on the bench.

Familiar, yet altered.

Taran looked alert, but apprehensive. He had showered and his damp black hair was glistening. Wearing a vacant expression, Patty stared into her coffee.

Bow mustn't have mentioned the new weapon. Good. A chance for a quiet breakfast. With viewers at home having had their thrill, studio bosses too, the pressure eased a little. Jay's breathing came more freely. Apart from the air seeming less dense and the light more vivid, the place felt safer. At least for now.

Jay sat. Nobody spoke. Not even when Taran poured sugar on the table. Bow dodged his offer to sweeten her tea. She swiped her tumbler from under the spoon he offered, scooped up the spill and threw it in the sink, all without a word.

Sonny's chewing noises became the morning's soundtrack. He drained black tea from his blue cup and vacuumed cereal from his bowl. He contemplated the peanut butter on the knife and, with messy slurps, licked the knife clean. His teeth puréed his toast into a bolus, visible to all.

Patty looked up, dark rings under her eyes, and ruptured the silence.

'One step closer to death.' No matter that she spoke quietly, Jay registered the message like a scream. 'You all look like you know what you're doing. Everyone seems so …' She gestured outside. 'Look at those two. You'd think they were old friends.' She shook her head. 'I can't run. I physically cannot run.' Sonny's squelching stopped. 'I have no one out there. All taken from me.'

Jay reached for her forearm, but he stopped short of touching her. 'No details. Later.'

She withdrew from his hand. 'I have nobody. Come for me, whoever you are. My husband was –'

'Stop.' Jay bumped the table. Was a quiet cup of coffee so much to ask for?

'No.' Patty searched for eye contact from the table. 'Nothing. I've got nothing. I don't even have my knitting with me. My family are knitters. My grandmother knitted for the troops. And her mother, the war before that. We did our share. My knitting group is my world. We meet in the community centre. Talking and knitting.'

'This could all be lies,' Sonny said, with a smirk. 'We'll never know the truth.'

Patty went to reply and Jay jumped in. 'Don't. He's goading you.'

'What about your dog?' Walt asked. 'He's waiting for you.'

Jay gave up trying to stop Patty from divulging information and took a piece of toast.

'Señor Bones? My sister will take him from me. Along with the house. She's been after that for years. I got the family property and she was left the café, which folded the minute she stepped inside.'

'You might win,' Taran said. 'You'll have money to buy all your friends a home.'

'My family were my friends.'

Walt changed the subject. 'How did Señor Bones get his name?'

Patty sunk with the memory and rolled her empty tumbler in her fingertips. 'No matter how much we fed him, he never gained weight' – she nodded – 'not unlike young Tarzan here.'

Taran flinched. He gathered his breakfast and executed a smooth departure.

24

Nicky realised they had an audience inside and deposited her cup on the grass. She threw the blanket that she'd whipped from the sofa around her and tied a knot.

'Come with me.'

They headed for the solitude of the woods. It was cooler among the trees, where the sun's warmth had yet to reach, where the ground chilled their feet. A rich scent of flora drowned the aftertaste of Nicky's coffee. Blanket flapping like a cape, she pointed at low branches and spoke to her apprentice over her shoulder.

'Everything is a weapon. You run out here, break a branch over your knee and go for the face.'

After a moment, they settled on a spot. Nicky untied the blanket and Saoirse spread it under a tree, where they huddled with their feet jutting onto the path. Nicky took out three straws, twisting a pink and red one together.

Glassy eyed, Saoirse lifted her head to look.

'You should see what some women produce,' Nicky said. 'Amazing, their eye for design.' She grappled with the straws as if they opposed her efforts. 'Wasted inside.' Next, Nicky's tattooed fingers worked the green straw. 'Wait for it. You've got to be – careful. Too forceful, you crush it.' Saoirse was examining her tattoos. 'You want to know why "HARD CELL"?'

'No.' Saoirse diverted her eyes.

She presented Saoirse with a paper flower.

Saoirse ran a finger over the red and pink petals. She pecked Nicky on the cheek. 'I didn't know Rosa was a killer. She looked so … normal.'

'I didn't know you were a lesbian.'

Saoirse kissed the flower. 'I'll struggle to work out who killed my daughter.'

'Quiet. You'll get yourself killed. Don't mention that person again.'

'My daughter –'

Nicky squeezed Saoirse's forearm. 'I can get you out of here. But you must listen.'

'You're hurting me.'

'That's nothing compared to what might happen.' Nicky let go.

'What's your problem, Jailbird?' Saoirse turned away, massaging her skin.

'Jailbird?' Nicky chuckled. 'What movie's that from? This jailbird will keep you alive.'

'You'll end up being my target. That's how cruel life is.' Saoirse dropped the flower on the blanket.

Nicky whispered, but spat her words. 'Two things, Smarty. My clue said I could trust you. And my crime involved a man dying. You're safe with me.' She shoved the flower into Saoirse's hand. 'You trust me, right?' Saoirse twirled the flower. 'I made you something. Trust me.'

'Who did you kill then? Your father?'

'Keep it down. This is serious.' Nicky growled, causing Saoirse to withdraw and raise a palm in truce. 'I didn't set out to kill anyone.'

'Christ, is everyone innocent here? Taran said the same thing.'

Nicky waved off the comment. Bird tweets filled the silence, and the sun found a hundred gaps in the leaves. After a moment, she studied Saoirse. Her mass of hair, sad eyes, tears of sunlight on her cheeks, her timid way of being in the world. Nicky wanted to squeeze her so tight, but Saoirse might easily break in her grip.

Saoirse brought the flower to her nose. 'Can you make it smell real too?' She linked arms with Nicky. 'I'm sorry. Please keep your promise. The one about keeping me alive.'

'I'll see what I can do.' Nicky brought her elbow in tight, trapping Saoirse's arm against her.

'My son's birthday is in a few days. I want to be there. He's studying law. Both my children are.' Nicky glared at Saoirse for sharing more personal details and Saoirse mouthed, 'Sorry'.

Nicky leant in. 'I helped with a job. A bank.'

'A bank robbery? How –'

There was a rustle of branches metres away. Nicky turned to block Saoirse, who covered her flower.

'Isn't this sweet?' Sonny said. 'Someone's been murdered and the lovebirds are huddled together.'

'Piss off,' Nicky said, making a display of gawking at his scar.

He angled his head. 'You missed Scot's update. We've got the day off. We're about to watch a film.'

Nicky shooed him away.

'Don't shoot the messenger.'

25

One hand dancing through branches, Bow rounded a curve in the path and saw the studio ahead. The house and garden sat tranquil in the summer heat, in contrast with the foliage swaying at her touch. From rolled leaves she'd fashioned a cigarette, which she drew across her nostrils. Unlocking memories. Teasing her body. Daring the irritability of withdrawal to start more trouble. It was there. Hiding inside. Waiting.

Taran was sunbathing on the lawn, legs and feet off the towel. His skin and hair glistened with the only visible moisture. Bow joined him by the flowering gardenias, where she could make out movement inside the house. 'It's me.'

Eyes closed, Taran mumbled a welcome.

Avoiding the screams of her dry joints she sat, legs folded to one side. 'Ooh, stiff.' Walking barefoot on marble wasn't helping, she explained.

'You and Walt won't be creeping up on anyone.'

Bow's knotted fingers kept rolling her leaf cigarette,

perfecting the green cylinder. She admired the gardenias beside her. Even in the sun, their dark glossy leaves looked wet. 'This garden has been loved. Such healthy leaves.'

Taran made a sound.

'Gardens are beautiful,' Bow said, anchoring one hand in the grass. 'They're like children. Begging to thrive.'

'Do you have kids?'

'Not yet.'

Taran rolled over and propped up on his elbows, catching sight of Bow's dirty feet. 'What were you doing in there? Digging your way out?'

They fell silent. Bow heard nothing but birds talking, plenty to discuss. So many topics were off limits with the housefriends. Their hobbies, their routines. Their pasts, their futures. If they had one.

Possibly sensing Bow's caution, Taran drew on the safety of the mundane. 'Thanks again for lunch. That sauce was delicious. You didn't use a recipe.'

'I never do.' Bow waved off the idea. 'I cook on the fly. No need for books.'

A minute passed.

'Have you read the rules in your bedroom?' Taran enquired.

Bow shifted her legs to the other side. 'What?'

'House rules. On the screen.'

'I didn't bother. Anything important?'

'Not one for reading much, are you?' Taran busied himself with the grass, stroking the blades.

Bow let him see her looking at the house. She changed the subject quicker than a thief fleeing a crime scene. 'We're being spied on. Don't look.' She lowered her head to appear more secretive.

'Who by?' Taran went to turn his head.

'Don't. They're looking. Guess.' Bow's lips hardly moved. She stole another glance at the house. Taran asked for a hint. 'Let me see.' She focused on her rolled leaves. 'This person wants to be everyone's friend.'

'Easy. Jay.' Bow nodded. 'Mister Try-too-hard, isn't he?'

'Although, he did come to Rosa's aid the other night.'

'He wasn't sticking up for her. It was a chance to be the good guy. With cameras rolling.'

'You don't miss much,' she said. 'Thankfully, we're on the same side.'

'There are no sides.'

Without warning, Taran squealed and pointed.

'Don't move!' Sitting up, he held out his hand. A rabbit, brown as a bear, hopped to him. 'Hello little one. How did you get in here?' He scooped it up and looked around.

'It must've come for the vegetables,' Bow said, leaning in to stroke it. In the sunlight, its fur appeared damp.

'It's shivering. You and me both, bunny.' Studying the rabbit from all angles, Taran showed Bow a twist in its left hind joint. 'This leg doesn't sit right.'

'Poor thing. It doesn't seem to be in pain.'

They heard humming – a man's voice – coming from the woods and Jay appeared. He waved to them and retraced his steps along the middle path.

A disbelieving look came over Taran. At a snail's pace, his eyes tracked from Jay to the house, to Bow and back to Jay disappearing into the wood.

'Oh.' Bow's cheeks were heaters. She brought a limp hand over her eyebrows and squinted at the house. 'It can't have been Jay I saw.'

She leant towards Taran to stroke the rabbit. 'What will we do with it?'

'I'm keeping it. Now I have a friend,' Taran said, claiming ownership.

'A pet for the house.' Watching Taran nuzzle into the fur, Bow couldn't know who felt more comforted – him or the rabbit.

With it clutched to Taran's chest, they headed inside to consult Scot. Squeezed sideways into the chair, they took turns stroking the rabbit. 'Look what I found. Its back leg's wonky, but it's not in pain. I'm keeping it.'

'Can you tell the sex?' Bow asked.

Scot told Taran to hold it up. He gripped it under the front paws, its bottom wriggling.

'Female.'

Despite Taran's squeal, Bow felt sure he would've made the same sound had it been a buck.

'She's come to save my bacon.'

*

At dinner, Jay made sure he sat opposite Taran at one end of the table. He'd been banking on Harriet's killer living in Sydney. So when Taran disclosed he liked swimming, Jay tried to find out if he preferred the pool or the sea. His thinking was Taran might confirm that he lived nowhere near the coast. But Taran was distracted by a cardboard box in the corner and could only muster an occasional 'uh-ah' and 'if you say so' in response to conversation.

Before long, Taran's distraction got the better of him. He went to the box and returned holding a rabbit. 'Everyone, meet my – bloody hell, Sonny, you eat fast.'

Eyes turned to Sonny's empty plate and couldn't miss his chin caked in gravy. These seemed more interesting than the live animal at the other end of the table.

'Prison. Can't leave your grub too long.' Sonny wiped his

face with his sleeve and burped. He got up and hurled his plate and cutlery into the sink.

'Why not?' Walt asked.

Taran raised his voice and stood tall. 'Everyone. Meet my new friend.'

'Because of flies,' Saoirse said, ignoring Taran. 'I bet the prison windows have no screens.'

Sonny's roar of laughter startled everyone. He stumbled past the table on the way to the sofa, pausing to lean on Bow, who shook him off like an annoying insect. 'Flies!' He clutched his chest as he spoke-laughed. 'That's the first thing the screws warn you about, Saoirse. Fucking flies in your starter.'

'Look this way, please. I have an announcement.' Jay watched Taran try again. And fail. Just like the first night with the cups. Another attempt to get attention, to command the mundane, to steal the light. A confidence thing. Not too much. Too little.

Patty shook her head. 'Saoirse, what Sonny means is his companions might steal his food.'

Patty waited for confirmation of her guess from Sonny, who only cackled more.

'Companions? What the fuck!'

'They spit in it,' Jay said.

Sonny dried his eyes. 'Spit, on a good day. Try any other body fluid. Range of colours. Like your cups.'

Jay put down his yellow one. He held his breath. Across the table, Saoirse drew the red tumbler from her lips and, before she could scrunch her eyes shut, spotted Bow's green cup.

With no hope of getting their attention, Taran carried the rabbit around the table.

'Her fur is so soft. Those ears. I want my dog with me.'

'Keep that filthy animal away from the table.'

'Did Scot give us a pet for company?' Walt asked.

'No. She's mine,' Taran said. 'I found her in the garden. She bounced right past Bow and came to me. Didn't she, Bow?'

'Straight to him.'

'I'm good with animals. Not creepy-crawlies. But proper pets, you know. I bond with them extremely easily.'

'You'll get on well with Sonny.' Nicky stroked the rabbit with her inky 'D' forefinger.

Saoirse snapped at Taran. 'Stand further back. Can't we eat dinner in peace? It will be unhygienic with the droppings.'

'Get used to her,' Taran said, indicating the box. 'Scot gave her a home.'

'Its own little Scot Free house,' – Walt pretended to tremble – 'ooh, the suspense. Will she get out alive?'

'She's not eating our food. Scot will have to provide greens,' Jay said.

'There's an entire wood out there, dumbarse.' Taran promenaded over to the sofa. 'Sonny, look. A bunny. Open your eyes.'

'Seen one before.'

Taran addressed the rabbit. 'Don't mind Sonny. He's a big softie.' Sonny lashed out, but Taran recoiled in time.

'What's her name?' Walt asked.

Taran made a face at Bow. 'We forgot to name her.' He bounced the rabbit. 'Do they come when you call them?'

'We'll all be fucking dead by the time it learns,' Sonny said.

'Let's choose a name,' Jay said.

Taran didn't hesitate one bit. 'I'm naming her "Alice". After my friend.'

'You made that up.' Jay frowned. 'You started at "A" and chose the first name that popped into your head. I bet there's no friend called that.'

'I've got lots of friends. Meet Alice. Or piss off.'

'What's a good name for a female rabbit?' Jay asked them all.

'"Totalitarian",' Patty said, finishing her meal.

Taran's eyes bulged. 'Over my – I am not calling her that.'

'Totali – what?' Sonny said. After Jay explained the word, he drummed the sofa. 'Fucking cool.'

'Not fucking cool. I've named her already. Alice is a girl. Totalitarian sounds like a boy's name.'

'Don't be daft. How can a regime sound more like a boy's name?' Jay clapped for attention. 'Let's vote on it.'

'I found her. I choose.'

'Hands up for "Alice",' Jay said. Saoirse raised her hand, then lifted Nicky's. Bow followed. Shaking his head, Taran raised his hand. 'Now for "Totalitarian".' Sonny, Walt and Patty voted with Jay. A draw.

'My vote counts as two because I found her,' Taran said. He stamped his foot at Jay's shrug. 'For fuck's sake. There's no point choosing a name longer than "rabbit".' His pitch climbed. He buried his nose in her fur. 'This is Alice.'

'Totally,' Jay said.

26

On Monday, Saoirse stopped outside the measuring room. There was a tightness across her chest and her throat burned like acid. Sonny was inside.

'Stand there,' she said, pointing to the wall furthest from the door. She stepped in and the door closed. The temperature dropped and the room shrank. With little more than standing space, it was smaller than the bedroom. She caught him watching her throat as she swallowed.

He signalled the tablet. 'Taran used that. You do that bit. I'm meant to show you how to measure up.'

'I'll do that myself.'

'Fine by me, darling.' He tried on the jacket he and Taran had measured. It fitted well. Only a choice of logo design and name tag remained.

'Give me the tape measure.' Saoirse's voice was loaded with false bravado.

He threw it at her. 'Not got your girlfriend now.' She looked up at the camera. Scot wasn't far off. Neither was Nicky. 'Scared?'

To calm herself, Saoirse counted the numbers on the tape measure. Twenty-one. Twenty-two. Twenty-three. A 'no' would surely escalate things. No point provoking him. Appeasing him was so simple. She nodded. Controlling her shakes, she took her measurements and entered them on the tablet, standing side-on so she could face him still.

'What happens if Nicky ends up being your match?'

'She's not. We've already –'

'Liar.' He stepped to her. 'Your eyes hit the floor quicker than a faggot in a punch-up.'

He snatched the tape measure. It was around her wrist before she realised. With one hand, he pulled on it, forcing her arm down. Whatever material it was made from, it wasn't normal paper. More like rope. He batted her jaw to make her face him. Her gaze rose to his dirty scar and savage eyes. His head tilted side to side as he pondered his next move. 'If only you could trust Nicky.'

Saoirse finally wrenched her way free, grabbing the tape measure. 'There are worse people in here.'

'There's one way to know for sure if she's your match, but Scot might not like it.' He turned to the workbench. 'Okay, back to work.' He hummed and looked through the material samples. 'Don't worry. This is really simple to do.'

'How?'

'First, you choose this bit –'

'Not that. Tell me how I find out it isn't Nicky.' As she spoke, Saoirse's insides shifted. A craving shot through her limbs, bowling over any fear in its way. Sonny's lure was like a drug, promising peace. To know for sure would put an end to the exhausting, guilt-ridden back and forth.

Sonny averted his eyes. 'Forget it.'

'Tell me.' Saoirse moved close to him. She could smell his coffee breath.

'I don't want no trouble.' She dug her nails into his forearm. 'Whoa. You're not as weak as you look.'

'Bloody tell me.'

'You want to know she didn't kill your relative? Simple. Put her name in the weapon dome. If she's safe, it won't open.'

She released his arm. 'We only have one go. It's too important to play with. How careless.'

'Exactly. A terrible idea. Forget it. Trust Nicky. She's a good kid. Keep your options open …'

Saoirse didn't hear Sonny's final words. Nor did she feel the tape measure come to rest on her feet when she dropped it. She wasn't aware of opening the door to leave, but she must have because she was now in the corridor. Only her vision was lucid – struck by a startling clarity. There was one way forward. There was no going back.

Had she turned around, she would've seen Sonny wink at the camera.

*

Squatting, Jay pitched potatoes into a basket. A camera was at treetop height. He tapped his glasses up his nose and swore. Why the hell was he with Walt? Another hunter. Time with the convicts was vital if he was to uncover anything.

'You okay there?' Jay couldn't keep his voice neutral.

A grunt came from Walt, steadied against a tree and pulling carrots with one hand. Very few were in the basket. 'I feel off.'

'Let's take –' Jay was interrupted by a vomiting sound. He stepped closer, but Walt's palm came up. Jay hid his surprise from the camera to protect the other man. 'They're watching us.'

'Goddammit. Keep your trap shut and don't tell the others.'

Walt kicked soil over the patch of sick.

'What's going on?'

'Shush.' Walt spat and wiped his face with his sleeve. 'Fuck.'

His panting intensified. He sat on the ground, hunched over, legs splayed. Clutching a carrot, he fiddled with the root and greens. As though motorised, his chest jerked upwards with each breath. His face was that of a sad clown. 'It's getting worse. Vomiting, swelling.' He hitched up both trouser legs.

Jay recoiled. 'Jesus.' Apart from his toes, Walt's feet were like balloons. Smooth and bloated, rubber stumps ready to burst. 'Kidney failure?'

Walt nodded. 'I have to get out of here. I'm on a transplant list.'

'The studio?'

'They know.' He smoothed the carrot greens, like a doll's hair. 'I vomited the day they came for me. I'd gone to the hospital because I felt so awful, and Maisie and I reasoned if I got onto a ward, I'd be safe. As soon as I registered, the hospital must've alerted these bastards. We were waiting in Emergency and they showed up. I got sick over myself. They moved us to a private room to freshen up and I changed into the suit they had for me.'

Half-listening, Jay kept an eye out for the others. 'Lower your trouser legs.'

Walt did so and continued. 'Maisie and I hugged and prayed. Then they took me off. We had a long drive. Felt like vomiting the whole time, but I didn't.'

'When the time comes you'll have the energy to fight, yeah?'

Walt tossed the carrot at the basket but missed.

*

Saoirse crept along the corridor, where her perspiring feet weakened her hold on the marble. Nicky and Patty's voices travelled from the kitchen. She'd need to pass them unseen if she was to reach the weapon room.

'Did you not learn home economics?' Patty asked.

'It's clean.' Nicky sounded fed up.

'That's filthy. While the lamb roasts, we'll clean up. Do not make that face, young lady.'

Saoirse grinned, picturing Nicky's scowl with her petite features wrinkling. She peered around the corner. They were between the island and the sink, backs turned. There was no one else around. Saoirse had to act. All she had to do was move from the sofas to the table to the island and vanish down the other corridor. She tiptoed to the nearest sofa and crouched. Her heart was thumping in its cage. Move it. She took two more sweaty, slippery steps. If the pair turned now, they would see her.

'Wait, Nicky,' Patty said. 'Before we put the recipe book away, remind me when we turn the veg.'

'You open the oven door and poke them with a fork.'

'Let's do it properly. Find the page and read it out to me. Then we're done.'

Saoirse reached the table. She could hear Nicky tutting.

'Saoirse to the chair.' Scot's voice, which seemed amplified tenfold, boomed. Saoirse looked at the nearest camera and wagged her finger in front of her snarly mouth.

Nicky gave a huge sigh. 'What now?'

Squeezed into a ball by the bench, Saoirse winced. Was she that much of a burden on Nicky's shoulders? Saoirse pictured Nicky hunched over under the weight.

In a flash, Nicky ran towards the measuring room, where she'd find Sonny alone. Saoirse took her chance. Not bothering to check if Patty saw, she ran to the far corridor and headed to the weapon room.

It was empty. Low lighting displayed the centrepiece: the unit with its thick glass dome. Saoirse's interest lay not in the steel mallet underneath, but in the keypad with its screen, buttons and thumbprint scanner. Her fingers twiddled out of control.

'Saoirse to the chair.' Scot's voice rang out again.

'Shush! I have to.' She squatted out of view and rested her thumb on the scanner.

A tinny, automated voice instructed her to select one of the names and press a green button, or say the name of a housefriend. Saoirse crossed her fingers. She whispered the name of the woman who had befriended her so swiftly. Beautiful Nicky. With her tattoos, spiky hair and boundless confidence.

'Repeat the name clearly,' the voice said.

'Jesus Christ!' Saoirse thumped the dome.

'Unknown name. Please choose from the list.'

27

Alan walked past the labs, three levels above the housefriends and the ever-vigilant television cameras. Here, in his eyes, colourists and video technicians performed digital miracles. It was the part of the Scot Free complex he least visited and it was the most deserted. He stopped outside a video suite. With a bit of luck, Everton, the elusive video and telecine specialist, would be inside. Lab staff never responded when he knocked. But he still gave them the courtesy. He rapped smoke-stained knuckles on the door, opened it and called Everton's name.

In the half-light, Everton slammed his laptop closed and curled up to hide himself. Alan stopped in his tracks and stared, not looking away for one moment. Watching Everton's pathetic attempt to cover up was sure to make him even more uncomfortable.

'What do you want? Knock first, would you?'

Alan didn't bother pointing out that he had. To restore a little privacy to the suite, he closed the door. Even in the dark, he spotted Everton's uncoordinated attempt at looking busy with an unbuckled belt, unzipped jeans and a box of tissues. 'Best to leave that until you're home. If that laptop's work equipment, she'll have that over you. And if she catches you herself, she'll skewer you with her favourite blade.'

Everton mumbled through his thick beard. 'She doesn't need proof to have something over me, dude.'

'Your job is to –'

'Your job is to keep her away from here,' Everton said. 'What do you want?'

'Good news. We still don't have your finish date and we went live days ago. You don't want her in here breathing down your neck. I've come instead.'

'She's the walking dead. She doesn't breathe. Breath hardly leaves her lips.'

In the dark room, Alan felt freer to join in. 'Yet it smothers.' He leant on the door poised to leave, careful not to touch anything Everton might have. 'Well?'

'I told you – I told her. It's coming along beautifully. Almost done.' Everton's tone warmed.

'We knew that weeks ago. I need to go back with something more than "It's coming along nicely" and "I'm busy with porn".'

Everton swivelled round. In full view, he did up his jeans and belt as calmly as he would wipe food off his T-shirt. Alan's gaze veered off to the equipment stacked around the room in uncoordinated piles of black and chrome. Machines used to copy, to restore, to refine. He inhaled deeply. There was something soothing about the glue smell of recently unwrapped gadgets. At least the equipment in the room was clean, reliable and good quality, even if the staff weren't.

'Tell her she'll have it by Friday,' Everton said. 'Of next week.'

'That's too close to the grand finale. Adolpha isn't comfortable being at your mercy. We're relying on your expertise –'

'Of this week.'

In the corridor, Alan took several deep cleansing breaths. He pulled out a pocket bottle of sanitiser and squirted a lavish amount into his palm. It would remove all kinds of filth. The sharp, vinegary smell alone made him feel cleaner. Opposite him, the glass casing of a notice board cast his reflection. He admired himself and ran the excess gel through his hair. Looking good.

*

Nicky rushed in and saw the screen.

'Who isn't a match?'

Saoirse retreated to the wall and shrank down, pointing at her.

'You didn't?' Nicky grabbed her hands. Under the downlight, Saoirse's skin appeared paler than usual.

'We can work together now. It's better,' Saoirse said, leaning in for a kiss.

Nicky pulled back and bellowed up at the camera. 'Scot! She deserves another guess.'

'It's going to be all right. You don't understand. Myra did. She got to face the person who killed her family member. I had to know.'

'We can get out of this, but you have to trust me.' Nicky's voice moderated as she tidied the straggly waves of Saoirse's hair. Could she look any more vulnerable? If she embraced Saoirse now as tightly as she wanted, she would shatter. 'In case you hadn't noticed, Myra had a huge knife. All you have is a paper flower. Where is it?' She patted Saoirse down.

'Safe. In my room.'

Nicky felt a playful desperation help soften her frown lines.

'I'd better make you another one to keep your hands away from mischief. The trick is to blend in. Be like Bow. Or Jay. This little stunt makes you stand out. In a bad way.'

Nicky followed Saoirse's line of sight to the encased weapon.

'I will not spend my time seeking out mallets,' Saoirse said. 'When you're not too angry to give me a hug, I'd like one, please.'

'Oh, Saoirse. This way.'

Nicky towed her to the other side of the house, where she accessed the women's bathroom with her thumb. Inside, she ran a hot shower and let the steam build up before undressing. 'You're getting in with me.'

'I am?' Saoirse's eyes were as big as her gaping mouth.

Leaving Saoirse to undress in the vapour that became a fog, Nicky stepped into the shower recess and adjusted the water temperature. Over one shoulder, she saw Saoirse, swathed in steam. They shared the water stream.

Nicky looked into Saoirse's flashing eyes and brushed water from her thick hair. Sounds from the shower would surely muffle any conversation. 'I've spent my life around abusive men. Family, work, everywhere. I'd been hanging around with this guy, an all-round bad seed, set to rob a bank with buddies. They needed a fourth person, a driver. That's how I ended up in this mess.'

'You didn't go into the bank? You were … chauffeur?'

Nicky nodded and gave her a peck on the lips. 'My job was to stay put, armed with a crowbar.'

'Who did they kill?'

Nicky stepped behind Saoirse, lathered her back and spoke into her ear.

'Nobody. We took off and –' Nicky paused at the painful memory. 'We'd been arguing the whole morning. Before we got in that car. On the way. Parked outside. So much tension. It was unbearable.'

'What about?'

'Everything. Who was getting what cut. Who was going to kick things off inside the bank. What to do if it went wrong. Everything. Plus, one of us was new to the group. Recruit on the fucking day? That's the worst thing you can do. He turned up wearing a balaclava, so I didn't even know what he looked like. I was the only one caught, so I still don't. Anyway, the tension in the car was building and building.'

'But didn't you have a plan? Tell me it was planned.'

'Things kept changing. They were saying we'd leave by one street, and that kept changing. But they got out of the bank, got in and we took off. And for the briefest of moments, we were all so bloody happy. Three of us screaming. Balaclava guy silent next to me. In the back, they were hugging. No fighting. Then we stopped at the lights.'

Saoirse reached behind her to Nicky's thigh. 'Then what?'

Nicky rinsed Saoirse's back and buttocks. 'This moron slammed into the back of us. Our car was a mess. Shattered windows. We were bashed about. We smashed into the car in front and the fucking thing wouldn't start. And. That. Was. It. I got out and saw the driver holding his mobile and I fucking lost it.'

'What did you do?' Saoirse positioned Nicky under the water and shampooed her hair, keeping her ear close to Nicky's mouth.

'I grabbed the crowbar. They took off with what money they could, but I made a beeline for this guy. I was furious. He'd ruined our plans and our two minutes of joy. All because of his shit driving.'

'In front of everyone at the intersection – what did you …?'

'I circled his car, smashing it up. I was on the passenger side and he got out and ran. Cunt still had his mobile in his hand. So I chased him. I had the crowbar. He looked behind and he ran into a car and got shredded.' She took a long breath. 'I'll never forget it. His body crunching against the car, the screeching noises.' Nicky paused to let the water rinse her clean. 'There I was, all ready to hit him with the crowbar above my head. And he was on the ground, all broken up. I dropped the bar and the sound kept echoing round and round. Everyone looked at me. Like the noise was disrespectful to the dead.'

'Did you get a good look at him? Who's his relative?'

Nicky shrugged. 'He was about fifty. Jay's build. Walt's colouring.'

'Bow could be his daughter.'

Nicky caught Saoirse's eye. 'Bow's a target, not a hunter.'

'Oh. How long did you get?'

'Eighteen years. This happened about two years ago.'

Saoirse did a double take. 'My children will be in their thirties by the time you get out.'

'Don't worry about me. We need to keep you safe.' Nicky held her finger up to get Saoirse to wait. She increased the force of the water and the noise grew. 'My plan is to get out way before your kids hit their thirties.' She kissed Saoirse's open mouth in three bursts, then focused on her earlobe. 'Close your eyes. Enjoy.'

'It's tickling.' Saoirse's shoulders came up in futile defence.

'Eyes closed.' Nicky planted more kisses and whispered. 'I've got an escape plan.'

Nicky told her why she didn't need to win the show to go free, all the while trailing a hand over Saoirse's thighs. Gentle groans mingled with the gushing water.

28

On Tuesday afternoon, once the direct sunlight had deserted the garden, Jay started practising handstands. Within thirty minutes, he was red-faced and his arms were tiring, and he hoped his garden workout would be broadcast. In between handstands, he traipsed around the lawn finding angles where he could see who was sitting on the sofas. Taran. Patty.

Jay was waiting for Patty to go so he could question Taran. But it had to sound spontaneous. He did a couple more handstands then headed into the cool air, where he found Taran and Sonny on the sofas. He grabbed a cup of icy water and sat with them.

They stopped talking. Sonny stretched out and closed his eyes. With Alice in his arms, Taran developed a sudden fascination for her fur.

'I'm not used to this heat. Is this normal Sydney weather?' Jay waited to see how the lie landed. It would need a long conversation to arrive at specific details surrounding Harriet's death.

Sonny opened one eye. 'You're so noxious.'

'Thanks. You might mean obnoxious.'

'You might get punched.'

Taran spoke to Alice. 'Time to get you some lettuce leaves, young lady.' He walked outside, leaving Jay with Sonny's chesty breathing that soon turned to snoring.

Jay rapped on the sofa armrest. Definitely not the way to approach the targets. His thoughts drifted. If only the targets spoke as freely as the hunters. Like the day before in the wood, collecting vegetables. Walt wouldn't shut up. But … wait. Something about Walt's words wasn't sitting right. It hadn't registered at the time, but now Jay had the feeling it didn't fit. What had Walt shared? Jay waited, expecting it to spring to mind. Nope.

It would come.

Scot's voice rang through the house, announcing that the next round of clues would appear after the tone.

*

Jay found wall space next to Patty and waited for his clue. With such little headway in identifying Harriet's killer, he was counting on some useful information.

A friend killed her

It must have looked like Jay was glued to his spot. He had wanted progress, but the clue hit like a tornado. He stood at the wall, using it to hold him up. Waves of shock pounded his skull from the inside, crashed to his legs to destabilise him and shot back to his chest to do it all again.

Poor Harriet. To be betrayed by a friend.

Jay had been interstate when he'd first heard the news. On his return, the police had only given him patchy details, which was law enforcement policy. Harriet had died alone in a shop doorway. And now this. Killed by a friend.

There were four possible suspects. Bow, Nicky, Sonny and Taran. Jay was having a hard time picturing Taran and Harriet as friends. But the others, quite possibly. Maybe Harriet's addiction, bonding over drugs, brought her in contact with Sonny or Nicky.

*

Taran was cuddling Alice at the wall, holding her brown nose to the screen that would soon display his clue. Next to him, Sonny was taking up his position when Nicky barged him into the wall.

'Thanks for helping to kill Saoirse, arsehole. With your stupid idea.'

'What are you talking about, Shorty?'

'Putting it in her head to check my name. She' – Nicky looked around and lowered her voice – 'is totally exposed now. Leave her alone or I'll give you another scar down your ugly face. She's not like you. She needs a weapon.'

'Piss off.'

Nicky gave him another shove. 'Fucking men. Always ruining it. Screw up everyone's chances of getting out of here alive and walk off with the money.'

'They are the actual rules of the show,' Taran said, sticking his head around Sonny. He heard the tone to signal their clues were coming and he faced the screen.

> Your hunter doesn't know what else
> you did to their relative

'Fuck.' Taran closed his eyes as if the clue was blinding.

Alice earned a flurry of pecks on her head to hide his searing cheeks. He welcomed the coming distraction by his side, Sonny pulling his finger from his nose and shouting.

'That's it? Trust dumbarse Nicky? That's a shit clue.' He pointed at her. 'I already know she's a target. Look at her. She looks more like a criminal than me.'

She flashed her capital 'E' at him.

*

Jay watched Patty heave herself up the steps to the decking and settle on the edge of the hot tub, her back to everyone. He followed and sat with her, not too close. 'I found these. I was peckish.' A bag of cashews jiggled in his hand.

He stared into the garden and checked their reflections in the glass. Patty's eyes were down, shoulders fallen. After about two minutes of sitting quietly and sharing his snack, she explained her mood. 'The person who killed my son claims to be innocent.'

'A houseful of wrongful convictions, it seems. I'm so sorry. Is a clue like that meant to fire you up and provoke anger?'

'It hasn't worked.' She gave her head two short shakes. Left. Right. 'What's the point? They've taken everything from me. But, apparently, innocent. They can't bring me in here and tell me that.' Her voice faltered. 'It's like Scot's trying to make me feel sorry for them. My clues aren't firing me up about revenge. They're turning me against Scot. I'm not able.'

'I wish I could help,' Jay said.

'You want to help someone? Who's most afraid? It isn't me. Go help them.'

'That's Saoirse. But she has Nicky.' Jay's eyes went to the four targets at the table, waiting for dinner. 'We're all scared in here.'

'I've moved beyond all that. This innocent person, whoever they are, can do their best. Come rob me of the last thing I have – bitter air in my lungs.' Jay offered his hand. Patty squeezed it. 'We'll sit here and wait to die.'

'Let's find something to do.'

They scoured the room, the wide empty space, the cameras, Saoirse and Walt cooking dinner.

'I'm not even allowed to be productive. I could be knitting. I miss it so.' Patty corrected herself. 'I miss my dog and my knitting. They're the two things I wish for. They'd make this place more bearable.'

'I've got an idea.' Jay stood. 'Come with me.'

He guided her along the corridor to the room with the chair. Once she'd settled herself in the seat, Jay called Scot's name. 'I'm here to ask for something. Patty would like some knitting.'

There was a pause.

'Er – yes. It's true.' Patty held her breath.

'It's against the rules,' Scot said. 'Needles are weapons.'

Patty sat forward. 'Wait. I don't need needles. I need wool. You can give me two makeshift needles. Plastic ones.'

'Her knitting will calm her, Scot.'

'Better you socialise with your housefriends and don't isolate yourself with a hobby.'

'But we watch films out there,' Jay said. 'There's nothing more solitary than staring at a screen in silence.'

'I want my knitting.' Patty whacked the armrests.

Jay pleaded. 'Look at how relaxed Taran is since he got Total … Alice.'

'Please return to the communal area.'

'No. There are different needles,' Patty said. 'Make them out of rubber. Or I can knit in the round. Children's ones. Bendy ones. I don't care which. You can't hurt anyone with them.'

'Please leave the chair.'

Patty stood, patted Jay's arm and left the room.

Jay took her spot. 'What if we all got something? Taran has his rabbit. Why not give us all a pick-me-up?' In the extended silence, Jay realised how unworkable the request was. For the entire show turned on keeping the outside world out.

The microphone came to life. 'I agree. Let's pick everyone up. Thank you,' Scot said.

Jay cried out.

'Please ask the housefriends what small gift they would like and return here alone. This mic shuts off in two minutes.'

29

A breeze rattled the venetians and the cicadas forced the volume up. In their usual seats, Frank and Eleanor Carlisle were watching Scot Free. A quick wriggle of excitement lengthened Eleanor's back and she leant towards the screen, which showed Jay beckoning to the others. 'Hurry!' she shouted.

An unseen narrator's voice blared.

'Jay has to explain everything to the housefriends, get their requests and relay that to Scot in two minutes. Will he make it?' A promo clip played.

Eleanor yelled again. 'Shut up so we can hear what they're saying! Why do they do that? They ruin it.'

'I wonder what Bow asks for,' Frank said.

Eleanor stirred her gin and tonic with a finger and slurped it dry.

'Picture of you?'

With his eyes locked on the television, Frank drank his beer. He blew across the top of the bottle in time with the jingle. He ignored her. That's how she knew her comment had hit the mark.

Seconds later, the show resumed with the narrator still drowning out the housefriends' words. Onscreen, Patty's hands were shaking frantically and Jay leant on the island counting off everyone's requests. Nicky was massaging Saoirse's shoulders.

'Those two seem very friendly,' Eleanor said. 'They're always together. Saoirse's the older one, but Nicky acts like the parent protecting her. You'd expect things to be the other way. It's good to see women making friends in such a hostile environment.'

'Oh Ellie. It's not a parent–child relationship. They're more intimate than that.'

'Can't I watch my show in peace without you policing every comment?' She pointed at the screen. 'He's going back to Scot! Quick, Jay!' She sighed. 'He's a real gentleman. He cares, you know?'

*

Like spider limbs, Adolpha's fingers twitched over the button that activated Scot's voice. She had a leg up on the edge of the console. Clad in black leather, it was still but primed for attack. Her prey was on its way. Alan watched her as she lay in wait in a web of wires. The sound equipment only added to his unease. Rows of magnified eyes all around them.

'It's working. He's bringing them together,' she said. Adolpha's decision to let them have gifts meant he had to stay in the suite. He was desperate for the cigarette he played with out of sight.

From several camera angles, the pair watched Jay zip back to the chair. A close-up of his face appeared on the wall-mounted screen as he sat and looked straight at the camera. Settling his glasses, he panted and spoke. 'I've got everyone's choices.'

Adolpha pressed the button to transform her voice into Scot's. 'Well done, Jay. Taran has Alice and Patty gets some knitting. What about the others?'

'Nicky and Sonny want cigarettes.'

Adolpha screwed up her face. Alan knew exactly what she would say to that. Tobacco smoke seeping through the house? No chance.

'They can only smoke outside. Please tell them.'

Alan stopped himself from crying out. Onscreen, Jay continued.

'Walt wants a mat to do yoga. He says the marble's too hard, and lying on grass itches his skin. He also asked for the mat not to carry your logo or any branding. Bow wants a novel – *La Pista Equivocada*, something like that. It's by Susana Casa de Sal. She said it has to be in Spanish, not translated.'

'Clever woman,' Adolpha said to Alan. She activated Scot's voice. 'Saoirse?'

'She wants a hair dryer. Well, Nicky wants her to ask for one. Saoirse really wants a pic of her children. But that's not safe, is it? They've decided doing her hair will lift Saoirse's mood.'

'All that in two minutes? And you? What would you like?'

Jay was staring directly into the camera. 'I'm like Patty. I want something to do with my hands. A Rubik's Cube, please.'

'Consider it done. Thank you, Jay. Know that the housefriends will appreciate your courage.' Adolpha lowered her leg and wheeled herself closer to the mic. 'It is comforting to see you taking charge. Not all the hunters have that mettle. There are some strong personalities' – onscreen, Jay sat tall – 'but they're targets, undeserving of such a privileged position. The group looks to you for guidance. If you're clever, that will serve you well.'

Adolpha removed her finger from the button and gave a thumbs-up to Alan.

Jay went to leave the chair, but he stopped and asked, 'When will the gifts arrive?'

'When would you like them?'

'Tomorrow.'

'Then you can tell everyone their gifts arrive tomorrow. Go lightly, Jay.' Adolpha cut audio to the chair and swung to face Alan. 'And that is how it's done.'

'Snared,' Alan said. 'He doesn't suspect a thing.'

Time for a smoke.

'It's happening, believe me. This will be some of the best television our viewers ever see. We are gearing up to that one stand-out moment people will talk about for years. Years. Come the grand finale, if we pull this off, I swear you'll hear the whole country gasp.'

What could Alan meaningfully add to that? 'I hope so' was all that came.

She tapped her phone on the console. 'He's all over the socials. He's the hero.' She swayed her head as she spoke. 'And nothing ever, ever, ever happens to the hero.'

30

On Wednesday, Nicky kissed Saoirse and waved her off. She watched her cross the lawn with Bow and take the right path into the woods. Saoirse didn't look over her shoulder. Nicky ambled to the measuring room. Her toes gripped the cold marble with each step. Metres from the door, she stopped. Walt was inside. Saoirse had warned her how suffocating a space it was, and his height made the room look even smaller.

He pushed a button and the door opened. 'There you are. Come on in.'

Once the door closed behind her, she started shuffling from side to side. 'Is there any way to make that stay open?'

Walt shook his head. 'Not unless we keep hitting the button. We'll be quicker if we just get on with it.'

'Get on with it, then.'

He pointed to the wraps of thin cotton and the tape measure coiled over them. 'We take this and this and we enter the details here.' He stepped closer to her.

She raised her fists. 'Young Nicky, you're blocking the screen.'

'Don't call me that.'

'That's where we enter our details.' He indicated the wall tablet behind her and grabbed the tape measure. 'You first. Arms up.' She obeyed, standing as rigid as a crucifix, and held her breath. He began measuring up. From the look that flashed across his face, he must have felt how stiff her limbs were.

Saoirse had warned Nicky about the tape measure. She knew Walt was gripping more than tailoring equipment – he was holding a weapon. Nicky watched where he placed the start of it, how tightly he held the thick, glossy tape. Only when he stepped to the tablet and she lowered her arms did her breathing ease somewhat.

'We get our presents tonight,' she said.

'We'll see. They'll say anything because they have a television audience to maintain. Turn around please. I'll do your back.'

Nicky inched around and faced the door, her gaze fixing on the corridor. 'What have they not been honest about?' She looked over her shoulder as Walt came close with the tape measure. Her panic rose again and she found her mouth agape in a silent scream as she tried to restart her breathing.

He tilted her head. 'You're angled. Face the front. And stand still. This is hard enough for me.' He measured her shoulders and turned to the tablet. She spun round and kept watch, her eyes glued to him. Next, he waggled his finger in a circle so she would turn away once more.

'Hurry up,' she said, giving him her back.

'Jay is convinced we're getting presents. Whatever they said to him in the chair last night, he doesn't doubt it.' He exhaled long and slow. 'Now your neck.'

'I'll put my hands around my neck and then I'll place them

against the tape measure.' She faced him, hands up like she was strangling herself. She took them away and showed him. 'It's about this long.'

'No, let's do it properly. I'm not going to –'

'I don't like things around my neck.'

'Trust me.'

'But –' Her chest raised and a cough erupted.

Walt gripped the tape measure and tapped the ends together like a pair of cymbals. He stepped towards her. She swallowed and held her chin down. His hands came up and she stiffened, the tape measure lurching around her shoulders as he passed the end from one hand to the other. Much taller than her, he looked down, widening his stance in an exaggerated way as though the task needed exceptional precision. A pair of mismatched dance partners. He chuckled and rested his wrists on her shoulders.

'What?'

His head fell sideways to catch her eye. 'You're going to have to lift your chin. I can't get under there otherwise.'

With her chin touching her chest, she followed his every move. But straining to see made her eyes water. She blinked the moisture away, but it only made her vision worse. In the corner, the ceiling camera went blurry and she closed her eyes. Fuck! She felt his hands caress the sides of her neck, where Saoirse had kissed, where warm veins throbbed. She gasped for air. The coolness of the tape sent a chill through her limbs. She opened her eyes to find him staring right at her, his saggy, yellow face inches away. Around her neck, the tape tightened. A burst of energy coursed through her and her arms shot up. She thrust him away, causing him to lose balance and fall to the wall.

'I'll do it. You're giving me the fucking creeps.'

*

It was a cool and cloudy day. Christy stepped off the bus at the end of her road, dying to scream. With her lungs about to explode, she let out a controlled shriek, her first since leaving the hospital. Nobody heard, for it was safely drowned out by the *vroom* of the departing bus. She increased her pace. There would be more squealing to come.

Clamped in her hand, safe in the pocket of her flimsy summer jacket, was the folded paper. She couldn't have gripped a million dollars more firmly. At the front door, the key wouldn't find the lock and her hand battled to steady itself. Finally, the lock turned, she flew inside and she slammed the door. That's when the serious screaming began, as she ripped through the place like a tornado. She pulled the paper out and threw her coat aside as if she'd never find a use for it again. She was strong, powerful, made of steel. This was the first time she had ever carried a baby long enough to attend a second ultrasound. A second ultrasound! And how well it had gone. They'd said so at the hospital. She'd never forget the sonographer's words.

'It's all good, Christy. It's all really good.'

Sonography. Her new favourite word. She repeated it aloud and gazed at the picture of her baby. Jay's baby. Head, body, legs, the gentle curve of its spine.

In the living room, with her back to the television, she admired the image for so long the monochrome shape started blurring. She diverted her eyes to refocus.

It had been ages since she'd needed to find a place for a photo. Her perfect, healthy fetus deserved to go on display in a special spot. It needed to be the first thing Jay saw when he walked in. After three miscarriages, the image she was holding was too important to go simply anywhere.

She scanned the room until her eyes came to rest on the photo of Jay and Harriet. The one he had swapped the day he was taken. It was out of its frame in no time. She folded the edges of the ultrasound image to fit the frame and closed the back, smiling. Her hand knocked the photo of Jay and Harriet off the shelf. It fell behind the large, heavy unit, where it would stay for a long time, among the electrical cords, dust and dead bugs.

A smile spread across her face. Rubbing her belly, she took a step back and admired the image. How healthy the baby looked, how cocooned, how protected.

She was jerked from her thoughts by a ringtone in the room. But not from her own mobile. It dawned on her that Jay's phone on the side table was ringing.

It was an unknown number.

A wave of alarm came over her. Maybe it was a friend who didn't know Jay was on the show. Breaking that news was not a task she fancied, but she answered it.

'Hello?'

There was no response.

'Hello-o?' She waited. A look at the screen confirmed the seconds on the clock were advancing, so the line was active. She could make out faint mumbles. It sounded like someone debating whether to speak. She might coax a response from them by putting on an upbeat voice.

'This is Jay's phone.' Her put-on voice came out overfriendly. But before she could correct herself, the line went dead.

31

The garden doorway to the studio closed behind Jay. Shoulders back, he crossed the lawn carrying a black box that bore the Scot Free branding. A thin red line and a bloodied dagger. As the sun faded from Wednesday, the interior of the house bathed the waiting housefriends in unforgiving studio light. They hovered on the decking and the stairs like an eager wedding party, standing aside to let him pass to the dining table.

Patty was beside him in no time. She couldn't keep her hands still. It looked as though she was warming up to start knitting instantly.

Taran stood away, bobbing Alice in his arms like a proud parent. He whispered in her ear and chuckled as he straightened up.

'You've started talking to it now?' Jay asked.

'Her, Jay. Alice is female. She'll have that box when you're done.'

Jay removed the lid and the others swarmed in.

'Me first, please,' Patty said.

'Here's the wool.' Jay handed a bulging paper bag to Patty. A black pouch swung in his other hand. 'These might be the needles.'

Patty went to take them, but Sonny snatched the pouch from her. 'Needles? Grandma got a weapon? Are you for real?'

'Give them to me!' Patty said. 'They're knitting needles. They're not dangerous, so you won't have any need for them.'

Sonny looked inside. 'They're plastic.' No more dangerous than their cutlery.

Patty snatched the pouch back from him and let out tiny cries as she withdrew the needles. 'I'm going to make you a jumper, Jay. See. I have enough wool. Oh, thank you, Jay.'

'Give me my fucking smokes.' Sonny held his palm out and Jay handed him a carton, which he tore open as he walked off. 'Oh, thank you, Jay,' he said, mimicking Patty. Jay fished out a box of matches and hurled it at his head. 'Oi!' Sonny picked the box off the floor.

Clambering to his feet at the other end of the table, Walt steadied himself as he shook a finger after Sonny. 'Don't even think about smoking inside. Move far from the door.' Any power in his voice was betrayed by his sluggishness. 'I don't want to smell it. Or see the ash. Or the butts. If I get so much as a whiff, I'll shove it down your throat.' He yelled at a camera. 'They're a bloody hazard, Scot!'

'Fuck off, old man,' Sonny said, traipsing up the steps.

'It'll damage your health, Sonny,' Patty said. 'We wouldn't want that.' She chuckled to herself and squeezed the skeins of black and red wool, which were good quality. Soft but firm.

'No chance. Fit as a fiddle, me. Got one of the highest fitness levels in prison. Doctors can't work it out. They love testing medicines and treatments on me, and I always score well. If another inmate gets six, I get ten. If they score forty, I get fifty.

They say it's my genes.'

'Fifty what?' Jay asked, resting his arms on the box.

'How the fuck should I know?' Sonny's voice rose. 'Just fifty. Ten more than the others on the bloody test. Endurance, immunity, bone strength, whatever. Why pick at my words? I explained something, but you always gotta pick.'

Nicky came over and beckoned for her carton of cigarettes.

'Only one box of matches,' Jay said. 'You'll need to share with the Medical Marvel over there.'

Sonny's annoyance continued as he stepped outside. 'Trying to make me look stupid. Accept a man's word and get fucked, all of you.' He slammed the sliding door.

Next, Jay removed a glaring yellow exercise mat. He abandoned his post at the box to place it by Walt. 'I told them no branding. Like you said.'

'Yoga in a house full of smoke doesn't appeal.' Walt left the mat untouched.

Saoirse shouted to Nicky, who was heading outside. 'Where do you think you're going? Don't come back inside smelling of tobacco.' Nicky snarled at her playfully and went outside.

'Here you go, Saoirse. Your hair dryer. Still in its box.'

This got Walt's attention. 'For god's sake. Another weapon?'

'Says here it's plastic,' Jay said. 'She won't be using it on you. I think you're safe.'

'Always the voice of reason.' Walt grabbed the mat. 'Time for yoga after all.'

Coming to stand next to Jay, Saoirse studied the glossy package in his hands. She turned to the mirror and smoothed her hair, as though checking whether a hair dryer might come in useful one day.

Jay pulled a sad face.

'Sorry. No exchange, no refund.'

Without a word, Saoirse retraced her steps to the sofa, the gift remaining unopened by her feet.

'Almost done,' Jay said. Out came the last two items. A book and a Rubik's Cube, both new. 'Bow, this is yours.' Jay called out the title and author, mispronouncing almost every word. '*La Pista Equivocada*. Susana Casa de Sal.'

Rubbing her palms on her trousers, Bow approached him. A mechanic wiping her hands to take a customer's keys. She took the book, flipped it and ran her finger over the back jacket. Anyone would think she was refreshing herself on the plot. Jay studied the cover. 'Murder mystery?'

'Yes. In English, the title is *The Wrong Clue*. This book is my favourite book.' Jay was puzzled by the awkward way Bow spoke. 'I was reading this when they collected me.'

'Do you remember your spot?'

Bow made a face. 'Er – what?'

'Your spot, you know, in the book. Do you remember the page you got up to?'

'Oh. That. I'll find it. I've read it so many times, it won't matter what page I start.' For an extended time, Bow stood at the table drumming the book with her fingertips and looking around at the others.

'Look. My Rubik's Cube.' Jay unwrapped it and rolled it in his hands. 'Do you remember where you were when these came out?'

'Earth,' Bow said.

'I'll take this for Alice,' Taran said, grabbing the empty Scot Free box. 'She won't know the significance of the gruesome logo.'

'Thanks, Scot,' Jay shouted. He tried starting applause, but nobody joined in. After five claps, he gave up.

*

It was one in the morning. Alan would be back in the studio by seven, but he couldn't sleep. His mouth was dry, the discarded bottle of vodka beside him even drier. That went an hour ago. Resisting tiredness, he lit another cigarette. He sent a drift of smoke rings to the television, which played a murder reel of all the Scot Free seasons. At full blast, the montage made his screen vibrate, which gave the blood-curdling screams a staccato disco rhythm.

The television was the only light source in the room. Each flicker – like lightning in an imminent storm – illuminated him, pinned to the sofa and draped in tobacco smoke. The cigarette pack and ashtray balancing on his belly rose and fell steadily through the footage of stabbings and stranglings. Always after a new angle on old kills, his hungry eyes stayed glued to the screen. He'd watched them so often that it was hard to know when the reel ended, when his dreams began, what was fiction, what was a movie, what was work. He enjoyed the kills more with the volume cranked up. If he burst into tears, it meant his neighbours wouldn't hear. Funny things, tears. They came out of nowhere.

'Rewind.' He mumbled the command loud enough for the system to respond. It wasn't until the video began rewinding that he heard banging at the front door. 'Pause.' A frozen image. Rosa in the chair. She looked spectral in the green and grainy night vision. Moments from death.

His neighbour was knocking. Complaining. Again. The young mother from unit twelve.

'Mister Coldbreath? Alan? Please turn that down. It's really late.'

Always the same pleading tone aimed at keeping him from getting worked up. He took a long drag of his cigarette.

'Mister Coldbreath, the boys are trying to sleep. They have camp tomorrow. We agreed that weeknights you would keep it low. Remember? Can you stick to what we agreed? Please?'

'Volume five. No, volume six.' One more murder before bed. 'Play at half speed.' Onscreen, Rosa shrank into the chair. Behind her, a washed-out Myra rose into view, brandishing the knife. Alan's eyes flickered. Hard to believe that from such silence and slowness, such ruin would come.

32

On Thursday, after the group enjoyed Saoirse's lunch of warm salmon salad, the clouds came threatening rain. Nicky and Saoirse endured the sultry heat outside. For the others, the air conditioning was too appealing. Bow, Taran and Sonny absorbed themselves in a film, and Jay, Walt and Patty huddled at the dining table. Safety in numbers.

In agony, Jay watched Walt fumble with the Rubik's Cube. Seeing Walt miss glaring opportunities to line up the colours was making his chest hurt. He reached across, holding his hands up like a statue. On standby, ready to intervene. In the end, his hands inched so close to Walt's that it looked like they were both doing the cube.

Patty's clicking knitting needles drowned out almost all of Walt's tutting. She lowered them, the train of black fabric settling in her lap, and surveyed the area.

'It feels like Sunday.'

Walt raised an eyebrow.

'I'd hate to see what your Mondays look like.' He checked under the table. 'Who's knocking the bench? Stop it.' His voice heavy with irritation, he showed Jay the complete green side of the cube.

'Great.' It took Jay a lot of effort to sound authentic. He'd seen primary kids do the entire puzzle quicker than Walt had done a face. His tight chest eased the moment he took the cube back.

'It's his leg. Don't show them you're nervous, Jay,' Patty said, starting to knit again.

'I filled up on coffee. That's all.'

'Right. Are you nervous, Walt?' Patty asked.

'It's not nerves,' Jay said. 'More worried. That I won't find out why all this happened. I want to know why.'

Patty leant in close and brought her elbows onto the table. With nowhere else to go, her needles came together in front of her face and the knitting covered her mouth. 'Do you have any idea, you know, who?'

'I wouldn't be sitting here if I did,' Walt said. 'Do you?'

Patty's fingers worked the wool with the calm assurance of an expert, and she shook her head. 'Knowing my luck, it will be Sonny.'

'You think there's a luckier option sitting over there on the sofas?' Jay asked, keeping his head down.

Making herself seem smaller, less visible, Patty scrunched her back. 'Sonny's so stupid, yet he could wipe out my entire family. I've no chance against a powerful, stupid man.' Her precise movements with the needles drove home her comments. 'When he talks, which isn't often, thank god, I have to check I'm not laughing.' Now she spoke through clamped teeth. 'I forget where I am and I think he's joking. He is actually a dunce.'

She stopped knitting once more.

Her pause got Jay and Walt's attention.

'This morning at breakfast, I poured juice for Taran and him. Two glasses but Taran wanted ice. Clunk, clunk.' She added the sound effects of ice splashing into a cup.

'Next thing I know, Sonny's complaining that Taran has more juice. Two of them sitting right here and Sonny behaving like a kid. I said the ice is making it look like there's more liquid. But the fool wasn't having a bar of it. We were there for ages. Honest to God. Ages.' She dropped her knitting to the table and gripped Jay's forearm. 'I'm a patient person. At church, we all know Father Billsborough can be' – she pondered her words – 'trying. Sonny makes Father look like a saint. It took so long to explain the difference in the level of orange juice and he could not get it. How is that possible? Even crows understand displacement.'

'Careful. He'll hear,' Jay said. 'Whatever you say makes its way into every corner. The acoustics are like a cathedral.'

'Lord have mercy.' She resumed knitting. 'Pity the soul that gets sent to heaven by his hands. And not least because he spends most of his time trying to hide them up his wretched nostrils.' She nodded to the sofa area. 'See what I mean?'

Jay and Walt followed her line of sight in time to catch Sonny reversing a digit out of his nose.

*

'They're talking about us,' Sonny said, wiping his index finger on his T-shirt and reclining on the sofa.

With a sweep of the ceiling, Bow's gaze hopped from camera to camera. There was no point reminding Sonny about them. She drummed her Spanish novel, with its sprig of leaves bookmarking her spot. Anyone who checked would see at that moment she was on page eighty-eight.

'Patty's lips are moving. They're probably sharing information to see who's matched to who,' Sonny said. 'My hunter is a parent. Could be her.'

'We know. You read your clue out,' Bow said.

Taran squeezed Alice closer. 'All of us could be parents. Don't automatically think the hunter is much older. You might attack the wrong person.'

'Unless you know how old your victim was,' Sonny said. 'Well?'

'Well what?' Bow asked.

'How old was the person you killed?'

Like it was yesterday, Bow could feel the wind buffeting her face, its howl drowning out the world. An image of the skyscraper shell. She let that same wind carry the picture away as quickly as it came.

Staring right at her, Sonny and Taran waited for her answer. Sonny, mouth open. Taran, head angled, ready to distrust what she might say next.

She fingered the pages of the book. 'It's complicated.'

'Get me back to prison,' Taran said, changing the subject. 'This is hell.'

'Do you want me to help you leave next then?' Sonny asked. Only he laughed. He punched Taran, who let out a yelp. 'What a sissy. Let's toughen you up. Women don't like softies.'

With a side glance, Bow caught Taran's eye.

'Come on, Tarzan,' Sonny said. 'Let's help you get out. Share your clues and we'll work out who's who.'

'Not now.'

'You know mine. Share. What did yours say?'

Taran grimaced. 'I have a safe person and the second clue said –'

'What?' Sonny sat up.

'Someone I can trust, it said. So, if I disregard you two, and Nicky, and this other person, it leaves three people.'

'You got a fucking name? I get shit.' Sonny's face was a nose away from Taran's. He had to come in close to compete with Alice. 'Who is it?' His voice became overly aggressive, but all Taran did was nod. 'Right.' Sonny grabbed Taran's wrist and bent it back, making Taran howl and drop Alice in his lap. Sonny gripped Alice's neck. 'Tell me or Total gets –'

'Walt.'

Taran massaged his hand and stole Alice from Sonny's slackening grip. He put his mouth next to her furry ear, with the pretence of whispering, but his voice was firm and clear. 'Is Sonny a good or bad boy?' Alice sat still, nose twitching. 'Ooh. Jury's out.'

'And you, gorgeous? What have you worked out?' Sonny said to Bow.

'That the shower works best if you turn the cold on first.'

'How old is the person you killed?'

'I'd love to tell you what was in my clues, but I can't. And I have nothing you can threaten.'

'Wanna bet? Give me a few minutes and I'll straighten those legs of yours.'

'The only way you'll get near my thighs is if I'm choking you in a headlock.'

'Say the word, eh, Tarzan?' He locked eyes with Bow and dug a playful elbow into Taran, whose flinching seemed to frighten Alice.

'Come for a walk, bunny.' Taran stood up.

'Time for a smoke,' Sonny said. His hands searched under him for his cigarettes. No luck. They weren't behind the cushions either. He jumped to his feet, grabbed Bow's hand and pulled her upright. 'You must be sitting on my pack of smokes.'

His hand dived under her legs.

'Watch it, you,' she said, moving out of the way.

A quick search of the area turned up nothing and he stood over Bow, forehead creased. 'Where did I last have them?' He shouted to Taran, who was passing through the sliding door into the garden. 'Oi, did you take my cigarettes?'

'I don't smoke. Neither does Alice.'

33

Later that night, Jay spotted rabbit droppings on the floor. With a wave of his hand, he got Taran's attention on the quiet. Saoirse didn't need to know. They were about to eat. Taran kicked the droppings to the nearest wall chute and activated the vacuum, which drew the pellets across the marble and up the shaft.

Jay was last to sit at the table. Three bowls the size of steering wheels sat in the centre. Salad, curry, rice. Jay helped himself to salad. 'Thank you, Taran and Nicky.'

Patty smacked her lips. 'Wait until you try the curry.'

'Lamb,' Nicky said.

'This salad dressing is tasty,' Jay said. He looked across to see Sonny examining the meat on his fork. Curry sauce was already running down his fingers.

'Lamb of Nicky, you take away the sin of the world,' Sonny said. He ate the forkful, shredding the meat loudly, mouth open. 'But sometimes you bring it.' Sonny puckered his lips at Nicky.

Jay didn't see her reaction but, whatever she did, Sonny met it with a snort of derision.

They ate without conversation for a while. No clinking of metal cutlery on ceramic plates. Only the soft scraping of plastic on plastic and Sonny's wet chomping. Jay was about to start speaking to drown out Sonny's noises, but Patty beat him to it.

'Has everyone seen the jumper I'm knitting for Jay?'

'Course we have,' Sonny said, chewing wildly. 'You don't shut up about it.'

'I'll knit you something next. A bib.'

Sonny snarled at her, then stared at Taran, who had unwisely chuckled at Patty's comment. Still swallowing food, Sonny started on the topic likely to cause Taran the most grief. 'I spotted Total's wonky leg' – burp – 'sticks out at an angle when it stands still. It's in pain.'

With a napkin over one finger, Taran dabbed his mouth. 'No, Alice is not in pain, thank you. Alice has a twisted joint in her hind leg. Alice hops differently. That's all. And Alice's name is not Total.'

'If it's in pain, you kill it.' Sonny said. 'What might look like a wonky joint is probably causing it agony.'

'She's not in agony. No open cuts, no pain. Leave Alice and me alone. You're looking for a fight. You're irritable because you lost your cigarettes.'

'Stolen. Someone's nicked them.'

'Ask nicely and Nicky might give you one of hers to tide you over until you can get into your bedroom for the carton.'

'It was probably her who took 'em.' Sonny pushed his empty plate away. 'When I worked on a farm, any animal that slowed you down would've been straight for the chop. We ran a farm, not a fucking shelter. If it can't keep up, it'll only hold you back. Your rabbit's buggered with that injury. Best kill it.' He indicated Jay with a sharp nod. 'Let's ask our leader. We keep things alive because it makes us feel better, right? Sign of wisdom knowing when to stop helping someone who ain't set to make it.'

Jay avoided their eyes. Images flashed through his mind. He felt the stab of painful memories. Wishing he could have done more. Harriet. Emergency room. A drip. Her arm. Harriet sitting up in bed. Jay lifted his head. 'You don't kill someone because they're different. You don't do that to someone you care about. You help your family and friends. You do what you can to …' He swallowed hard, an imaginary piece of food threatening to block his airways. 'There's nothing wrong with Totalitarian.'

Leaning forward to face Sonny, Nicky interrupted. 'You've got an injury.' Her finger traced an invisible scar on her face. 'Does that mean we kill you? Are you no good to us with your scar?' She returned to her meal. 'Yum. Delicious. If I do say so.'

Jay stopped chewing. That was the first time any of them had commented on Sonny's scar in front of him. Sonny was spoiling for a fight. This might not go well. Eyes down, Jay helped himself to curry.

Walt, too, busied himself with another serving of food. 'Delicious, indeed. You'll have to give me the recipe.' He pointed at Sonny. 'How dare you sit there judging who or what should live? Hypocrite.'

'There's only one thing worse than a hypocrite.' Nicky licked her spoon. 'And that's a scarred hypocrite.'

'Oh, dear.' Saoirse covered her mouth.

'Okay, let's leave it for after dinner, shall –' Jay said, but Nicky spoke over him.

'Why don't you tell us, Sonny? How did you get that very-hard-to-notice scar on your face? Did your victim fight back?'

Jay realised he was holding his breath. He exhaled and looked up. Sonny's eyes bore into Nicky. He was ready to pounce.

'Got this in prison, where you meet some nasty types.' Sonny's head bobbed. It looked like he was giving everyone time to absorb the news. 'Gang leader thought he could teach me a lesson. Mongrel was thick as cow turd. You wouldn't believe someone could be so fucking stupid.' Patty coughed into her meal. 'Thought I was lying, making a fool of him. Dumb dog whipped out a razor. Cutthroat.'

A loud gasp drew everyone's attention from Sonny. 'A what?' Saoirse asked. 'A weapon? In prison? How on earth –'

'Oi! I'm talking.'

Jay found himself frowning at Saoirse. Sonny's story was too interesting. Her interruption too irritating.

Sonny continued. 'So out comes this blade and he goes to slice me up. I moved and he got me here.' His finger traced the length of the welt. From the middle of his forehead to the side of his mouth. He finished his drink with a slurp. 'Didn't feel the blade. Even with its broken edge. All too quick. Just my eyes filling up with blood. Warmer than you'd think, blood.'

There were groans around the table.

'You were lucky to escape with only that,' Jay said. 'It's close to the socket.'

'Quick reflexes, me.'

Out of the corner of his eye, Jay saw Patty shifting in her seat. He avoided eye contact with her.

'Ease off with the sympathy, everyone. What did you do to provoke this "dumb dog"?' Nicky asked.

'Nothing. I was telling him when it's winter here, it's summer in other places. And when it's summer here, it's winter there. He thought I was lying. But who the fuck doesn't know that, right?'

Nicky roared with laughter and sent a wave of giggles around the table. 'You point out a geographical fact to some idiot and he ends up disfiguring you? Because he thought you were taking the piss? My god.' She held on to the table to lean back.

Sonny looked at each of them. The food on Patty's plate had her mesmerised. Taran and Saoirse were watching Nicky fall apart and Bow was gazing at her drink as though she'd never seen liquid before. With his cutlery down, hands clasped, Walt stared outside.

Nicky's laughter eventually slowed, like a car on the last of its petrol. She took a sip of juice and stared at Sonny, almost willing him to replenish the tank with more of his stupidity. 'What a pathetic sight that must've been. There you are, standing around thinking you're a know-it-all on the solar fucking system and this dude slices your ugly chops.' She jiggled the last drops of juice in the cup. 'But it was a special occasion for you, right?'

Sonny leant back and crossed his arms. 'Keep going, Shorty.'

'Finally meeting someone thicker than you,' she said.

Sonny slammed his fists down and fixed them on the table as he stood. Puffed chest, prowling eyes. 'Your last warning, cunt. That goes for all of youse.' Breathing through his clenched teeth, he hunted for someone daring to make eye contact.

Jay got to his feet too, but more slowly. 'Let's finish dinner. Please. We can all calm down. Save the fighting for later.' He took his seat, hoping Sonny would copy him and sit down. But no luck.

After a few seconds, Patty stirred the bowls of salad and curry. 'Who wants more of Taran and Nicky's lovely curry? Salad, anyone? We're on a culinary tour of the globe tonight. India, Greece. Both countries have given so much to the world, haven't they? I'm not talking purely cuisine. Great thinkers, education. Greece has some breathtaking natural beauty. But

I've not stepped foot in India.' She couldn't see Sonny glaring down at her.

'I'm on this show 'cause I murdered someone with these hands,' he said. His cheeks scorched like hot coals and his scar creased like old rope. 'And I'll do it again.'

Nicky watched him, mouth wide open, glint in her eye, almost inviting him to make her laugh some more.

34

On all sides, the trees and crops held beads of rain from the morning sun showers. The droplets were a million eyes watching Jay and Saoirse work. Wet grass underfoot, Jay stood with his hands around a pear, which was still attached to the tree. He was absorbed in thoughts of the previous night's dinner. Sonny's eyes full of rage. In Jay's belly, a rock had formed and it now felt like a boulder. Heavy, cramped anxiety. On top of Sonny's outburst, Walt's comments in the woods the other day still eluded him. Whatever Walt had said was bugging Jay. And it bugged him even more that he couldn't recall it.

Next to Jay, Saoirse yanked a pear off the tree. She studied it like it had an inscription.

'Do rabbits eat fruit?'

'What?'

She dropped the pear into the tub. 'Taran really cares for Alice, doesn't he?'

'And you care for Nicky.'

With a slight nod, she ran her fingers through her hair. 'What a mess looking after so much hair with this humidity. Nicky's offered to blow-dry it later. I never do it right myself. I can't get the style how I like it.' She brushed her hair over her shoulders, altogether fed up with it.

Jay stayed watching her. Saoirse always seemed most assured when sharing what she couldn't do. He looked around them. 'I want to ask you a question. Do you have any inkling about your target?'

Eyes blank, she shook her head. 'I forget to pay attention to what the others say and it's hard to know who's who.' A look of shock came over her. As though she hadn't realised that she had to find out who her target was.

'Careful, I could be here to get you.'

'You? You couldn't hurt anyone. Nicky and I both know that.'

Jay's gaze lowered. 'I'm sure my exes would disagree. Christy too.'

She reached to him and touched his shoulder. 'What on earth are we doing here?' she asked.

How good that moment of tenderness felt. He couldn't meet her eye directly though. His throat burned. They stood barefoot in matching outfits, picking fruit in the grounds of a television studio. His mouth opened, but words wouldn't come easily. His half-smile was an attempt to hold back the tears. 'Officially, I'm going to −'

'Kill someone? I don't think so. You're not the type.'

'You noticed.' He distracted himself by lifting the tub of pears. It wasn't too heavy. They could add more fruit. 'Apart from having no desire to kill, I have no idea who my target is. And is killing that person really going to bring justice for my relative? She −'

He stopped. Best not to start talking about that. Had Saoirse registered what he'd just divulged?

Saoirse paused, about to place another pear in the tub. She turned to him. 'I asked Scot to pair up with you today.'

'Did you? You're better off pairing with targets, so you have a chance to get information. Wait. Why? Why me?'

Saoirse seemed to change the subject. She sniffed the pear. 'Nicky helps me. She takes care of me. I need to watch what I say in here, she says. Play it safe, like they do in prison. She's adamant. In here, speaking gets you killed.' She nodded several times. 'A good soul. Nicky cares for women. She doesn't kill them.' Jay held Saoirse's gaze and they nodded together. 'She's doing my hair later. Did I tell you that?' Her pear joined the others in the tub.

Jay did a double take at Saoirse's absentmindedness. 'Yes. A minute ago.'

'She'll do a good job. I need cheering up. My son's birthday is next week. What day is it?' In a split second, her face changed and she buried her face in her hands. 'There's so much tension. I feel it building.'

'Saoirse? Why did you ask Scot to pair us up today?'

Saoirse huffed and panted with increasing intensity. 'It's that blasted Sonny. It won't be Nicky's fault if something happens. She hates him. He's going to lash out at someone. I know he is. I need your help. We must keep them separated. Or she'll get herself killed.'

35

Bow woke curled up on the sofa. Slowly, she extended her legs. Bones creaking like never before. That was the last thing she needed. A body like a bag of abandoned tools. Her ankles were spanners locked from lack of use, her knees rusted hammers. How well her prison cultivating had worked: having daily weed kept her joints gliding easily, as if soaked in lubricant. Stop. Carlisle and his prison were not going to enter her mind. Slaps to her legs brought her back into the house, which was oddly quiet.

There was a soft clicking noise, source unknown. But the chlorine smell that came to her when she took a deep breath was recognisable. It was the hot tub on the decking above. A gentle soak would soothe her limbs.

Bow got to her feet, clenching her jaw to stop tell-tale groans of pain escaping. Patty was hunched at the dining table, her plastic needles working hard. That explained the clicks. Bow climbed the steps and spotted Taran outside, doused in soft sunlight, talking with Jay and Sonny. Once she had his attention, she pointed at him, then to herself and the tub. He returned a thumbs-up.

She headed to the showers to change and almost stepped on Walt doing yoga in the hallway. He was lying facedown on his mat, elbows propping him up like a sphinx.

'I love yoga. Hatha?' she asked.

Walt changed position. With only his backside touching the mat, his hands and feet pointed to the ceiling.

'Ooh, boat pose,' Bow said. 'Good for the kidneys, that one.' She tapped her lower back.

Walt lost his balance. 'Yoga isn't a team activity.'

'What's your favourite pose? Mine's –'

He brought a finger to his lips. Not a traditional yoga posture.

'I'll go in there,' she said, tiptoeing past and entering the bathroom with her thumbprint.

Inside, Saoirse and Nicky were standing at the double sink wearing startled expressions. They watched each other in the mirror, then faced Bow.

'Is that your new hair dryer?' asked Bow, checking out the box they seemed to be guarding. 'Ooh. And a brush. It's brand new. You haven't even removed the plastic.' Through its wrapping, the dryer gleamed.

'Have you come for a shower?' Saoirse asked. 'We – I was about to wash my hair. Maybe come back later.'

Bow explained her plans, grabbed a swimsuit and towel from her shelf and dipped behind a screen. As she changed, she addressed Nicky. 'Join us in the tub if you like. While you're waiting for Saoirse to shampoo.'

'That's an idea.' Nicky's voice was mechanical.

A minute later, wrapped in a towel, Bow stepped out from behind the screen. Neither of them had moved from their spot, but Nicky was shoving something into Saoirse's back pocket.

'Everything's a weapon,' Nicky said in a hushed tone. Bow cleared her throat and made a breezy exit.

'See you out there, Nicky.'

At the tub, she tied up her hair and slithered into the warm water, avoiding the metal jets that glistened beneath the surface, her feet getting purchase on the slippery base. She turned to sit with a view of the garden and felt instant relief. How quickly the buoyancy stripped away the weight of days of tension. With the water stream on low, the hum of the pump drowned her contented sighs. She wiggled her toes. Her breathing slowed. She couldn't help asking herself why she'd waited so long to take a dip.

Unexpectedly, Nicky appeared, swimsuit on. She got in, making ripples that lapped at Bow's shoulders. This sent tickles up and down her neck and, for a moment, Bow felt as far away from the show as she might get. Life had paused. Possibly the aim of the tub. To slow down moving bodies, to prevent housefriends from hunting, attacking, killing.

Bow waited for Nicky to look over before she spoke. 'You made an enemy last night. Not sure that's wise. We're better off together.'

'Allegiance is a mirage. Has prison taught you nothing?' Nicky asked.

'Why create –'

'Here I am,' Taran said. 'Make way, make way.'

'Oh, you. I didn't recognise you without your bunny,' Nicky said.

'I could say the same about you.' He settled himself under the water.

'Saoirse won't like you referring to her as my bunny.'

'Don't tell her.' He reached under the water. 'What's sticking up my bum?' He inched towards Bow. 'Who'd put a metal fitting there? This show designs everything to piss people off.'

'Room for two more?' Jay was outside the tub, Sonny behind him, and both were clad in swimming trunks. Jay stepped in carefully and sent a small wave around the tub.

'We started a trend,' Taran said. 'Budge up, ladies. The more the merrier.'

'It's too crowded. Come back later,' Nicky said, holding up her palm.

'There's a spot,' Sonny said. His muscular frame, lean from prison-yard exercise, descended into the wash. Poseidon arriving to lay claim to stormy seas.

'Thank god for gyms,' Taran said into Bow's ear.

Despite her easing joint pain, Bow's muscles tensed. She drew her legs in close.

'I'm done.' Four pairs of eyes watched Nicky stand. No sooner did she climb the first step than Sonny leant forward and tripped her. She slipped, swore and clutched Bow's shoulder to avoid toppling back in. 'Arsehole.'

'Stay.' Bow gave Nicky's hand a little squeeze, but she pulled herself free.

Taking Nicky's vacated spot, Bow shifted towards the steps. She glanced around her. Three men. Only one was a hunter. Jay. Seemingly safe.

Jay swirled his hands underwater. 'It's so refreshing, isn't it? If I remember rightly, the last hot tub I sat in had salt water.'

'Oh, the ocean,' Bow said. 'Imagine swimming in the sea, bobbing, catching waves.'

'Bliss,' Taran said, closing his eyes. 'There's something about swimming that I find so soothing.'

'That's right, you're a swimmer. At the beach or pool?' Jay asked, his voice neutral. There was no answer. Jay persisted, his submerged hands swaying. 'Did you swim at the beach or the pool, Taran?'

'Please. Not now.' Wetting his face, Taran moved away from Jay. 'It's downtime.'

With a violent skim of his hand, Sonny splashed Jay full in the face. 'Knock it off. He sees what you're doing. We all do. Trying to work out where he lives. If he doesn't want to answer your questions, he doesn't want to answer your fucking questions. Go back to your friends. No hunters allowed.'

Bow's eyes were planted on the ceiling. The imagined beach far behind her, she was back in the centre of the prison food hall. A throng of heads and prison greens. No easy escape if a fight were to start. But with the water so restorative, she couldn't get out yet.

'Heaven,' Sonny said after a moment. 'Sitting in a tub with a babe inches from me.'

'Which one of you is he talking about?' Bow signalled Jay and Taran.

Sonny clicked his tongue. 'You, Bow. Can't control myself.'

'Something tells me you will.' Propping herself up, she squeezed her scruffy hair bun. A stream of water deserted the strands.

'Don't be so sure, gorgeous,' Sonny said. 'Hey fellas, why don't you leave us alone? Bow and I are going for a skinny dip.' His hands went underwater. A second later, up they came, his swimming trunks swinging. 'You don't want to miss out, Bow. Quick. Before Nicky sinks her claws into me.'

'Sonny – clothed – to the chair.' Scot's clipped tones echoed around them.

In a second, Sonny pulled on his trunks. 'Sorry, Scot,' he shouted. 'I forgot it's a family show. Murder's in, nudity's out. Gotcha.'

Having appeased Scot, Sonny made himself comfortable in the water again and quiet descended on the tub for a moment.

From her elevated position, Bow saw Nicky and Saoirse reappear from the bathroom and drag a bench to the wall mirror. Saoirse sat and twiddled the hairbrush, a towel covering her hair. Behind her, Nicky plugged the hair dryer into the extension cord normally saved for the toaster.

'Forget the hairdressing, ladies. Get in,' Sonny called.

Saoirse's hair dryer screeched to life. Nicky held it at eye level, her knuckles white.

'They're almost a married couple,' Taran said, over the dryer.

'It's like a real salon,' Bow said and turned to face the garden. It was time to leave the women to themselves.

Too subtle a hint for Sonny, he remained an avid spectator – his chin propped up by his arms on the tub's tiled ledge and his eyes fixed on Nicky. She cut the hair dryer to say something to Saoirse and the noise abruptly stopped. Sonny grabbed the opportunity. 'Come and join us, Nic. Bring your lover.'

'Stop,' Bow said.

Sonny shouted out again. 'Nicky, love?'

'Piss off.' Nicky turned the hair dryer on.

Bow waved a hand at Sonny. 'Leave them. That's enough.' His taunting wouldn't end well. She wished Taran and Jay would speak up, but they stayed silent. Her limbs were now so tense there was no benefit to being underwater. That stiffness in her body of late was coming back. She bobbed onto the underwater step.

'Give it a rest, Bow. I'm enjoying myself,' Sonny admonished quietly, then flicked his gaze back to Nicky. 'No point doting on her, Nic. Waste of time.' Not getting a reaction, he raised his voice again. 'Hey one thing, Nic. Have you told Saoirse about your girlfriend inside? She's got a right to know …'

Bow heard the screeching getting louder behind her. She realised Nicky had left her makeshift salon. Dining table, steps, hot tub. In a flash, she was standing above them with the hair dryer, the extension cord a deadly snake trailing behind. They immediately sat to attention. Nicky dangled the hair dryer over the water and all four of them flinched. No one was close enough to catch it if it left her hand. Nicky turned it on and off nonstop, like a hoon revving a car.

'Please, Nicky. He didn't mean it,' Jay said.

'We didn't mean it!' Taran screamed. He clawed at Bow as he tried steadying himself. His hands found the sides of the tub.

'Nic, don't do anything silly.' Sonny's voice was smooth and placating, as though he had experience asking killers to rethink a massacre. 'I was joking. Course I don't know whether you've got a girl inside. Toying with ya, that's all.'

Seemingly unaware of the other three in the water, Nicky glared at him. She panted through gritted teeth. Bow hadn't seen Nicky's jaw that rigid. Like an axe head.

In the fraught silence, the water pump hummed and the bubbles danced around them. Bow's heart thumped in her chest, making her voice vibrate. 'Nicky, don't do this.' She spoke softly as she stepped up from the water. Only one of her calves remained below the surface.

Jay crouched next to her, looking ready to spring up.

'He's not worth it,' Patty called out from the table, untangling a section of wool.

Nicky's gaze didn't shift from Sonny. She raised her hand, with the dryer swinging between her index finger and thumb.

Sonny stepped towards her. 'Stop.' His tone had changed. 'Listen, cunt.'

'Stay back, dickhead.' Nicky wiggled her hand. 'You're dead.'

Taran screamed and slipped, nudging into Bow. She slipped back and was again up to her waist in water. Reaching out to steady herself, her fingers found one of the metal jets. She moved her hand away, but the tub's surface was silky smooth, like it had a coat of oil.

In one slow move, Nicky opened her hand.

A descending dryer.

A churning tub.

A roaring quartet.

Limbs thrashed in all directions. Bow jumped up the steps, adrenaline temporarily taking charge of her aching joints. Jay leapt towards the edge, knocking Sonny underwater. Taran fell over Sonny's flailing form and they fumbled with each other as they sought to right themselves. The hair dryer hit the water. Bow made it out of the tub and moved away on all fours.

The thrashing and splashing eventually died out, as did the shouts, leaving only the water bubbling gently around Sonny's legs. It wasn't electrified. All four were unharmed. Nicky checked to see who had removed the cord, but it was still attached.

'They must've cut the power,' Patty said, without a pause in her knitting.

'Filthy fucker!' Sonny lunged for Nicky, catching her leg before she could retreat from the hot tub's edge. She fell to the decking, steadied herself with her palms and kicked her legs. Within seconds, Sonny had wrapped the cord around her foot. But she was cannier, pulling on the slack cable trailing back to the kitchen. He lunged for her arm and she looped the cord around his head.

Saoirse now joined the scene, having been rooted to the spot in her salon chair when the chaos unfolded. She took up the loose end of the cord and yanked it taut. Still in the water, Sonny choked and spluttered as the women pulled in opposite directions. His face reddened and Saoirse's eyes widened. His wet hands frantically tore at his neck but they couldn't grip the cable. With no luck manoeuvring himself out of the noose, he tried lunging for his captors. But he went for Saoirse, and Nicky dragged him away with brute force. Then Saoirse did the same, each violent tug cutting short his screams.

'You'll kill him!' Jay shouted.

'Stop it, Saoirse,' Nicky said in a jeering tone. 'You'll kill him if you're not careful. Stop it, Saoirse. Stop it.'

Her tone was jeering. In rhythm, the pair dragged Sonny through a gruesome tug of war. His face went purple. His eyes bulged. His legs gave way. His head hit the hot tub's tiled ledge.

The women wrenched him upright with the cord.

With Sonny no longer fighting, Saoirse became uncertain. She looked to Jay. Whatever she saw in his face, she released her grip on the cable. 'We can't.'

Bow stepped in and cut the pump. Sonny's phlegmy hacks were the only sound once the water stream died.

Nicky let out a roar of laughter as she too let go. She crouched down near a spluttering Sonny, on his knees in the water. 'We've decided to let you live.' She stumbled backwards until she hit the sliding glass door, laughing more loudly each time she heard him cough. 'You're pathetic.'

Before Nicky could pull her away, Saoirse removed the cord from his head, revealing a neck scorched with welts and blood blisters. Sonny stayed motionless. He could have been a pilgrim bathing in holy water.

Asking for forgiveness.

Washing away his sins.

36

Eleanor Carlisle took a risk topping up her gin so late in the ad break. She couldn't miss a second of the show. 'I'm coming,' she sang, more to the television than to Frank. Scot Free was back on by the time she entered the living room, the light from the side lamp guiding her. She passed between the screen and Frank, who ushered her through the tight space. His other hand cradled his bitten pen, but his newspaper crossword sat unfinished in the kitchen. She settled into her usual spot. Slippered feet on the coffee table. Gin resting alongside.

'Maybe the next housefriend is dead,' she said, again mulling over the evening's promos that had teased her with a shock development in the house.

Frank mumbled a retort.

'What's that?' she said, sipping her drink. A whack of gin. A bite of tonic.

'Shush.'

Frank leant closer to the television.

Onscreen, Scot greeted the eight housefriends, who were silently eating dinner, the camera showing each face in turn. There were no obvious signs of the earlier fight, but Nicky and Sonny were at opposite ends of the same bench.

'That voice is creepy.' Eleanor pretended to shiver.

'Ssssshush.' Like a punctured tyre, Frank's quiet command was drawn out.

Scot's voice filled the small living room, holding the housefriends and the Carlisles equally spellbound. The housefriends held still. Eleanor and Frank overlooked their drinks.

'An opinion poll is now running for twenty-four hours. There's a prize for the housefriend with the most votes, and the two housefriends with the fewest votes receive fitting punishments. We air the results this time tomorrow.' Scot signed off.

'Is that it? A poll?' Eleanor said. 'Hardly shocking, Scot. I thought someone was dead.' A large gulp of gin was charged with lifting her spirits.

'Count them,' Frank said. 'They're all there.'

'Okay, okay. I'm not a savant. All those camera angles. Changing too quickly.'

'Eight of them. Like the gins you've necked.'

'Frank, please! I don't neck anything. Least of all the gin.' She agitated the melting ice in her glass. 'But we've paid to see the gory bits. Get on with it, I say.'

On the television, the narrator spoke softly as if the housefriends might overhear. 'What we can reveal for home viewers is what's in store for the winner and the bottom two' – a pause in the presenter's commentary gave Eleanor enough time to excitedly look at Frank, who didn't return her gaze – 'tomorrow night. To the housefriend who polls last, we'll administer a fast-acting truth drug. And the housefriend who comes in second last gets the unenviable task of mowing the lawn. Our most popular housefriend wins a phone call to the outside. Download the app and get voting.'

The camera remained on the housefriends. With Bow appearing onscreen, Eleanor studied Frank again. His bushy grey eyebrows knitted, his chest hardly moving, his pen still in his grasp. Once the camera moved off Bow's face, he spoke. 'She's not too scared. Good. That's good. Very good.'

'Chill out. It's unlikely they'll call out her name. She's always on best behaviour. Is she like this with you?' Eleanor held up her glass, with its drowning lemon wedge. 'I bet she could do with a drink though.'

'Bow doesn't enjoy alcohol. It aggravates her arthritis.' He demonstrated the condition by wriggling his wrists unnecessarily.

'Bow and me are different then, because this seems to help my stiffness.'

'Or maybe your self-diagnosis is wrong.'

A clip of Bow started rolling. It had been recorded within hours of her arriving at the studio. She sat alone, swaying on a stool and looking at someone behind the camera.

'If I win?' She looked up and a chuckle-cough allowed her to think. 'If I win the show, I'll hide away in Thailand. Beaches and more beaches and anonymity.'

'Liar!' Frank roared, grinning wildly.

Eleanor jumped. She checked her drink hadn't spilled. 'Good lord, love.'

'That's a tactic. She hates the beach. She's self-conscious about her legs,' Frank said, animated in his seat like it was on fire. 'What did I tell you, Ellie? She's bloody good.'

Eleanor checked her own legs, extended and crowned with shabby slippers. She couldn't remember the last time he'd commented on them. Legs that had stepped them through thirty years of marriage. 'Which is a bad thing, honey.'

Frank's eyes lost their cheer. He sat back and seemed to ponder the implications of Eleanor's comment. It wouldn't hurt to spell it out for him.

'That clip was filmed before the show began, and she was already using a strategy. If she plays that same game with the housefriends, lord knows what she'll accomplish. You may not see her back at Barton.' She buried her smile behind a gulp of gin. 'Now, who will get my vote?'

37

'Hold still.'

On Saturday evening, Jay stood with his back to Patty, letting her drape the work in progress over his back.

'You're a fast knitter,' he said.

She smoothed the material on his shoulders, each hand stroke relaxing him. A childhood memory came. Winter in the Blue Mountains. He was six. His mother had knitted matching jumpers and thrust them over the heads of the three children. Jay, Harriet and their brother. Despite keeping him warm, the wool had restricted his playing. Thick and itchy, that jumper had been so uncomfortable. Luckily, the wool now caressing his neck didn't have the same texture.

Nearby, Saoirse was cuddling Nicky, who was cradling Alice.

Taran played with the Rubik's Cube, having no luck beyond the orange side.

Sonny rubbed his washboard stomach under his T-shirt, his neck blotchy from the previous day's assault.

Walt and Bow were squeezed at one end of the sofa watching a film. Walt looked tired and grumpy, his cheek resting in his cupped hand.

'Do we need to be concerned about tonight's results?' Patty murmured in Jay's ear as she arranged the knitting over him.

'If you haven't tried to attack someone in the last twenty-four hours, I think not.'

'Housefriends. Good evening.' Scot's voice made them stir. 'We are ready to reveal the results of the public vote.'

Jay felt Patty quickly remove the knitting from his shoulders. They sat together on the bench. As though expecting trouble, Taran dropped the Rubik's Cube, seized Alice from Nicky and popped her in her cardboard home.

'We can now reveal the two housefriends with the fewest votes.'

Jay was certain his would not be one of those names. Anyone would be hard pressed to show where he'd stepped a foot wrong.

'The housefriend with the lowest number of votes is Nicky.'

Saoirse let out a gasp and hugged Nicky, who lowered her head. No surprise there.

'And the second lowest is Sonny. Punishments to follow.'

Nicky lifted her gaze and patted Saoirse's knee. No reprimand for her, at least.

Drawing a cigarette from behind his ear, Sonny wandered outside. Walt turned to Nicky.

'Trying to electrocute half the house clearly didn't go down well with the public.'

'If you think that was made public, you're more gullible than you appear,' she said. 'Aren't you going to have a go at Sonny too?'

With a huff, Walt returned to the film.

'I need cheering up. Something sweet,' Bow said, heading to

the pantry. She came out eating a chocolate-chip cookie, caught the crumbs with her free hand, and rejoined Saoirse and Nicky on the sofa. With her cheeks full of biscuit, she gave Nicky a consolation kiss.

'We are ready to announce the winner of our public poll,' Scot said. 'This person will receive a two-minute phone call from a family member. Tonight.'

'It's not me then,' Bow said, between chews.

In an instant, Jay's mind went to work. Bow had no family. Or Bow's family wanted nothing to do with her. Only since her conviction? Or had it always been that way? With no family contact, that could mean Bow had relied on friends instead. What if Harriet had been one of those friends?

'And the winner is –' Scot's extended pause made them all look up at the cameras. There was silence, which was broken by Sonny's shouting from outside.

'Get on with it. For fuck's sake!' His voice was croaky from the assault.

'Patty,' Scot said.

Jay worked at putting a smile on his rosy face. He clapped for Patty, who was as confused as he was disappointed.

'Me?' Little creases in her forehead sharpened. 'Who wants to –' Her mouth hung open. Absently, she restarted her knitting.

'Patty to the chair, please.' She stayed still until Jay tapped her arm.

'They're waiting.'

*

Blank screen opposite blank eyes. Patty folded her arms.

'Patty? It's me, Elizabeth. I have Señor Bones with me. He's been well behaved. No barking, no growling.' Patty could almost hear the cuddle Elizabeth gave him. 'He misses you. For two whole days, he sat by the front door.'

Patty's chin wobbled and her hands searched for her knitting, which was out with the others. Her restless fingers clawed at the leather chair with its concave steel armrests.

'Say hello to mummy, Señor Bones,' Elizabeth said, breaking the long silence. No bark came, but Patty heard a clinking sound. His collar with the red studs shifting under Elizabeth's strokes.

Patty's body ached. How she longed to cuddle her dog.

'How are you, Patty? I've been watching the show at times.'

Patty sniffed quietly. She was sure the microphone wouldn't pick it up.

'Not up for speaking? It must be overwhelming. You'll be home in no time. Please tell me you're getting enough sleep. Everything is fine here. As you left it. I – you won't mind. I don't think you will. I moved the large lamp to the corner beside the sofa. You told me not to sit in George's chair, and I don't. But I need a light for my evening reading and I look around me now and I think the room looks better with the lamp away from the armchair. Too similar in colour, aren't they? You can change it when you –'

Patty swallowed hard.

'Are you still there, Patty? There's no news. Well, you did get one letter. I opened it. I had to. You see, in the rain we had last week, the envelope got wet. Ruined. That's because I forgot to check the mailbox the day before. Anyway, I took out the letter and I laid it flat to dry. Quick thinking, wasn't it?'

Patty's chest felt like it was crushing inwards. She couldn't breathe.

'A developer wants to meet you, Patty. They're interested in the land, and they suggested you act quickly. Isn't that wonderful? I'm sure you won't mind. I followed the instructions in the letter. I called them. A lovely gentleman is coming by tomorrow. He says he's on our … He's on your side. I'll keep Señor Bones in the garden when he knocks. To be safe –' The call ended.

Patty rocked in the chair. Her voice cracked. 'Please don't.'

38

Adolpha threw open the production suite door, mobile to her ear, and took a seat beside Alan at the console.

'Walt is not dying, Doctor Ellis. I can assure you. He vomited from food poisoning. Between you and me, Jay needs a cookery class.' She formed a yapping mouth with her free hand. 'I do take this seriously.' She listened. 'Wrong. Other housefriends did get sick, but we chose not to air it because there's so much material. We also –' She let the doctor interrupt her. 'Way ahead of you. He's booked in to see our specialist on Monday morning. We'll have Walt out of here as soon as possible.' She ended the call and spoke to Alan. 'Which, I suspect, may be sooner than the doctor thinks. Are we ready?'

Fists on the desk, Adolpha straightened her back.

Alan nodded. 'Oh, yeah.'

'Then what are we waiting for? Let's give 'em a show.'

*

Click. Scot was there. Listening.

Nicky watched her reflection in the dark screen. Too slumped? She corrected her posture. If she appeared remorseful, a more lenient punishment might come her way. Unlikely though.

She settled herself into the leather, still warm from Patty sitting there moments before, and let her arms fall to the metal armrests. Besides the rasping sound of her breath through her nostrils, the room was quiet.

'Well? Do I get a phone call too?' Her usual steely tone was absent and an edgy voice betrayed her unease.

'Why do you think you ran last?' Scot asked.

'Payback for yesterday?'

'Those events probably had an impact.'

Her forearms rolled in the armrests. 'Hurry up. What's my punishment?'

'Stand up.'

'Huh?' She shrugged. Scot was fast becoming as annoying as the guards at Burranul. She tried to stand, but only her head and torso moved. Her forearms wouldn't budge. Something in the chair gripped her limbs. Tendons popped up, but her arms stayed put, even as her hands formed fists. 'What the fuck?'

'Excellent,' Scot said. 'In a moment, you'll feel a slight prick in both –'

'Ow!'

'Oops. Sooner than I thought.'

Nicky broke free. She jumped up, rubbing her arms and checking where the injections had gone in. There were two pin pricks. Without touching the armrests, she studied the metal. Not only did the soft light hide where the needles had jutted out, it revealed no sign of the mechanism that had trapped her arms.

'You're free to go.'

'What did you give me?'

'Something to stop you withholding information. Off you go. You have questions to answer out there, I'm sure.'

'What's going to happen?'

'You'll relax and you won't lie. It's a truth drug. Clinical name –'

'Fuck.' She splayed her fingers checking for signs of tremor, of sweat, of anything.

'You'd better get out there. My advice – act normally.'

'How long before –'

Click. Scot was gone.

In the corridor, Nicky made the sign of the cross and took small steps back to the others. She already felt jittery, which could be the drug working or her panic taking over. Shaking both arms and taking several deep breaths did nothing to calm her. She made fists to steady her hands but changed her mind. They'd notice. Best to look normal. Scot had said exactly that. Act normal. Or was that Scot setting a trap? Trying to act normal might draw attention. But was that paranoia? And was that ordinary paranoia, given the situation, or drug-induced paranoia? Her mind raced away.

She covered her mouth and lips, which felt oversized, like a grouper fish. Ready to shout each word that her conveyor-belt tongue would spill out. She stood still and the internal rushing became more noticeable. A swaying between calm and panic. Mentally, she addressed each organ that could betray her in speech. Tongue, vocal cords, teeth, lips, jaw.

No words. Let them bank up, like a traffic jam.

She pictured herself stepping into that traffic, like a lollipop lady with a stop sign. Cars full of words, honking to move forward and leave her mouth.

Fuck. Vulnerable. Danger. Saoirse.
More words, more memories sat further back in the traffic.
Van. Trip. Chummy. Watchful. Moccasin. Card.
'Shit.' Not that memory.
Forget the card. Don't mention the security card.

39

At the threshold of the open area, Nicky stopped, hand on throat. Everyone was present, but the only sound was Patty's needles clicking. They could have been right by Nicky's ears. Inside her head, the revving of the word-cars created a cacophony. But all she had to do was take her seat next to Saoirse.

She advanced, acutely conscious of her movements. One leg in front of the other. Silent lifting and landing of feet. Hips losing their rhythm. At the sofa, guiding herself to sit became complex. She misjudged and sat on Saoirse, who started to speak and stopped.

Nicky held a trembling finger to her inflated lips. They stared at each other for an eternity. For the first time, Nicky was the more frightened of the two.

'What's wrong?' Saoirse mouthed.

Draped over a beanbag, Bow threw the Rubik's Cube, with only the green side complete, back to Jay. 'Infuriating.' She looked up. 'You're back. What did Scot want?'

Nicky's voice wasn't her own. 'Needles – pointless – task.' Her voice seemed amplified, distorted. She squeezed Saoirse's hand, cleared her throat and coughed.

'It's going to be all right,' Saoirse said, avoiding anyone's gaze, eyes to the floor.

A rush of warmth travelled through Nicky and softened her limbs. Her shoulders relaxed and she rolled her head to soak up the slackening. 'It's not,' she said. She spoke a little too loudly.

Passing behind them, Taran stopped. 'It's not what?' he asked.

'Nothing.' Saoirse shot him a glare.

'It's not going to be all right,' Nicky said. She tried rolling her shoulders, but Saoirse held her still.

'Sonny to the chair.' Scot's voice came loud and clear.

'What won't be all right?' Taran walked around the sofa and faced the two of them. With a lift of her eyebrows, Nicky gave him a 'hi'. Unlike Saoirse, who waved him away.

'Tomorrow's punishment. Tough work involved, but Nicky will be fine.'

Then Sonny appeared next to Taran. 'What are they making you do tomorrow?' He must have picked up on the pair's new dynamic. Saoirse's intense hugging, Nicky's surrendering frame. 'What the fuck's going on?'

'Nothing. Scot wants you. Go. Nicky has work to do tomorrow,' Saoirse said.

'No, I don't. That's a lie.'

'What?' Sonny's face screwed up.

'Stop, Nicky. Don't speak.' Saoirse nudged closer to her. The more relaxed Nicky felt, the more distressed Saoirse appeared.

'What happened in there?' Sonny's eyes widened. 'What've they done to ya?'

Saoirse shoved him back with a foot.

'Scot wants you.'

'To the chair, Sonny.' Scot's voice boomed through the house, but Sonny gave his middle finger to the cameras.

Lollipop lady Nicky stepped aside and the traffic started flowing. 'They injected something into me. Scot said I will tell the truth.'

'Stop!' Saoirse screamed. 'You leave her alone.'

Getting to her feet, Saoirse rushed at Sonny, knocking him away.

'Hey, everyone,' Sonny said. 'They've given Nicky some kind of truth drug.'

In seconds, Nicky had a full audience. Jay, Bow, Patty and Walt gathered, which kept Saoirse away. Seeing their quizzical looks, Nicky took this as a signal to explain what had happened. She told them about her arms locked on the armrests and feeling the needles pinch.

Sonny claimed the sofa space next to her. 'Time for questions, I reckon.' He rubbed his hands together. His big smile reminded Nicky how many teeth he was missing. 'An easy one first. What do you think of me?'

'You're the dumbest, most chauvinistic cunt I've ever met.'

'Whoa.' Sonny's palms came up. 'They've given her loads.'

'Not necessarily,' Patty said.

'Oi!' Sonny lashed out. 'Watch it, lady. It's fast acting, whatever it is.' He looked Nicky up and down. 'She's ...' He hunted for the words.

'Exceptionally forthcoming?' Jay asked.

'Leave her alone.' Saoirse forced her way forward and pulled at Nicky, whose limbs and trunk seemed lifeless. Walt grabbed Saoirse's arms from behind. 'Let go, Walt. You're hurting me.'

'Right. Answer this.' Sonny had another question. 'Have you been stealing my cigarettes?'

'No. I have my own.'

'Shit.' Sonny nodded his acceptance of her answer. 'I thought you were the thief. It must be Bow then.'

'I told you I hadn't stolen them,' Bow said. 'Stop being a dickhead.'

A wounded look crossed Sonny's face. 'Why are you being horrible? They drugged her, not you.'

'Let go of me! I need to –'

Saoirse was struggling to free herself from Walt's grip. It seemed to give Sonny an idea. He addressed Nicky again. 'What do you think of Saoirse?'

A silence fell over the room. Deathly. Even Saoirse and Walt paused.

Nicky found Saoirse towards the back of the group, still in Walt's grip. 'She's a lovely soul, but she's too weak to make it in this place.'

'Stop, Nicky!' Saoirse wriggled an arm free and elbowed Walt in the gut. He yelped and let go. She forced her way forward and gasped at the strange sight. Nicky, hands limp by her sides, and Sonny, hungry for details, were almost huddled together, like lifelong friends. Yet, the day before, Nicky had held a cord around his neck.

'What?' Nicky asked.

Sonny angled into her more and, with an outstretched hand, sought space and attention. 'Here we go.' He waited until Nicky looked his way. 'How did you get on this show?'

'They collected me from prison.'

'I mean where did your crime take place? Which country?'

'Here.'

'What happened?'

'I was driving.'

Walt, who had been leaning against the wall rubbing his stomach, stood upright.

'And?' Sonny continued. Nicky did a sweep of their faces, hunters and targets waiting to hear her story.

'Don't speak!' Saoirse implored.

'I was driving a getaway car. We were hit from behind. I chased the driver.'

Walt walked around the beanbags, so he could see Nicky face on.

'He ran across the road and a car hit him. It was his own fault.'

Walt howled. 'My brother!'

From the sofa, Nicky saw the group part, making a pathway for him. Her instincts took over and she launched herself at him in a low charge. They staggered off together, with Walt grabbing and punching her back. She yanked her head up so quickly that she slammed into his chin and severed a chunk of flesh from his tongue. He screamed. They tumbled over a beanbag and came crashing down. With her arms gripping him, her head hit the floor first. Her skull felt like it would crack. An intense pain blinded her. She could feel the ache extend over every bone ridge and surface in her head. Slow to move, she paused on her hands and knees. A wave of the drug tore through her and the house spun. She was unsure if the smeared blood on the floor was hers, but her heart thumped, every beat amplifying her headache.

Nearby, Walt spat blood onto the marble. He gripped the steps to pull himself up. One hand cradled his bleeding mouth as he stumbled to the far corridor, leaving bloody prints on the walls.

Still under the drug's influence, Nicky gasped an announcement. 'He's going for the mallet.'

'Get up!' Saoirse said.

Nicky stayed on all fours facing the corridor Walt had taken. 'Come here, you fucker!' The shouting made her wince, but she continued. 'Your brother got in my way. Ruined everything.' Then she fell silent. She breathed in and out. To the others, it would have looked like she was doing a macabre yoga stretch, surrounded by blood. She searched for the strength that had always shown up. A fighter, she was. 'Come on.' She wasn't calling Walt but waking something inside.

A loud gasp from Saoirse signalled Walt's return.

He advanced clutching the steel mallet. Spitting a mouthful of blood on the top of Nicky's head, he raised the mallet high. 'You're dead.'

Before he could swing, Nicky shot up, fists clenched. She punched both his eyes before he could react. But it was the pummelling to his stomach and kidneys that wrecked him, the mallet hanging by his side useless.

He threw up. But Nicky didn't let up.

She knocked him in the side, and he slipped on his vomit and fell. She pounced on the mallet. A second later, she was over him. There was a quick pause to catch her breath and regard her half-dozen spectators menacingly. They huddled in the kitchen, unsure what to do. Even Sonny retreated a step. But they all kept looking. Transfixed by the horror. Determined to bear witness to Walt's suffering, but thankful it wasn't their own. Buoyed by the promise of a fellow contestant breaking free.

Nicky turned to a camera. 'Are you watching?'

She swung for the dead centre of Walt's head and he slumped down. One more swing crushed his temple, splitting his eye socket. Her compact frame lent power and speed to her blows. She stepped back from the marble turning red. Her rasps eased off enough for her to hear Saoirse whimpering. Nicky shuffled to the sofa and dropped the mallet. It clattered to the floor, and the fog that had engulfed her dispersed with the sound. Only a second ago, she had been on the sofa with

Saoirse. And now she was covered in blood. She had killed –

A loud keening filled the room. It could have come from a wild animal.

Walt was alive.

He writhed and he howled, almost willing his fury to take over. His body raised off the floor.

Frame by frame, Nicky's world moved in slow motion. She picked up the mallet, its warm handle slick with blood. From the corner of her eye, she saw Saoirse turn to face the wall. What at first looked like Saoirse unable to abide what was coming next was, in fact, Saoirse watching the reflection in the marble wall. A makeshift cinema. A silver screen of tiles giving a veneer of distance. Reflected images and make-believe.

Nicky stood over the man whose role in the drama was coming to an end. She brought the metal down with tremendous force and saw Walt's skull lose its shape. He collapsed, but she kept going, six more hits punctuating her message.

'Get.' *Wallop.*

'Me.' *Whack.*

'Off.' *Thwack.*

'This.' *Crunch.*

'Fucking.' *Crack.*

'Show.' *Splat.*

The third blow had killed him.

Part 5

Show stopper

40

Jay lay awake, staring at the ceiling. His list of prisoners was down to three: Bow, Sonny, Taran. It was exhausting going over who most likely fit the profile of Harriet's killer. And poor Walt. If –

He stood up, leant forward and pressed into a handstand with such control he didn't need to remove his glasses. There was a slight wobble in his trunk, but he held position. Upside down, it was easier to block the previous night's horrors. He came down and caught his breath. Faster than coffee, the exercise woke him instantly.

His bedroom door button turned green. Free to leave, he threw on his top and headed out, marching past where Walt had died. All traces of Nicky's attack had vanished. Gleaming tiles, spotless walls, fragrant air.

A new start, a new dread, a new weapon.

He quickened his steps along the far corridor and stopped in the doorway of the weapon room.

There was a fresh weapon secured under the glass dome.

He lurched back as though an invisible hand had shoved his chest.

After a moment, he went in. Under the thick casing, a black snub-nose revolver sat, cylinder open. With a synthetic grip and matt-steel barrel and cylinder, the gun showed no marks or fingerprints. Never handled with bare skin. Two of the five chambers contained bullets. Jay had to step back again. The dome could have been giving off skin-flaking heat. His lungs shrank to the size of one of the empty chambers. This house wasn't big enough for bullets and guns and people untrained to shoot them.

Seconds later, Sonny walked in. 'You've got to be kidding.' He tapped the glass. 'Smith & Wesson J-Frame.'

'You know the correct name for it,' Jay said.

'Work of art.' Sonny stepped around the dome, gawking at the gun. 'Next to no recoil. But it will need a steady hand.'

'Two bullets. How thoughtful of Scot.' Jay moved around the dome to remain opposite Sonny.

'I'll only need one. But if you're my match, I'll use the second one for fun.'

Jay swallowed. It was hard to know when Sonny was joking because the scar distorted his expressions. 'You've fired one, then?'

Sonny looked at Jay like he was the most pathetic person alive, even more pathetic than the guy who'd slashed his face. 'Beautiful firearm. I can't imagine the others firing it.' His snorting turned into a laugh. 'Patty? Jesus! She wouldn't have the strength to pull the trigger. Or Tarzan. He can barely hold Total.'

'He'll shoot through the wall and kill one of the crew,' Jay said.

'Fuck, yeah!'

Jay felt himself relax, ever so slightly, as they bonded over the common target of Taran. But the camaraderie was fleeting.

Sonny rapped his fingers on the digital display and Jay's heart rate soared. 'Why don't I enter your name and see if it opens?' He placed his thumb on the thumb reader. 'Are you my match?'

Jay stepped back. 'Don't mess around.'

'Welcome Sonny.' An automated voice sounded. 'Choose from the list of housefriends' – Sonny's glare was intense – 'or say a housefriend's name.'

All uncoordinated movements, Jay was at the door. 'Stop. You don't know if I'm your match.'

'Calm down, Scaredy. Your face.' Sonny cleared the screen. 'I'll come back when I know my match. But that gun is mine. Tell the others.'

Jay shuddered at the image of Sonny walking around armed.

'I'm not leaving yet. Not until I've had Bow,' Sonny said, resting his chin on his folded arms as he leant on the stand, inches from the gun.

'Will that … ordeal … be consensual?'

'She flirts with me.'

Flirt. Jay cursed under his breath. One word he didn't expect to hear in the house. As if people played around here. He was unsure what troubled him more. A gun in the house or Sonny with seduction on his mind. His thoughts switched to Christy and where she might be in that moment.

'What's up, Pretty Boy?' Sonny asked, noticing Jay's expression.

Mouth open, Jay stopped. Sonny providing emotional support? 'I doubt you're interested in my –'

'Try me.'

'My world is out there.' Jay pointed at the camera, a tiny door to the real world. 'My girlfriend's on her own.' Sonny limited his response to an almost imperceptible shrug and returned to admiring the gun. 'We're going to have children. One day, we'll be lucky. We'll start our own family. She'll make an amazing mother. She's warm and … patient.'

'If you say so.' Sonny's voice climbed. 'But you as a parent? Jesus, you'd be one galactic pain in the arse.'

'Nobody's perfect.'

'All the bloody questions.' Sonny started mimicking Jay in a posh voice. 'Where were you last night? Who's on the phone? Second? You came second? I don't care it was the whole school. You bring shame to this family.'

Jay rubbed his forehead. It sheltered his eyes. 'People in here have lost their −' His voice cracked. 'How sad not to see your kids grow up. Before they −' He stopped. No point. Better to put the focus on Sonny. 'Are you a father?'

'Possibly, dickwad. Possibly.'

*

During breakfast, Jay stood on the deck and watched sheets of rain obscure the garden and woods. No wonder a sombre mood encased the house. Like the others, he wanted to deny what had happened yesterday, but the horrific scene continued to cast a pall. With two fewer housefriends around, the remaining six had more space. Which had to be a good thing. But Jay was adamant the house was shrinking. Walls loomed and cameras appeared closer, if only by inches. At the same time, the area had never seemed so exposed. There were almost no hiding spots from a flying bullet. Not to mention needles that poke out of armrests.

He dared not think what else Scot had lurking.

At the table, Saoirse cupped her coffee, eyes fixed on her straw rose. She looked like she was guarding it, should Nicky appear and demand it. Opposite Saoirse, Patty did her knitting.

More focused than ever.

Taran ate breakfast on the ledge of the hot tub. He seemed transfixed by the rain lashing the windows. And in the kitchen, Bow waited for her toast, hip resting on the cutlery drawer. She gave her wrists a workout. Sonny approached and grabbed her waist to move her out of his way. She elbowed him and pointed at the cutlery on the kitchen island. Her toast popped up. She settled for it dry and retrieved her paperback from the island.

Jay went down the stairs and met Bow on her way to the sofa. She scared Alice, who hopped into Jay's path and received an accidental kick. He scooped the rabbit up and mouthed 'Sorry' into her ear, waving her paw at a camera. Taran saw nothing.

Then Sonny's tutting caught Jay's attention. Balancing on one foot, Sonny had a dropping stuck to his sole. 'Total is shitting everywhere. Clean up after that fucking rabbit.'

'I've picked it all up,' Taran said from the deck.

'Bullshit!' Sonny plucked the flattened dropping from his foot and lobbed it at Taran. It struck his head.

'Jesus. I'm eating.'

The exchange seemed to waken Saoirse, who lifted her mane of hair and addressed nobody. 'I've seen droppings around. It's not healthy.' Her tone was lifeless, her eyes vacant. All the vigour with which she had previously defended her hygiene standards was gone.

'Dear me,' Taran said. 'Turn on the vacuum. It sucks things up in no time. Everyone does their bit to clean up Alice's shit. Oh, that rhymes.'

Sonny gave him the finger. 'Pass me something blunt to hit that fucking –'

'Sonny to the chair.' Scot's voice rang out.

'I'm eating. What now?' Sonny wiped buttery fingers on his T-shirt and headed to Scot.

A bout of coughing from Bow silenced the group. Still eating toast, she clamped her mouth shut to stifle the coughs.

Jay sat down. 'Here,' he said, half-turning to her. In his palm, he had the jumbled Rubik's Cube. 'Take your mind off coughing. I didn't think you smoked.'

She threw him a look and took the puzzle. Coughing some more, she answered Jay's unspoken question. 'A tickly throat.' She tried the puzzle with jerky moves.

'Don't Harriet,' Jay said.

'Harriet?'

'Don't hurry it, I said.' He paused. 'Who's Harriet?' he asked, lowering his voice and observing her eyes.

A strand of hair fell over Bow's face, causing her to flick her head. She left his question unanswered and threw the puzzle into the air a few times.

'A friend put me on to the Rubik's Cube,' Jay said.

A half-nod from Bow. 'It's not for me. Or my friends.'

'Do your friends know you're on this show?'

'Do yours?'

'Some, I guess.' He kept her gaze. 'And yours?'

Bow held the cube up, almost brandishing it at him. 'Why did you ask for this? Of all the things Scot could have given you. Why this?' Jay sipped his drink. It was his turn to fall silent. 'Every time you appear with it and pass it around, you ask prying questions. I see what you're doing.'

'What? I didn't –' He pointed at her book. 'Why did you ask for a book?'

She sat up straight. 'I like it. I love this book. Good characters.'

'It's usually in your room. You hardly ever read it, but the bookmark moves around. One minute it's in the middle. The next it's at the front.' He tried to get a better look. 'Today it's at the back. Anyone would think –'

Bow threw the Rubik's Cube at Jay and returned to the kitchen. Her face was flushed and her body shook. He shrugged to himself and locked the cube's yellow face into place.

When he next looked up, four housefriends were in the kitchen area. Something told him a scene was about to unfold. Zombie-like, Saoirse shuffled around the sink, navigating the area with Taran, who had abandoned the deck and was scanning the floor for rabbit droppings. Patty walked up to Bow, stared at her and mumbled something.

'What?' Bow snapped. She grabbed a pot of Greek yoghurt from the fridge and wrestled with the lid.

Patty mumbled to her again, but Jay couldn't hear properly. Then the scene changed swiftly. No sooner had Bow eaten a spoonful of yoghurt than she was covered in a shower of Taran's coffee. A scream from Saoirse made Jay start. His eyes worked hard to understand what had happened. Taran's cup lay on the floor. Patty was frozen in place.

Bow shook her hands to remove the excess liquid and wiped off her wet hair. 'Jesus. What's going on?' she said.

'Get away from me. Don't come near me!' Saoirse pointed at Taran, who was gawking at his empty left hand, which moments earlier had held his cup. The coffee was everywhere. Slow drips fell from the island surface. Saoirse's rose lay on the floor.

With his jaw hanging down theatrically and hands now on hips, Taran looked around for support. 'It was an accident. Calm down, Saoirse. Look what you did.'

Saoirse picked up the flower and popped the stem in her trouser pocket, the red petals poking out. Then she changed her mind and held it close to her chest.

'We bumped into each other and she flipped,' Taran said. 'Clean knocked the cup out of my hand. Lucky the water here can't boil.'

'Stay away. All of you.' A pained look invaded Saoirse's face. 'There's no need to touch me.'

'No one's touching you,' Taran said.

'Liar!' Saoirse brushed hair from her face, a panicked look in her eyes. She seemed to gauge where she was. 'Scot.' Her voice was a whisper.

Taran pointed behind her. 'That way. But Sonny's in there.' He waited until she'd gone before twirling a finger at his temple.

'My poor book,' Bow said, wiping droplets from the cover. 'I need to clean up.' She ran off.

41

Saoirse reached the door, fingers trailing the walls. Sonny was inside. Bathed in alabaster light from directly above, he looked angelic in the chair. She tapped the button to open the door, keeping her spot at the entrance. Sonny growled at her and she retreated a step.

He faced the screen and continued chatting. 'You'll leave a mower out tomorrow then, Scot?' He flapped his feet. 'Will I get shoes?'

'No,' Scot said.

'I'll be extra careful with my toes.'

Sonny thumped the armrests and stood. He walked to the door, where he checked Saoirse over. 'You look terrible. Don't let yourself go because your sweetheart's gone. Smile more – cameras are everywhere.'

Saoirse lifted her head until she saw the bottom of his crescent scar. Her words came feebly. 'It takes no time to tidy your appearance. Fixing internal mess is harder.'

'You're off the planet.' Sonny walked off. 'Tell that shit to Scot, not me.'

She went inside. With the door closed, her breathing settled. Her first time there. There wasn't much. A chair, a blank screen from which Scot's voice came, and ceiling cameras. Dim lighting played tricks with the walls, making them appear slanted. Shadows danced in the darker corners and the ceiling seemed to move. She looked around quickly, hoping to catch the shadows out.

Instead of heading straight to the central chair, she explored the perimeter. She had to prove to herself that the swaying walls were solid. Her fingers traced their cold surface. Fingertips almost numb and deadened. With half the room covered, she stepped towards the chair.

'Hello?' Her voice lingered for a fraction so that the echo suggested she had company. Like several people were in the same predicament. Once the sounds died, she was alone again. Her focus went to the chair, where she spotted the armrests and recalled Nicky's tale of injections. She brushed a finger across the metal searching for telltale holes. Nothing.

'Good morning.'

Saoirse cried out and spun around.

'I'm sorry. Did I scare you?' Scot's voice warmed. 'Welcome. This is your first visit. Would you like to –'

'I'm not sitting there.'

'It's safe. I'm glad you came.'

She took out her paper rose. It was keeping its shape. She brushed her cheek with it, tracing the path Nicky's fingers had taken. 'How's Nicky?' There was no answer. 'Don't worry about me. I'm fine. Is she okay?'

'No outside news, I'm afraid.'

'Did she make it back safely? That's all.' She gave a huge sigh. A wave of exhaustion swept over her, much stronger than her distrust of the chair. She sat gently on the edge, feet together, arms close. 'Is she back in her cell?' Nicky had told her about the long drive from the prison. Plenty of chances to flee.

'Where else would she be?'

Saoirse looked around. 'What do people do in here? Why is this room so dark?'

Scot turned up the lights. 'They check in with me. I make them feel better. I hope to see you more often.'

Saoirse yawned, covering her mouth with the flower.

'Did you sleep well?' Scot asked.

'Last night, I watched someone –' She cleared her throat.

'That's where I can help. A cloudy head is no good to you here.'

'Huh?'

'If you feel low or sleepy, come here and I can help,' Scot said. 'Nicky had a calming effect on you. She's gone, but I have support. If you need a pill to get you through, we place a yellow one in your room. And if you think you need two' – Scot's voice got chirpier – 'well, we leave you two. Simple.'

'Do the others take them?'

'We respect their privacy.'

'Did Nicky take any?'

'We will respect your privacy, too.'

Saoirse grunted and fiddled with the flower. 'I – I want …' She closed her eyes, the huffing continuing. 'Do you know what I want?' Her eyes stayed closed and a hand came up in capitulation. 'Nicky. I want news of Nicky.' She opened her eyes.

A frosty silence crammed the room again. It could almost burst through the walls. Scot kept a neutral tone and repeated the rule – no outside contact. 'As people depart, the house can seem more menacing.'

Saoirse gulped. Her reflection in the blank screen was fractured in the half-light. 'It feels like the first day again. No, it's worse. I have no friends out there.'

'I'm not surprised you feel that way, after what Taran tri–'

'You saw that? You saw what he did to me?'

'The whole country saw it. They're not good people out there. Are you scared, Saoirse?'

'Do you televise these chats? Can everyone at home hear?'

'We mute these catch-ups sometimes. Or halt the cameras. There's someone at home?'

She nodded.

'You would rather your children didn't know?'

She nodded again. Seconds passed before Scot spoke.

'Okay, Saoirse. There you go. No cameras for us. One pill or two?'

42

Under construction, the skyscraper had been a skeleton building in a skyline of glass. Bow worked alone on the twenty-fifth floor, filling bags with waste from the installation of the ventilation ducts. As far as she knew, no other woman worked on the fifty-storey site. Her hair was tucked under her hard hat. A friend of a friend had secured her the job, but being unskilled excluded her from all but basic tasks. At least the money came in.

The exposed frame of the building afforded her almost three-sixty-degree views of Melbourne. A furious wind ripped around her from all sides. Coupled with rustling from her protective clothing and the flapping of canvas bags, it drowned out the world.

A hoist had begun its creep up to the top floor.

She took a rest. Her wrists were stiff, so she took out an unfinished joint. A couple of tokes would see her through until the shift ended.

Despite the wind, the joint lit quickly and she held in the vapour for as long as possible.

A smooth burn rushed through her, the wind died down, the view stood out. She marvelled at the dormant ocean to the south. It seemed not to move. Settled. Like her. Apart from the chasm opening in her belly. Damn it. Her food was below. She finished the joint and threw it into the pile of rubbish she would shortly bag.

Unexpectedly, the second hoist appeared from the lower floors. With a screech, the metal gate opened and the foreman stepped out with five visitors. He shouted at her as he hit the button to call the upper hoist.

'Where's Bench? What are you doing up here alone?'

'He went up to fifty. Minutes ago. A cable's come loose on the crane and they called him for help. I'll go to the ground floor now then.' She felt her stomach grumble and placed a hand on it to conceal the noise. No way would they hear it above the wind. This idea brought on the giggles.

'You won't be smiling if it gets out that you aren't following regulations.' The upper lift arrived and the foreman directed the visitors into it. 'I'm taking the project team up for a quick look around and I'll send Bench straight down. Back to work.' He started the hoist and all six occupants disappeared upwards, part by part.

Heads.

Trunks.

Legs.

Bow stepped over to the hoist shaft cautiously and watched the car rattle out of sight on its slow ascent. With her nose touching the security fence, she glanced down. It didn't seem too high up, but the powerful wind told her otherwise. Dust and cold air blew into her face. She blinked and looked up the hoist shaft.

Without warning, high above her, there was a ferocious crashing sound. A clattering of metal ricocheted down the shaft. Then came screams, bringing an end to her drug-induced tranquillity. Through the intercom, the foreman shouted.

'Bow! Are you there?'

She went to the unit mounted at the upper shaft. 'What happened?'

'A hook block's broken off. It's damaged the shaft. We're trapped on fifty. We can't get out and we can't get the lift to go down.'

She looked at the hoist to the lower floors. 'I'll go for help.'

'There's no time. We've got a ruptured gas tank a metre from us. Open the panel. I'll step you through the override and you can call us down. I'll give you the code.'

'Code?' She staggered backwards. It dawned on her what he was asking. Her mind became a swirl. 'I can't —' Her limbs froze yet her insides churned. Waves of panic ran from head to toe. In a flash, a layer of sweat appeared between her skin and her overalls.

'Are you there?' the foreman asked. He bellowed through the intercom. 'I've got the code.'

Hands shaking, Bow opened the panel. What she saw made her chest tighten. A keypad with indistinguishable numbers and letters. Each key was grey with white shapes and markings. She dry retched, but her empty stomach had nothing to give. Her mouth felt so dry that she grappled to speak.

'I see a keypad.'

'That's it. First press "Off" to start the override. It's seven-eight-three-four. Got that?' He repeated it. 'Quickly. There's gas.'

She pressed random keys and the unit beeped. 'Slower, please. Say that again.'

He yelled for her to hurry.

'There's something you must –' she gasped. 'You'll need to repeat it once I –'

An explosion sounded overhead, roaring through the hoist shaft and killing the intercom. Bow choked.

Through dusty air, the hoist car blasted down to her, revealing six crumpled bodies.

Legs.

Trunks.

Heads.

43

She knew. Patty knew alright. She waited at the table. As soon as Bow came back from the shower, Patty's eyes were on her. With rigid limbs, Bow went to Jay, Taran and Sonny, who were on the sofas absorbed in a film. She hovered there for a moment, pretending to catch up on the plot.

Patty watched on.

Then Bow hummed all the way to the sink, poured herself some water and stole another glance towards the table. Patty pointed to the garden and walked off with her tea. Bow had no choice.

Outside, a cooling drizzle battled with the steamy heat. Small puddles remained on the bench. Patty was unsure where to stand for the impending confrontation.

A short time later, Bow came out and closed the glass door. She wet her lips with her tongue, dried them with her hand and reached for the greenery of a branch.

A breeze enveloped the women and the trees quivered.

'The rain … Good for washing things away,' Patty said, lifting her face to the drizzle.

A few steps away, Bow cleared her throat and spoke in a low guttural tone.

'Was it your husband?'

Patty's pain could have been one day old. She waited until her voice felt ready. 'Our son. Our only child. But in the end, George died too. It took its toll on him. When we buried Pete, George lost the will to go on. He'd sit in his chair. "I can't breathe, Patty. Open the windows." And when I did' – her voice broke – 'he'd get the guilts about breathing. He'd cry in that chair in the suit he wore to Pete's funeral. Then he wore the same bloody clothes to his own service. George as good as died the day you took Pete from us, and I wasn't strong enough to carry him through.' Almost over her shoulder, she whispered, 'We couldn't both rot in that front room.'

Bow stepped closer. 'I'm –' She stopped. 'I'd do anything to bring them back.'

'When you kill me, that'll make all three of us. A whole family you'll have wiped out.'

'I won't do that.'

Patty scoffed. 'That's right. You're innocent, aren't you?' Her head bobbed melodramatically. 'Taran too. Both innocent.'

'Not fully. I was there when your son died. But the company used me as a scapegoat.'

'Not true. Your error killed them. They came to the house. They told me a worker didn't know what to do, couldn't work the machinery properly.' Bow went to object but Patty silenced her. 'I won't hear it.'

For a while, neither woman spoke. Patty finished her tea and shook her cup dry. Bow caressed leaves in the tree and kept her head down.

'So, now you know we're a match' – Patty motioned behind her with a nod – 'was that my last meal? Toast and a cup of Irish Breakfast before you execute me?' She put her cup down.

'How did you find out?'

'Elimination. One clue told me the person was illiterate. Another said to look for someone who denies responsibility.' She paused and raised her eyebrows. Bow turned away and she continued. 'One night at dinner, Sonny admitted he'd killed someone. Plus, he reads his clues out, the fool. It couldn't have been him. Taran does say he's innocent, but he can read. Now that Nicky's gone, there's nobody else left, young lady.'

'Easy for you. None of us targets get such helpful clues.'

'Good. I hope you –' Patty covered her mouth. 'What would Father Billsborough say if he could see me wishing harm on a fellow human?' She turned to Bow and studied her face. 'Look at you. You're so young. You'll have to carry what you did for years. Years.' She shook her head. 'And your family? What do they say about it?'

'Don't. Please.' Bow breathed deeply through whistle lips and repeated her earlier promise. 'I'm not killing anyone.'

A crisp tut came from Patty and her tone turned harsh. 'Then I'm stuck here. I don't want to live – there's nothing to live for – and I can't take a life.'

'Jesus fucking Christ. You must have some reason for living.'

'I'll make you kill me. I know what. I'll tell the others we're a match.' Patty took two defiant steps to the glass door. She saw the men watching the film and the absurdity of the scene struck her. Jay tumbling the Rubik's Cube in his hands, Sonny caressing his stomach muscles, Taran bobbing one leg over the other.

'No.' Bow blocked Patty with her arm. Shocked that Bow had dared to stop her, Patty froze. An instant later, Bow moved aside. 'Go on. Tell them.'

Up close, Patty peered into Bow's eyes. The muscles around them were too tight for her comments to be anything but a bluff. She went to grab the door handle, but Bow shoved her away. They struggled, with Bow keeping one foot blocking the door. Hitting Bow's upper arms, Patty cried out. 'Don't touch me!'

'They'll see. Get away from the door.'

Patty gave up and staggered back. She picked up her cup and threw it against the glass. 'You!' She screamed out her pain. 'You ruined everything!'

'I can get you home. Let me help.'

'I want you dead! I can't think of Father Billsborough this time. What would he know about loss?' Patty's strength was fading, her voice weak with exhaustion. 'Oh.' She sat on the bench, oblivious to the rainwater.

Behind them, the door slid open and Jay poked his head out. 'Is everything okay? We heard –'

'We can handle this.' Bow waved him back inside.

'Patty?'

Patty could feel him studying her eyes. He wouldn't tell tears from rain. But her blank look, features too heavy to fake a smile, might give something away.

'Piss off, Jay,' Bow said. 'Stop making it about you.' He retreated inside and she thudded the door shut.

They stayed silent for a half-minute. Patty blew her nose and whimpered.

'Poor Señor Bones. He must miss you. I'll make sure you get your life back.'

'My what?' Patty said. 'It's gone, remember.'

'You can still do things. Your knitting. Jay wants his jumper.' Despite Patty's eye roll, Bow persisted. 'Whoever you had the phone call with.'

Elizabeth.

Patty didn't want to think about what her sister was doing with the house. Getting rid of it, no doubt. Liquidating the family asset. An image invaded her mind of a fast-talking auctioneer waving rolled-up papers at the bidders. Sold!

With a nod, Patty motioned inside. 'Go on. Get the weapon.'

'Stop,' Bow said. 'Look at us. We're not like the others. We haven't pounced on each other. There's a camera up there. We're not allowed to collude so I'm not planning anything with you. Okay? I'm merely saying. Right? There are six of us now. Soon, two people will fight. Someone will die and someone will leave the house. When there are four left, then two more will eventually fight. Understand? Then we can walk off this show. Through there.' She signalled the garden door that led to the studio. 'That's how close you are to going home.'

'I'm not making plans with my son's killer. For you to go free. You're so crafty.' Patty went to heave herself up.

'Sit down!' Bow jabbed a finger her way and shouted with clamped teeth. 'It will hurt to admit but, right now, you are safest with me. Do you know what the best thing is to get bits of eggshell out of raw egg? Eggshell itself. I put you in here – I can get you out.'

'Oh, how clever.' Patty put on a mocking voice. 'A nice little food analogy to fool gullible Patty. Let's bamboozle her with talk about eggs and eggshells, and she won't realise she's making plans with her son's killer.' She took a breath. 'We are not making a deal. I am not planning anything with you.'

'Excellent.' Bow gave a forceful nod, like she'd finished a week's work. 'Let the others do the fighting. None of them will negotiate. They'll kill straight away. Saoirse too. But we have an advantage.'

'Are you listening to me, you selfish cow?'

'Name-calling I can live with.'

'It's easier if you kill me and head back to prison.'

Bow must have been pondering an incarcerated future, for she stared into the distance. Finally, she shook her head, picked up Patty's discarded tumbler and held it out for her. 'Remember that you can do whatever you like with the winnings.'

'I don't want money. I want you dead or back in prison.'

'Gun's in there.'

Getting up slowly, Patty glared at her. She stepped over to Bow with her palm open and raised to head height. Bow flinched despite her recent bravado and braced herself for a slap. Patty's hand swooped down and snatched the cup away.

44

On Sunday evening, with the rain stopped and windows open, fresh cool air gave the house an expectant feel. Wearing Jay's jumper and track pants, Christy googled baby names during the ad breaks. With Scot Free on its tenth night, she had a routine. She absorbed as much of the nightly show as she could from the sofa, and there were few interruptions. Nobody visited. If she was lucky, she would hear Jay's voice and see him often. He might even visit the chair, where the camera sat directly on him. Even as a pixelated face, his image on telly made her want to move the sofa closer to the screen.

Jay's mobile phone rang. For a moment, the ringtone made everything at home seem like before. Jay could have been in the bathroom or getting dressed.

An unknown number. It looked like the one from the other day. Her silent caller.

'Hello?'

'Hi. Pleased to meet you.' A woman's voice, confident and upbeat.

Puzzled by the greeting, Christy tried to sound natural. 'Who is this?'

'Who are you? I know you're not Jay' – the chuckle sounded forced – 'because he's on television. I've been watching.'

'I'm his fiancée. Christy. Who are –'

'Let me explain,' the woman said. Her voice took on renewed enthusiasm. 'I saw the show last night and I had to call. Jay's in the last six. That's fantastic news. There are four murders each season, and there's already been two, so Jay's –'

'Stop, please.' Christy squeezed a palm to her forehead and took a pause. 'One day at a time for me. It gets overwhelming otherwise. You called last week?'

'No, I didn't.'

'This number came up.'

'Let me see' – the voice hummed – 'I remember now. I got nervous, wasn't sure if you'd like the company. But my thinking has changed.'

'You did ring then?'

'Are we going to let it go? I answered the blooming question.'

Christy gasped. 'I'm not done yet. How did you know someone would answer Jay's phone? He's on the show.'

'A woman was bound to pick up. Jay always has a girlfriend.'

'Stop right there. You still haven't told me your name.'

'I'm Teddy.'

'How do you know Jay?'

'I was best friends – once – with Harriet.'

That name again. Christy sighed before she could stop herself, then turned it into an utterance of sympathy. 'Such a tragedy, wasn't it?' But there was no one called Teddy at the funeral. 'You weren't at the service. That's a pity. Being her best friend.'

'Jay's one of the viewer favourites. You know from comments online and the amount of screen time he gets. He's involved in everything. But he always was. Always on his terms.'

'Why didn't you go to the funeral? If you were such good friends with Harriet?'

'You're lonely, aren't you?' Teddy said.

'A little.' The admission was out before she could stop herself. 'What's that got to do with anything? Why couldn't you make it to the funeral of your best friend?'

'You wouldn't understand.'

Christy swore under her breath and let the silence draw out. It paid off.

'When friends' – Teddy paused – 'clash, if that's the word, they separate, they think things over. But you wouldn't understand. You're way too nice. Too … compliant to clash with someone. You and Jay make a great couple.'

'How the hell do you know I'm –'

'I wasn't born yesterday. You're such a –'

Teddy hung up. Christy stared at nothing, struggling to understand what on earth had happened. All she could do was chuckle. A more chaotic conversation she had never had.

Jay's mobile rang again in her hand. She answered.

'See?' Teddy's voice sounded chirpy again. 'I hang up on you with no explanation and when I phone back, you answer the call? What sort of person does that? A lonely, compliant one.'

Christy took a deep breath and did her best to ignore the jibe. 'Where were we? Aren't you going to say why you didn't attend Harriet's funeral?'

'Would you drop it, Christy? Gee whizz. I thought I had trouble letting go.' A long dramatic sigh travelled down the line. 'I had plans to go, to say my goodbye. But memories surfaced and I questioned if it was the right thing to do. Anyway, back to the present. Who do you think is Jay's match? It's Sonny, isn't it?'

'What do you know about Harriet's death?' Christy stopped. 'Wait. First tell me how you got Jay's number.'

'Whoa. Okay, this feels like a big mistake. All the questions, straight up rude.'

'What the hell? You rang me.'

'Fact check. I rang Jay's phone. Next time, I'll start charging you a dollar a question.' Teddy put on a squeaky voice. 'Got to go now. Bye-ee.'

'Wait. I want to –'

45

A glaring sun greeted Sonny. With the rain gone, the ground had lost its dampness. Ideal weather for mowing grass. He was glad to be outside. Sitting around talking to that lot bored him out of his skull.

As Scot had promised, the lawnmower appeared overnight. A nifty piece of machinery, it looked brand spanking new with its black body and familiar red stripe. There wasn't a surface that Scot Free branding didn't reach. Barefoot and shirtless, hands on hips, Sonny surveyed the lawn and devised a strategy. Up that right side, back down that way. His toes wiggled on the grass. Green blades stroked his skin.

Two kookaburras, perched high on the camera wire, began their mocking laughter. Sonny had always been puzzled by how such small birds could make that racket. The mower would surely scare them. He flipped it over. Fixed on a central axis, the blade was a slab of bevelled steel. Gleaming. He tapped along its edge.

Right in front of him sat the sharpest object in the house.

He put the lawnmower the right way up and set its electrical cord clear of the frame. Good. With the grass catcher secure, he wheeled the mower to the top right corner of the grass and faced the house. His hand came up to block the sun's glare. Three cameras were filming. His squinting masked the faint curl in his lips.

A dog at its master's heel, the mower was ready to work. Sonny flicked the power button to stir it awake and the crisp sweetness of cut grass immediately tickled his nostrils. It was years since he had smelled that scent. Morwell had concrete everywhere. Exercise yard, corridors, dining hall. Cement. Rock. Metal. Glass. Korydallos Prison in Athens was the same. Add to that the whole time he had lived in Athens and it had to be close to a decade.

He moved slowly and carefully in a straight line, determined to achieve a neat edge. He paused at the return to scrunch his toes into the moist clipped grass and admire his handiwork. If a job's worth doing …

Under his mighty flick, the power cord bounced out of his path. He pushed his way back to the house. The angle of the sun made him squint again, and for a metre or so he couldn't see his footing. Yet he walked as if on a catwalk. Spine straight, shoulders back. At the start of his third lap, he spotted a rogue clump of clippings that had fallen onto his tidy green. He cut the engine and went to retrieve it.

Stepping lightly, he pushed forward, turned and doubled back. Each time, a powerful whip of the electrical cord sent it safely out of harm's way. He emptied the catcher, taking care not to scatter clippings on the tended section.

Halfway along his second to last lap, the engine sputtered. As it chugged and hiccupped, Sonny slowed to a crawl and willed it to continue. He sighed with relief when the engine roared again. But seconds later, about a metre from the end, the engine cut completely.

'Shit.'

His line was uneven and the entire lap would need a rework. That's if he got the bloody thing to start again. He pressed the power button a few times. Nothing. He walked over to the wall socket to make sure it hadn't come loose. Plug firmly in the wall, switch on.

Lifeless, the mower sat on the green.

He killed the power and returned to the mower, only treading on uncut grass. A swift nudge and the light machine was on its side, revealing a motor tattooed in damp snips of grass, where the scent was even more intense. Sonny knelt and leant in towards the cutting blade. There was no apparent obstruction. When his fingers were millimetres from the steel, he pulled back. He wasn't going to take any chances.

The orange electrical cord ran snake-like from his feet to the wall. He stared into the camera above. Trust nobody. He wound the cord around his hands and yanked the plug from the wall, causing the snake to strike the air and hit the ground dead.

Sweat and dust caked his face and his lips were salty. He tapped the blade and took his finger away as though testing a steaming iron. Hot metal.

Rubbing his hands together helped dry his fingers, which would give him a better grip. He nudged the blade and it moved lightly.

Nothing was blocking its motion. Whatever caused the engine to stop, it wasn't a faulty cutting blade.

Sonny stared at the blade as he considered his next move. It glinted in the sun and all thoughts of neatly mown edges left his mind. There before him sat his weapon, its destructive beauty mesmerising. That steel would slash a throat like a knife through a watermelon. Or it would crack the weapon dome so he could get the gun.

He looked around to check he was still alone. With both hands, he gripped the long, hot blade on either side of the axis. It burnt his palms, but that wasn't stopping him. A vigorous shake of the mower confirmed there was no way he could remove the blade without tools. Damn it.

He leant in again, hoping to see deeper into the mower's workings. A bit closer. His panting echoed inside the cutting dome. Closer. Eyelashes of one eye brushed the blade. He knew he had gone as far as he could when his nose touched it too. He set his fingers to work feeling around the mower's inner landscape: smooth metal parts, thick bolts, uniform grooves.

Along with the scent of grass came the smell of oil, and a memory surfaced. The prison workshop. A hydraulic press and a pack of cigarettes. A hand reaching. A button pressed in retribution. The wet crunch of multiple bones being crushed.

Remote control. The press had been operated by remote control. In a fraction of a millisecond, Sonny realised that pulling the mower's cord from the wall socket had made no difference. No difference at all. He had been set up. The motor he was hugging like a newborn was not within his control. Someone, somewhere behind the whirring cameras, had their finger on a button.

The muscles in his arms mobilised for an emergency evacuation from within the mower's belly, as his brain reconnoitred the route they would need to travel. Off the central shaft, past the disc, away from the spinning blade. Beads of sweat flooded his forehead.

The engine let out a low chug.

His adrenaline surged.

The blade spun only a little before it hit his wrists, burning and cutting. He tensed his body and groaned. Having both arms trapped within the mechanism had stopped the blade's full motion. For now. He looked on helplessly as the metal ate into his flesh, the vibration digging the blade in further.

'Help!'

No response from the house, but the kookaburras cackled overhead.

Wisps of smoke rising from the motor told him the engine might soon cut out. But he wasn't sure how long he could keep his hands there. It was best to risk pulling them away. He would have to extract both at the same time.

'Help me!'

No more shouting. He needed his energy to hold on, and nobody would reach him in time. His grip was weakening. Clamping his teeth, he curled his fingertips as much as he could to protect them. No time to lose. He pulled his hands away, his palms and fingertips shredding, the blade slicing through skin and knuckles. Dark blood spurted across his face, finding his exposed teeth and tongue.

The motor's roar intensified as Sonny rolled away howling. He cradled his mangled hands at his chest as though in prayer and rocked to the pain. His screams echoed through the air with the kookaburras' laughter.

46

Alan sat twirling an unlit cigarette. He would've been puffing on the balcony in a flash, but for voicing Scot. Although he was alone, the buzz through the studio after Sonny's accident was so tremendous that he felt like he had company. The show was trending on the socials and Alan had already sent a video file to his home system. No loss of life, but … blood, gore, flesh sliced and diced. Plus Sonny's rat cunning going up against – and losing to – Adolpha's diabolical shrewdness. One to watch.

He faced the large screen, which showed Sonny writhing in the chair, hands draped in stained tea towels, his bare chest smeared in blood. Even with the screen blowing up Sonny's image, Alan still managed to look down his nose at the wretch. He spoke into the mic to deliver the unfortunate news. 'You'll live.'

'My fingers! I've lost me fucking fingers!'

'Stop exaggerating. I can see ten,' Alan said, as he held the button to speak. 'Maybe eleven.' He cut the mic.

'You fuckers! Pray I don't get out of here. If I ever get my hands on you!'

'I doubt that.' Alan activated the mic again. 'What were you doing fiddling with the underneath of an automatic mower? Who in their r–'

'The fucking thing was off!' Sonny screamed through wet sniffs as he rocked in the seat. 'How did that happen?'

'You turned it on and off several times. It was recharging. That cord you pulled out was the charger, not the power. I've watched the footage. It shows you –'

'You fuckers set me up! How was I to know it was automatic?'

Alan removed his hand from the console and spoke to the room. 'You weren't. Serves you right for grabbing the boss's arse. Twerp.' Next, he spoke to Sonny. 'Is the pain relief working?'

Eyes closed, feeling sorry for himself, Sonny nodded like a child. He whimpered. An injection in each forearm had morphine swirling around his system and mixing with gratitude. His head came up and he looked into the camera. 'I can't go back to prison like this. They'll crucify me.'

'Let's get you bandaged up then. No doctor can enter the house, I'm afraid.'

'Aww.' Sonny's whimpers were like those of a mournful puppy.

'We've arranged for Saoirse to do the bandages.'

'Her?' Sonny scrunched up his face, which sent tears down his cheeks. 'Might as well do it myself. She's fucking useless.'

'Ah, Saoirse, there you are. Sonny would like your help.'

Onscreen, over Sonny's left shoulder, Saoirse stood. She nodded wearily, staying behind the chair. Alan ordered them to the measuring room, where he'd left medical supplies.

'You'll find everything you need. Suture strips, bandages and so on. Get up, Sonny. Shake a leg.'

He killed the mic before Sonny could respond and popped the cigarette in his mouth. The quicker they finished up, the quicker he could go for a smoke.

*

Sniffling, Sonny sat and watched Saoirse sort through the supplies. Despite the injection deadening his sense of touch, his hearing remained acute. A rustling of wrappers. A stretch of rubber gloves. He watched closely. Saoirse was almost on autopilot. Before she laid a finger on him, she had everything organised on the worktop.

She began by inching the bloodied tea towel from his left hand. They locked eyes. He noticed the flecks in her irises, her crow's-feet, moisture on the eyelids. Gloomy, but determined. She would do her best, they seemed to say. Saoirse paused before she peeled the cloth fully away. With no bin available, it hit the floor with a squelch. If she was battling to keep the shock off her face, she lost. 'Don't look.'

He had no strong desire to see the damage, but he glanced all the same. Like pineapple tags, flaps of flesh sat away from his hand. One knuckle looked like it was about to join the tea towel on the floor. He hoped that was bleeding and swelling playing tricks.

'You're losing lots of blood.'

'Hurry up then.'

She cleaned his hand. But the second she wiped away blood, more appeared and ran down his forearm. Finally, wound glue and suture strips covered all the major cuts, pulling in the untidy shredding. His right hand received the same treatment.

'That's the tricky part over,' Saoirse said. 'But you really need stitches. It says on the packet these strips reduce scarring. That's the last thing you need. More scars.'

Sonny flinched.

'Now for the bandage.' She unravelled a section. 'You might not have a doctor nearby, but these supplies are some of the most advanced that exist. This is the toughest material you can get.' She stretched the bandage with both hands until it looked like it might break. It bounced back into shape with no sign of distortion. She held the bandage to his skin to start binding. 'They won't let you back into prison wearing these bandages.'

'Why not?'

'They're so tough you could scale the walls.'

Sonny was surprised by Saoirse's attempt at a joke. He looked up at her in search of a wry smile to accompany her words, but she hadn't quite mustered the energy for that. He rolled his eyes.

'Get on with it. I ain't got all day.'

'Yes, you have. I'll bind the fingers as one but bandage your thumb separately.' With his left hand wrapped, she paused. Her head shook slowly as she studied his face, his marked neck and his blood-smeared chest. 'What a state. It's had scrapes and bumps, this body of yours. You're travelling around in a well-dented car indeed. Your hands make the scar on your face seem like a freckle.'

He wasn't sure what had caused her openness towards him. Seeing his blood flow, his raw pain? He stared at her. 'And your scars? What about the dents in your car?'

'They're inside, on the dashboard.' She unravelled the second bandage. 'Luckily I've got tinted windows, so they're not visible.'

Sonny snorted. 'You're kidding yourself. You need a darker tint.'

'Right one,' she said. He raised his hand, which she wrapped as thoroughly as the left. 'This material is as durable a bandage as you'll find. Built to last.'

'Yeah, yeah. You said.'

He watched his mangled hand gradually disappear under swathes of cloth.

'All done. They're waterproof too, but you ought to keep your hands dry. Don't lift anything heavy, obviously.'

Sonny rotated his hands, forearms high like a boxer. 'Where'd you learn that?'

On his left hand, an edge of bandage jutted out. Saoirse tucked it into place with two soft taps. 'I'm a nurse.' She scrunched up the packaging of the medical supplies. 'You're done.' When Sonny didn't respond, she snapped her fingers. 'Now that's something you won't be doing in a hurry.'

Sonny did a double take. He forced a smile. 'Do that again. The finger thing.'

Looking down at her hands, she stepped back. 'What?' Her eyes darted to the camera.

'Again, I said.' His tone was surly.

She raised one hand inch by inch. She snapped her fingers in her idiosyncratic way, using her thumb and ring finger, and quickly hid both hands behind her back.

He laughed. The lengths the studio had gone to to conceal the identity of each housefriend. Tests, clues, control over weapons. And here was a simple hand gesture that confirmed the woman standing in front of him was Aggy's mother. All the guessing was over. And his fucking hands were out of action. Great.

'It's different,' he said. 'Only met one other person who snapped their fingers like that. Show me again.'

Saoirse made no attempt to follow the order. His eyes bore into hers like a surgical drill. He nodded to signal that she should do as she was told. He made to get off the stool. She brought her hand up and the two of them fixated on her ring finger and thumb coming together.

Snap.

'It's no big deal,' Saoirse said. 'We're all done here.'

She wiped her forehead as if her skull ached. 'I don't want

any trouble. If you know who's after me, tell them from me – not today.' Rather than shaking, her head rolled. It could have been made of stone.

'Okay. I'll tell them to leave you alone.' He followed up with a forced chuckle.

'Do you know who –'

'Joke. I only know I killed a man – my best friend – in a hunting accident.'

'Oh.'

'I will live with it forever.'

'Did he leave behind a family?'

Sonny nodded his lie. Saoirse winced, drawing small lines over her blotchy cheeks. 'They must miss him.'

47

'Drop it.'

Sonny stared into the darkness, enveloped by the roar of the waves. Next to him on the rocks, Aggy wound the cloth beach bag over her forearm. She wiped sand from her sunburnt skin. They were a short walk from the main beach area. But every so often, holidaymakers strolled by, their faces illuminated by mobile phones.

'I'm cold,' Aggy said, fumbling for his arm and forcing him to cuddle her.

'I'm too hot. It's summer, fuck's sake.' He freed his arm. Again.

A few moments later, she returned to her interrogation. 'I want to know where you stayed. That's all.'

'How many times?' He gripped her shoulder and brought his face close to hers.

'Don't raise your hand to me. You promised. And don't get cross with me because you can't get your story right.'

'I told you. I was at Reggie's watching the football.'

'Honey, Reggie's is closed for renovations. It has been for weeks. You must have drunk a lot if you didn't even know which bar you were in. How are we meant to work out where you spent the night? You must have been so –'

Blood boiled in his head. A ferocious heat swept through him. Despite the sea breeze, he could feel sweat building on his forehead. His hand shot up in the blackness squeezing her cheeks into her teeth. 'All right, detective.'

'You're hurting me.'

He eased off. 'I ought to …' He brought up a hand, which made her flinch.

'Stop. That's not nice,' she said, massaging her cheek and checking her jaw. 'But you're right. I'm sorry. I've jumped to conclusions.'

Convinced he hadn't heard the last of it, he looked her way. Only a fool would dare bring it up again. 'No more. I'm telling you. Or' – he huffed out some air – 'there's no saying what I'll do. And there's nobody around to rescue you tonight.'

He was running out of alibis and losing track of where he'd already claimed to have been the night before. He knew it sounded ridiculous, and Aggy was too persistent to let it go. The darkness had dulled her usual confidence, but she wouldn't stop.

'It doesn't add up. First, you thought you were in the Odyssey, but Colin didn't see you.' She snapped her thumb and ring finger together, marking the demise of the first alibi. 'Then you said you were with Pete. But Terri says no way. She was with him.' Another snap, another alibi down.

Sonny's chest tightened. Each snap detonated a landmine in his head.

'It can't have been Stavros's because they don't have screens anymore, and you watched the game.' A third snap.

Sonny gripped his head, now a decimated battleground.

'Now you say you were in Reggie's, but –'

He pounced before her fingers could come together a fourth time. In a split second, hands of steel locked around her neck. He would have felt like a boulder crashing from above. She was powerless. His body trapped one of her arms, already tangled in her cloth bag, between them both.

He felt her stop struggling. That was her signal for him to ease off. But that wasn't going to happen this time. How many chances had he given her?

'Pleas–'

He growled through gritted teeth. He had to make the problem go away. 'Shut your mouth.'

Her voice. Her words. Her nitpicking.

His hands. His fingers. His ten digits – with the power of twenty – squashed into her throat, keeping the air from her lungs and imprinting the blame on her skin. Her legs twisted and kicked, but not for long. Only when she fell limp did he release his hands. Her body slumped against the rock.

Sonny's fitful breathing mixed with the crash of the waves.

'Fuck.'

Aggy's mobile vibrated next to her body. Sonny shook out his hands and checked the screen.

One word. Mum.

He hurled the phone into the sea.

48

Man with a purpose, a shirtless Sonny strode past the others. Jay and Patty were on the sofas, and Bow and Taran were preparing lunch. All four speechless, surprise plastered across their faces. Less than an hour before, they'd come to Sonny's rescue, tending his wounds and bearing his weight as he stumbled through the house, covered in bloodied cloths, to the chair. Not unlike a biblical scene.

Now here he was, a new man. Padded hands swinging freely, his recent discovery about Saoirse had taken his mind off the pain more than one of Scot's injections. One thing was for sure. As soon as he was armed, the house dynamics were in for a radical change.

'Nobody move!' he said, before taking the corridor to the weapon room. He looked back. He was alone. Those fools knew better than to try it on with him. Were it not for the bandages, he would have rubbed his hands in anticipation. Without interference, he would put Saoirse's name in the weapon dome and *bam!* – the glass would open and he'd have the gun. Firing the fucker was another matter.

He elbowed the green button to open the door and entered backwards. There was still nobody tailing him. He chuckled to himself at how the pieces had slipped so neatly into place with one small action. Mother and daughter snapping their fingers the same weird way. Fancy that. And Saoirse had no inkling that he knew her identity. He closed the door with his forearm. Only then did he turn around.

The dome was empty.

No gun. No bullets.

He blinked to clear his vision, in case the injection was messing with his eyes. But the gun was gone. 'Fuck!' He rammed a knee into the wall, circled the dome and cursed some more. One of those idiots had it. Hands by his sides, he stooped down in a clumsy bow and rammed his head into the solid glass. In a fraction of a second, the pain returned and stole his attention. His hands throbbed, his head even more. 'No. No. No.'

*

'Who's got it?' In the main area, their puzzled faces stared at him. 'My fucking gun. Which one of you?'

Without speaking, Jay stood from the sofa and shook his head. He hadn't checked the weapon room all day. Nobody else responded.

Sonny shook his big white gloves. 'Was it you, Scot?'

'Gone?' Patty said, bunching up her knitting. Someone might take that too. 'This is all getting out of hand.'

'Trying to be funny, Grandma?'

'We're not safe,' Patty said. 'Someone is armed.'

'Who's got it?' Sonny bellowed.

On the other side of the island, Taran clutched Alice close and stroked her ears flat. He couldn't help looking at Sonny's oversized hands. 'You giggling at me, Tarzan?' Sonny shot round the island and bared his teeth to him. 'What are you hiding there? Guilt written all over your fucking face.'

'Stop picking on me.'

'You've got it under Totaliser. Show us.' To check underneath the rabbit, Sonny elbowed Taran's arms upwards.

'See, nothing there. Leave Alice alone. Poor thing's terrified of you. We all are. Help us, Bow.'

Bow came between the two men and nudged Sonny, who retreated a few steps but only to give himself a better view of everyone. 'To the fucker who stole my gun, there are two bullets. One for my target and one for you.'

Patty came to her feet. 'You two listen to me. Taran, you do not speak for me. Sonny doesn't terrify us all. Not me, anyway.' She addressed Sonny. 'Shut up, you fool. That gun doesn't belong to you. You belong in prison, but don't kill innocent people along the way.'

'Innocent? None of you are innocent,' he said.

'Don't come at me with your bullshit.' She looked straight at him. 'What kind of fool puts their hands under a –'

'Careful. I can still –'

From nowhere, Bow blocked Sonny's view of Patty. 'We haven't got the gun. You've had a rotten day. Sit on the sofa and I'll get us a beer.' A promise of female attention and alcohol seemed to work. 'Go on.'

Sonny sat on the free sofa and waited for Bow to join him with two cups.

Jay watched him take a drink like a circus bear doing a trick, cup raised awkwardly to his lips. Liquid spilled down Sonny's chin and his bloodied chest.

'One moment.' Bow disappeared and returned with a T-shirt and two small towels, one dry, one rinsed in hot water. She sat next to Sonny. He faced her, chest puffed, with his fat hands resting in his lap. She put his cup on the floor and cleaned the smeared blood off his chest with the wet towel.

Sonny mumbled, but Jay could hear. 'Scot did this. Fucker wants me dead.'

'Why?' Bow asked. She dried his chest with the other towel and handed him his drink.

'I done nothing.' With a slurp, he finished his beer and tossed the cup on the seat. He inched closer to her, a forearm on her knee. 'I'm lucky to be here.' He shook his head, as though the severity of the accident was just dawning on him. 'You almost lost me.'

Bow drained her cup and made a face. 'Ooh, that went down the wrong way.'

'If that had been one of you out there, you would've died. The motor on that thing was fucking powerful.'

'You've got the muscles.'

With little nods, Sonny agreed. 'Not only that. Strong bones too. Prison doctors keep telling me that.' Like a boxer facing a career-finishing fight, he kissed his bandages. 'Thank you, Jesus.'

Bow fumbled for the T-shirt and gripped it around the neck. 'I'll help you with this. I grabbed the largest size I could find so the bandages fit through the sleeves.'

They got to their feet.

'You wouldn't laugh at me. You're not like the others,' he said, placing his hands on her hips as she worked the shirt over his head. She thumped one of his hands with her elbow and from under the fabric, he shrieked in pain. He was the only one who couldn't see Bow grinning.

'Oh, I'm sorry. I didn't see you there. You've got to be careful. Best keep your hands to yourself or you might get hurt.'

49

The next day, Jay waited until everyone else started on their daily tasks. With the door locked, he sat in the chair, fiddling with his Rubik's Cube. An age passed before Scot arrived and asked what was wrong.

'I'm worried,' Jay said, rubbing sore eyes.

'Worried? Who for? Not for yourself' – there was a pause – 'obviously.'

He rattled off names. 'Saoirse. Patty. Now Sonny, with, um, yesterday's accident.' He looked to the door. 'On the day the show started, I overheard a woman say she would injure Sonny. You … fixed it.'

'Fixed it? Nobody asked him to flip the lawnmower and grip the blade.'

That news stopped Jay. Sonny hadn't shared any details. 'Well, now he's got a weapon. Attached to him. His hands are like sledgehammers.'

'Sledgehammers?'

Jay lifted his gaze. 'Are you going to say anything apart from echoing me?' For a moment, the only sound was him shuffling the faces of the cube into place.

'Sonny can't pick up a thing,' Scot said. 'Under the dressing, his skin is shredded. Saoirse did a good job, didn't she?'

'He only has to grip someone's neck.' Jay forced the coloured squares around. 'Saoirse is not good. She's not sleeping –'

'We're monitoring her.'

'And Walt. You're meant to help the hunters.'

'Nicky was drugged and Walt had a weapon. We were as surprised as you.'

Surprised? That wasn't the first word that came to Jay's mind. 'When Walt died, was there a viewer backlash?'

'Backlash?' Scot echoed again.

'Stop it, Scot. Of course, there's no point asking, is there? No outside news.'

'Put down the cube. Look at me.' There was no 'me', but Jay obeyed. He crossed his arms. 'The game's progressing, the stakes are higher. Is there doubt growing behind those resolute eyes? A woman died. Are you fully prepared to discover the truth about Harriet? What if it uncovers more pain? Are you feeling guilty, Jay?'

A shiver ran down Jay's back, but he tensed his body to hold still. 'There's Christy to think of.'

'Consider your position. Very few victims of crime get to be where you are now. Thankfully, our closed courts shield the country from the horrors, from the criminals. Our state manages the violence. But on this show, you get to flex that coercive arm. You're one of the privileged few. A ticket to revenge. Don't let your fellow citizens down by squandering this chance to right the wrong done to Harriet. You must draw on your fear, your doubt and your killer instinct.'

Jay swallowed hard. His heart beat like a gavel pounding in a courtroom.

'People at home need to see that it is best for the government to manage this side of life. They think they want that burden. They don't, not really, deep down. But you must show them what it takes to wield that power correctly. Viewers must understand what's at stake. Christy may be the one who ends up feeling guilty.'

'But I'm no closer to working out who killed Harriet.'

There was a drawn-out pause before Scot responded. So long that Jay was already on his feet.

'Poor Harriet.'

50

The next day, Bow was preparing dinner, with a bandaged Sonny failing in the role of sous-chef beside her. He watched her organise the ingredients for a beef casserole with garden vegetables. They were planning a fruit flan with fresh berries for dessert, and Taran and Saoirse were in the woods with instructions on what to pick.

'I feel useless,' Sonny said. 'I can't even scratch my balls. Will you help me?'

'There's no time to look for them.' She stayed counting out meat portions for six. 'We've got dinner to prepare.' She indicated the telly. 'Put some music on. Something quiet.'

After fumbling with the remote for a full minute, Sonny found a station playing a thumping dance track and grinned. Bow sent him a cutting look and he raised his padded hands, signalling his helplessness. He ditched the remote on the sofa. Making the most of her attention, he then ran his eyes down the length of her frame. As she moved away to use the tethered knife, she could feel them lingering on her.

'Delicious,' he said. When she turned to confront him, her face stern, he motioned innocently to the ingredients.

Bow held a large carrot and locked eyes with him. 'If you ruin this meal' – the carrot snapped in her grip – 'there will be consequences. Chop up or shut up.'

Sonny beamed. 'You're tough with me. I'm not used to being so –'

'Weak?'

'– helpless. I come from a family of labourers and farmers. We get stuck in.'

'Good genes run in the family, do they?'

He looked her up and down again, more quickly this time. 'Yours too.'

Bow turned her wrists to loosen them. Her arthritis suggested something other than strong genes. She put the thought from her mind, returned to her chopping and soon had the casserole simmering on the stove.

'What happens now?' Sonny asked.

'Dinner cooks. We wait.' She wiped her hands on a tea towel and walked to the sofa.

Sonny settled himself into the beanbag next to her. He covered himself with a blanket and moved his feet to the music. 'Who has the gun, d'you think?' He elbowed the beanbag. 'Come down here with me.'

'No. Patty and Jay are around that corner doing their suits and the other two will return any minute with a tub of fruit.'

'Nothing's going on. Come under here.' He lifted the blanket. 'I need attention is all. Look what they've done to my poor hands.'

'No funny business,' she said, sliding onto the beanbag.

He pulled a sad face as they resettled the blanket.

She inspected her fingernails and repeated his question. 'So? Who has the gun?'

'Can I have a kiss?' She angled her head away from his advances. 'How long do we have off our sentences for getting this far in the show?' he asked.

'About fifty per cent.'

'How much is that?'

'Half,' she said, looking at the camera in disbelief. The good genes hadn't reached as far as Sonny's brain.

He nodded several times. 'Kiss?' They fell silent momentarily, the music filling the void. Under the blanket, Sonny's legs locked around Bow's. 'I only want a kiss. Can't I –'

She pecked his scarred cheek. 'There.'

'Look at the state I'm in. I need someone to change my luck.'

'That's not how it works.'

'Want to know a secret?' he asked.

'Of course I do.'

Sonny chuckled and looked around. He hid his mouth from the cameras. 'I know my hunter.' Movement at Sonny's side made him turn and he missed Bow tensing at his revelation. Alice was ambling her way around the beanbag.

'You're kidding me.' Bow's voice stayed calm. She sat Alice across their laps, allowing Sonny to stroke her fur. His massive hands looked like they could crush her.

'Aren't you a lovely bunny, Alice?'

Bow gave a glance to the camera. Her look said, *Are you getting this?* She gestured for him to share his secret. 'Who is it?'

'Not saying.' He looked at her from the corner of his eye, his mouth turned down in a playful smirk.

She patted Alice and shook her head. 'I have no idea who mine is. Terrible clues. Is it Jay? I assumed your match was Jay.'

'It's a woman,' he said through stony lips, head down.

Bow tried not to react as the last two matches clicked into place in her head. Sonny with Saoirse. Jay with Taran. 'Patty?'

'Not saying,' he said, stroking Alice with the back of his huge hand.

'Saoirse?'

'Not saying.'

'Are you sure you know? Or is this all a wild guess?'

'I'm willing-to-kill-and-get-off-this-show sure. I saw her do something and I knew.'

'You're lying. Otherwise you'd go after her.'

'Look' – he raised his hands – 'I can't go back to prison like this. I'm waiting for a good moment. Anyway, you're here. I want to be friends.'

'Get me a bucket.' Her hand came up to make a gagging gesture, but she thought better of it and scratched her cheek. She pretended to still have doubts. 'That's odd. I was certain you were matched with Jay. And you're sure about this woman?'

'Sure as the boner in my pants.'

'That's not creepy at all.' She stroked Alice and fell silent, lost in thought. It was time to act. She might not get another chance. 'I reckon that clarifies who has the gun.'

'Huh?'

'Scot. Think about it. He works out you know who your match is and steals the gun before you get to it. They're fucking with you. You said yourself they'd set you up with the mower.'

'Bastards,' he said, but without much conviction. Bow's warmth beside him was sapping his interest in the cat-and-mouse game of the show. He leant closer. 'All I want is a kiss. Please.'

'Stop. I'm thinking. Turn the music down.' He used his nose to lower the volume on the remote. She took a few breaths, checked nobody was around and braced herself. 'Right. We'd better get a move on. I say what goes on and when. If I tell you to stop, you stop. If you don't, I will hurt you. Majorly.'

She could see he wasn't following. 'You can't undress yourself because you can't get dressed quickly if someone comes, and I'm not doing it for you. But you've got to come inside me.' She unzipped his trousers. 'How long will you be?'

'What? Jesus! Fucking hell. Not long.' Sonny tossed Alice aside so forcefully that she bounced off the sofa opposite and hit the floor.

From under the blanket, Bow removed her clothing. 'Wait. You can't help me come. Your bloody hands.' His tongue shot out. She forced his head between her legs and used the blanket to block as much as possible from the cameras.

Pleasure travelled through her body. Her limbs twitched as she fought to contain her climax, puffing out through pursed lips. Then she pulled out his erection and turned away from him. 'It's easier this way.'

From above, they formed a Y. Their legs twisted together for control, not intimacy. Their breathing quickened and his thrusting intensified. 'I thought you said you were close.' Shortly after, a deep intake of breath and a flurry of mechanical thrusts from Sonny signalled the end was nigh.

'Here it comes.' His body tensed, then went limp. Because he had no grip, she pushed into him.

Several minutes passed before they spoke. She dressed under the blanket and stuffed tissues in her knickers. 'Nobody saw, did they?' They looked at the cameras and laughed. 'I didn't hear any footsteps.' She stretched her arms up, enjoying the calm in her body, the temporary relief from her joints. 'They won't televise this bit, surely?'

Sonny shrugged. 'Let's use the showers next time.'

'Next time?' As a distraction, she reached for Alice, who had been cowering under the sofa.

Sonny turned to her, propped up on his elbow. 'You're gorgeous. D'you know that? Your eyes. They're Astraean.'

Bow's cackle erupted in his face. She wiped her saliva from his cheek. 'Sorry. I'm not laughing at you. What does that mean?'

He waited until her eyes met his, to give the definition the solemnity he felt it deserved. 'Like the stars.'

'Oh. That's a good word to – er – have up your sleeve.'

'If someone gives you a compliment, you're meant to take it.'

Bow got to her feet adjusting her clothes. 'If you give me a compliment, fine. If you're expecting me to accept a compliment, you can shove it. Look at me. Look at Astraean Eyes. You don't give me any rules.'

Forearms and elbows doing the work, Sonny fought to sit up. 'Maybe it is time to get out of here.'

Standing over him and tightening her ponytail, Bow stared at him and predicted his future. 'Look at your hands. You're not leaving this place. Alice will get out of here before you do. Watch the food please. I've got to freshen up.' She walked off, staring into the nearest camera and pointing at the fool behind her.

51

Sonny's face hardened. Fuck did Bow pile on him. He went to rub an itch on his scalp, but his hand ached. He tried with his wrist. Fucking hands. Fucking house. Fucking Scot. He glared into a camera. Everyone was playing games with him.

Alice, having forgiven him his recent attack, sniffed around the beanbag. Drawing her closer, he trapped her with his padded mitts. She had a watchful eye on him. He also knew a few games.

He squeezed. Alice wriggled.

His hands moved along her body to her neck. 'Stay still, Total. Which name do you prefer? "Alice" or "Total"? Or "Totalitarian"?' Her black eyes, ever cautious, looked on. He tightened his grip and sucked air through his teeth to stifle the pain in his hands. Alice's powerful legs thumped about, but he squeezed even more. He growled at the ache in his hands that came from rabbit bones breaking under rabbit ligaments and muscles.

Alice lost her fight fast. Her head fell forward.

Below his grip, everything stopped moving: the fat belly and the dangling legs. Inert curves and fur.

He spent a clumsy half-minute standing up, shedding the blanket and keeping hold of dead Alice. He had to be quick. The best way to skin a rabbit was manually, which for him presented a problem. His years of farm work had seen him master the task. Done well, it took no effort and led to minimal blood and mess.

At the sink, he bit a chunk out of her hide near the neck and spat it in the bin. He knelt on the neck and did his best to work a fork into the fresh hole. What used to take him one go now took several. He winced with each yank of the hide, but he got there. Once the fork did part of the work, he grabbed the hide between both hands and a final tug did the trick.

His hands were ringing with pain and beneath the bandages, his fingers felt damp and sticky. Fresh blood.

Seconds later, Alice's fur was off, tail too. He used his teeth to remove the guts. His bandages got less bloodied as a result, and his hands were spared more pain. He checked the liver. That wasn't going to waste. No white spots – safe to eat. He chewed it well before swallowing it.

In the bin, he buried the incriminating hide and viscera. A rinse of cold water removed most of the blood from his bandages, and he shifted some of the material to cover what was left.

With his elbow, he pressed the button for the tethered knife and chopping board. Humming to the music and awkwardly using his body weight rather than his hands, he separated Alice's carcass into six pieces. Front legs, back legs and body in two. They joined the beef and vegetables in the bubbling pot.

*

'Did you cut yourself?' Bow was back in the kitchen, her wet hair off her shoulders. 'You've got blood on your cheek.'

'Tomato sauce,' Sonny said, stirring the pot and sending the ingredients below the surface. 'Hey, hold still.' He ruffled her hair until he held a few strands between his mitts. Before she moved off, he tugged on them.

'Ow! Piss off.' She whacked him.

He added one strand to the pot and let the others fall to the floor.

'Gross. What are you doing?'

'Secret ingredients.'

'Ingredients? Plural? What else did you put in there?'

'Shush.' He brought his finger to his lips.

'Golden rule – don't mess with dinner. What else went in?' She called out. 'Scot! What did he put in the cooking?'

'Shush! You'll give the game away.'

'What's in there?' His eyes shifted to Alice's box off to the side and Bow's mouth fell open. 'No!' She ran to the box. 'Where is she?'

Sonny pointed at the pot and chuckled.

'You fucking animal. What happened? Why?' She fished around the pot with tongs and held up a leg, its bone attached. 'What's this?'

'Always cook rabbit on the bone.'

'Are you out of your mind? Taran will – oh fuck. No, no, no. We don't need this.'

'It's only a rabbit. Taran'll see the funny side.'

'He most certainly will not. Why on earth?'

Sonny stirred the pot. 'All good chefs add a dash of something special.'

'You're not a good chef, and now dinner includes human hair and someone's pet. Jesus.' She checked the freezer drawers and slammed the door shut. 'We don't even have meat to cook something else.'

'Fuck that. They're eating it,' he said.

Bow huffed. 'I've seen worse go into food, I suppose.' An image of the kitchen at Barton Correctional Centre came to her, which she thrust from her mind. Sonny went to speak, but she stopped him. 'Don't even think about tampering with my dessert.'

*

On his way back from a smoke break, Alan bumped into Adolpha in the corridor. To avoid being grilled about Everton's work – Alan had no fresh news – he commented on Bow and Sonny's tryst. 'Interesting development.'

'You stink of smoke.'

'I slipped out for one on the balcony.'

'It's disgusting. You're disgusting.' Adolpha covered her nose. 'Stand there.' With a flick of her hand, she shooed him away.

Alan was grateful she wasn't carrying her fencing foil. Once he'd taken two steps away, she lowered her hand and went on, 'What's her story shagging that monster?'

'I'm unsure what she's up to.' Maybe nothing clandestine lurked behind Bow's decision.

'Update.'

It wasn't a question, but a command that Alan had heard countless times. 'Let's see. Saoirse. The team's worried she could take her life. Now that she's lost Nicky.'

Adolpha made a face like she'd eaten something that didn't agree with her. 'Suicide? On my show? She wouldn't dare.' She took a moment to swallow down the awful taste. 'Ugh. People do make me sick.' She walked off and raised her voice. 'If Saoirse even hints at it, I'll creep in there myself and put a pillow on her face.' She laughed and stepped into the lift.

Alan remained in the corridor alone. Ringing in his ears was Adolpha's threat of murder.

52

Christy found a shaded barbecue table in sunny Centennial Park. Her colleagues at the bank no longer asked after Jay or accompanied her to lunch. Two mouthfuls in and Jay's phone rang in her bag.

'Oh my god!' Teddy blurted, as if ringing an old friend. She recounted the morning's events, which allowed Christy to eat more of her sandwich. 'You're outside?'

'I'm with colleagues. Can't stay long.' Christy expected a prickly comment given the lack of background chatter. She would say she'd stepped away to take the call. But Teddy didn't challenge her on it. Instead, she was thrilled to share the delicious details leading to Alice's death.

'All because Bow brushed him off after sex?' Christy asked.

'I'm not lying. She's a cold one. Yet the promos make out Sonny's accident turned him nasty.'

'It's fair to say Sonny's character explains Alice's death, if you ask me.'

'I didn't,' Teddy said. 'You'll see. They keep showing him choking her.'

A woman arrived at Christy's table and asked to sit. Christy nodded. 'Ugh. Sonny's a pig. I bet he killed Harriet. Was there footage of Jay?'

'Forget him. I'm interested in who'll eat the rabbit. Taran won't.'

'That's obvious,' Christy said.

'Oh, is it? Excuse me.'

'Sorry. I didn't mean it like that.' There was a pause in the conversation. Christy watched a couple walk past, each with a terrier on a lead. She sipped her soft drink.

'Take care with them there words, missy.' Teddy's voice was sharp, making Christy tense.

'Maybe Bow will warn them,' Christy said, returning to the topic. She took out a slice of lemon cake and nibbled on it. 'If Saoirse eats any, she'll go off the deep end.'

'Patty too, with her dog and all. They'll puke. Lord, I am not missing tonight. What about your dear boyfriend?' Teddy said in a taunting tone.

'He won't eat it. Jay's too –'

'He will.'

'No.' Christy's voice held firm. 'He knows it will hurt Taran.'

'Wrong. Jay's all about the future. He's a what's-done-is-done type. He's practical, doesn't hold on to stuff.'

Christy felt the burn in her blood. It wasn't good to get so worked up. 'I think I know my own partner.' Across the table, the woman looked away. 'I'd better get back to my colleagues.' There were still questions she had for Teddy, but they'd keep.

'We should meet for lunch,' Teddy said.

'No.' It came out before Christy knew it. The last thing she wanted was to meet Harriet's peculiar friends. Nor did she fancy strangers knowing about her pregnancy. She wasn't through the tricky period. 'I mean I don't work in the city. Erm, sure. Do you work?'

'Not now.' Even with Christy staying silent, Teddy didn't elaborate.

'What did you do today then?' Christy asked.

'Had my morning fix of Scot Free, went to my favourite post office –' Christy's laughter drowned out the rest of her sentence. Teddy tutted. 'What now?'

'Sorry. I must've misheard. It sounded like you said you were at your favourite post office.'

'Yeah. What's so funny?'

'Oh. They're all the same, aren't they?'

'"They're all the same," she says. God give me strength,' Teddy said.

Christy's voice cracked as she held back laughter. 'I've got to … go.'

'Whatever. Let's watch the show together. Call me. I do all the phoning.'

Christy hung up and held her belly. Her cackles drew the woman's attention and covering her mouth did little to stifle her hysterics. 'Favourite … post …'

Her bench companion also laughed.

'Who is that fucking fruit loop?' Christy asked, wiping her eyes.

53

Bow topped her flan with the fruit that Saoirse and Taran had picked that afternoon, trying not to gag as she arranged the blueberries and strawberry halves. They might as well have been the size of potatoes. Hard, unswallowable, ready to choke. She was praying Taran would come down with a bug and not show for dinner.

Nearby, Sonny ladled the casserole into six bowls, apportioning chunks of Alice with unusual care. Bow angled herself away. She could only imagine what he had planned.

'No meat for me. I'm not hungry,' she mumbled under her breath.

'More for the others,' Sonny said.

Jay rapped on the dining table, Patty and Saoirse next to him. 'We're starving here.'

In a few trips, Sonny brought the starter of bread rolls, creamy butter and dips to the table. He nudged Patty. 'Believe me, you'll eat well tonight.'

'What's cooking?' Saoirse asked sleepily. 'It smells lovely.'

'It's a surprise, apparently,' Jay said.

'I'm surprised we're eating at all this evening,' Patty said, choosing a bread roll. 'When I looked earlier, it wasn't cooking I saw.'

Bow's cheeks seared like a barbecue. She dropped the berries in her hand and began babbling. 'No, no, no. We're ready. It's all set. Sonny cooked this as it's an easy meal for him to eat with a spoon. But don't feel you have to eat everything. Leave room for dessert. I'm making a flan from –'

The sound of cheerful whistling made Bow stop. Taran was returning from his shower, damp hair glistening. He headed for the rabbit box and loosened the lid. Bow's heart dropped, crushing her stomach even flatter.

'Stop right there!' Sonny shouted. He came behind Taran and held the lid down. 'Leave her. You're clean. We're eating now and we're all starving because of you, late back with the food. Totalitarian can totally wait.'

Obeying, Taran joined Bow at the island, giving his back to the others. 'We were late because Saoirse stood in the tub of fruit and crushed everything. Hours of back-breaking labour ruined. She's in a permanent daze.' At the table, Saoirse's angled head and vacant eyes supported Taran's words.

'Has anyone seen my Rubik's Cube?' Jay asked. Nobody had.

'I can't remember when I last saw you with it,' Taran called.

'I've lost my flower, the one Nicky made me. I left it here this morning.'

'That's missing too then,' Bow said. 'I've been here all day and I haven't seen it.'

'Who would do that?' Saoirse's tired eyes scanned the group.

'My pack of smokes went,' Sonny said.

'My puzzle, the flower,' Jay said, eyes on Bow. 'It looks like we have a thief in the house.'

Placing the last of the berries on the dessert, Bow locked eyes with Taran. Surely vengeful relatives and convicted murderers living together posed a bigger concern. A glint in Taran's eye suggested he'd had the same thought. Bow showed him her dessert.

'Yum, a fresh tart,' he said.

'It's a flan. Made with the fruit Saoirse didn't step on.'

Taran waved her off. 'That's not a flan. Flans are more covered. It's a tart.' He turned around. 'Anyone? Patty? Help us over here please. Tart or flan?'

'Come and tell him, Patty,' Bow said. 'It's a flan. It's got no solid base.'

Patty got to her feet at her usual slow pace and walked to the island. She studied the dessert from several angles, then held Bow's stare. 'You're dead right, Taran. It's a tart.' Bow shook her head, but, unblinking, Patty nodded. 'Trust me. I know a tart when I see one.'

Bow's cheeks reddened for the second time. 'Yes, well, we'll eat it later, however we call it.'

'Come on, come on,' Sonny said, shepherding Patty and Taran to their seats.

Bow joined them, leaving Sonny to serve the meals alone. A waft of casserole meat hung over the table, encasing everyone. Bow picked at the vegetables in Alice juice. Dice of carrot, bit of potato.

Sonny took a deep breath. Only when the others started chewing did he tuck into his meal, squelching loudly. Each time an empty spoon left their mouths, each time they swallowed, each time they licked their lips, he gave a little nod. A blob of gravy landed on Saoirse's chin. To alert her, he tapped his own, a wide grin on his face.

'Beef, definitely.' Patty was the first to guess. 'Succulent.'

'Yes,' Sonny said. 'And something else.'

'It's quite gamey,' Taran said, examining the meat on his spoon.

'Good one.' Sonny nodded to Bow, who shook her head at his antics.

'Wild guess. Pheasant?' Jay asked.

'Snob.' Sonny chuckled. He dipped his roll in the stew and sucked juice off the dough and his bandages.

'It's lodged between my teeth, whatever it is,' Taran said. He worked it out with his knife. 'Tasty though.'

Sonny watched Saoirse gawking into her meal. 'Oh gross,' she said. 'A hair.' Everyone turned to see a long blonde hair, coated in gravy, hanging from her spoon.

This made Sonny cackle like a child. He lurched back, then fell forward, slapping the table. 'Common mistake, love. People often confuse the two.' Bow frowned at him but that set him off even more. 'It's not hare. It's rabbit,' he said.

It dawned on Bow why he'd placed a strand of her hair in the casserole.

Taran dropped his spoon and spat onto his plate. 'No!'

'What's going on?' Jay asked. He lowered his spoon.

In a flash, Taran dashed to Alice's box and tore off the lid. There was only a brown cushion inside. 'Tell me you didn't.' Taran looked around and called out. 'Alice! Come to me!'

'Yes, I did.' Sonny resumed eating.

'I don't believe you.' With pain in his voice, Taran shook the cushion. 'Where's Alice?'

Sonny patted his stomach. 'In Wonderland, son.'

'Stop, everyone! You're eating my rabbit. They cooked my Alice.'

'I feel sick,' Saoirse said, pushing her plate away. She hurried to the kitchen and vomited in the sink. 'You're an animal,' she said to Sonny. Each time she spat, Sonny laughed more.

'I had no hand in this,' Bow said.

'Not cool.' Jay was shaking his head. 'What's Scot's take on this?' he asked. Neither Sonny nor Bow answered. Jay stood and strode to the chair.

With Sonny and Patty continuing to eat, Taran moved his spoon through his bowl, as though expecting to recognise Alice. 'Patty! Think of Señor Bones. What if it was your dog?' Sobbing, he hurled the cushion at Sonny and threw himself onto the sofa.

'I'm not wasting it. It's lovely, Sonny.' Patty herded more stew onto her spoon. 'The mix of herbs and meat, along with the veg. It's quite Mediterranean.' She leant to Sonny and whispered. 'I'm all for any endeavour that keeps your fingers out of your nose.' Sonny raised both bandaged hands. His fingers weren't going near his nostrils anytime soon.

Patty spoke and chewed, sucking her teeth dry. 'Why would I think of eating Señor Bones? I don't think of him when I eat chicken. Look where we are, Taran.' She licked her lips and sat up straight. A serious expression swept over her. 'We must put things in perspective.' She took another spoonful. 'You can't tell me what to do.' Her voice became firmer. 'I'll eat whatever I choose. I'm sick of people ordering me around.' She banged her fist on the table, catching Bow off guard. 'When I get out of here, I'm going directly to my sister and I'm telling her what I think of her.' She prodded the table. 'I'll demand Señor Bones back. He's my dog! It's my house! Stop telling me what to do.'

Taran lifted his head from the sofa cushion, his face wet and blotchy. 'You're horrid, Sonny. A brutish, unfeeling murderer.'

'And you're not?' Sonny said through his squelching.

'I'm nothing like you. I'm innocent!'

'Pull the other one, Tarzan.'

*

'It's disgusting, Scot. Sonny's a monster.' With white-knuckled fists, Jay paced around the room. He had no intention of sitting in the chair. 'That's all he knows. But you? You could have told us they put Alice in the fucking dinner. What will people watching at home say about you? I'll tell you what they'll say. Evil. It's fucking low.'

'Let's not argue, Jay.' Scot's voice stayed calm and placating. 'You know the rules. I can't pass that information to you. Sonny broke no house rule when –'

'Taran formed a bond with Alice.' Jay punched his own palm for emphasis. 'Have you no conscience? Everyone knows how much he cared for her. And you just stood by and watched while Sonny fed his own pet to him. Any trick Sonny pulls, I bet you'll go along with him. Good for the ratings, eh? Bastards.' Jay's breathing was erratic, his face and throat scarlet. 'I'm bloody hungry. What am I meant to do?'

'Eat your dinner. I don't want to fight with you on this.'

'You set the standard out there. Low tactics like that will encourage bad behaviour in others. We don't deserve this. I want an apology.'

'Jay, I am very sorry.'

Jay tensed at the insincerity. He jabbed at the button to open the door, but before he left, he directed a final comment at the useless blank screen. 'Because Sonny is suffering, he wants us to suffer too. You set him off with that lawnmower stunt. You enabled that prank with Alice. God knows what else he has planned.' He stormed out.

Except for Taran's sniffles from the sofa and Patty's cutlery scraping against her plate, the main area was quiet. Jay returned to his seat and pulled his plate closer.

'Forgive me, Taran. But I need to eat.' He scoffed the meat smothered in gravy. His elbows rested on the table, hands clasped. He chewed. Tender meat, rich sauce. He kept his back rigid to make it seem like he wasn't enjoying it. A sip of red wine added to the experience. He had to stop himself from moaning with pleasure.

54

During the adverts, Christy stifled a yawn and checked the call duration. Twenty-eight minutes. That's how long she and Teddy had been watching the show together, with Jay's phone on speaker. She felt too exhausted after a day's work to hold a mobile. And her eyelids wouldn't remain open much longer.

'Holy smokes, you got that wrong,' Teddy said, referring to Christy's claim that Jay would not eat Alice. 'Do you know your boyfriend or what?' Teddy tutted and went back to crunching on her crisps.

'You clearly know him.' Christy waited for the munching to stop. 'Listen, Teddy, could you do me a favour? I like our chats, but if you're going to eat while you're on the phone, can you choose quiet food? Like chocolate or yoghurt.' Teddy's crunching stopped. Hoping Teddy would speak, Christy stayed silent. She had to wait only seconds.

'You make a right pair, you and Jay. Couple of divas. If you're going to start dictating what I eat −'

'Shall I hang up so you can eat without bother from me?' There was no response. Christy huffed as loud as she could. 'What do you mean by that comment? "We make a right pair." You're rude. You know that? You know nothing about us.'

'I –'

'I haven't finished,' Christy said, steeling herself to pose a question she'd wanted to ask days ago. 'Did you and Jay date?' She grimaced but didn't know why.

'What's that got to do with the show?'

'Answer me. Did you and Jay have a relationship?'

'Yes.' Teddy gave an exaggerated huff. 'God, you're such a –'

'When?'

'A long time ago. I'm sorry I never told you. I enjoy our chats. They're fun and I don't want them to end. I want us to be friends.' Christy was about to tell Teddy to fuck off. 'News of Harriet's death saddened me. Then all this with Jay and the show. I had to call. You don't know how much it meant to me when you answered his phone.'

Christy calmed herself with a few breaths. 'You could work on your phone manner. I'm going to become very busy soon. I'm not what you're –'

'I lost my baby.'

Christy gasped. Absently, her hands found her belly. She still hadn't shared her pregnancy with Teddy, nor her miscarriages. Her voice cracked. 'Oh, Teddy. Did you get support? When – was this?'

'Harriet proved invaluable. I couldn't have done it without her.'

Christy's eyes widened like saucers, her tiredness gone. She must have misheard. Harriet? Jay's sister? Invaluable?

Teddy carried on, her tone staying neutral and buoyant. Like a newsreader.

'She arranged it all. Booked me in. Took me there. Made sure I went through with it.'

'Harriet? I don't understand. She made sure you went through with – what?'

'My abortion.'

'Oh.' Christy stopped, puzzled that Teddy had referred to the procedure as losing a baby. 'How kind of her.' It was astonishing that Harriet had been so organised, so supportive, given that her addiction tended to get in the way of so much.

'It was her idea.'

*

Frank Carlisle returned to the living room with a cold beer. His favourite way to switch off from work. Barton would be there in the morning. Regrettably, without inmate Bow. His trusted viewing seat took his weight. He rarely noticed the ridges left by his backside, which came to rest like a device sliding into its dock. Scot Free was on, broadcasting the catch-up of the day's events.

On the sofa, Eleanor lay almost horizontal, except for her head and shoulders. Her fourth gin was working nicely. She watched Frank briefly before she spoke, her speech slow.

'What's not to like about Jay?'

Frank snorted and raised the volume.

The footage showed Jay storming through the house on his way to the chair and the audio came from a narrator. 'Jay's heading to Scot to complain about Sonny and Bow.' Frank and Eleanor listened to Jay's outburst, unaware they were hearing a heavily edited version that had excised his protests about Scot's behaviour.

Jay's voice bellowed onscreen, 'Disgusting, Scot. Sonny's a monster. That's all he knows. Evil. It's fucking low.'

'See, love?' Eleanor said. 'Finally, someone with heart on the show. That man's got a conscience.'

In the shot, Jay's hands flailed. 'Taran formed a bond with Alice. Everyone knows how much he cared for her. Sonny fed his own pet to him.'

Then Scot spoke. 'Sonny and Bow have crossed a line.'

'Low tactics like that will encourage bad behaviour in others,' Jay said in the footage. 'I want an apology. We don't deserve this.'

Scot's voice was animated. 'Then go and demand your apology.'

Eleanor slurred her words. 'Jay's perfectly right. Bow and Sonny were awful.'

'It's nothing to do with Bow,' Frank said. 'She didn't kill the damn rabbit and she wasn't there when Sonny threw it in the pot.'

'She knew.' Eleanor squinted at Frank. 'It's left to Jay to have a conscience.' Next, the footage showed Jay returning to the others. 'Watch this. He's about to give that pair of troublemakers what-for.' She shouted at the television. 'Sort 'em out, Jay.'

Onscreen, Jay sat at the table and finished his meal. He said nothing to Sonny or Bow. Eleanor hitched herself up.

'That's odd. I thought he planned to get stuck into those two.'

'He's a bloody hypocrite,' Frank said, waving his beer at the telly. 'Behind closed doors, he's mouthing off about how bad Sonny and Bow are. Yet out there to their faces, not a word. That two-faced turd you like so much has cast himself as Scot's favourite, strutting around like he owns the joint. Sonny and Bow are right there at the table with him, and he hasn't said boo. And you like him? Mark my words. That little stunt is going to cost him a lot of public sympathy. People don't tolerate double standards.'

Eleanor took a gulp of gin and stared at him. Eyebrows raised, she waited for his glare to come her way. 'You're just grumpy because your inmate-slash-colleague had sex on national television then helped cook the pet rabbit.'

55

Sunlight cast harmless shadows over the furniture, and Jay enjoyed his first cup of coffee for the day upright at the island. His thoughts drifted. Lie-ins with Christy. Cool sheets, warm limbs, lazy cuddles. Nudging each other out of bed to make the coffee.

Now, the house was church quiet.

Saoirse was awake but slumped at the table, hair unkempt. Jay hadn't spoken to her when she'd shuffled out. Instead, he had made her a coffee and placed it by her hands. Limp and empty without Nicky's flower.

After the previous night's ruckus with the rabbit, it was understandable if the others were loitering in their rooms. Alice's cardboard box had gone, and with it the last trace of her. But a strange charge hung in the air, like a housefriend had died, not an animal. What made this different was that Alice hadn't died as part of the game. Her death had come from a crueller place, which Jay hoped Sonny kept hidden.

Slapping footsteps in the bedroom corridor stirred Jay from his thoughts. Someone in a hurry. Taran, stern-faced with fists pumping, came past and raced straight down the other corridor. Jay was glad to see he had moved on from last night's sadness. No doubt Scot was about to receive another serve and Jay hoped Taran wouldn't hold back. Scot needed to hear it.

Jay sighed. Breakfast was unlikely to remain as quiet. He removed his glasses, wiped them with a tea towel and threw the cloth over his shoulder. Time for food and more coffee.

Taran returned minutes later and started preparing breakfast. His anger was palpable. He threw plates and tubs down on the island with as much force as he could muster, almost willing them to break. But the plastic merely thudded onto the marble surface. Not to be thwarted, Taran brought his fist down on a tub of honey and droplets splattered across his face.

'Sonny was alone when he killed Alice. Where is he? That bastard deserves to die.'

'Perhaps you should –'

'Stop with the peacemaking, Jay,' Taran said, slapping his cup down so violently coffee spilled over the rim.

'That's cool, buddy. I'm here if you want to chat. Sorry about Alice.'

'You finished your plate though. I hope she didn't disappoint.' Taran threw him a withering look.

It crossed Jay's mind to share how delicious the meal had been.

'Have you had pets before?' Jay asked. 'You clearly love animals.'

'Have you ever eaten a pet before?'

'What I meant was –'

'What did I do to him?' Taran struggled to control his voice. 'It's not fair. She didn't deserve to die.'

'If you're after a sensible explanation from Sonny, you're wasting your time.'

Taran stepped forward. 'I need this.' Yanking the tea towel off Jay's shoulder, he shot outside and paced around, head down. He picked up something and bounced it around as if testing its weight. Jay groaned. A pebble. Taran found another one. And a third. He returned inside with the stones twisted inside the cloth.

'Think this through,' Jay said, holding out his hand.

'You think this through. What have I got to lose? When Sonny gets up, I'll smash his skull in, and I'll go back to prison and rot in my cell. But at least he'll be dead.'

Jay mentally awarded Taran top marks for originality in weapon choice, but low marks for practicality. 'They're small stones. They won't do any damage to someone's head, least of all Sonny's. He survived a run-in with a mower, remember.' Jay's tone was calm. 'It must be tough serving time for something you didn't do. Was it a colleague from the bank that died?'

Taran huffed. 'You persist.' He tightened the twisted cloth, making the stones bulge in the tea towel like dislocated bones under taut skin. 'Someone's been feeding you rubbish. Or you're bluffing.' He held Jay's gaze. 'It wasn't a colleague.'

'G'day,' Sonny said. Eyes barely open, he stood rubbing his belly.

Taran leapt into action and rushed at him. He launched his makeshift club at Sonny's forehead before the other man could block him. But even with a weapon, two functioning hands and the element of surprise, he had no chance. Sonny used his thick forearms to shove him backwards and pin him to the wall by his neck. Taran squealed and dropped the towel.

'I oughta kill you right here, cunt,' Sonny said, his nose brushing Taran's jaw.

Saoirse watched on, mouth open.

Jay kicked the tea towel away and turned on the wall vacuum, which sucked the cloth and the pebbles quickly away up the chute. He then stepped in to end the melee and braced himself for a whack from Sonny. But surprisingly, the thug let himself be pushed back. Taran spluttered his way to the sofa.

'Jesus,' Sonny said. He checked his cut forehead in the mirror. His collection of injuries was growing. Hands, neck, forehead. 'This place is worse than prison.'

56

That afternoon, Saoirse took a long, warm shower, partly to escape Sonny's snoring from the sofa. In the bathroom, behind a locked door, she felt isolated but safe. Not another soul around. Each time she grappled with her wild locks under the water spray, she remembered Nicky and the hair styling that hadn't gone to plan. Her hair dryer ending up in the tub. Dead.

A towel dry and brush of her mane would be all she could realistically manage on her own. She should've had her hair done before coming on the show. But the kids had been her focus. What little relief the water spray afforded faded at the thought of her children. Even through the haze of Scot's pills, her body ached so deeply that the steam had no effect. With luck, her friend was still texting the children using Saoirse's mobile.

She turned off the taps and, moving slowly to keep her balance, reached beyond the screen for a towel. Slippery floor, wet feet. Perhaps the shower wasn't as safe as she thought. With needles in armrests and rabbits in dinners, only God knew what other parts of the house Scot had booby trapped.

She towel-dried her hair and listened out. There was a muffled sound from within the bathroom. It could be bare feet on tiles. She wrapped the towel around her.

'Who's there?' Her very question made her chest restrict. A man hiding maybe. 'Taran?' Her voice cracked. 'You must leave now.' She dried her feet on the mat. Ear cocked, she left the cubicle. But nobody was around. She was almost disappointed. If her imagination was playing tricks, that wasn't a good sign. She moved to the mirror to grapple with her hair, then screamed.

Behind her, Bow stood squeezed next to the shelves. Saoirse's first thought was to run, but Bow blocked her exit. 'Quiet!' Bow held her arm.

'Please don't hurt me. I'll scream again.'

'You want to see your children, right?' Bow held Saoirse's gaze until she nodded. 'You're going home right this minute.'

'What?' Saoirse said, trying to wriggle free. 'Leave me alone.'

'Listen.' Bow wedged something into Saoirse's closed hand. 'Take these. I know who your target is. It's Sonny.'

Saoirse uncurled her fingers to find two pieces of metal. Her face twisted. 'What are they?'

'Bullets,' Bow said, holding up the pistol.

Saoirse jumped and the bullets clattered to the floor. One disappeared under the shelves and the other, aided by the sloping marble, rolled to the drain, a steel grate with thin bars and large gaps. It teetered on the edge inches from Saoirse's foot.

'Don't move.' Bow dropped to her knees, gripped the bullet and pulled it to the marble before picking it up. She retrieved the second bullet and forced both back into Saoirse's hand. 'You're shaking, poor thing.' Bow leant in and hugged her. 'We don't have much time. Sonny knows it's you. You've got to kill him.'

'I don't believe you,' Saoirse gasped and batted the gun away. 'I've never fired one of those.'

'You have to. You take this, you load it and you kill him. Then you leave here and you see your children. You see Nicky.'

'Nicky.' Saoirse smiled. 'Yes.'

'Good woman.' Bow patted Saoirse's hand, only to have Saoirse pull away.

'How did you find this out?'

'He told me. Something you did. He guessed. You have to act quickly. Do you understand, honey? You are in unbelievable danger. You're alive only because he doesn't want to rush back to jail. He plans to kill you.' Bow stepped back to assess Saoirse. Her wet hair and pale skin, her thin limbs and her hunched shoulders brought her a forlorn air.

'You killed Alice.'

Bow huffed. 'For fuck's sake. Sonny killed her. For absolutely no reason. That's who you're dealing with. Forget last night. Forget Alice. I've given you a gun.'

'Use it yourself. I've got a weapon.'

'No, you haven't.' She grabbed Saoirse's arm again. 'It's too late for me, but you can live.' With every word, she shook her. 'You must kill him.'

Saoirse looked Bow up and down. 'You're lying. Sonny said he wouldn't hurt me. He killed his friend, not my daughter.'

'The fucking pig's lying.'

Saoirse wrestled free. 'I told him I wanted to get out for my son's birthday. It's this weekend.'

'Good. Let's make sure you're alive to hug him.'

Saoirse steadied herself against the wall. 'Why are you helping me?'

'Because I don't want you hurt. Sonny's dangerous. You mustn't tell anyone about this. They will take the gun from you. Then you're less safe. Okay?' Saoirse nodded and Bow continued. 'He's asleep out there. Shoot him. But get close. Have you heard of point blank?' She jammed two fingers into Saoirse's belly, making her flinch. 'Up close. That's so you don't miss. Grip with both hands. Use both bullets.'

Saoirse checked over the gun. 'Where do I aim?'

'Get the head or heart. Then run outside because he'll try to kill you. Scot won't call a doctor. If Sonny doesn't die straight away, he'll bleed to death. But you must get to a safe distance. Understood?'

'Has he got Nicky's flower?'

'I don't think he's our thief. But if it makes you hate him more, let's pretend he's got it. Time to go home. Creep up to him and blow his fucking brains out.'

She added as an afterthought, 'There won't be much mess.'

*

Sonny was still on the sofa. He looked like a half-finished mummy with his bandaged arms crossed over his chest. The nurse in Saoirse spotted the open cut and bruising on his forehead, and she longed to put a bandaid over the dried blood. But despite the contusions and his concave scar, Sonny's sleep appeared peaceful. She inched nearer. His snores came uniformly, but they stopped when she was in line with his waist. She reached out, but he blocked her with a bandaged hand.

'What are you up to?'

'You're bleeding.' She tapped her head. 'Checking you're okay.'

'Don't lie to me.' He swung his legs off the sofa to sit up, but Saoirse shrieked and ran outside.

57

Jay was half-watching a film, which Taran, snoozing on the other sofa, had dredged from the digital library. At the table, Patty worked on her knitting, examining the stitching like a jeweller inspecting diamonds. Her nose and forehead wrinkled. Jay couldn't see why knitting would need so much focus, but Patty seemed dedicated. She caught Jay watching and her features softened.

In the garden, on Walt's mat, Bow held the warrior pose briefly. Then she returned inside, her desire for exercise quashed by a steady gaze from Sonny, who was sunbathing nearby. Bow almost tiptoed down the stairs by the hot tub, narrowed eyes peering through her loose hair, shooting a furtive glance to Patty. Interest aroused, Jay propped himself up. Bow sat down next to Patty, who turned away. Hearing only their mumbles, Jay saw Bow reach out and Patty raise a hand in warning. Then as quick as it began, the exchange ended. Patty stood in a huff and approached Jay.

'What happened there?' he asked.

'Um – the rabbit. She won't let it go.' Jay doubted her explanation because she appeared to doubt it herself, avoiding his eye. Patty changed the subject. 'Stand up. Face me, please. Let's measure you up while I have you here.' Jay got to his feet. 'How are you today? Not your usual self, I see.'

Jay raised his arms. 'I'm okay. Sore stomach. Something I ate, I suppose.'

'We all ate the same food for breakfast, so that can't be it.' She flattened the knitting on his arm, checking its reach. 'Incredible how much you remind me of my son.'

'Why didn't you say so before?'

'Not looks. Personality. When something troubled him, he couldn't talk about it directly. Like he lacked the words for negative emotions. Instead, a physical grumble was forever getting to him. Sore limbs, bad sleep, painful chest. I'd have to work out what was going on.'

'And could you?'

'Always. I was his mother. If his chest was tight and his head ached, he felt angry. Obvious, right? If he was sad, his energy went and he wouldn't leave the couch. Not even for a game of rugby.' She tilted her head searching for more memories. 'Loss of appetite meant he was worried. And fear showed as a sore back.'

'How?' Jay's attention went to the design taking shape in Patty's needlework. A wall of brown with a central yellow disc. 'Is that the sun?' She covered it with her hands. He'd have to wait to see the finished pattern.

'The stress made his back hurt.'

'But you said he played sport. What if his back ached from a game?'

'If that was so, there was no need for a grown man to tell his mother. It was his way of communicating.'

'I'm unsure that logic holds up.' Jay resumed his seat on the sofa.

'Never failed. I'd sit and let him talk about his aches and pains. Asking how it all started. And there would always be some trouble with a friend or a woman, you know. He couldn't make the connection between the two. His hidden spots, I called them. But with distance, I saw it. "What's wrong?", "Nothing."' Patty shook her shoulders impersonating a tough guy and lowered her voice. '"Then eat the damn dinner I cooked." He would truly deny it. Symptoms would appear and only days later, after a chat, would the penny drop for him. Funny.'

Jay nodded. 'How out of touch can someone be that they can't say what's on their mind?'

'Has there never been a time when your girlfriend was upset with you and you didn't know why?'

He gave a short whistle. 'A few more than I care to remember.'

'Your hidden spots.' She wound a loose stretch of wool around on itself. 'What did you just tell me? You've lost your appetite, have you?'

Jay went to speak. He laughed at Patty's attempt to liken him to her son. 'Very good. But it really is physical. A bad stomach.' He cast her a look. 'You seem in good spirits today.'

'I'm fine. I slept well. I'm going to buy Señor Bones a new collar. My memory of my son and husband gradually disappears. But every now and then, life sends me a joyful reminder. Today, you helped me remember my son.' She chuckled. 'See?'

But Jay did not.

'We're not talking about you again. Good deflection.'

Jay chuckled.

'You radiate joy when you speak about your son. I want to experience that. To know a world that unlocks for me when I become a parent.'

'You're a parent in here, that's for sure. How you sort things out and get results with Scot.'

Jay stole a glance at the cameras and lowered his voice. 'I'm not so sure about that. Things have changed in the last few days.'

'How?'

'Scot's acting differently, and the mess with the rabbit. Narky comments. Do you sense it?'

'I don't go to the chair. There's nothing to say.' She picked at a stitch. They fell quiet.

'Do you remember your relative easily?' Patty asked, a moment later.

Jay nodded. He paused. Taran looked fast asleep and nobody else was around. 'I have' – he took a big breath – 'things to remind me. At home, there's something. Only I know about it. Tucked under the bed.'

Patty leant in, resting on an elbow. 'Why only you?'

Jay wasn't going to mention Christy. 'There was tension and I got fed up with advice from all sides on how we should have handled her.' He whispered now. 'Harriet was special. Our family failed. We didn't find the time to save her.'

'That's a pity. What things of hers are you keeping secret?'

'A small box of her belongings that the police handed over.'

'Aww, that's sweet. You're lucky. What's in the box?'

58

Christy stretched her legs towards the television, with the Scot Free catch-up playing. Finally, her usual way of sitting on the sofa – legs bent in – was too uncomfortable. Her body was changing. Change. How wonderful. Even though she saw no glaring difference in the size of her tummy.

In her hands, she held one of Jay's Rubik's Cubes, with only the green side complete. Next to her, Jay's phone sat on speaker. Christy still hadn't given her own number to Teddy. 'I called you last night,' she said.

'Couldn't talk. I had a thumper.'

'Poor you. Teddy, I wanted to ask –'

'Not now. There's Jay with Patty.'

'They're only talking about her son.' Christy heard the volume increase on Teddy's television. 'Ooh, you might lower that a bit please. I like following your insightful commentary.'

Teddy's tutting came through the phone.

Christy cleared her throat and held the cube steady. 'You

and Jay dated.' Her stomach felt as twisted as the puzzle she held. 'Was it serious?'

Teddy didn't answer straight away. 'Huh? Harriet introduced us.' Christy bristled at the name. Harriet. Everywhere. 'Nothing serious. It was never going to work. Harriet saw to that. She brought us together, then made sure it finished once it became an inconvenience for her.'

'Inconvenience?'

'Patty's so sweet,' Teddy said. 'I wish she was my mum.'

Christy fiddled with the cube but kept an eye on the screen, where Patty and Jay were still chatting. She battled to conceal the impatience in her voice. 'Teddy? You were saying. Jay and you. Inconvenient?' A quiet line. 'Teddy?'

'Yeah, yeah. I'm trying to watch this. Harriet saw Jay gaining a good friend and she saw our friendship changing. If Patty'd been my mum, I would've made better choices.'

'You had Harriet for support. Like you said, she helped you with the abortion.'

Teddy scoffed. 'Got that right. She practically forced me into it.'

Christy grunted in sympathy and waited, allowing Teddy a few seconds to watch the show in peace. 'I wonder why she was so keen for you to have it.' There was no answer. 'Teddy? Did Harriet –' Christy paused, unsure if she wanted the truth. But how satisfying to get a 'no' from Teddy. 'Did she know the father?'

'Sometimes I wonder if you call only to find out about Jay and Harriet. You don't want to speak to me. If I must answer the bloody question, yes, she knew him. Shush. I'm watching.'

Christy's mouth was stone dry. 'Do I … know him?'

'Christy! Look! Listen to Jay and Patty!'

Onscreen, Jay was talking about a box of Harriet's belongings, with Patty asking what was in it. Christy froze. Mouth open.

Jay's face filled the screen. 'Everything she owned. Rather, everything they found on her. It all fits in a small box. She had' – he took a big breath – 'nothing. I sit with the box at times. The items in it are special to me. Insignificant objects, but special nonetheless. When I open it, the first thing I smell is tobacco. Awful to think that's the association for treasured memories. Tobacco. But everything she died with is close to me.'

'Christy! Can you hear this? Go get the box. Don't hang up.'

Christy went straight to the bedroom, her legs wobbly with the news. 'Tell me what else he says.' She knelt on the floor, stretched flat on her side, trying not to squash her belly, and wriggled under the bed. There it was. A tin the size of a child's pencil case. Christy reversed out and leant against the bed with the box and phone in her lap. A memory came to her of the day Jay had gone. He'd tried to tell her something. But she'd told him she was pregnant, he hadn't believed her and they'd argued. This could be the thing he'd wanted to reveal. His secret to share.

'Open it.' Teddy's voice came through the phone.

'I'm trying. It's hard to –' Christy struggled with separating the lid and the base. 'Got it.' The tin opened silently and Christy closed her eyes.

'What's in it?'

'This is terrible. I'm snooping in my own home.' Her heart was thumping. She closed the tin. 'I'll ring you back.' She ended the call midway through Teddy's swearing.

Breathing deeply, she opened the tin. Jay had been right. She instantly caught a tobacco smell. Inside, there were coins, a hatpin, a lighter and a grey object the size of a house key. Christy guessed it was a kind of fob, giving access to a shop or office or warehouse. She held it up.

It looked like a plastic teardrop.

Surely Harriet hadn't had a job before her death. Had she been storing something? Drugs? Apart from a hole for a cord or keyring, the fob had no markings.

Jay's mobile rang next to her, but she ignored it.

Christy next took out the grungy pack of rolling tobacco, which was almost empty. She tested the orange lighter. It worked. Always smoking was Harriet. With the base of the lighter, Christy batted the coins around the tin as if they were concealing something. She couldn't remember the last time she'd made a purchase with coins. Finding a shop that still accepted them was near impossible. Sad that Harriet had died with less than five dollars on her.

She picked up the plastic hatpin, which would have secured Harriet's auburn frizz. The tobacco smell was strong here too. She sniffed it. Perhaps it doubled as a tool for picking locks. Maybe it came in handy for self-defence in strange homes, getting wasted with unfamiliar men. Christy closed the box and rang Teddy.

'What are you going to do with it?' Teddy asked.

'I'll hold onto it for now. When Jay comes home, I'll –'

'You should put it back. It's private. It's meant to stay –'

Christy cut Teddy off a second time.

59

From the sofa, Bow kept an eye on everything. Waiting was murder. Like being in the queue for the prison phone. She pretended to read her novel, but she was close to bursting. Nothing seemed to go to plan. For a start, Sonny was alive, sprawled on the other sofa and definitely not in a Scot Free body bag with a bullet in him.

For the life of her, she couldn't explain the hold-up. Saoirse was helping Patty prepare a dessert. She appeared to be doing her best to keep her distance from Sonny and to avoid Bow. Patty ran the cake-making and Saoirse orbited her, looking lost. They barely exchanged a word.

There was a slim chance Saoirse was holding off killing Sonny until the evening's clues arrived, which Scot had earlier announced. Saoirse's clue might confirm Sonny as her target. She would whip out the gun and shoot, and Bow would be a step closer to freedom. Bow pictured Sonny's blood spilling over the marble floor.

His final wound.

Then there was Patty. Stubborn, wilful Patty. Would she keep their secret? At least she seemed to be going along with Bow's request for now.

Stirring from her thoughts, Bow looked down to find she was crumpling her book. She eased her grip and flattened the pages. Then she spotted Jay watching her from the dinner table. His damn spying. He must have seen her observing the others. Without blinking, she glared at him – even as her eyes watered – until he averted his gaze. What a jerk.

The moment Scot's voice sounded through the speakers directing the housefriends to get ready to read their clues, Bow's heart sped up. She steeled herself for trouble.

Saoirse shuffled into position, taking a spot near the kitchen, and Bow chose a section of wall near the far corridor in case gunfire broke out. She waved at Taran, who was returning from the garden. He managed a sluggish nod and Bow's cheeks went rosy. The memory of Alice's tragic end was still fresh.

Five of them stood waiting, only Patty ignoring Scot's request. She stayed where she was, icing the sponge cake. Bow had never seen her look so calm. Pleased with her culinary efforts. But Patty needed to keep up their charade.

'Hurry up, Patty,' Bow said. 'Our clues.'

Patty mouthed, 'Get fucked.'

Bow spun to the wall, shaking. Her blood boiled. She drew a breath and, with all her power, shouted to the ceiling. 'Fuck you!'

*

With Bow's words echoing through the house, Jay glanced over his shoulder. He half expected to find Sonny harassing her, but they were metres apart. Sonny was jogging on the spot and wriggling his arms, like a boxer about to enter the ring, and

Bow stood inches from the wall, as though she was cursing the décor itself.

Jay quickly faced the wall again to catch his clue. These words were his best chance of getting answers about Harriet.

View it as murder and the culprit is revealed

Jay felt the air and energy leave him. He slumped to the wall, no idea what it meant. Past the point of caring what signal he might give to the others, he barely registered Sonny approaching him.

'Looks like we both got shit. Telling you something you know already? Mine's old news.' Jay ignored him, staring into space. 'Wake up, weirdo,' Sonny said. He gave Jay an almighty elbow to the stomach, which sent him sliding down the wall before he could catch his balance.

'Leave me be,' Jay said from the floor.

*

Taran faced his screen with low expectations and the pose of an insolent child. Long arms folded high on his chest, shoulders back, eyes ready to roll at another useless clue.

You can trust Bow

It didn't disappoint. In fact, a less helpful clue didn't exist. He'd known Bow was a target for over a week. He shot up the stairs and headed back into the garden.

*

Saoirse gasped. She rubbed her eyes to check her vision. Her clue remained visible long enough to read it again.

Beware the one with the welts

She turned on the spot and leant against the wall. Nobody was allowed to see her clue. She cradled her head. There was so much information to remember. She peeked from under her thick fringe, the temptation to look at Sonny too great. He was rubbing his scar at that very moment. Its ridges of raised skin, red and round, looked like welts. Saoirse whispered to herself. *The one with the welts.* Not *the man*? Bow might still be telling the –

Saoirse's mind froze as she saw Bow walking up to her, a questioning stare on her face. Why hadn't she killed Sonny?

'Are you okay, Saoirse?' Bow asked, her voice unnaturally loud. 'Is it a headache? Come with me and we'll –'

'I'm fine.' Saoirse pushed herself off the wall and moved to the kitchen, placing Patty between her and Bow.

60

'Good morning. How are you?' Scot's chirpiness contrasted with Saoirse's movements. She'd shuffled to the chair, her small steps making the room seem bigger than it was. Cupping her elbows, she sat down and scowled. She was still sleepy. Her gaze stayed low. Her unkempt hair sat higher than usual, extending in all directions.

'Too obvious.'

'Pardon?'

'How's Nicky?'

'We have no contact with the outside.'

'Has she asked about me?' She shifted back into the cool leather. The large, quiet room added to her feeling of cold. A chill bit at her shoulders. She shivered. 'Let me go back to bed.'

'Ooh, that's not allowed. We're on television, remember? What's on your mind?' She shook her head. 'Ah, I understand. You've come here to step away from it all.'

'It's too obvious. Last night's clue.'

She raised a limp hand to signal her face. 'Sonny's scars. "The one with the welts." Too obvious.' She fell quiet again. 'The welts on his face and neck. His hands. We've all got scars. Even me.' Peeling back her clothes, she showed a horizontal line centimetres below her belly button. 'Caesarean. Aggy.' She tapped the scar. 'That's thirty-one years old.' She examined it. After all this time, there was more to notice about it. 'Trauma in' – she covered herself up – 'trauma out.' She sat up straight. 'My kids are safe? My son's birthday's coming up.'

There was no response. Scot was not going to bend on his rule. Saoirse looked to the door. She really ought to stand up and leave and make a cup of coffee. She sat quietly for a time, deep in thought. 'He was cruel.'

'Who?'

'Sonny. He was very unfair to Taran. He's not a nice person.' Her tone was matter of fact. She batted away unpleasant images of Sonny and his aggression. 'Someone's going to explode.'

'Best not to interfere.'

'Yes.'

'Best to keep away.'

'Exactly. Those two want to kill each other. I heard them.'

'Leave them to it, I say. You have your own person to find. Let those two battle it out. You should focus on who you –'

'Aggy,' Saoirse said, absorbed in her own thoughts.

'Let Sonny and Taran fight. Ignore them. Who does that leave you? To avenge Aggy, who do you need to choose from?'

Saoirse lowered her head. A skull full of swirling thoughts was too heavy to hold up. 'I don't know. It's all too complicated.'

'Let me help. You have three people to choose from,' Scot said.

'Three? How many are in the house?'

'Six.'

'But you said I need to choose from three?' She blinked repeatedly. 'Why only three?'

'You said yourself that Sonny and Taran will kill each other. That leaves four people. Excluding you leaves three.'

Saoirse mouthed the number. She lengthened her back more and held three fingers out.

'See? Your task's easier already. Is Jay your match?'

Scot's comment was met with a light tut. Saoirse said, 'You know full well he's not a target. He's a hunter. Like me. That leaves –' Her mouth hung open as she held up two fingers.

'That's right, Saoirse. That leaves –'

Her eyes widened. 'Patty and Bow.' She leant forward and whispered to the screen. 'I have the gun.'

'Do you?' Scot whispered too.

'Bow gave it to me.'

'Isn't she helpful?'

'But she wants me to kill Sonny.'

'Hold on a minute.' Scot's tone became exaggerated. 'Seconds ago, you told me Sonny and Taran want to kill each other.'

'They do. I saw them fighting the other day.' She closed her eyes. 'I don't trust Bow.'

'Listen to your instinct not to trust her. She wants to stitch you up. You trust you.'

'Is Bow my match?'

'Would she give you the gun if she was?'

'Oh yeah.' Saoirse lowered her middle finger. Only her index finger remained extended. 'That leaves –' She looked at her finger like it was someone else's, as if the word was tattooed on her skin.

'– Patty.'

61

'Ooh, smell that.' Patty offered the bunch of basil, rosemary and thyme to Taran, who closed his eyes and sniffed. 'Have you been to Italy? No? That smell, young man, places me instantly back in Tuscany. A table with olive oil, bread, a fruity red. A sunset – deathly slow – and Mediterranean air.'

Taran's face changed. He indicated over his shoulder to Bow at the dining table with her novel and Sonny on the sofa. 'We're not alone,' he said.

'Don't worry. I can look after myself. Keep stirring.'

Taran shrugged. If Patty insisted on sharing personal details, it was her choice. 'How long ago was that?'

'George and I went there on our honeymoon, among other places.'

'Where did you go for your honeymoon?' Sonny called from the sofa.

'Italy. Do you know where that is? Shaped like a boot.' Patty tapped Taran's arm. 'Heat down a bit.'

She turned and caught Bow's eye. Bow smiled, but Patty looked through her.

Sonny raised his voice further. 'Where else did you and George go? He sounds like a lovely man.'

'I'm cooking now, Sonny. Later.'

'Greece?'

'Yes, there too.' She leant to Taran. 'What's with his questions?'

'Don't know. Best to ignore him. He wants trouble.'

Sonny stood up and stretched his neck and back. 'What part?' he asked.

Patty ducked into the pantry and, after a few moments, came out holding a can of sundried tomatoes. 'I knew I'd seen these somewhere.' She made sure not to look at Sonny, who was moseying towards her.

'Oi, Granny. What part of Greece?' He stood opposite Patty on the other side of the island, his injured hands resting on the marble.

Inexplicably, Patty felt her nerve abandon her. Sonny, so close, asking odd questions. 'What's next? Let me think,' she said. It felt like she had arrived new to the kitchen seconds before and had to take stock of goings-on. A tray of condiments caught her attention. Arranging the olive oil and vinegar was all she could think to do.

Without a word, Sonny knocked a colander to the floor. He wore a smirk that any second would become a menacing smile.

Patty looked to Taran and Bow, whose expressionless faces unsettled her further.

'Go on. Tell us,' Sonny said. 'Which part of Greece?'

'Why do you' – Patty cleared her throat – 'want to know?'

'He's baiting you,' Taran said in a whisper. 'He's bored.'

'Shut the fuck up, Tarzan.' Sonny skirted the island to reach her. 'Well?'

'What does it matter?'

'Getting to know you, Patricia. Too much time on my hands, that's all. Time to kill.'

*

A cool change was coming, welcome after the day's humidity. Jay strolled around the lawn, avoiding the patches where Sonny's mowing remained unfinished, where his blood had dripped from the grass and seeped into the soil. Ahead, the three paths to the woods beckoned. After checking no one was following, he took the middle one. Only him, his footfalls, his thoughts.

He'd gone over his latest clue countless times. It was nonsense.

His sister had been murdered and the police had confirmed it. What was he doing in this bloody mess if that wasn't the case? All part of Scot's twisted game, no doubt.

With tree branches either side rustling in the breeze, he ran his fingers over the leaves and ventured further from the house.

The path curved and narrowed, some sections as cramped as his room. But the fresh air and clear sky staved off any feelings of claustrophobia.

He stepped on something firm. A used cigarette butt. Sonny and his damn smokes.

Smoking.

Jay thought of Harriet. One of the last times he'd seen her alive, they'd been chatting in the beer garden of an Inner West pub.

*

Liquid rings glistened on the wooden table. His beer was almost finished when Harriet arrived.

'Missed the train,' she said. 'Christy not coming?'

'She's not well.'

Harriet sat on the bench opposite. She took a pouch of tobacco from a grubby cloth bag and set to work on her rollies, bringing undeniable method to the task. Tobacco in front of her, filters to the left, papers to the right. She nudged both sleeves up her arms, looking around. 'It's packed here. I'll save our seats. You get the drinks.'

Jay did so. He returned with two schooners to find three hand-rolled cigarettes lined up on the table. Harriet was putting the finishing touches on a fourth, packing loose tobacco in the end with a plastic hatpin. She pointed to where her glass should go, like she had an in-tray.

Jay stopped himself from shaking his head in judgement and took his seat. If only Harriet put all that focus into something worthwhile. He wanted to lean over their drinks, crush the cigarettes and shout that if she made walls or furniture or art to that standard, she'd be her own boss. But he'd sworn he wouldn't give her grief about finding work, taking drugs, living her life. Time to be grateful she'd at least turned up and only kept him waiting an hour. Casting aside negative thoughts, the sight of the rollies offered him a little comfort. He had no clue how long the four would last, but it meant she planned to sit there for some time.

She caught him staring. 'Want one?'

'I still don't smoke.' Jay backed away from her offer. 'They kill you.' The moment it came out, he regretted it.

'Have two then.'

'That's harsh.' He cleared his throat. 'I'm sorry.'

He changed the subject and lied. 'You look well. It was

Mum's birthday on Tuesday. Please call her.'

'It's too late. Her birthday's gone.' She lit her first cigarette.

'She wants to know how you are.'

'You can tell her you saw me in one piece.'

That unified piece consisted of many disorganised parts. Knotted hair. Ringed, bloodshot eyes. Dry skin. Cuts and bruises on her legs. Insect bites at her wrists.

'When you see her, does she go to yours?'

'No, I go there. Why?' he asked. They went silent, pub noise taking over.

'You've still got a spare room?' Harriet sipped her beer.

It sounded like she was after somewhere to stay. 'For when we start a family.'

'Your place is clean. That's important for raising kids.'

Jay shifted his weight in the seat. 'It was great to see you last Christmas. Christy enjoyed having you around.'

'I bet she did.'

'Erm – the day you left. You didn't pick up some money by mistake, did you?' Jay gulped his beer. 'Refreshing.'

Harriet took an interest in their surroundings, her eyes glancing in every direction. She played with her lighter. 'Not me. I wouldn't do that.'

'It was a large amount.'

'You shouldn't leave it lying around.'

Jay agreed, which only added to his irritation.

*

Bow ate Patty's pasta alone at the dining table that evening. Sonny made mulch of his meal on the sofa, and everyone else ate outside. Patty had claimed the bench for herself and Jay, Taran lay on the mown grass and Saoirse had disappeared into the woods. Bow studied the empty table spaces. When the show began sixteen days ago, dining together had brought them a certain safety. But since Sonny had cooked Alice, group meals had fallen out of favour.

Sonny's burping woke Bow from her thoughts.

'Your cigarettes are here,' she said.

'Yep. I fancy one now.' He came to the table, left his plate, grabbed the cigarette pack and went outside.

'Close the door. I don't want smoke getting in,' Bow said. 'And call Saoirse in. Scot wanted her.' She counted on Sonny not realising the speaker system reached everywhere. If Scot had really wanted to speak to Saoirse, both she and Sonny would already know it.

A short while later, Saoirse appeared from the garden. Ignoring Bow, eyes down, she carried her plate and cutlery to the dishwasher. In an instant, Bow was by her.

'Why the hell is Sonny still walking around?'

'Leave me alone. Scot wants me.' Saoirse's hair fell across her face, shielding her eyes. It stayed there.

'Where's the gun?' Bow hissed. 'It's not in the bathroom.'

'It's in my room.'

'Quickly. Give me the bullets before the others see you.' She held out her open palm.

'I haven't got them. They kept jangling in my pocket so I put them in the gun.'

Bow clamped her jaw to contain her anger. She spoke through her teeth. 'There's no point keeping a loaded gun in your locked room. You're supposed to get Sonny. What are you waiting for?'

Saoirse shot her a glance and looked away. 'Does Patty have any scars?'

'What the fuck are you talking about?' Bow shook her arm roughly. 'I want the gun. Are you listening?'

'We don't trust you anymore.' Saoirse was cowering and her voice trembled, but the words hit Bow with unexpected force.

'What?' Bow peered outside. Who did Saoirse mean? Had she teamed up with someone else? Bow thought about the gun she'd placed in Saoirse's hands, and she shook her head at her own foolishness. Then her gaze fell on a camera and a more troubling explanation surfaced. She let go of Saoirse's arm as though it burned.

62

Christy woke herself up from a snooze calling Jay's name and her head sank back on the pillow. She'd fallen asleep on the covers clutching the box of Harriet's belongings. Hunger tore at her insides, as if she hadn't eaten for days. A rummage through the kitchen cupboards and she was sure to find something.

Minutes later, noodles were boiling. Christy was humming, with Jay's secret box open next to her on the counter. She stirred the pot and her engagement ring caught her eye. As sparkly as the day she first wore it, the diamond glinted. Jay had given it to her without warning. She'd been impressed by how he'd secretly chosen and sized it. It was exactly what she would've picked had they shopped together.

She nudged Harriet's things around in their box with the handle of her wooden spoon. Coins, fob, lighter, tobacco, hatpin. Nothing precious in that collection.

No wedding band, no diamond ring, no photo of a special someone. This pathetic assortment may have had a grip on

Harriet – on Jay even – but Christy didn't see it.

She used Jay's phone to call Teddy and fired off a question. 'Hi. How did you and Harriet meet?'

'Are you nosing around Jay's box again?'

'No.' Christy checked the blinds were closed. No way was Teddy spying on her. Just a lucky guess.

'I know you're lying.'

'Answer me.'

'I used to attend evening classes and she worked on reception. We got talking.'

'Was it a big place?'

'Why do you want to know? Go on. Tell me. What's in the box?'

Christy shook her head as she caved and revealed the contents. 'Tobacco.'

'What else?'

It wasn't right to share this. Yes, Jay had mentioned the box on television. But that didn't mean he wanted others knowing the contents. Christy visualised her own purse and rattled off a few items. 'A travel card, a door key, a pen.'

'Is that all?'

'What do you mean?'

'Harriet was so controlling. I'd expect there to be lists and columns of names and the debts these people owed to her. Ticks and crosses. Due dates. All that.'

Christy caught herself nodding. There was Teddy confirming what she'd suspected. Harriet the controller. 'When did you last see Harriet?'

'About two or three years ago.'

Christy stirred the noodles and added vegetables. The conversation had stopped. She felt sick but couldn't tell if it was hunger or nerves. 'Was …' Her words wouldn't come smoothly.

She had no right to ask her next question, yet Teddy could hardly object to meddling. 'Was Jay the father of your –'

'No.'

Christy paused to let Teddy say more, but the waiting didn't pay off. At least her nausea eased a little.

'What are your plans? Are you and Jay getting married?' Teddy asked, changing the topic.

Letting her engagement ring catch the light, Christy pictured the near future. 'We'll be very busy after he gets back. Lots to discuss. This is the longest we've been apart. I don't remember the house being so quiet.' She stopped. 'Do you live with someone? Have you got people to talk to?'

'No.'

'I can't stand Jay's computer games and I never thought I'd say this, but I miss him playing them. Yesterday, I turned on the Xbox just to hear the theme music.'

'Sounds like hell,' Teddy said. She hung up, leaving Christy's unit quiet as a cathedral.

Christy moved to the table and picked at her dinner. Alone with the noodles, a glass of water and the box of mementos Jay had decided to share with the world before her. She really shouldn't wallow in the past, in Harriet's past. There was the baby to think of. Yet, it was odd Jay hadn't told her about the box.

They didn't have secrets. That was one of their things, as a couple. Oh well, now she knew.

She wiped her lips with kitchen towel and recalled her own mini-secret. No big deal in comparison. And it was far from being a secret because Jay knew about the event. What he hadn't been aware of was Christy's intention. Not for certain, anyway.

Christy recalled last Christmas, when Harriet had been going through a difficult patch and she'd stayed for a few days. All to ease Jay's festive guilt. Christy hadn't fought the idea too much. She'd placed almost four hundred dollars in plain sight.

Plastic notes leaning on a plant pot, steadied by a giant panda figurine. As far as Jay knew, she'd forgotten to bank the money. Lo and behold, the cash had disappeared the day Harriet left.

'Why did you leave it out? You had loads of time to go to a cash machine,' Jay had said.

Standing with her back to him, Christy had thought of saying, 'What are you insinuating?' But if Jay had persisted and if she'd turned around, her expression would have given her away.

At the big, lonely dining table, Christy sipped her water. No regrets. It was a good bargain. Four hundred dollars to make sure Harriet never came to the house again. Christy had soon been more at ease. Jay, too. Their sanctuary was restored.

Now, the money was gone. Harriet was gone. And so was Jay. Which hadn't been the plan. But thank god for that shitty box of worthless keepsakes. With a flick of her hand, Christy knocked it to the floor.

Useless Harriet.

63

On Sunday morning, Patty made tea, which she drank on the hot tub ledge. An endless blue sky cradled the garden and warm air swept through the open door. She pictured Señor Bones outside playing with a stick. She sighed.

She'd be home soon. And even though the house would be the same – barring any unimaginable changes by her sister – it was she, Patty, who would have changed. Those days of people pushing her around were over.

She owned the house, not Elizabeth.

Señor Bones belonged to her, not Elizabeth.

It was that simple. She would take control of her life.

From her elevated position above the common area, she looked for her knitting. It wasn't in its usual spot, tucked between the sofas. Then it dawned on her she hadn't had it the previous evening. Sonny's questions about Greece had been too unsettling.

She asked the others.

Taran denied seeing it and Saoirse seemed too groggy to respond properly.

'I hope our thief hasn't taken it,' Jay said. 'You only had a little bit left to do.'

Sonny appeared from the garden, smelling of smoke. Before he said a word, Patty accosted him. 'I want my knitting back.'

'Piss off.' He stepped around her and went to the kitchen. She followed him.

'I don't mind if you took it. You know, your silly games. But I want it now.'

'I don't have your bloody knitting. You didn't answer my question about Greece.'

Patty grabbed him. 'Drop it. Honestly, you're a child. Is that why you took it? Because I won't let you pick on me? You mustn't steal. It wasn't me who swiped your cigarettes.'

'Scot!' he shouted. 'Let her check my room.'

Patty made a face. The very thought.

Next, Bow appeared, adjusting her hair into a ponytail. She too denied having the knitting, then looked at Sonny.

'I thought the same.' Patty said. She began searching the cupboards.

Sonny prepared coffee and shouted a question. 'Do you know what I'm doing today?' Nobody answered. 'Finding out where Patty went in Greece.'

'Leave it,' Bow said, tutting.

Trying to appear unfazed, Patty shook a finger at Sonny. 'You're in the mood for a fight. You ... you can pick on someone else.' Her heart racing, legs weak, she controlled her walk along the corridor to the chair.

Once inside the room, with the door closed, she called out.

'Scot! What's Sonny up to? I don't know what's going on. God, I'm shaking.'

She offered her quivering hands. 'He's gunning for me and I can't find my knitting.'

'Would you like something to calm you?'

She shook her head, sat down and caught her breath. 'Keep him away from me. That's good enough. He's not my target. Why's he picking on me?'

'You revealed personal information yesterday.'

'What did I say?'

'You told him you'd visited Greece. Several times.'

She raised her hands high. 'And?'

'It could be key for him.'

'But I'm not matched with him. I know who my person is.'

'Maybe he wants to toy with you. It would be fair to say Sonny likes causing trouble.'

'Fiddlesticks. Taran tried to warn me.'

'I have a suggestion. If he raises it again, lie. He's trying to trap you. Flat denial is best. You were never in Greece.'

She nodded, then stopped. 'Won't that make him worse?'

'With Sonny, it's the best approach. You can stop him in his tracks.'

'I doubt that.' She went to leave.

'Patty?' Scot's voice was calm. 'We want you safe.'

64

At the mirror, Saoirse wearily brushed her damp hair. *Everything is a weapon*, Nicky had instructed when they'd unwrapped the hair dryer where Saoirse now stood. Nicky sure had got creative with the dryer and its extension cord on the day of the fight in the hot tub. Saoirse removed hair from the brush. Maybe she would be attacked with it. Everything was a weapon.

Fuzzy-headed and weak from a bad night's sleep, her remaining strength went towards raising her arms to style her hair. A long shower hadn't cleared her mind. At least extra time in the bathroom meant being away from the others. As soon as the bedroom doors opened that night, she would catch up on sleep. She rubbed moisturiser into her face and neck, then rinsed her hands. Funny – the water running into the sink seemed to call her name. She put it down to lack of sleep, but it sounded so real. Even with the tap off, the sound remained.

'Saoirse, Saoirse.'

It was calling her! She bent forward as far as she could, with one ear close to the plughole.

'Saoirse, Saoirse.' She recognised the voice.

'Nicky? Is that you?'

'Saoirse, Saoirse.'

She spun around. Her lethargy disappeared. Head angled, she tried to pinpoint where Nicky was calling from. 'I'm in the bathroom. Where are you?' Her limbs had a renewed bounce. She whacked the button to open the door and stepped into the hall, which was noticeably darker than usual. So dark that blinking rapidly did little to improve her vision. 'I'm here.' Her hands reached for the walls. She listened. Nicky continued calling her, each time saying her name twice.

Behind her, the bathroom door closed, the loss of light plunging the corridor into almost total darkness. Heading right would lead to the main area, but Saoirse went left, feeling her way deeper into the corridor. Nicky's bedroom was the last on the left, five doors along. Saoirse felt her way, fingertips tingling with excitement. Scot must have brought Nicky back! Saoirse banged on Nicky's door with both palms. 'It's me. Open up.' Nicky kept calling out. 'Come out, Nicky.'

Saoirse felt the air on her neck shift. She wasn't alone in the corridor. There was movement behind her. She turned. 'Nicky?' She could just make out a short figure in front of her. Spiky hair. But it was too dark to see features.

The figure thrust something to Saoirse's chest. Instinctively, her hands came off the walls to stop whatever it was from dropping. Clothing of some sort draped in her arms. She squinted to get a better view, but it was impossible to see what she was holding. There in the dark, it felt like she was losing her balance and she leant on the wall for support. When she looked up, the figure was gone. Nicky couldn't have entered someone's room. She must have run out to the others.

'Nicky! Wait!' She gave chase and rounded the corner to bright light, joining the housefriends. Sonny was shouting at Patty.

'Just tell me where you've been and don't change your story,' he said.

Patty gasped. 'Where did you get that?'

Saoirse's eyes stung as they adjusted to the light. 'Nicky was here. Where is she?' She was more interested in finding Nicky than seeing what she was holding.

'I told you I didn't fucking have it,' Sonny said.

'What have you done to the jumper? My jumper?' Jay asked.

'Would you look at that,' Taran said.

'Who gave it to you?' Bow asked.

Saoirse realised what she was carrying. Patty's knitting. She held it up to see what the commotion was about. The ends of the arms and the neck had been unravelled and frizzy wool sat bunched in her hands.

'What happened?' Jay asked.

'Nicky gave it to me in the hall just now. She must've come this way.'

'Liar.' Patty snatched the jumper away and whimpered. She showed Jay the mess. 'How could you?'

Saoirse looked about her, still expecting Nicky to appear. 'We'll ask Nicky. She gave it to me.'

'We've been here the whole time,' Taran said. 'No one else came from the corridor. Where could they have gone? Our bedrooms are locked.'

'She's unravelled the arms. All the welting,' Patty said, taking a seat. 'Why?'

Under the weight of everyone's stare, Saoirse felt forced against the wall. Jay rested a hand on her arm. 'Are you okay?'

Saoirse held back tears. 'Nicky was calling me.'

'This was a gift for Jay.' Patty flapped the fraying ends of the sleeves. 'I'll have to redo the welts.'

Saoirse gasped. She came off the wall and made her way to Patty. 'What did you say?'

'Welts. A trim on a jumper. I'll have to do them all again. Thanks to you.'

'Welts,' Saoirse said.

Her latest clue. *Beware the one with the welts.*

Patty stiffened. 'What's – wrong?' She fidgeted with the weave, not meeting Saoirse's glare. 'It's – it's okay,' she said. 'I can fix it. I'm sorry if I upset you.'

Saoirse's eyes widened with every movement of the loose wool in Patty's hands. Patty placed the knitting to the side and stared straight ahead. 'I'll fix it later.'

'Get out of the way, Saoirse,' Sonny said. 'Patty's got some explaining to do about where she's been in Greece.'

Jay stepped in and shoved Sonny away from Patty. 'Leave her be for a moment.'

Staring ahead, Patty swallowed. 'I've never been to Greece.'

Sonny persisted even as he threatened Jay with a bandaged hand. 'You have. You told me and Taran you loved the place and the food. Where have you been in Greece? Tell me.'

Patty looked at Sonny, then Saoirse. 'I've never been there' – she wet her lips – 'ever.'

Saoirse let out a cry. Head down, her splayed fingers shielding her eyes, she scuttled to the weapon room.

Heart thumping, Saoirse leant against the empty dome. Fire coursed through her. 'Patty said that word.' She pressed her thumb on the digital panel.

One word flashed up and the automated voice spoke. 'Invalid.'

'Let me check her name.' Saoirse tried again. 'I want to make sure, Scot.' She slapped the glass. 'Pleeeease.' One final bang on the dome made her hand sting. 'Answer me!'

The door opened, but nobody entered.

Above her, the camera kept watch. It seemed to flicker. She looked to the exit and back to the camera. She moved to the doorway and looked out at an empty corridor of darkness. Opposite her, the door to the chair glided open and the lighting came up a touch. An invitation to enter. She ran to the chair. With her body hot and clammy, she slumped into the cold leather.

'It's all too much, Saoirse,' Scot said, voice theatrically breathless. 'How did you correctly work out it was Patty?'

'She looked so guilty out there. But I want to be certain.'

'Do you remember some days ago you used your guess on Nicky?'

'I want another try. I want to go home. Nicky was here.'

'I have bad news,' Scot said. Saoirse's mouth turned down. She fought back tears. She guessed what was coming. 'That wasn't Nicky.' Saoirse nodded. 'Your housefriends pulled a stunt. They were fooling you.'

Face shielded from the cameras, she composed herself. How silly to think that Nicky would return and hide from her. 'You're a fool,' she said, under her breath. She whacked the armrest.

'They tried to stitch you up.'

'They stitched me up.'

'They were needling you.'

'That's cruel.'

'They won't stop until you come apart at the seams.'

She checked her hands, almost needing to confirm her stitching was intact.

'Good luck with that.' Her trembling fingers told another story. She made fists.

'How did you correctly work out it was Patty?' Scot asked again.

'My clue. And she denied ever visiting Greece, but Sonny caught her out. She's a terrible liar.'

'She is.'

'Bow too. Nicky sure was right. Trust no one.' For a few moments, the only sound was Saoirse's fitful breathing. Her head came up. 'It's my turn to –' Her breath took her words. 'If – if I do this, I can go home?'

'Hold the gun with both hands, pull the trigger and leave.'

'Easy. I can do that.' She frowned. 'But why? Why did she kill Aggy? Will she tell me?'

'It's too late for explanations. Patty will deny it and while you're distracted, someone will grab the gun. It's your time to leave. You have all the clues you need.'

'My head is spinning.'

'There's work to do, Saoirse. We're not speaking. We're doing.'

'I can't work a gun.' *The gun!* She patted herself down frantically. 'It's in my bedroom.'

Below the screen in front of her, a panel opened.

Saoirse lifted herself up and wobbled over to see inside. Her limbs wanted to move in different directions. It took a moment to work out the crashing in her ears was her pulse. There was the gun. Looking small and compact, like it held the fetal position. As though normally it was bigger, longer, braver. Only when she picked it up did she realise how damp her palms were. She wiped them on her trousers. No matter how much she tried, she couldn't slow her breathing. It felt like, from nowhere, her body had a million working parts. Beating, thumping, rushing. A symphony of sound. She couldn't hear herself think. Maybe a good thing.

In the screen, Saoirse almost caught her reflection, gun in hand. But she looked away and headed to the door.

'Saoirse,' Scot said. 'Today is your son's birthday. Aggy can't be there, but you can.'

She gave a start. 'So soon?' Still holding the gun, she squeezed her head between her palms. How long had it been since she'd had a clear mind? 'I thought it was −'

'Saoirse, the party at yours started an hour ago. You can still make it if −'

She didn't hear Scot's next words. A bolt of energy seemed to come through the floor, up her legs and sear every pore in her body. She boiled on the spot and smashed the gun against the door.

'Aargh!'

65

A five-way argument was in full swing. Jay, Bow and Taran were ripping into Sonny, who was relentless in antagonising Patty. Perched on the sofa edge, she was increasingly uncomfortable being the centre of the fuss.

Normally the calming influence, Jay had had enough. He bellowed. 'You leave her alone. You're a fucking thug.'

'Drop it!' Taran said.

He followed with a high-pitched scream of frustration from the kitchen, which caught even Jay off guard. The half-orange that Taran was juicing got a violent squeeze, before being hurled across the room.

It hit the wall next to Sonny's head and fell to the floor.

'She's lying.' Sonny stood over Patty.

'Stop it!' Patty shrieked.

'You're such a prick,' Bow shouted. 'Stop this silly game.'

'What's it to you anyway, Sonny?' Jay asked.

'Piss off. What's her connection to Greece?'

Sonny's forehead wrinkled with impatience. But his soft mouth and relaxed eyes suggested at any moment they would join to form a smile.

Patty sniffled and examined the knitting. 'Jay, come over here. I want to measure you up again.'

Sonny leant in, teeth bared. 'You told me the other day you'd been there. And now you deny it.'

'Jay! I told you to come here,' Patty said, glassy-eyed. She held up the jumper. 'I need to assess the damage.' On her feet, she pointed to where Jay should stand. In front, facing away, between herself and Sonny.

Jay squeezed between them and let Patty drape the knitting over his back. He felt her trembling thumbs smooth the weave across his shoulders. Her sniffles were right by his ear.

'This will set me back a fair whack. What was she thinking?'

Running footsteps from the far corridor made everyone stop. They went strangely quiet. Jay thought he could hear a metal object clattering along the wall, but most things in the house were plastic. Everyone else looked equally uncertain. Taran paused in the middle of sipping his juice. Sonny finally retreated another step from Patty, and Bow pressed herself so flat against the wall she looked like ribbon. Jay felt Patty freeze behind him.

Clack, clack, clack.

Saoirse appeared with both hands clasped in front of her, elbows to her ribs. She pointed the gun at their faces.

A collective gasp erupted.

'She's got the g–' Jay's jaw dropped and both hands came up, like a hostage. Patty's nails dug into his shoulders. He tensed at seeing the pain streak across Saoirse's face. Brandishing a gun fooled no one. Saoirse was terrified. From the corner of his eye, Jay saw Taran duck out of view.

'What the —' Sonny's eyes bulged. 'How the fuck did you get that?'

Saoirse's arms extended, which made the gun wobble. She settled her grip and waved the stubby barrel around. It now pointed at Jay and Patty.

Sonny raised his bandaged hands. 'Take your finger off the trigger.' Jay had never heard him speak so slowly. 'I'm not going to hurt you.'

Ignoring Sonny, Saoirse motioned to Jay. She wriggled the revolver. 'Move out of the way.'

Jay's heart clamped tight, his ribs seeming to crush it further in its cavity. 'Stop waving the gun.' He stayed blocking Patty.

'Step away!' Saoirse howled at him. 'Keep away, all of you!'

Jay tried moving, but his limbs didn't take him far. He wanted to scream at Saoirse, but that might startle her. With the jumper still on him, he stopped centimetres clear of Patty.

'Me?' Patty said. 'What did I do? You're overreacting, Saoirse. It's just knitting.'

'You know what you did.' Saoirse's face screwed up. 'Why?'

Patty howled. 'I don't know —'

'Say it!' Saoirse fought back tears and lifted the gun a tad. She fired.

The shot was deafening. Jay felt it in both eardrums.

'Ow!' Saoirse cried out. She rubbed her hand on her leg.

Jay didn't dare turn around. He had to keep watching Saoirse. Patty was still by his back. It sounded like the bullet lodged in the wall by the television. Only he and Patty stood in Saoirse's line of fire. There was one bullet left.

'Rookie error,' Sonny said, roaring.

'Stop pointing it at us,' Jay said, his tongue sandpaper-dry.

Saoirse brought the gun up again. Fighting tears, she sniffed like a tormented child.

'Out of the way, Jay.'

Over his shoulder, Jay saw Patty had placed herself behind him again. 'Move!' Saoirse ordered. He nudged left.

'What did I do?' Patty said, whimpering.

Saoirse pulled the trigger and fired the second bullet.

66

Jay crept to the body. He felt sick. There was a bloodied hole in Patty's chest and she wasn't breathing. Rumbling thunder enveloped the house and roared to a crescendo. Jay cocked his head. No, it wasn't thunder. It was the crowd outside. He tried to picture the size of the mob that could make that sound. His chest tightened more. He had never expected to feel safer inside the Scot Free house than out. A chill down his back stirred him from his thoughts.

'She killed my Aggy,' Saoirse said, dropping the gun.

'No,' Jay said. 'Patty was a hunter.'

Saoirse spotted a ceiling camera. 'Scot, I can go now.' She turned away from Patty's body. 'Please. I want to see my children.'

'Is she alive?' Bow asked, approaching Jay. 'Try CPR. Scot! Get a doctor.'

Sonny came forward and led Saoirse away by the shoulders. 'Come with me over to the table. Let's sit you down. This way, that's it. They'll look after Patty. Easy does it.'

He forced Saoirse backwards onto the bench.

'Leave Saoirse alone,' Bow said. 'I'll take care of her.'

'Did I get the right person?' Saoirse asked. 'I had no more guesses at the machine.' She leant sideways around Sonny, a stricken look on her face. Sonny's hands were on her shoulders.

Jay knelt by the body. 'Patty? Can you hear me?' He placed a hand under Patty's sleeve. He shook his head. 'She's dead. It's no –'

A choking sound made him stop. He looked around. It took a moment to process what he was seeing.

Sonny had Saoirse by the throat. She spluttered and gurgled and tore at his bandages, but he towered over her. He growled as he gripped her neck. The pain in his injured hands must have been horrendous. His face was as red as Saoirse's. She clawed at him and part of his dressing came loose. But her fingers lost their grip on the fabric and Sonny continued unperturbed.

Helpless, Jay exchanged a look with Bow. It was against the rules to intervene. 'Stop! Wait!' Jay shouted. Ridiculous. Sonny wouldn't comply.

Saoirse slipped from the bench and Sonny was forced to let go. Her chance for escape had come. She scrambled away, clambered to her feet and dashed around the island, coughing. Sonny gave chase. Saoirse turned in time to bat his hand away. She circled the island again, using the marble corners to launch herself away, putting more distance between them. But her pace soon dropped off. She struggled for breath.

Sonny also slowed to a walk, as though confident of his imminent catch. 'Your turn, Saoirse.' He wound the loose bandage around his hands, but it fell free again when he lowered his arms. With a menacing smile, he pretended to lunge at her.

She whacked his hand away with a cry. There was no time for her to regain energy.

They were as close as dance partners now. Sonny went for her neck, and she did nothing more than lean to the side. That was all he needed. He grabbed her around the trunk and they fell to the floor, hitting their heads on the marble. They both lay together for a moment, entangled on the floor, as they oriented themselves.

Saoirse let out a weak cry. 'Scot!' Her face was inches from the flap of bandage trailing from Sonny's hand. She grabbed it. There was enough to wind round his neck. But Sonny was too strong, immediately wriggling free and punching her cheekbone. She screamed. He howled but was on her again in a flash.

Mouth open, Jay froze, watching the pair roll around and smash against the wall. From the corner of his eye, he saw Bow kick something across the floor. It was the half-orange Taran had hurled at Sonny minutes before. She punted it to the wall, inches from where Saoirse and Sonny lay scuffling, and she started the wall vacuum. Like a feather, the orange shot up the chute and Sonny's loose bandage followed. With one bandaged hand not enough to hold her, Saoirse wriggled free from his grip.

Flattened against the wall, Sonny shouted up at Bow. 'What the fuck are you doing? Turn it off!'

Bow rested her back on the wall. She covered the switch. Sonny took a swipe at Saoirse, but she backed away. He let out a roar and brought his right hand to the wall outlet to pry his left hand free. But the suction trapped that hand, too. 'Turn it off!' he repeated. He managed to crouch on his feet. As much as the material stretched, it didn't rip. He pulled with all his might, but the bandages were trapped. It was the only thing saving the women from his rage. 'When I get free, you cunts are dead.'

Her energy spent, Saoirse spluttered and started to crawl away. Her face pulled along the marble, spit trailing from her mouth.

Sonny gave Bow a vicious smile and she could almost see the lightbulb going off in his head. His teeth clamped together. He stopped fighting the suction and moved his wrists in circles, feeding the chute. It devoured the bandages as the dressing on both hands unwound. Within seconds, his shredded hands would be free.

'Run, Saoirse!' Bow screamed. 'Get up!'

Jay's heart pounded in his chest. Saoirse wasn't moving fast enough and Sonny's bandages had unravelled to the point that fresh blood was showing through. It was too late for Saoirse to escape. Now Bow was in danger too.

'Run, Saoirse!' Jay shouted.

Saoirse gasped on the floor. 'I – can't.' She let out a grating cry. 'Nicky!'

Fighting tears of frustration, Sonny laughed and spat through his words. 'I'm going to fucking kill …'

Beside him, Saoirse took a few deep breaths. 'Everything is a weapon!' she roared. She sat up and pulled a plastic bag from her back trouser pocket. The wrapping from the hair dryer.

In a second, she was behind Sonny and pulling the bag over his head. She wrestled him to the floor and the yelp he let out betrayed his surprise. He writhed furiously, bandages still caught in the vacuum chute. His legs thrashed around. He whipped his head from side to side, but Saoirse used her weight to keep the bag in place and tightly closed at his neck. Inches from her face, his violent panting snapped the plastic in and out of his mouth.

Jay watched on as Sonny instinctively tried to bring his hands up to his face. But the chute remained a fierce opponent and only his forearms came anywhere close. He paused for a split second, lacking the strength to unwind the bandages, break free from Saoirse's grip and fight for air all at once. In that pause, Jay saw horror fill Sonny's eyes through their plastic shroud. Sonny knew what was about to happen. Jay held his own breath.

Saoirse, by contrast, found a last reserve of strength and pulled the bag tighter around Sonny's head. With the plastic stretched over his mouth, his chipped teeth couldn't tear it. She held him steady in a head lock, his hands still trapped in the chute. A safety sign was plastered to his cheek: Keep away from children. *Whoop*s, thought Saoirse as she locked eyes with him, upside down.

'Breathe. Come on. Big breath, Sonny. You've got this,' she taunted and blew onto his face.

A weak grumble came from under the bag. Sonny's eyes closed.

Saoirse caught her breath, then yanked his head back. 'Wake up.' His eyes didn't open. She shot Bow a look, then slowly loosened the plastic bag.

'What are you doing?' Bow said.

Sonny's eyes opened a fraction.

'First time was for Aggy,' Saoirse said. She tightened the bag again.

Sonny's body shook violently, yet Saoirse stayed clamped onto his head. She and the bag moved with him. Condensation lined the inside of the plastic at his mouth and his frantic tongue wiped it off.

Jay noticed that the convulsions in Sonny's chest had calmed. His bloodied right hand was now free of its dressing and lying lifeless by his side. Saoirse's grip held strong. She waited.

She stayed where she was, even as Sonny's whole body went limp. She could have been hugging a loved one. 'Second time, for me.' She eventually exhaled.

Trembling, Bow turned off the wall vacuum.

Once more, Jay heard the howl of the crowd, hungry for

death, settle around them. It seemed to stir him from his shock. With Sonny dead, a wave of relief passed through him. He breathed more deeply and looked around. Three housefriends standing, three on the floor. Saoirse now completely spent, Patty and Sonny dead.

In the kitchen, Taran emerged from his hiding place. Jay locked eyes with him and Bow. All three stood perfectly still, waiting for confirmation that the bloodbath had come to a stop. Even the slightest movement might cause more mayhem to unfold.

Jay felt something tickle his neck and gave a start. He pulled the knitting off his back, where Patty had left it, and let it fall.

67

In the production suite, Adolpha came off her seat and punched the air. She high-fived Alan on the way down. 'What did I tell you about Saoirse?' She jabbed a finger at his face. 'You do not mess with that parental instinct.'

'She certainly has drive,' Alan said.

'She also had a plastic bag.' Adolpha pointed to the screen, where a still of Sonny's shroud flickered. 'A fucking plastic bag, Alan?'

He lowered his head. 'It was all last minute. In the rush, the gifts didn't pass through our usual vetting. I suggested confiscating it while she slept –'

'Excuses. You're lucky it worked to our advantage this time. What have I told you? If we control the weapons –'

'– we control the game.'

'Exactly.' She spoke into a mic. 'Prepare Saoirse for exit.'

'You're letting her go?' Alan asked. 'She'll discover her son's birthday is actually in two days.'

'What's she going to do? Lodge a complaint?'

'We'll bring her back for next season?'

'I have a better idea – of course. We release her and she leads us to our little escapee. It's Nicky I want for SF seven, not Saoirse. Tonight worked wonders. I couldn't have asked for a stronger finish to the weekend. What do families want as they tuck into a Sunday roast? Mint sauce and a double murder.'

'It's trending already,' Alan said, glancing at his phone. 'We're close to pulling off the surprise of the season.'

'Excuse me? You mean the surprise of the show's entire fucking history.' Adolpha threw him a look and paused. 'Our new arrival. Update.'

Alan coughed. 'Yes. I've been thinking. I suggest keeping Jay, Bow and Taran isolated until Wednesday.'

'No. That will kill ratings.'

'They can leave their rooms one by one for meals. We'll make it look like we've postponed the normal set-up for a day or two, like we're deciding how to proceed on the back of Saoirse's mistake. If we launch straight into things, it'll attract attention.'

Adolpha's lips formed a snarl as she pondered, almost tasted, her mouthwatering options. After a pause, she shared her plan. 'She goes in on Tuesday. They wake up with her.' She lifted a manicured eyebrow, daring Alan to oppose her. 'I want to meet Everton that day for a run-through. He's promised he'll be done. Finally. I was ready to strangle him.'

Alan nodded.

She leant into the mic. 'Put the house on mute. Any live footage for the rest of the evening is muted. Visuals only. Did you get that? Let's get Saoirse out of there. Put her on stage, but I want a five-second delay. She mustn't mention the clues. They're off limits. And we isolate the other three. Are you ready with that amended script? Let's get it out there that this is unprecedented.

Say it four times. Make out the studio's in a spin, but we'll sort it.' Adolpha sat away from the console and sighed, satisfied lungs ushering out the air. Then she leant forward to use the mic once more. 'We promised four murders and we've already hit that target. Point that out, but be delicate.' She cut the mic and spoke to Alan. 'It never hurts to keep the advertisers happy.'

*

Jay spun round to watch the door to his room close. Alone and safe. In the confined space of the bedroom, even with its limited air, he took in more oxygen. He hadn't breathed fully since Saoirse had appeared with the gun. All the tension that his body had been holding eased, perhaps too abruptly. His stomach flipped and he reached the sink in time to vomit.

He moved backwards until his legs found the bedframe. Eyes wide and disbelieving, he collapsed on the mattress. His heart pounded in his chest, each thud lifting him from the bed.

There were only three housefriends remaining.

Two targets: Bow and Taran. One of them his sister's murderer.

*

Eleanor Carlisle trotted into the living room holding a gin and tonic, and Frank's icy beer. 'Here.' He sat so low in his armchair he looked stitched to it. With his newspaper in the kitchen, he clicked his crossword pen nonstop. His eyes locked on the screen where Saoirse, wearing her exit suit, had joined the presenter on stage.

Into Frank's free hand, Eleanor wedged the beer. She sat down and retrieved her phone from under the cushions. Time to get back to voting, which, wisely, she hid from Frank. She sipped her drink, smacked her lips and strained to hear the television over the clicking pen. 'Saoirse's suit fits well. Sonny helped her make it,' she said.

On the television, the presenter draped a long arm around Saoirse. 'How do you feel to be out alive?' she asked.

Saoirse nudged herself away. A bruise was showing on her cheek where Sonny had hit her. 'I want to see my children.' Saoirse got twirled around by the presenter until both faced a huge screen. A montage of her best scenes aired.

Eleanor kept one eye on Frank. He wasn't touching his beer. With her right hand, she placed a bet on the season winner. Then fresh odds flashed on the screen, so she put another twenty dollars on Jay.

'Ellie, what am I going to do? Bow's not coming back,' Frank said. He looked close to tears.

'Don't talk like that. She'll return.' She placed a bet on Bow to win. 'It's not over yet. Drink your beer.' Frank's face hadn't shown so much emotion in a long time. Whatever gloom she saw reflected there was at least better than the blank look he usually brought home. If only their marriage could generate a reaction. Eleanor tucked her phone back under the cushions.

'I feel ill,' he said, leaving his beer on the side.

A still of Sonny's pained gaze, wrapped in plastic, took up the television screen. Saoirse's final act as housefriend. Next, the footage showed her leaving the stage and the presenter reminding viewers the season had already seen the four predicted murders, even with one week remaining. She announced the latest betting odds.

Frank groaned as if his insides were corroding.

*

'If you keep shutting me up, I might as well put the phone down.'

Christy brushed off Teddy's comment by swiping the air. On speakerphone, Jay's mobile perched on the arm of the sofa. 'Shush! I don't want to miss anything.' Christy had been on her feet stepping side to side since seeing the first bullet whiz past Jay. Her heart still hadn't settled. 'I don't believe it,' she said, multiple times.

The television screen divided into three segments to show Jay, Bow and Taran confined in their bedrooms.

'They look frightened,' Teddy said.

Christy stared so hard at Jay's image that his face disintegrated into fuzzy pixels. 'You're wrong. Jay's okay.' Teddy didn't know Jay the way she did.

Teddy's scream came through the mobile. 'My god, Christy! Jay's the only hunter left. Does that mean only one more person has to –'

'Stop.' Christy sat down, her legs no longer able to support her. 'Please don't. It's too soon for that.'

'I can't do anything right.' There was a long pause.

Christy's voice was all but a whisper. 'Don't you see, Teddy? He might have to kill to come home,' she said, her gaze landing on the picture of the ultrasound. She gave her belly a slow rub.

'He'll still be Jay,' Teddy said. 'Cross that bridge.'

*

Four thousand kilometres away, in a Mount Magnet bar, Nicky watched a television mounted over a battered cash machine. The volume drowned out the pub noise. She wore a cap, shirt and pants pulled from a charity bin. A half-schooner of beer abandoned near the pokies now belonged to her. She occupied herself making a flower from three black straws in her lap. Her tattooed fingers remained hidden. The bar's regulars would have thought she couldn't care less about the Scot Free recap. Her gut still churned from watching Saoirse overpower Sonny.

'Dramatic scenes earlier, when the Scot Free household halved within minutes. Our three remaining housefriends are in their bedrooms as we have an unprecedented situation unfolding here. Never before has the Scot Free house witnessed events like these. For those just tuning in, Saoirse has killed a hunter by mistake. As you can imagine, the house is in turmoil. Rather, the studio is in turmoil. We're trying to discover what went wrong. This is totally unprecedented.'

She finished the beer and ditched the flower in the empty glass. There were plans to put in place, and she'd need to wait before making contact. She pushed herself through the pub doors into a cool, cloudless night. Lungfuls of fresh air cleansed the tension from her limbs.

Saoirse was going home.

Part 6

Show down

68

The next morning, Jay pressed his ear to the locked bedroom door but heard nothing. Pacing around his poky cubicle did little to relax him. His mind raced as he considered where events would next lead. Bow or Taran could be outside, armed and set to pounce. A locked door was a blessing.

He did handstands to calm himself. The feeling of weightlessness left little space for worrying thoughts. Upside down, he spotted the green light that signalled the bedroom was unlocked. Then, automatically, the door slid open. Waves of panic caused him to lose balance and crumple to the floor. He clambered to his feet and held up his fists, ready to defend himself. His skin flushed hot and cold.

'Hello?' he said.

Out in the dark hall, the other doors were closed. He left his room and, without stopping, sped across the living area, which sat empty of the living and the dead.

On finding the weapon room locked, he cursed and opened the door to the chair.

'Scot, what's going on?' Jay sat on the edge of the chilly leather, staying clear of the armrests.

'Good morning, Jay.' Scot's automated voice conveyed nothing of the previous night's horrors. 'How are you?'

'You've locked the weapon room.'

'You face an extraordinary situation. Only three house-friends. Which is not enough for the weapon dome to operate. Even if you enter the wrong name, you can work out the identity of your match. Where's the fun in that?'

'What the fuck happened yesterday? It was all so quick.' Under his glasses, Jay rubbed his face. He relived what he'd seen. 'Poor Patty. And how the hell did Saoirse get the gun?' His legs began bouncing. 'Crazy.'

'That's a fair assessment.'

'One of those two' – Jay gestured outside for Bow and Taran – 'killed Harriet.' Moments passed. His knees jiggled. 'I've sat with them for dinner. They aren't strangers now.'

'Your role in this house is to kill. For Harriet. You must avenge your sister's death. This game ends when only one target remains.'

'I get it!' Jay's shouting echoed through the room. 'There are two targets now, right?' A lengthy silence let the question drift off. 'Right?' Jay tutted at Scot's silence. 'Jesus, Scot. Why so fucking cagey? There are two left. Bow and Taran.'

'What does Jay make of this?'

Scot's phrasing caught Jay off guard. He waited, but Scot didn't elaborate. 'I can't imagine it's Bow.' Jay's voice cracked.

'Circumstances push people to their limits. It's at these limits where the inexplicable becomes the –'

'Bullshit. And Taran wouldn't hurt a fly. Look what

happened with the rabbit.'

'Now I'm confused,' Scot said. 'Only two targets remain? Neither one killed Harriet?'

'Taran's claimed his innocence all along. Maybe Harriet's killer isn't in the house.' He paused. 'What if the courts got it wrong?'

'How much simpler if that were so,' Scot said. Jay folded his arms. 'Listen, Jay. Your reaction is understandable. Raise doubts about the housefriends' guilt and let that doubt justify your inaction.' Scot's pacifying voice cocooned Jay from all sides. It was inescapable. 'You feel guilty, selfish. You're alone. Only three left? Why, the game's as good as finished. Overnight, avenging Harriet's murder has lost its appeal. You thought yourself brave. But passion gives way to fear.'

Scot's voice became firm. 'Jay, the nation waits for you to end this game. To cross that line. To murder.'

*

Bow woke up cold. A draught on her face told her something wasn't right. Even with the light on, her eyes needed a moment to adjust. Her bedroom door stood open. Her heart started pounding and she bolted upright. How quickly her breathing shifted from drawn out and steady to short and fitful. A sharp pain spread across her chest. Battling stiff limbs, she got up and hit the button to close the door. But nothing happened. She got dressed and peered into the corridor.

'Taran? Jay?'

She crept to the main area, which was deserted. A coffee smell lingered and triggered her hunger. On a shelf in the fridge, she found fruit salad and croissants. She prepared coffee and devoured the lot on foot, peering around without straying far from the island. With a top-up of coffee, she headed to Scot.

In the chair, she drank in silence, moving her ankles in circles.

'Good morning, Bow. Finally awake. You slept well. Eleven hours.'

Her eyes bore into the screen ahead. 'Did you drug me?'

'You're hilarious. You must've needed the rest. It was a big day.'

She winced at the understatement. 'Have I won? Did Jay and Taran fight?'

'They're in their rooms. You'll go back to yours soon.'

'Patty wasn't meant to die.'

'Many things occurred yesterday that were not meant to.'

Bow blinked and moved a lock of hair away from her eyes. 'Oh?'

'When the state gives permission to kill, nobody overrules that. Sonny had permission to kill Saoirse.'

'Saoirse had permission to kill Sonny.'

'And you intervened. Under whose authority did you act?'

'I didn't overrule anyone's permission. I turned on the vacuum to clean up and Sonny became entangled. I had no obligation to free him.' She sipped her coffee. 'Don't worry, Scot. I won't be acting further. I'll wait and see what Taran and Jay do to each other. I'm safe' – she shifted in the chair – 'I guess.'

'Unless one of them makes a dreadful mistake. Like poor, poor Saoirse.' Exaggeration came through in Scot's tone.

'How did she hide the gun?' Bow asked. 'I searched everywhere. It wasn't in the bathroom.'

'You're not giving her proper credit. She played you all. You saw what she whipped from her pocket when the time came to kill.'

*

'I'm hungry,' Taran shouted at the camera above his bed and repeated his mime, patting his stomach and bunching his fingertips at his mouth. He flopped on the bed and stared at the camera. Half the country could be watching him live. If only his parents could see. Imagine! Moved from prison for murder to a studio where he was begging for food. His family had been appalled at his arrest for shoplifting years ago. A murder charge had been the last straw. How he longed to be back with his insufferable parents. Given another chance, he could easily endure their controlling, nagging and manipulating.

A glint came to his eye. His hand darted under the bed and came up clasping Saoirse's paper straw rose with its pink and red petals. What a scene that had caused. Saoirse had totally flipped and coffee had gone everywhere. He rubbed the petals and looked at the camera. It hardly mattered who knew now. His fingertips tingled. That addictive rush of accomplishing a goal, of possessing things that belonged to others. Gripping the green stem, he carefully placed the flower back under the bed.

His hand came up again, now with Jay's Rubik's Cube. Its six complete sides gleamed under the light. He cupped it in both hands. Holding his breath and with delicate moves, he shifted a red row around to join the orange side. Six orange squares and three red ones. Underneath, the opposite: six red, three orange. He exhaled. With amateur precision, he reversed the moves to restore the puzzle and rolled the cube in his palms, like it was spherical. Days ago, he'd sat on it by accident. He was proud of collecting it that day, with all the colours done. No point taking an incomplete puzzle when he couldn't finish it himself.

He put the puzzle back in its hiding place and next retrieved a pack of cigarettes. Sonny had taken a while to notice they were missing. Taran opened the lid and eased one up until its filter sat outside the box. He offered it to his closest imaginary friends, shaking the pack at them when they refused. 'Suit yourselves. More for me.' His thumb flicked on an imaginary lighter, which managed to stay lit on the third go. He brought the cigarette to his lips.

Smokers pondered their future as they puffed, so he did too. There were only three people left in the house. Maybe he would survive after all. He could be back with his awful family within days. If he won the show, the bank might even let him return to work. Customers would recognise him, and they'd all mention Alice, and Taran would get sick of it. He pictured himself holding court in the staffroom. He'd say, 'If another soul mentions that fucking rabbit, I'll grab their hand and activate the security screen.'

Sliding open by itself, the bedroom door shook him from his daydream. His cigarette fell on the covers. He nestled it in the pack and lobbed the box under the bed.

'What's going on?' he said, half-expecting the camera to respond. 'Is it safe out there?' His questions were met by silence. He impersonated Scot. His voice became guttural, digital. 'It's one hundred and fifty per cent safe, Taran.'

He came off the bed slowly. His hunger drew him to the kitchen. He craved toast and coffee, but he wolfed down cereal while the toast cooked. Dirty plates languished in the sink. Bow and Jay had already been out of their rooms by the look of things. Standing on tiptoe, he confirmed the garden was empty. He buttered the toast, scoffed both slices and prepared another. With coffee and toast in hand, he strolled to the weapon room and chair. He stopped in front of both doors.

Invitingly, the door to the chair slid open.

Taran eyed the camera over the doorway. Standing firm, he slurped his coffee and bit off a piece of toast. He chewed slowly and washed it down with a gulp of coffee. With a smooth turn, he sauntered back to the kitchen.

69

Five floors up, against building regulations, Alan sat smoking on the external fire escape. Each drag warmed his lungs as the night air worked to ruffle his lacquered hair. He had an uninterrupted view of the floodlit studio complex, where all was quiet. No crowds, no journalists, no Adolpha. Three guards at the gate. A dark stretch of landscape beyond the grounds offered little to see. He took a long puff on the cigarette and coughed his chest empty.

About half a kilometre away, lights appeared in the darkness and the foliage. Great. They were on time. The van snaked towards the studio and passed through the gate. One last drag and Alan flicked the butt over the railing. He hurried down the external staircase, smoothing back his hair and buttoning up his suit jacket. A guard climbed out of the front passenger seat and stopped at the side door. She did a double take at seeing Alan by the van.

'Where did you spring from?' she asked. Alan glared at her.

'We weren't expecting to collect anyone else this season,' she said. 'This one's on us.'

Without a word, he wagged his finger at the van door for her to get a move on. He was reluctant to draw attention to this arrival. Best they worked in silence. With a low rumble, the van door slid open to reveal a darkened interior and two occupants. A guard came out first.

Alan glanced in at the second occupant, the season's eleventh housefriend. She was wearing the cream suit and moccasins. Against the dark interior, she almost sparkled, as though she had her own light source. He had to stop himself from smiling while he gawked. A royal watcher standing inches from a princess. Unsure if it was the buzz of tobacco or excitement or rushing down to the van, Alan felt light-headed. His skin tingled.

Extending her arm, the first guard offered her hand to the housefriend-in-waiting. But the occupant launched herself from inside the van, landed in a squat and stood up. Alan flinched and stepped back.

'I'll take things from here,' he said, dismissing the guards. He escorted the new arrival inside. 'I hope they took good care of you.' He looked her up and down, but she merely stared ahead at the double doors blocking their way. Alan swiped them open. They passed along a corridor flanked by meeting rooms and office windows. He ushered her inside a room, keeping as much distance as possible between them. She must have smelled smoke on him because she grimaced when she passed by. Instead of taking the chair that Alan offered, she sat facing the door. He took a seat opposite her. There was silence. He watched her, his dark eyes stealing the light. She took in the surroundings, her striking blue eyes reflecting light.

She looked out to the corridor and finally spoke.

'Where are they?'

Alan pointed behind him.

'On the other side of this wall, in their bedrooms. You're not going in until the morning. After we finish the paperwork here, we'll do some promo clips. Then you'll go to a private bay. That'll be fun.'

Alan wasn't sure she was listening.

He fumbled with his phone and called Todd, his assistant. 'We'll do the promos and the interview now. She stays in the temporary wing tonight. When can you get here?'

He ended the call and they sat in silence again. At a loss for words, Alan drummed his fingers on the back of his other hand. He studied her but hoped he didn't come across as a creep. She had a long body and a thick neck, developed through training and sports, according to his research. Her hands were small, but the fingers solid. Speed and agility would be her assets.

Alan's stomach was a cauldron. So much was riding on the next few days going to plan.

'Ooh, water,' he blurted out.

'Pardon?'

'Would you like some water? No, what am I thinking? You prefer fizzy drinks, don't you? But not this late at night. One of the housefriends, he was a target. He had a terrible diet. Not to mention poor dining habits. I was forever thinking the prison dentist would kill him if he made it back. Which he didn't – he's dead now. Sweet food, sweet drinks. I never once saw him brushing his teeth. Admittedly, in his last days, he couldn't hold things correctly. An accident' – Alan took a breath at last – 'happened. Please eat and drink sensibly while –'

Her stare drilled him into a short silence.

He continued. 'You'll have everything you need. Remember to brush your teeth twice a day. Do you brush –'

She tutted and pulled a face, inadvertently hitching up her top lip.

Alan caught a peek inside her mouth. 'I knew it. Milky white.' He cleared his throat.

Seconds later, the door opened and Todd appeared.

'Great,' Alan said. 'We can get on.'

70

A morning storm woke Jay. Thunder reverberated in his chest and ears. He stayed under the warm covers and let his mind wander. He imagined nestling in the clouds among the peals of thunder. Lightning strikes danced around him, but he felt oddly at ease. Far below, next to the lush woods, the Scot Free house throbbed like a beating heart. Its lights beamed up at him through the rain. The thought of the large droplets washing it clean brought him comfort. A freer soul on the planet could not be found.

Jay blinked and the ceiling camera came into focus. As his daydream evaporated, his body felt like lead flattening the mattress. He would have to get up, leave the room and live someone else's day.

At the sink, he splashed water on his face and grabbed a fresh towel, which smelled of citrus. Their linen at home had the same scent. He wondered if that were deliberate. Glasses on, he checked himself in the mirror. His hair looked like a serif font, all tufts and wedges. He dressed, opened the door and waited, but the house was silent. He poked his head out. Nothing. Only the empty, dark corridor and dim natural light at the far end. To guide himself, he tapped his fingertips along the cool walls.

A figure at the dining table made him yelp and swear at once. His skin turned icy. It was a woman. Brown hair past her shoulders, she sat with her back to him, head down. Jay rubbed his eyes. She stayed there. Nothing else in the house seemed out of place, no clue about who she was. Then she moved and the sounds were real enough. Crunching as she chewed cereal and scraping as she moved the spoon across the plastic bowl. All his arm hair stood on end and he shivered. Positioning himself ready to sprint off, he stammered out a single word.

'He-llo?'

At this, the figure became more statue-like. She stopped eating but didn't turn around. He made a face at the nearest camera and mouthed a question – 'What the fuck?'

He retraced his steps and lightly rapped on Taran's door, then Bow's. Too much noise might cause the mystery woman to follow. Taran's door opened first, but Taran stayed out of view.

'It's started again,' Jay said, whispering from his spot in the corridor.

'What?' Taran said.

'There's someone out there.'

'Who?' Taran asked. Jay shrugged, but Taran wouldn't have seen. More light came into the corridor once Bow's door opened and her raised fists appeared.

A loud clap of thunder sounded directly over the house. Jay felt it through the floor tiles, his legs growing a little weaker. He spoke in hushed bursts. 'Someone's out there – a woman – eating breakfast – she won't speak.'

'What the hell's going on?' Bow asked.

'Come with me,' Jay said. He stepped ahead of them. Bow placed her hand on his shoulder and removed it as quickly. From the way she was angled, Jay guessed she and Taran were holding hands. With the bedroom doors now closed, the corridor went dark again. They snuck along as quietly as they could.

'Let's go to Scot,' Taran said. Jay flapped his hand to silence him.

They reached the main area. Bow and Taran gasped. The tall female figure was still seated at the table, facing out to the garden, her back straight as a wall. Her breakfast bowl and spoon sat to the side. Like the other housefriends, she was barefoot.

Rain pelted the windows. Lightning made shadows bounce over the kitchen, dining area, sofas and hot tub. For a second, Jay thought the woman was moving but soon realised it was just a trick of the light. They were yet to glimpse her face.

'Hello,' Jay said. With only a few metres separating them, it seemed rude not to talk. All three circled the table to face her.

'Careful,' Taran said. 'She might be armed.'

'Maybe's she's only visiting. Or part –' Bow stopped.

'Jesus fucking Christ,' Jay said. His stomach did somersaults. It wasn't an adult at the table. He was looking at a child. She couldn't have been more than sixteen. A blotchy yet unblemished round face, which experience had yet to scar, framed natural, overfull lips. She had a wrinkle-free button nose and large eyes that stared back at them, as if the three housefriends were the recent arrivals in her living space.

Beside Jay, Bow began swaying and bellowing. Her head shook so much he expected her to fall over. She collapsed onto the opposite bench. 'No!' she shouted. Where their footsteps had failed to rouse the girl, Bow's shouting succeeded. Even though the girl sat still, her eyes widened further and her lips parted a fraction.

Jay could tell Taran was as confused as he was by Bow's overreaction. He watched on as she stared at the girl. Did Bow recognise her? Jay cleared his throat and stepped forward, head angled.

'I'm Jay. Who are you?' He blinked and waited, like a teacher with a lost student. 'What are you doing here?'

She met his gaze. Her tone was flat, her words well-articulated. 'I'm here to kill one of you.'

71

Bow stumbled through the door. Her body couldn't carry her to the chair. She slid down the wall and hit the floor, her eyes vacant. Her tears wouldn't come. Crying needed energy that she could no longer generate. All hope of leaving the house had vanished.

'Good morning, kiddo. How are you today?'

'Fuck you. I can't kill a child.' She thumped the floor. 'How old is she? Twelve? Thirteen?'

'I can't share that information. Only Olivia herself does that.'

'You put a minor on the show.'

'She's old enough. Please don't assume too much. It could lead to … disastrous consequences.'

'She's Patty's replacement. We had it all sorted, Patty and me.'

'Then Saoirse went and killed Patty with a weapon you handed over.'

Bow shut her eyes at Scot's painful reminder. Her plan.

So bloody simple, how could it not have worked? She opened her eyes and found a camera. 'Out there is Patty's granddaughter. Or she's related to one of the others who perished.'

'Remind me, please, Bow. How many people died in that catastrophe?'

Bow broke her gaze at another comment that stung.

'Congratulations.' Scot's voice perked up. 'You're in the final four.'

'And?'

'You'll die, return to prison or walk free. If you're the next person to kill someone, you'll return to prison with' – Scot's voice intensified, like someone making a sales pitch – 'a seventy-five per cent reduction in your original sentence.'

'I can't go back to Barton. They won't honour any talk about a reduced sentence.'

'Balderdash. Superintendent Carlisle is in possession of the facts. The state dictates –'

'You don't understand.'

'I'd start thinking about where you want to escape to, if you are the last remaining killer. You get off scot free – clue's in the title.'

Bow knew where she wanted to end up. A picture of the location formed in her mind. Without a doubt, the last place reporters or aggrieved relatives would look.

'What's on your mind?' Scot asked. 'Let me guess. You're thinking, "Can I negotiate with my match for a second time?" Good question, Bow.'

She propped herself up slightly and sat stone-faced.

'Would the hunters out there be willing to sit tight and wait, like you convinced Patty to do?'

Bow got to her feet.

'There's only one way to find out,' she said.

'Attagirl.'

'Fuck off.'

'Go mingle with Olivia. She's dying to meet you. But don't jump to conclusions about who's matched with who.'

'If she's not my hunter, then Jay is. Which means you had two people in the house hunting me – Jay and Patty. That's unfair.' Seconds passed. 'Scot? Are you there? Wait.'

*

Alone in the production suite, Adolpha settled the collar of her shirt. There was nothing more to say to Bow. On the large wall-mounted screen above the console, live footage showed Bow returning to the main area. Adolpha swigged her coffee and waited. She'd been involved in Scot Free from the start, time enough to know she wouldn't need to wait too long. And she was sure who would stop by next.

One of the console's side screens displayed Taran strolling, seemingly casually, to the chair. Adolpha couldn't stop a devilish grin from forming. Their new addition to the household was already having the desired effect. Adolpha sat up straight. Her index finger took up position at the console, set to activate Scot's voice.

Now appearing on the main screen, Taran sat on the edge of the chair. He angled his head and body to the left and his eyes avoided the camera. His shoulders were back, his chin high.

Adolpha pressed the button and spoke into the mic. 'Let me guess. You've come to explain that, as a murderer with standards, you cannot possibly condone the killing of a minor for entertainment.'

'I'm not a murderer.'

'You needn't worry. I believe Olivia's up for slaying someone.'

Taran's palms came up to head height.

'This is sick. It's that woman's daughter, I suppose? She's here to avenge her mother. And Patty was my match?'

'To avoid a train wreck out there, I strongly advise against making assumptions. There's too much at stake. Remember you can only kill the relative of the woman you brutally murdered.'

'Stop telling your twisted audience I killed her.' Taran's voice rose sharply, but he still averted his eyes from the camera. 'She was dying when I found her.'

'You –'

'It's not true, Scot!'

'You're on this show because of it,' Adolpha said. 'You're in prison for it.'

'One day, the truth will come out.' Taran pounded the armrests.

Adolpha tutted. How boring. A conversation about clearing someone's name. She shook a bangle along her forearm and sipped her coffee. Time to provoke.

'Congratulations. You're through to the next round.' Taran's image looked like it had paused and he was quiet. 'Oh, Sourpuss,' Adolpha said.

'I've been wrongly imprisoned for murder. I almost got electrocuted and I ate Alice. Excuse me if I don't seem elated.'

Adolpha stifled a laugh. That would make a perfect montage for Taran's best bits. She regained her composure and activated the mic. 'We care about you.'

'Ha! Until your script says get rid of me.' There was a prolonged silence. He turned to the camera, jaded eyes looking straight at Adolpha. 'So, when is it?'

'When is what?'

'When does the script say, "Dispose of Taran"?'

She took a breath and paused for effect. 'Very soon.'

His startled jump brought a smile to her face. 'That ill-fated night, what else did you do to the woman you apparently didn't murder?'

The screen showed Taran scurrying from the room. 'Leave me alone,' he said.

Adolpha wheeled her chair away from the console.

'That has to be the unluckiest man in the world.'

72

By lunchtime, the storm was losing intensity. Grey clouds clogged the sky, but the rain had stopped. From the dining table, Jay kept an eye on everyone. Olivia did exercise drills on the decking. Press-ups, arm dips and the plank on the hot tub ledge. From the sofa, Taran watched her every move, but feigned nonchalance. In the kitchen, Bow had muffins in the oven. The sugar-sweet scent of chocolate and vanilla hung in the air.

Jay caught Olivia's eye after her fifth set of press-ups and beckoned her to follow him. She didn't move.

'Come with me. I want to show you around. Best you know the layout so you aren't at – so you know the place as well as we do. We've been here for two weeks. Have you been watching the show?'

She descended the stairs. 'I'm not allowed television.'

'If you've got strict parents, you'll fit in well here. There are rules for everything,' Taran said.

'I don't have parents. My –'

'Stop!' Jay cut her off. 'Don't give out personal information like that.' He led her away.

With a burst of energy, Taran ejected himself from the sofa, topped up his coffee and followed them. Bow, after a quick peek through the oven door, was not far behind. Jay spoke to Olivia as though he was welcoming a roommate. He pointed at the doors on either side. 'Shower's there, and here you design your leaving clothes. Scot needs to get you started on that.'

'What are those doors?' Olivia asked.

'Our bedrooms. They open again tonight,' Jay said.

She turned to Bow and Taran, pointing a steel-like finger. 'Show me your rooms.' Bow, surprised by an immediate urge to comply, signalled her door.

'Don't tell her,' Taran said, his words a whisper, his eyes fixed on Olivia. She grinned impishly, almost enjoying his fear. Even Jay was unsettled, but he continued with the tour. 'This place is like a horseshoe. Let's double back. You can see the other side.'

Flattening themselves against the wall for Jay and Olivia to pass, Bow kept her eyes to the floor and Taran covered his coffee, as if Olivia might deliberately spill it.

'Is it always this dark here?' Olivia asked.

'In the corridor, yes. Don't worry. I'll protect you.' Jay gave Bow and Taran a frown as a warning.

'You? Protect me? Who from? These two?' Olivia laughed, long and loud.

Images of the previous killings flashed across Jay's mind. Myra chasing Rosa with a knife, Nicky splitting Walt's head open with a mallet, Saoirse raising the shaking gun at Patty, Saoirse again with the bag over Sonny's head.

Had Olivia deigned to look at him properly, she would have seen both the trauma and the determination in his eyes. She wouldn't understand yet what it took to survive. He ushered her back into the living area, pointing out the garden and woods.

They took the other corridor, where Jay opened the door to the chair. But Olivia peered into the weapon room. 'What's in there?' she asked, pointing at the dome.

'It's locked. Scot places weapons in there.'

In a flash, Olivia hit the button to activate the door. Nothing happened.

'He told you it was closed,' Taran said. He felt comfortable adding a quiet tut.

Ignoring him, Olivia studied the corridor walls. Her eyes followed the line of the weapon room's doorframe. She reached out and touched the thick glass of the door. She could have been there for a fit-out. Only a notepad and pen were missing. She ran her hand over the doorframe, then the thumb scanner. 'Who put this place together?' she asked, tailing the others into the next room. 'The architecture leaves a lot to be desired.'

Inside, Taran and Bow stuck to the perimeter, hiding in the shadows. Jay explained that Olivia could speak to Scot in this room, but that she would need to lock the door each time she came in.

They watched Olivia approach the chair.

'Sit in it,' Bow said.

'Why?'

There were more tuts and huffs from Taran. Olivia did a lap of the chair without touching it.

'Can you cook?' Bow asked.

Olivia kept her eyes on the chair. 'Can you?'

'We take turns preparing meals,' Bow said.

Taran kept his voice low but clear. 'Can we swap her for Sonny?' He came away from the wall. 'I have a question for her.'

'You can talk to her directly,' Bow said, chuckling. 'That's not against the rules.'

Taran batted playfully at Bow. 'Olivia, who says you can't watch television?' There was silence. Jay shook his head for Olivia not to answer.

'I go to boarding school, where the prefects look out for us.'

'Ah,' Taran said, nodding sagely. 'Here, "look out for" means "control rigidly".' He gave his coffee a self-satisfied slurp, letting the others take in his translation. 'Drop the act. You can be yourself in here. We're more relaxed.'

Olivia scoffed. She scanned Taran from the long toes on his skinny feet to the top wisp of his messy hair. 'Tell me something I don't know. I've seen you eating.'

*

That evening, Scot's voice boomed through the house. A jackpot was about to launch, for the winning hunter and winning target to share equally.

High on the wall above the housefriends' heads, over the hot tub, the starting figure of thirty million dollars lit up. One blue three and seven blue zeros sat ready to climb. Scot explained the live total would remain projected on the wall for the rest of the week. Home viewers could bet on almost anything. Who would win the show, who was matched with who and who would leave next. Dramatically, Scot counted down to kick off the jackpot and open the betting.

Jay and the others watched on, chins raised, mouths open. Within seconds, the amount increased. Viewers were playing already. Jay gulped. In front of his eyes, the zeros vanished.

Twos became threes.

Eights became nines.

73

Constructed in the eighties, the building had only become a television studio when the Scot Free team had moved in six years earlier. Close to central Sydney but on an isolated property, the location kept plucky journalists and overzealous fans under control. Because floor space was limited, the offices, production suites and living space for housefriends sat dispersed over multiple levels.

On level four, which housed the post-production spaces, Adolpha and Alan strode out of the lift. They took the deserted corridor to Everton's suite, where it was time for the video specialist to deliver his project.

Adolpha's voice carried along the corridor. 'Unreliable tosser that he is, he's probably driving home. If he's not in his suite, I'm getting my foil and going after him.'

'I've let him know we're on our way,' Alan said, ever wary of the unzipped trousers and used tissues of his last visit. 'We should knock first.' He sped up to reach the suite door before

Adolpha and knocked. After a moment, he nodded to her and opened the door.

'Everton! You're here.' Adolpha advanced to where he was sitting at the telecine controls and Alan settled himself in an armchair. 'I was telling Alan how excited I am. I always like your work.' She squeezed his shoulder and crouched beside him.

'If you go back there with Alan, you'll get a better view when it comes on the large screen,' Everton said.

She patted his shoulder. 'This is kind of you.' She sat in an armchair next to Alan. 'We know how busy you are. Don't we, Alan?'

Alan nodded, tidied his hair and dropped a loose grey strand to the floor. He took out a cigarette and played with it.

'Ready for your private viewing?' Everton asked, without turning around.

Adolpha seemed to miss Everton's quip. Alan prompted her with a smile, but Adolpha's forehead creased. 'Oh, a joke,' she said. 'A private viewing. It is, isn't it?'

Alan thought he heard a grumble from the front. But it could have been one of the many buttons Everton played with. Ahead on an oversized screen, footage played. Instead of watching, Alan turned to see Adolpha's reaction. Her eyes widened at what was unfolding onscreen. She gave nod after nod to Everton's editing skills. Open-mouthed, her lips glistened. Death reflected in her eyes.

Finally, the screen went blank. Everton swivelled around to face them and his T-shirt caught Alan's attention. It carried photos of European tourist landmarks and a slogan, which Alan squinted to read. *Binge there, done that.*

'Outstanding, outstanding.' Adolpha was nodding. 'It looks so much better. Well worth the wait.' She gave another forceful nod. 'You had me worried you would screw up. Like others around here. Fantastic, isn't it, Alan?'

'It is.'

'I hope you realise what we've just watched.'

'A w–' Everton couldn't finish his sentence. Adolpha cut him off.

'I'm talking about its significance.' She edged forward in her seat. 'When this airs on Friday night, the whole country will go wild. Never again will funding be a worry.' She clapped with her knuckles. 'I can't wait. You'll be the hero of the grand finale, Everton.'

'The unseen hero,' Alan said.

'Ooh, yes. I like that,' Adolpha said. 'You stay hidden, Everton. But you're an essential service in this building. We only notice you when we need you. Isn't that terrible of us? You're like' – she looked around the office for inspiration to finish off her simile – 'like aircon. We only pay attention when you're not there.'

Alan looked at his cigarette. 'Like a fire escape.'

'Exactly like a fire escape,' Adolpha said. 'Virtually invisible, but bloody handy.'

'How kind.' Everton turned to face the control panel. 'That's good to go.'

Alan stood and went to leave. 'Adolpha, one thing. We're debating how to get the knife in there for Friday. I'm worried Olivia will go for the wrong person.'

'I don't care if she kills all three. Ratings, Alan. If she brings viewers, I'm more than happy to have her back for another season.'

'That's unfair.' Alan checked himself.

'A little late for you to develop a conscience.' Lengthening her neck, Adolpha smirked, unseen by Everton, who busied himself with the controls. Alan glared at her.

'Thanks, Everton. Excellent.' As he spoke, Alan could tell his voice sounded too forced for an innocent farewell.

'It will be excellent,' Adolpha said. 'Let's work on those opening shots.' She went over to Everton. 'Can we go back to the beginning? I want the tones just right for Friday's big screen. A couple of items need to stand out. When were you heading home?'

74

A day later, with the grand finale two days away, Jay helped Olivia work on her exit suit in the cramped measuring room. At the wall tablet, Jay brought up the screen Olivia would need. As soon as he stepped away from the wall, Olivia jumped forward. She cleared the screen and prodded impatiently at different buttons. Jay shook his head as she opened a cascade of windows, all incorrect. She punched the home key again.

Jay snapped. 'Slow down. You're rushing and you're getting it wrong.'

She let the tape measure slip from her hand.

He wiped his glasses on his T-shirt and took a few breaths. His voice softened. 'You were in the right spot about three screens ago.' He rolled his shoulders to loosen his back muscles. 'It's time to talk about the messy situation we're in,' he said. 'This show is relying on us leaping in and lashing out at someone. They want the ratings. You're impulsive. In here, that's a hazard.'

'I can look after myself.'

'No, you can't.' What Jay had seen in the last couple of weeks was enough to convince him. 'None of us can.'

But Olivia waved off his concern. 'I've been briefed.'

'Listen,' he said. 'I'm a hunter. You must be too. That means we're on the same side. Get it?' She retreated from him. 'Don't move. You're going to listen to this. I'm stepping through the logic to prove we can trust each other. Okay?'

She shook her head but said nothing, and he blocked the door and covered the exit button.

'You can't always trust that people will tell the truth. First, Bow and Taran are targets. They have killed people. You're in a house with convicted murderers. So, you must not trust them. Promise me that.'

Her promise came with blinks of her long eyelashes. He paused to study her face, smooth and unblemished by the disappointments of age. How young she was. A fresh wave of sickness swirled inside him at the thought of what she was caught up in.

He continued. 'I'm in here because I recently lost a relative. And you've also lost one. You can't possibly be a target. Scot wouldn't have introduced another target in the house. That would mean there are three killers in here.' He huffed a long breath out. 'The show would never end. That's how I know I can trust you.'

When Olivia spoke, it was the last thing he expected her to say.

'I'm sorry for your loss.'

He averted his eyes and waited for the ache in his chest to subside. So much loss. He blinked to stave off tears. 'Right. Where were we? I'm not telling you this to help you kill them. I am not going to let you kill.'

'My mother was murdered,' she said.

'Don't!' Jay shouted, which made Olivia recoil.

Her reaction seemed genuine. 'I didn't mean to scare you. I don't want to know anything about that. Bow and Taran will try to get information from you. To kill you. Withhold everything.'

'I'll get to them first. I want justice for my mother.'

'There you go again.' Jay picked up the tape measure. 'The show needs one more murder for the season to end. I'm getting out of here. But no way are you killing someone to secure my freedom. That is not happening.'

'By your logic, you have to kill one of them, then. Do your duty.'

'I don't want those two dead either.' He shook his head. The situation was maddening. 'Let's get on with our work.'

For the next few minutes, neither spoke. Then Olivia stopped what she was doing and stared ahead. 'There's no option,' she said. 'What you've described is a stalemate. You want neither to kill nor to be killed. You want to stop me from killing. Can you see the inconsistency in that position with only four people in the game?'

'Sorry to disappoint, but you are not killing anyone.' Creasing his brow, he held out the tape measure. 'Take this.'

'What other option is there? Dying?' she asked.

'We'll think of a plan.'

She turned away. 'I already have one.'

*

In the garden, Bow sunned herself facedown on a towel. The strength of the afternoon sun waxed and waned as clouds paraded overhead. A tumbler of juice and the remains of a muffin were beside her and, a couple of metres away, Olivia sat cross-legged on bare grass. They would have looked like mother and daughter relaxing together in a park were it not for

378

the distance between them. Bow had invited Olivia to sit with her. Only in her own time had Olivia moved from the bench to the lawn.

'You're in here because of an accident,' Bow said. 'Somebody killed the wrong person. And you're here to replace her. The woman who died was' – Bow lifted her head to see Olivia's reaction – 'Patty.'

Olivia squinted.

'Your grandmother? Patty? Patricia?'

If Olivia knew who Patty was, she wasn't letting on. She stared at Bow, sleepy-eyed. She seemed genuinely uninterested.

An image from the building site explosion flitted across Bow's mind. She cast it away. 'Your relative had an interest in heritage.'

'Are you asking or telling me?' Olivia said.

Bow watched for a clenched fist or a catch in Olivia's breath. Maybe she'd been trained not to react. Yet the child seemed so determined to attack, she couldn't be holding back. Maybe she didn't know Patty after all.

Bow took courage from there not being a weapon in the house. She scanned the garden. Nothing in easy reach that Olivia could attack her with. It seemed the right time to share more details.

'I believe you're here to hunt me. Patty and I agreed not to kill each other. To sit it out and let the others do all the fighting. So, how does that sound?' Bow sipped her juice. There was no response. 'She would want you to do the same. Understood?'

Olivia nodded, her eyes wide.

'Do you really understand? Or are you nodding for my sake?'

'Who's Patty?' Olivia said.

Bow let the irritation come through in her voice. 'For fuck's sake, I'm serious. I'm your target. If you're not Patty's relative, then you're related to someone else from that day. It doesn't fit any other way.' Bow came to a sitting position. 'Don't worry about the details. I say we sit back and let those two kill each other. You get off the show alive and I go home too.' Bow watched Olivia's face for a sign, any reaction. Her sparkling blue eyes gave nothing away.

'You liar,' she said, after an age.

'No! I can't be lying. If I wanted you to kill someone, I wouldn't offer you my name. I'd tell you to kill Taran. Jesus! Think, please.' Bow clenched her jaw shut and let birdsong fill the silence.

After a minute, she decided to take a more circuitous route to connect with Olivia and get her message across. She gently plucked two leaves from the gardenias in the nearby flowerbed. She kept her voice soft. 'Do you know what these are?'

'Leaves.'

Bow persisted. 'I love plants. The beauty in each flower, each petal.' She held out her hand. 'Look at that dark, glossy coat. Do you know which type of leaves these are?'

'Dead ones. If you love plants so much, why damage them? You remind me of my science teacher. He claimed to love animals, but I lost count of how many rats we dissected.'

Bow threw the leaves on the flowerbed and wiped her hands.

Olivia raised her voice over Bow's smacking palms. 'You have no self-control. You want something, you take it.' She signalled the discarded leaves.

Bow swore under her breath. 'You brainwashed little sheep.'

'Pleasure-seeker.'

'Foot soldier,' Bow said.

'Lost cause.'

'Killer-to-be.'

'I have a duty,' Olivia said.

'Ha! What duty could you ever have except taking up space in foster care?'

'And you in a prison.'

'If only you knew, kid. I keep that prison operating.'

Olivia pulled out blades of grass. 'Your family must really hate you.'

'Get fucked.' Bow's blood boiled at the truth. She pointed to the sky. 'I bet your relative's up there thinking, "Thank god, I got away from her."'

Olivia gasped. 'That's horrible.' She took off inside.

'Fuck!' Bow buried her face in her hands. That was not how it was meant to go. Once her breathing had returned to normal, she lifted her head and spoke aloud. 'Your conflict resolution skills are coming along nicely.'

Unsure where the cruelty had sprung from, Bow flopped on the grass and watched the clouds. They floated, neatly spaced across the uniform blue, nudged on their way by an invisible hand. A picture-perfect scene.

Indeed, she'd seen identical clouds countless times, in the photo of Tristan da Cunha above Superintendent Carlisle's desk.

75

On Thursday, lunch was lamb and vegetables. During the meal, Olivia raised a topic the housefriends had so far managed to avoid. Politics. She regurgitated the official line on how the Great Preservation had affected Australia. Sweeping social and political changes, which had pushed the country into a totalitarian state, were breathtakingly beneficial.

'Fundamental changes in security, welfare and health mean that we —'

'The financial sector is suffering,' Taran said, interrupting her.

'Because of foreign interference. If we operate independently, we will be great again. We now have hope.'

'Where did you learn all this?' Taran asked.

'Our school syllabus has never been stronger. Next year, I enter the armed forces and start a five-year degree in international law.'

Taran whistled. 'You can probably skip the first two.'

'Why would I do that? My school friends will be there.'

'It was a joke.'

'That comment was funny?' Olivia looked at Bow and Jay.

'It comes with age,' Taran said. He wiped the table with his sleeve, demonstrating how uncivilised he was. Olivia glared at the table like it was contaminated.

Jay leant in. 'I want to talk.' He glanced at the escalating prize money on the wall above them. Almost eighty million dollars. 'I'm not playing this game anymore. We lost Patty because of a horrible mix-up and now Olivia is here. It's changed everything. We need to protect her. We have to unify, to stop this, to refuse to take part.'

'I'm ready to do what I came here to do.' Olivia's head rose again.

'Maybe they've prepared you physically. But pitting you against adults is cruel.'

'What are you suggesting?' Bow asked.

'That we stage a protest. We outright refuse to play along.'

'How?' Taran said.

'We go to Scot and we show solidarity. Together, we pledge not to kill anyone and we force them to end the game.'

'One more person needs to die,' Taran said. 'It's too close to the end, and you have to convince them out there.'

'I think we can do that. There's no weapon in here. Maybe we're meant to come together, with Olivia arriving.'

'It's a test to see how we react?' Taran asked.

Jay nodded.

'Maybe. What if a terrible fate awaits the person who lays a finger on Olivia? She's only a child, for god's sake.'

Bow's long, drawn-out sigh stopped Jay and held everyone's attention. She had her head down, but she was listening. When the last bit of air was out of her lungs, Jay continued.

'I know what this means for you two. If the show does progress as planned, one of you is going to walk free. I'm asking you to put this young girl's life first.' Bow lifted her head and looked at Taran. Olivia sat scowling at Jay.

'What's your plan, exactly?' Bow asked.

'Tomorrow evening, when we're meant to end the show, we sit and we share our stories, the truth about why we're here, and we don't react. No fighting. I'll speak first. Then you two. Olivia goes last.'

'Do you realise the trust that would take? On everyone's part?' Taran said, head shaking. 'We can't rely on what people say. One of us will promise not to react, but later, they'll attack their match.'

'It's all we have, Taran. Can we all promise?'

Bow laid her hands flat on the table. 'This is my opinion,' she said. 'Let me be honest.' Jay sensed she wouldn't be mincing her next words and folded his arms in readiness. 'You think that you've got a privileged position with Scot because you're a hunter. You think you can control how the show runs. But you're mistaken. And I think your suggestion puts us all in danger. They want one more death. We have to give it to them. We have no choice.'

'At least let's try,' Jay said.

Bow brought her fists down on the table. 'Two of us are convicted killers. Do you think they give a shit about us? If we're going to plan something –'

'Hello, housefriends!' Scot said. Jay stiffened at the jovial tone. 'The next weapon is now in the dome and tomorrow, the fourth round of clues arrives.' Jay felt the energy zap from him. His whole body sank. 'A popularity poll starts now, with one lucky housefriend winning access to the dagger.'

Olivia immediately shot up from her seat and dashed from the table. The others hardly had time to blink before she disappeared down the corridor leading to the weapon room. Jay settled his eyes on the darkened passageway, as much to avoid Bow's gaze as to witness Olivia's return. Both were proving to be sticking points in his plan. Both seemed determined to play along.

'Pippi Longstocking's on a mission,' Taran said. 'I know who'll win that poll.'

Seconds later, Olivia reappeared. 'There's a knife this long.' Her hands were shoulder-width apart.

*

'We're not happy about this. How do we protest?' Jay asked, from the chair. 'The show has ratings to worry about, but this is outrageous. She's still in school.' He sipped his cola.

'Isn't she adorable?' Scot said.

'I'm serious.' Jay scrunched his face. 'Is she Patty's relative? She looks kind of familiar. Patty dies in the worst possible circumstances, and you bring in her granddaughter, or whoever she is? Get someone else to replace Patty, not a child. Are you that desperate for ratings?' Scot was silent. 'We want to formally protest. How do we do that?'

'One moment please, Jay.' There was another pause. Jay pictured people on the other side of the screen frantically dialling the mobile numbers of senior executives they had never met. Trying to find out if the protest could stand.

Finally, Scot returned. 'After consulting extensively, we have confirmed the policy. The approach I will outline applies equally to all those wishing to protest.'

Jay settled himself in the seat, nestling the small of his back into the leather. He stared into the screen. Progress, at least.

'If someone comes running at you with the dagger, stand still, hands by your sides, and close your eyes. We'll take that as a formal objection.'

Jay sat quietly, staring blankly, for an age. He heaved himself up and brandished his middle finger at the camera. In the doorway, he turned around. He hurled his tumbler at the screen. The liquid splashed across the wall.

76

As soon as Christy heard about the new weapon, she pulled the television plug from the wall. Best to protect the baby from stress. Her eye caught sight of the ultrasound picture in pride of place, and she cradled her belly. It felt good to be standing there, in their home. The apartment was silent and spotless after a day of spring cleaning. A new start. Their bed had fresh sheets, the floor was vacuumed, and the waft of lasagne emanated from the oven. Jay adored her lasagne.

There were three things Jay would notice when he walked in. First, he'd spot that she was pregnant. She had already laid out the right clothes. Skinny jeans and a tight-fitting sports top. Once Jay saw her, he'd know. She even knew the best place to stand. Near the television gave her a view of the front door. He'd rush in and they'd embrace.

Next, over her shoulder, the ultrasound photo would stare him right in the face.

The hairs on her arms stood on end.

Then, finally, he'd spot the box of Harriet's things resting on the table behind her. As if the old thing meant nothing. As though she'd found it that day. She could make out she had no idea what was in it. But it had been clutched, opened, inspected and closed hundreds of times since she'd unearthed it. He'd know the truth.

Jay's phone rang. It was Teddy. Christy explained she couldn't watch the show anymore.

'I'll text you any developments. There's a dagger in there now.'

'That's why I stopped watching.'

'Oh. I shouldn't mention it then. The jackpot's skyrocketing and Jay's alive. How's that?'

'Better.' Christy sat down. She considered her next comment. 'I've had three miscarriages. Jay and I have been trying. It's … tough. We're going to get through this.' A wave of emotion disrupted her thoughts. She steadied her voice. 'You deserve a baby, too.' Christy got no response. 'Do you regret your abortion?' she asked. 'Have you forgiven Harriet for pushing you to do it?'

'It was a long time ago and I wasn't ready to start a family,' Teddy said, letting out a pained sigh. 'I only think about it when people remind me. There's nothing to forgive for Harriet's role in it.'

'You're strong.' Christy stared at the ultrasound photo. 'I couldn't let someone get away with that.'

'Why do you hate Harriet so much?'

'I don't hate her,' Christy said, battling to keep defensiveness from her voice. 'She was … family. She stayed here once. I don't hate her.' She felt her voice climb.

Teddy tutted. 'Like I said, it's in the past. A decision had to be made. Harriet helped it along. And remember, it's Harriet we're talking about. She wasn't fully mindful of her daily life. Addicted to the end.'

Christy nodded to herself. She supposed it was the case that

Harriet had been using drugs up until she died, but she couldn't be sure.

She stopped. Something about Teddy's comment didn't sit right. 'Wait. How do you know?' The line was quiet.

'Answer me. How do you know?'

'Know what?'

'That Harriet was addicted "to the end"? You told me you hadn't seen her for years.'

'Someone posted something online.'

That made sense. Christy had an idea. 'Appearing from nowhere as you did, I think you and Jay should meet up some time soon. He'd like that.'

'How do you know he would?'

'You'll have things you want to share about Harriet and …' Christy left her comment unfinished.

'Nope. Nothing to say at this point.'

Christy reached for the box of Harriet's things. 'Don't worry, I'll have enough to say to him for a month. When he walks through that front door, I'm going to –'

'Whoa! You're waiting for him at home? That's madness. Go to the studio.'

'It's best if I wait here.' Christy had it all arranged, and she still hadn't shared her pregnancy with anyone. She couldn't do crowds.

'Go! Get a good spot. You're one of the laziest people I've met.'

'We haven't met and I'm not lazy.'

'You're splitting hairs, and only people with loads of time on their hands – that is, lazy people – split hairs.'

It crossed Christy's mind to call Teddy a fucked-up bag of shit. But she was meant to be staying calm. No television, Jay's imminent return, his favourite food. She wanted to sit with those things. It was time to cast off negative thoughts.

But Teddy was on a roll. 'If my man was exiting Scot Free, I'd be there to greet him.'

Christy's face flushed hot. 'If your man saw you waiting there, he'd volunteer for another season.'

Teddy hung up and Christy flopped onto the sofa. She commended her own wickedness.

Going to the studio. Of all the wild decisions. She googled the address, then it occurred to her she already had it. After rummaging through kitchen drawers, she pulled out a sheet of folded paper. The letter announcing Jay had been selected for the show. It was signed by Adolpha Martin, Executive Producer.

Christy flattened the page by placing the secret box on top. 'You're coming with me, Harriet.'

She went to text Teddy on Jay's phone, but it dawned on her Teddy still didn't have her mobile number. All their contact had been through Jay's mobile.

Using her own phone, Christy messaged Teddy, explaining she would go to the studio, and she and Jay would contact her soon.

Hopefully that was enough of a white flag.

*

Alan knocked at Adolpha's office and entered. She was on her mobile and jutting at the air with her foil.

'That's superb, Mister Bennett. I appreciate you calling me directly with such fantastic news. My team will be delighted. I'm thrilled to have met the quota of murders for the season, and we still have the grand finale to come.' She winked at Alan. Her jaw fell and the foil stopped moving. 'Hitting double figures for murders? In one season? Oh my! That's an ambitious target. I look forward to discussing this further with you. I'm glad we both see the potential in this format.' Her call ended.

'Bennett's just confirmed two more seasons. And we still have tomorrow to hit them with.'

'I've also got news,' Alan said. 'The jackpot's reached a hundred million.'

Adolpha had a glint in her eye. 'Wonderful. It's all coming together.'

77

On the day of the grand finale – the day Jay was stabbed – Alan screamed himself awake. His limbs were thrashing but tangled in damp sheets. It took a moment to remember that he hadn't made it home. Instead, he'd slipped into a holding cubicle, normally reserved for housefriends entering the show. He perched on the edge of the bunk while his thumping heart eased and the sheen on his skin faded. It was before five. He cradled his head. The close of season six awaited him, and if something went wrong today it would be disastrous. An image of Adolpha running at him with her foil was enough to get him moving.

After a quick shower, he grabbed a coffee and headed to the fire escape for a solitary cigarette.

From this spot, he could make out the treetops of the Scot Free woods to the south. Ahead in the distance lay the twinkling sprawl of suburban Sydney. A yellowing horizon heralded a clear, warm day.

Three cigarettes later, he returned to the production suite, twiddling an unlit fourth. He turned on screens and equipment, ready for when the housefriends woke up, and logged into the mic system. He pressed an override button to take control of voicing Scot. And then he waited. There was little else to do. Before too long, the beat in his heart caught his attention. A metronome to mark the day's orchestration, it picked up speed.

At seven, earlier than usual, he unlocked the bedroom doors for all four sleeping housefriends and permanently deactivated the locks.

No more locked bedrooms this season.

Waiting was the worst. He rolled the unlit cigarette in his fingers, watching live footage, from multiple cameras, of mostly empty rooms.

Olivia surfaced first and headed to the garden. Shortly after, the cameras traced her walking to the showers. Then Taran appeared, visited the weapon room, made tea and drank it in the garden. Bow and Jay rose soon after.

Onscreen, Jay, Bow and Taran moved about the kitchen in silence, like unacquainted hotel guests forced to breakfast together. Holidaymakers on the last day of a trip, dreading the return to normality. Their chatter was gone. Alan checked the volume was up and confirmed that the only sounds came from the plastic cutlery and bowls, and the microwave pinging. They were strangers again.

Bow had to make another cup of coffee after she spilled her first. Alan saw her look sheepishly at the camera. Like part of an imaginary queue, Taran lined up for the sink well behind Jay. Despite not speaking, all three ate breakfast at the table. Bow and Taran faced Jay, sitting so close it looked like the pair were touching elbows.

When speech finally came, it caught Alan off guard. He heard Taran clearly through the speakers.

'I stole everyone's things. They're in my room. But I'm not a killer.' Head down, he eyed his toast. 'I'm not.'

A camera caught Jay and Bow exchanging a glance. Their silence seemed to ask for an explanation, but Taran walked away without a word. Apparently, no further explanation would come.

Then, moments later, he reappeared with Jay's Rubik's Cube, Saoirse's flower and Sonny's cigarettes. He left them on the table. 'Here. I've been in trouble with the police before. I was convicted. My anxiety comes out and I see things and I –'

Bow picked up the flower. 'Nicky's a talented woman,' she said, twirling it in her hand. 'You weren't taking this stuff for monetary gain, that's for sure.'

Jay played with his Rubik's Cube, messing up the colours. 'If we had more time, Taran, I'd show you how to do it. Was it for attention?' His question went unanswered. 'I'm sure viewers will appreciate your honesty.'

Alan spoke to the empty suite. 'What good will come of that honesty now?'

Bow changed the subject. 'Don't know about you, but I slept terribly. Not sure I'll make it through the day.'

Opposite her, Jay nodded. 'Same. I had the strangest dreams. Turning all night. I can't remember half of them, but weird. They all featured a baby. It feels like they did, anyway. People were trying to hand me this baby, and my arms couldn't lift. I was trying and trying – you know, when you can't grab something – but I couldn't take it from them.' Jay forced a smile and kept talking. 'I hope my girlfriend's okay. We've tried a few times to have children.'

'By the way,' Taran said, 'the knife's gone.'

'What?' Bow said, exchanging a shocked look with Jay. 'When?'

'I checked on it when I woke up.'

'Why didn't you say so earlier?' Jay asked.

'What difference does it make?' Taran said.

Olivia appeared in the background and joined the others at the table. Jay directed her to sit next to him. 'Stay close,' he said. She helped herself to a piece of toast from the stack.

'Have you got the dagger?' Taran asked her.

Olivia took a bite of toast. 'Is it gone?'

Alan leant back in his chair. With almost everything in place, he was already thinking of his home murder reel, which would soon contain one more death.

78

Scot's voice boomed through the house.

'Afternoon, housefriends. We're live, so please watch the language. Your exit suits are on your beds and you have some cleaning to do before you leave the house. But now, your final clues of the season.'

With limbs weighed down by lethargy and tension, Jay shuffled to the wall in the kitchen and beckoned for Olivia to stand near him. But she skipped to the far end, by the bedroom corridor. All he could do was shake his head. He watched her warm up as if she was about to play sport. Swinging her arms and jogging on the spot. Ready for action. She was insufferable. Between him and Olivia stood Bow and Taran, spacing themselves out along the wall.

'Listen,' Jay said to the others. 'We can choose not to react to what we read.' Yet he knew how much he would welcome a clue that identified Harriet's killer.

They heard the tone signalling that their clues would appear.

'There you go. Not totally useless this time,' Taran said, seconds later.

Before he'd had time to consider his own clue, Jay sensed hurried movement behind him and turned around. Olivia was stomping over to Bow and she looked ready to strike her.

'You're a liar!' Olivia shouted.

Bow raised her arm in defence and Jay stepped in between the pair.

'She wants me to kill the wrong person!' Olivia said from around Jay.

Bow's eyes were as wide as saucers. 'I haven't lied to you. What did your screen say?'

'Don't answer that,' Jay said, before he was brushed aside by Bow, who was fighting to stay cool.

'If the clue contradicts what I said, don't believe it,' Bow said. 'Be careful. That's the show manipulating you.'

Olivia's eyes were watery. 'I know you lied to me.'

In exasperation, Bow growled. 'I've told you already. Patty and I were matched. You're my replacement hunter.' She looked at Jay and Taran, and nodded. 'Yes. That means you two are a match.'

Jay locked eyes with Taran. This man, who had claimed his innocence all along, had murdered Harriet? Sensitive, rabbit-loving Taran?

Jay was shaken from his thoughts by more shouting.

'Liar!' Olivia said to Bow.

'I'm not! Why are you doing this, Olivia? I know these two are matched.'

'Wait a moment, Olivia,' Jay said. 'Bow, how do you know that?'

'I just do, okay?'

She moved away and sat at the table.

'Not true! My clue said it's Taran,' Olivia said, following Bow to the table and standing opposite her, the confrontation far from over.

Taran yelped. 'Me?'

Bow tutted. 'Now she's lying. There is no way her clue said Taran.'

'It did. It did.'

Taran pulled himself together and went over to the table. 'Things don't add up here. So, for god's sake, nobody do anything right now. Olivia, to be frank, I'm sort of only talking to you when I say that. You're bloodthirsty. Don't lash out.' He turned to Bow. 'You're sure Jay and I are a pair?' Bow nodded. Then Taran turned to Olivia. 'And you're saying I'm your target?'

'Yes. My clue said it's a man.'

Taran shrugged. 'One of you is a —'

'They're playing with us,' Jay said. 'They're trying to cause confusion because they know whatever happens, they get a show. They get a spectacle whether we make a mistake or not. Olivia, be especially careful, please. Listen to Taran. Don't rush to do anything. You could make a gigantic error and it might mean you don't get out of here. Do you understand? Sometimes, there are odd clues. Like mine. I'm being told there's no statute of limitations for murder.' He stepped closer to her. 'None of us will attack you. We stick together.'

'Speak for yourself,' Taran said.

'Taran!'

'I'm just saying. Don't go telling Olivia that nobody will go after her. That gives her a false sense of security and the idea she can attack as she likes. I've been living with you and Bow for three weeks now and I'm pretty sure I can tell if Bow lies or holds something back. This one' – he pointed at Olivia, whose eyes were down – 'arrived days ago and I can't read her as well.

But if these clues don't add up, it means she's lying. They've trained her to lie through her sodding milk teeth.'

Olivia lifted her head and brought her finger close to Taran's face. 'I'm warning you.' He batted her hand away and, in a flash, the argument turned physical. They swiped at each other in an awkward dance of attack and defence. Olivia had lost some of her regimented precision in the heat of battle and Taran's lanky limbs had, at long last, found their calling in fending her off. Bow moved in to keep them apart and took a hit to the face. All three became entangled.

Jay turned his back on them. He could feel his blood boiling. He sucked in all the air his lungs would allow. Bent double, fists shaking, he yelled over the commotion. 'Fuuuuuuck!' His roar echoed through the house. 'Stop fighting!'

The three separated, moving metres apart. Bow ended up at the mirror, fixing her hair. She caught Jay's eye. 'We need to know who has the knife,' she said.

'I can help there,' Taran said. 'My clue said that my hunter doesn't have the knife. What do we make of that?'

Jay thought about it for a moment. 'That's good news,' he said. 'It means you're safe, Taran. Because Scot wouldn't lie about that. We might get useless clues, but never misinformation.' He turned to Bow. 'You're the other target. Either you have the knife or your hunter does.'

'No, wait!' Bow shouted. 'Taran might have it.'

Jay shook his head. 'No. Think about it. If Taran's armed, Scot wouldn't write a clue to him about his hunter not having the knife. It doesn't make sense.'

Olivia chimed in. 'Maybe Taran's bluffing.'

This earned her a glare from Taran. He hissed two words her way. 'Little cunt.'

Jay paused, lips pursed. He looked Taran over. 'No offence.

But you're not that quick-thinking.'

Taran wagged his head to show he half-agreed.

'Let's assume Taran doesn't have the knife,' Jay said. 'And from his clue, neither does his hunter. Olivia says her target is Taran. If that's true, then following on from Taran's clue, she mustn't have the dagger. Which leaves Bow and me. And I don't have it.' They turned to Bow. 'It's looking like you do.' Jay watched her eyes closely for a flicker of guilt. There was none.

'Way too many assumptions there.' Bow shook her head.

'It fits the other clues,' he said. 'You keep telling us Olivia is your match. If that's true, Taran's clue fits. His hunter – me – doesn't have the knife. Which is correct.'

'If I have the knife, why am I still here?' Bow asked.

'Look at that prize money escalating.' Jay pointed up at the jackpot, which now sat at almost one hundred and thirty million dollars. All three followed his gaze. 'It's in your interest to wait. More money and a chance of winning your freedom without killing someone. Like you planned with Patty.'

Olivia stepped up to Bow. 'What did your clue say? We've all shared ours.'

Three pairs of eyes watched as Bow's face flushed red and she brought a hand to her neck. 'I didn't see it in time. You interrupted me.'

'Such a terrible liar,' Olivia said.

Jay ached at seeing Bow's discomfort. She wavered as she looked set to draw on a lifetime of excuses. With hours until the show ended, there was no reason Taran and Olivia had to find out Bow was illiterate. Jay lied for her.

'That happened to me in one round of clues. They don't stay up long.'

79

'Pizza's here,' Frank Carlisle said, entering the living room. A waft of melted cheese mixed with the balmy evening air. He handed a plate to Eleanor.

'Look at the crowds, love,' she said, ignoring him. In one deft movement, she covered her phone with a cushion, pointed at the television and pushed herself into the sofa.

'I can't until you take this from me.' He shuffled back to his seat, watching the camera sweep across hordes of fans outside the studio. 'Unbelievable.' Still on his feet, he swigged his beer and ate his pizza. 'I can't sit.'

'I can.' Eleanor finished her gin and tonic. 'I'm not moving for the next few hours.' She was set for a torrent of repeated scenes, pre-recorded celebrity predictions and live crosses to the front of the studio. All intermingled with muted footage of the housefriends pottering around the house. 'Imagine being there with all those people.'

'I can't think of anything worse,' Frank said.

He discarded his crust on the plate and wiped his fingers on a napkin.

A voiceover on the television blared out. 'Download the app and start betting. The more you bet, the more they win.'

Now was a good time to get Frank out of the room. Eleanor could place another bet in peace. She brandished her glass, which only contained a drenched chunk of lemon. 'Make that wedge swim, you son of a gun.'

'Why is the volume so loud?' he asked before he left the room.

'Because,' she said to herself, with a chuckle. No point advertising the fact she was an avid Scot Free gambler. She checked her mobile, which poked out from under the cushion with the betting app open.

Frank returned with the drinks as the adverts ended and the jackpot flashed on the screen. He swore. It had more than quadrupled in three days. One hundred and eighty million for the last hunter and target to split.

Eleanor raised her hands to collect the gin and tonic that was heading her way. Even the small sip she took made her mouth sting. 'Ooh, Frank Carlisle. You should be in prison for that.' She raised her glass to him. 'You do make a good G and T.' Unseen under the cushion, she tapped Jay's photo on her phone to lodge another vote. A green tick appeared. She took a mouthful of drink, accompanied by a satisfied slurp.

'Keep your votes coming in,' the television presenter said. 'Four housefriends. Who is matched with who? Two lucky viewers will each win a car.'

It all seemed too much to Frank. He sank into his seat. 'Stop throwing bloody money at them!' he shouted, shaking a fist at the television and stomping his heel on the floor.

Eleanor didn't blink. 'Stop that, love. Why don't you have a minute in the kitchen to calm yourself down?' She tucked into the pizza as he heaved himself up again. 'You could fetch me another slice while you're there.'

*

The grand finale was the only day the public could access the forecourt of the Scot Free premises. A large area had been cordoned off and it now housed hundreds of devotees, every second one in fancy dress. A cinema-size screen was broadcasting live and a medical tent stood ready for when the tension, alcohol and humidity inevitably came to a head. For everyone outside the gates, another large screen carried footage from the house and the television studio itself, where the show's host entertained another, smaller audience.

Line after line of fans chanted and roared. Whenever the cameras panned over them and they found themselves onscreen, they raised their drinks skyward and their roars intensified.

From the studio, the host crossed to a presenter, who talked his way through the crowds. He batted away homemade banners and elbowed fans who came too close. A young man in stripy prison overalls waved a toy rabbit at him. 'Who have you come as?' he asked.

'Taran!' The fan shook the rabbit in the air.

'Is the real Taran going to win?' the presenter asked. He was answered with a roar and a rabbit launched at his throat. He swatted the toy away and moved on to a trio of women wearing school uniforms, their hair in pigtails. All three chewed gum. 'You've come as Olivias.' A swarm of people around him cheered.

One Olivia leant forward and blew a pink bubble. 'Olivia to win! She's been in there four days and she already owns the place.' She stuck her gum on the microphone and her friends laughed raucously for the cameras. With a frown, the presenter batted the mic to dislodge the gum until a second Olivia snatched it up and popped it in her own mouth.

Live on the screens, Jay and Bow moved from room to room, stripping the beds. Then the image cut to the kitchen, where Taran and Olivia emptied the fridge, separating rubbish and scraps for the compost. Olivia took a cup from the cupboard and filled it with tap water.

'No more. We've just cleaned those,' Taran said, out of shot. The camera panned back to catch him, hands on hips, standing in front of Olivia. 'Wash the cup.' Olivia guzzled the drink and spilled some as she returned the cup to the sink. 'You're sweating,' Taran said. 'I thought you'd be used to a bit of housework.' Olivia waved him off and he shrugged, then turned to grip the tub of food scraps. 'Help me empty this in the field.'

The pair manoeuvred the tub from the kitchen, up the steps and into the garden. Noise from the crowds died down.

80

Christy arrived at the studio with daylight fading. She gripped the box of Harriet's effects that Jay had kept secret. Jammed in her pocket was the letter from the studio.

As she nudged forward to the gate, a sea of people came at her in waves. The cotton T-shirt that showed off her pregnancy didn't prevent her from being jostled, and she felt she might be pulled under at any moment. She eased her way to the edge of the crowd and the safety of the railings. Ahead lay the red brick of the studio building, about one hundred metres away. If she was lucky, she would get inside the grounds. Each step was taking her closer to Jay. She nudged forward again.

Another few metres on and Christy found herself blocked by a Sonny – tall, muscular and as impassable as a tank. She gingerly tapped his shoulder and he turned to show off an impressive special-effect scar that hadn't yet smudged, despite the evening heat. Thankfully, he noticed her bump and thrust some people aside.

She moved forward and came face to face with Jay.

Glasses, brown hair carefully parted to the left, a Rubik's Cube and a can of beer. The man was so like her Jay, and yet nothing like him. She steadied herself using the people around her as a hush suddenly fell over the crowd.

The screen showed Olivia and Taran walking to the woods. They took the middle path to a clearing where the composter sat. Taran set to work feeding tomatoes through the hatch, while Olivia snapped celery stalks in half. Each snap echoed across the subdued spectators, who watched open-mouthed and mesmerised by the beads of sweat rolling down Olivia's forehead.

Picking up the empty tub, Taran turned to go back inside. Olivia loitered, her face shielded from the camera. 'Come back, Taran. I want to show you something. Look what I've found.'

Taran stopped some way off. 'What is it? Show me from where you're standing.'

'No, come here. Look. What do you think this is?' She pointed to the ground. Taran's tutting boomed around the studio forecourt and he stepped closer to Olivia, who was bending over. She spun round. She was gripping the dagger.

Christy screamed and grabbed the nearest person's arm. She closed her eyes. People gasped and cheered as Taran and Olivia struggled.

*

Inside the house, Jay trailed Bow across the common area. 'Where are those two?' he said, standing on tiptoe and peering out to the garden.

'Scrapping the food,' Bow said. She sat at the end of the sofa and turned to him. 'Sit down, listen and don't interrupt.' She wore a serious expression.

Jay scanned the area. He sat at the near end of the other sofa and removed his glasses to clean them with his T-shirt. His belly showed as he grabbed the cotton. It was looking flabbier than usual. Three weeks sitting around. Starting tomorrow, he had exercise to do. 'Go.'

Bow spoke clearly and slowly. 'I was telling the truth the other day. Taran is your match. Patty was mine. I know for sure because we discussed it. The day you saw her distraught in the garden …' She paused until Jay confirmed he remembered. 'That day I convinced her to sit tight and wait, so that we would win.' Bow wrung her hands. 'I gave the gun to Saoirse. I told her to shoot Sonny, but she killed Patty instead. Something went wrong. All that must mean Olivia's here to get me.'

'Is Olivia related to Patty?'

Bow's shrug was slight. She lowered her gaze. Jay could sense there was something Bow was withholding.

'Let me ask you. What was your crime?' he said.

Bow contemplated. Then she explained. 'I was responsible for several deaths.' She told him about the explosion on the building site, how she'd been stoned and failed to operate the lift.

'You're telling me you'd never met those people in the lift before?' Jay asked, rubbing his chin. Bow nodded. 'And you never discussed it with Patty in detail?'

Bow shook her head. 'We skirted around it. Had she asked, I would have talked to her about it. But whenever I saw the pain in her eyes, I couldn't bring myself to cause more hurt.'

'Do you know what this means?'

'What?'

'You didn't really confirm that you and Patty were paired. Neither of you spoke explicitly about the crime?'

'You think we've jumped to conclusions? Impossible. She was my match. And Taran is yours.'

'Wait. It makes no difference. I am not doing this. I don't care if I starve here. They are not going to make me kill. We're connected now. We've come through so much, you, me and Taran.'

'Talk of the devil,' Bow said, looking over Jay's shoulder.

Jay turned to see Taran nudge his way through the sliding doors. His face was expressionless as he fumbled down the stairs and flopped over to them. Jay jumped in his seat.

Taran was clutching his stomach and blood gushed between his fingers. He fell to his knees and toppled forward.

81

Jay rolled Taran over and gasped at the blood streaming from his stomach.

'Olivia's got the wrong fucking person! We've got to act now,' Bow said.

Jay locked eyes with her. He nodded. They knew what had to be done. 'I'll keep him breathing. Get the knife,' he said.

Bow dashed outside, calling for Olivia.

Jay leant forward, inches from Taran's face. 'Taran? Can you hear me?' Taran's eyes opened. 'Hold on, buddy. Stay awake.'

Taran lifted his head a fraction, caught sight of the blood and yelped.

'Look away. Look at me.' Jay placed his hand behind Taran's head. 'Please Taran. My sister, Harriet. She died a few months ago on a street in Glebe. What happened?'

'I never killed her.' Taran fought to breathe. He closed his eyes. 'I'm sorry.'

'Please Taran. Tell me.'

Glossy blood spread over the floor.

'There's not much time. How did you know Harriet?' He shook Taran's arm to get his attention.

'I didn't know her. When I arrived, she was on the ground bleeding.'

There were footsteps. Bow raced through the door and down the steps. She dropped the dagger by Jay.

Jay drew back to refocus. 'Go on, Taran. What else?'

Bow screamed. 'We need to fix this, or Olivia won't get out of here. You've got to do it now, Jay. His breathing's shallower. We don't have time!'

Taran opened his eyes. 'I never touched her. I crouched down. To see if I could help. Her things were on the floor.' He took a short breath. 'All bloody she was.'

Jay winced at the image of Harriet attacked and dying. He felt Bow nudge him.

'Hurry, Jay!'

Taran spluttered and winced. 'She opened her eyes. Blood everywhere. "Who did this?" I said and –'

'Taran, tell me.' Panic made Jay's voice rise. 'Open your eyes. Who did it? Did she answer you?'

Taran's eyes opened. 'No. She fell in and out of consciousness. She couldn't speak properly. Blood was pouring out of her neck. I put everything in her pockets.' Taran turned from Jay and whimpered. 'I'm sorry. Sorry.'

'Taran? Why are you sorry?'

'I put everything in her pockets. To help. I felt the money through her clothes.' Jay leant back, his hand resting on Taran's arm. Taran coughed. 'A … weakness. I took her money. I'm paying for it now. But she was dying. I didn't kill her.'

'Jay! Kill him!' Bow shouted. 'He's dying. You can save Olivia and end this properly. He's your target!'

'Wait!' Jay shouted over his shoulder. 'Taran, did you see anyone?'

'A car passed by and slowed right down. I went to wave, but it drove off. A woman driving.'

'Didn't you tell the police?'

'Yes. But it was no use. They found my DNA on the money.'

'At the trial, did any other suspects come up? Taran! Stay awake!' Jay flicked his cheek.

'Save Olivia!' Bow said, shrieking. 'When you kill him, it's all over.' Jay turned to Bow and shook his head. She pointed at the dagger. He had to act now. Beside Jay, Taran's twitching fingers found the dagger handle.

Jay sat back on his heels, his face in his bloodied hands. He choked through his breaths. 'I can't do this.'

'This is for Olivia.' Bow grabbed the dagger and thrust it into Jay's right hand. 'Look away, Taran.' She pulled Jay's left hand onto the knife handle and stepped back.

Jay whispered close to Taran's ear. 'Olivia must leave. There's no other way.' He prodded Taran's bony chest looking for a gap in his ribs. 'Don't look.' He twisted the blade into Taran's clothing to position the tip of the dagger. He looked to Bow, who nodded, and he thrust the dagger into Taran's chest. Taran let out a short and shallow groan as Jay scrambled away, bringing a trail of blood with him on his trousers.

In the quiet house, there were no flashing lights, no fanfare, no music to mark the occasion. Only Jay's disturbed breathing and sobbing.

'Something's wrong,' Bow said. She heard a sound at the top of the steps. Olivia stood there frozen, her eyes locked on Taran's body, the blade upright in his chest.

Jay was numb. His legs wobbled as he came to his feet. Lifting himself onto the bench seat seemed an impossible task, but he managed it. He turned away from the deathly scene.

82

Jay's breathing returned to normal. He cried out from his seat. 'Where are the goddamn balloons?' He held his arms up high, his fingers splayed to stop them sticking with Taran's blood.

'I did it!' he screamed to the ceiling. 'Happy? You got your final murder. I killed an innocent man!' A bolt of energy shot though him. He stood up. 'Who killed Harriet? It sure as hell wasn't Taran.'

Bow's voice almost broke. 'Scot? Talk to us. It's over. Why isn't it over?'

'What's going on?' Jay asked, staring up at a camera.

Then Scot spoke. 'Housefriends, the show ends when only one killer remains.'

Jay pointed at Taran. 'He's dead. There's only Bow left. She wins.'

Bow checked Taran's pulse. She nodded to Jay that Taran was dead.

'What's happening?' she cried, to a quiet house.

Scot's voice came slow and serious. 'Jay Perry Marsden, we find you guilty of murder.'

Jay frowned. He had no energy for more messing around. Bow stared at him with a blank look. Jay pointed to Taran's corpse. 'I had to kill him! He was dying anyway!' From the corner of his eye, he saw Bow nod. 'We did it to save Olivia.' Exhaustion weighed Jay's body down. 'Stop this. Whatever it is, stop it. Please.' He was losing his voice.

'You must pay the price for the woman you killed.'

'What?' Forehead creased, Jay went from camera to camera. 'I've never killed —' His insides turned to stone. His skin seemed to freeze in a second. 'Oh no.'

All the lights dimmed and a grainy image appeared on the wall above their heads. Footage, restored and coloured to give it a crisper quality, began to play. A woman in a bed looking into the camera.

Jay felt the air leave him. His legs became watery, incapable of holding him up, and he fell back into his seat. He recognised her instantly. Anita Lessing, who he had recorded killing herself fifteen years earlier. His words got wedged in the back of his throat. 'Je—'

In the footage, Anita's wasted body lay immobile under a bright red duvet. Jay, white gloves on, passed between her and the camera twice. He was younger, with shorter hair, no glasses, but it was unmistakably him. Through the house speakers came the sound of people knocking at Anita's front door. Jay's voice was clearly audible as he and Anita spoke about the baby in the room. Anita's screams for Jay to hurry grew louder. Her final words and her dying gasps filled the house.

Jay went to stand again, but his knees buckled and he landed on the floor. He cried out with his last remaining energy, steadying himself on all fours.

'That wasn't murder! It wasn't. You've set me up!'

In that moment, so many things made sense, like the final square on the Rubik's Cube slotting into place. He remembered the day he had been taken from Christy. Bundled into the van. That day in the woods, Walt had said he'd had time to farewell his wife. But Jay had been ambushed. No way could the show risk Jay not arriving at the studio. He was their plot twist.

His clues, too. All along, they had referred to Anita, not Harriet. Never Harriet. He recalled an early clue. When she had needed her friends most, they had deserted her.

He managed to get to his feet. 'Anita was dying, you fuckers! They wouldn't let her control her own life. I'm here for Harriet!'

'Assisted suicide is murder,' Scot said. 'You murdered a woman – a young mother – and you must pay. There is no statute of limitations for your heinous crime.'

'This is a set-up!' Jay said, spinning around, turning to each camera. 'Come on then. Who's here to kill me?' Bow made a noise behind him, and he registered someone close by. He spun around but it was too late.

In a flash, the dagger slid into his stomach. Sharp pain jolted through him and his vision darkened. Agony radiated along his limbs. He became aware of his entire body, from his toes to his fingertips, which twitched almost mechanically. He felt as though he'd been cut in half. He bent forward and gripped the handle. His hands found Olivia's. Their eyes met. Eyes he had recognised almost as soon as she'd arrived in the house. Only now did he admit to himself that they were so like Anita's. The baby from his dream.

'Liv? Is that you?'

If he'd had the strength, he would have stepped back to get a better view of Anita's grown daughter. Memories flashed through him. Changing nappies. Rocking her. Feeding her.

Burping her. Beneath the colossal pain of the wound lay a bed of regret. Had he refused to help Anita that day, perhaps he could've helped secure a better life for her child.

Olivia bared her teeth. She reminded him of Anita. Her round eyes, her jaw coming out slightly, a toughness softened by pink cheeks. Her hand relaxed under his grip.

'Let me go,' she said. She struggled to break free.

Jay shook his head, which only intensified his pain. She would have to finish the task. His teeth ground together. He dared not look down, but he could feel warm blood dripping onto his feet. Another wave of scalding pain ripped through him. He mouthed, 'Please'. Fifteen years ago, Anita had begged him to steal poison from his laboratory, to kill her. And now, here he was, pleading for her daughter to return the favour.

Olivia's fingers gripped the handle tighter. He took his hands away. Moments ago, his exit from the house had seemed so certain. Now, the marble walls seemed hundreds of metres off, the roof a mile high. He would never leave this place. There was no way out. Tears formed in Olivia's eyes and Jay closed his. An image of Christy came to him. But all too briefly, it was interrupted by Olivia wrenching the dagger out of his gut. Jay screamed. Holding his breath, he straightened himself up to present his body to her. He felt his wound stretch. Within seconds, the blade went in again. He lost his balance and his head came to rest on Olivia's shoulder. She shuddered and stepped back to let him slip to the floor.

Had he lived, he would have heard the music blare. He would have seen rainbow lights dance over the walls and balloons blow over the sofas, the hot tub, the dining table, the island.

He would have seen streamers float down over Bow, the winner of Scot Free Six.

83

In the studio forecourt, the crowd watched the streamers cover Bow. People roared and drowned out Christy's stricken screams. As she thrashed in pain, they thrashed in joy. Music thundered around them and fireworks lit the sky, raining red and green tears above her.

She had been carried away from the railings and was now adrift in the sea of bodies. She gripped Jay's box of mementos as hard as she could and kissed it. Pain shot through her body and she felt one knee scrape the ground. Her lungs burned. An intense heat erupted in her chest and she crumpled to the ground.

Only when a man stepped on her hand did people realise she had fallen. Two women helped her up. One shouted into her friend's ear and pointed at Christy's stomach.

Christy felt herself lifted away to the safety of the fence. She was handed to the security guards and they guided her to the nearby medical tent.

Inside, a doctor offered her a seat at a trio of chairs. She handed Christy some water.

'This place isn't for everyone. It's much more intense than it looks on the telly. Plus, you're pregnant. How many months?'

Christy sipped the water and looked around. There were two low stretcher beds across from where she sat. At the opposite end of the tent from where she had entered, two thick flaps of material covered another opening, which Christy guessed must lead on to the building.

'You sit there as long as you like. Do you speak English?' Christy looked to the exit. She bit her lips and nodded. 'You're pregnant. I can't give you much. Stay until you feel better. Who are you here with?'

There were shouts and footsteps outside. A security guard half-entered the tent. 'Doctor, we've got another one out here. He's collapsed.' The doctor followed the guard outside. They returned within seconds, propping up a man in a school uniform. His skirt was short, his blouse tight and his face heavily made up. They positioned him on a stretcher bed, then the guard left.

Christy looked around the tent again. She had to get to Jay, to see his body. She left the cup of water on the floor and eased herself up. Her legs already felt stronger. Her breathing was better. She took small steps backwards to the heavy flaps that led to the building and watched the doctor minister to the semi-conscious Olivia. When she felt the canvas behind her, she slipped between the flaps and turned around.

It was a trade entrance. She was standing in a brick vestibule, which meant she was almost inside the studio. A swing door blocked the way. She pushed it and, to her surprise, it opened.

But three metres ahead, a set of locked double doors with no windows stopped her. There was a security pass reader on the left wall. It was as far as she could go. She cursed.

Behind her, glass partitions in the door panels afforded her an unbroken view back to the tent. Nobody was following. It didn't matter. She couldn't advance.

She fought back the sting of grief. There was no way she was leaving without saying goodbye to Jay. She could try returning to the tent and demanding to see him, but that wouldn't get her far. Alone in a brick corridor with two routes. She didn't want to go back the way she had come and she couldn't advance on the route she wanted to take. Tears stung her eyes.

From nowhere came a burst of abdominal pain. It intensified and her legs wobbled. She grabbed her bump with her right hand and propped herself against the wall with her left, still clutching Jay's box. A sharp pain tore around her belly. Her hand slipped down the wall as she lost strength and the box bumped the security pass reader.

Click. The doors ahead swung open.

Christy froze. She thought someone was approaching. But there was no one around. Almost instantly, the doors began to close again. Pushing the pain aside, a burst of energy helped her step through the doors in time and they closed behind her. She wasn't in a trade corridor anymore. It was office space. She was inside the Scot Free studio.

She studied Jay's box, unsure what had happened. She waved it over the reader again. There was the clicking sound. The doors reacted on cue. She opened the box and her heart quickened.

The fob.

Jay's secret fob worked here, at the studio. Questions began swirling in her head, but now wasn't the time. She put the fob back inside the box and gripped it tighter. Adrenaline ripped through her body.

She took a huge breath and ran along the corridor, the

mementos rattling inside the box. Each time she got to a locked door, a wave of the box over the reader cleared her way. She stopped at the lift and pressed the button. She didn't know where she was going, but she would check as many floors as she could before she was found out.

The ping of the arriving lift echoed like a drum. Her heart pounded against her chest. She gasped when a man walked out.

'Oh, you scared me,' he said. 'Are you okay? You look a bit … well, you er … must be new? I'm Everton.'

Christy settled her hair. 'Tough start. Second day here. I'm lost, to be honest.'

'This is a staff exit to the car park. Where are you heading?'

She recalled the name on the letter from the studio. It was the most specific information she had. 'Adolpha. Adolpha wants me.'

'Adolpha?' He looked her up and down. 'Where's your ID?'

Christy noticed his T-shirt. Four cartoon computers in a circle linked with cables. She read the quip. *I know my boundaries. I'm a LAN.*

Christy looked directly at him. 'I lost it. She found it. That's why I'm after her.'

Everton whistled. 'You're lucky. She'll be in a good mood because we finished the season with a bang.'

Christy stepped into the lift before the devastation on her face could give her away.

'You won't find her in her office,' Everton said. 'She's in the suites. Third floor, the one at the end of the corridor. Knock before you enter. Bow and Olivia have just left the house and Bow's due onstage any minute. Before she vanishes.'

The lift doors started closing. She relaxed, but Everton stuck his foot between them. 'Are you armed?' He looked at her suspiciously.

'No.'

'She is.' He removed his foot and the lift doors closed.

In no time, she was outside the third-floor suite. She took another breath and put her hand on her heart. Whoever was on the other side of the door, inside the suite, might have heard the thuds in her chest. Over her shoulder, she looked down the long corridor, back to the lift.

She turned the handle.

84

At the far end of the suite, among the screens, microphones and desk controls, were two people. A lithe, brown-haired woman sliced the air with a fencing foil. She advanced to her seated male colleague, who was swiping his mobile screen.

Christy closed the door behind her. It was the only exit. She swallowed hard. Each thump of her heart hit her dry throat. 'I came to see Jay. Where is he?'

'Who are you?' the man asked, getting to his feet. He stood beside Adolpha stiffly.

Adolpha rested the foil over her shoulder. 'Alan, meet Christy. Jay's girlfriend. You can't see Jay's body. It now belongs to the state.'

Christy gripped the box tighter, feeling the thin tin shift under the pressure. She stepped further into the room.

'What did I just watch?'

An image of a young Jay, mid-twenties, flashed across her mind.

'You didn't know about Anita?' Adolpha grimaced. 'I'm sure Jay would've told you one day.' Her voice trailed off. 'Trust takes time.'

'How did you get hold of that tape?' Christy noticed Adolpha looking at her stomach.

'Authorities have had it for years, waiting for advances in technology. We restored the erased sections of the tape. Our film specialist produced the footage that you saw broadcast tonight. Unfortunately, Jay didn't make it through.'

Christy choked back tears. 'He never had a chance. You set him up.'

'He had a debt to pay,' Adolpha said.

'You murdered him!'

Adolpha inched closer. 'Excuse me. I saved his life!' She prodded her own chest. 'I cut the power in the tub. Nicky would've electrocuted them all.'

'He was a good person,' Christy said. 'He lost —'

'Helpful to a fault was Jay,' Adolpha said, giving exaggerated nods.

'He was my best friend.' Pain returned to Christy's stomach. She winced.

Adolpha's voice changed. She spat her words. 'He killed a woman, Christy. She took her own life with drugs he'd procured. All while he looked on. A lower act you cannot find. The state doesn't give us that autonomy.'

Christy searched their faces for any sign of compassion, any sign of remorse. Nothing. 'You're sick,' she said. 'It's not the law you care about. It's the show. You got hold of the footage and you waited.'

'I gave viewers an unforgettable treat. Tonight, audiences in every corner of this great land witnessed a defining moment in reality television. Where the justice system failed, Scot Free stepped up. I'm proud of the finale.'

Christy hardly heard Adolpha's words as she became aware of Jay's box in her hands. It all had meaning. She went on, almost to herself, 'And then Harriet got murdered. How convenient.'

Adolpha withdrew the foil from her shoulder and pointed it at the ground. She looked away. Alan gazed at the ceiling.

There was silence as Christy studied them. She started to notice a shift in atmosphere. Slight, but it was there. Something didn't sit right. Perhaps it was how close the pair stood to each other. Or their lack of movement, waiting for Christy's next move. But the longer they stood still, doing nothing and saying nothing, the more Christy's heart leapt. A chill made the hairs on her arms stand on end. Her stomach cramped.

'How did you get up here?' Alan asked, finally.

Christy's hand tightened around the box. She still couldn't see the connection between Harriet and the building fob. Yet, there had to be one. In her confusion, she thought aloud, 'How the fuck did Harriet die carrying a pass to this building?' She shook the box, making the meagre contents rattle about.

Alan's head dropped.

'What do you have there?' Adolpha asked. She pointed the foil at her.

'Stay away.' Christy moved backwards until she nudged the doorframe. Her mind was a muddle, but she knew she had to leave. Accessing the building had been a mistake. A huge one. She'd come to mourn Jay's death and now her life was in danger. The baby's life.

Adolpha and Alan stared at her.

Christy pictured her route out of the building. A dash to the lift, down to the basement, out through the medical tent. She breathed in. Her lungs felt strong, as did her legs. For now, her stomach felt fine. At her back, she grabbed the door handle without turning around.

'Would you like to see Jay?' Adolpha asked.

'We can arrange access for you,' Alan said. 'It's the least we could do. Take a seat.'

From the far end of the room, two pairs of eyes stared at Christy. Without warning, Adolpha chucked the foil in the air and grabbed it on its way down. She caught it like a javelin. With gritted teeth, she launched the foil across the room.

Christy spun round to open the door. She felt a pull on her scalp, where the tip of the blade caught strands of her hair. The foil hit the wall and clattered to the floor. Christy screamed and ran out, closing the door. She headed to the lift. Behind her, she heard the door open. Alan was chasing her and Adolpha watched on from the suite entrance.

Christy's heart pounded in her ears. The lift doors opened and she rushed in. She slammed her hand down on the buttons and watched the panel light up. In the rush, she dropped the box. The lid popped open and the contents spilled out. Both doors started to close, but Alan's hand appeared in the narrowing gap. She shrieked and scooped up Harriet's hatpin. With all her strength, she rammed it deep into the back of his hand.

He howled and fell backwards, clamouring to remove the hatpin from his skin.

The lift closed and began its descent. Christy gasped for air. In her panic, she had pressed too many buttons and the doors opened at each floor. 'Come on!' she screamed, shoving the remaining things back in the box.

After an age, the lift reached the ground level, one above where she had entered the building. There had to be a way out. People would be around. Security teams. Best to get out now. Outside the lift, there was only a right turn. A sign directed her past the reception desk to the main exit.

Sliding doors were straight ahead. Her chest eased and she

breathed more fully. A burst of warm, scented air enveloped her as she exited the building. Music and crowd noise filled the night. At the far end of a courtyard was the security screening point she had bypassed on her way to the medical tent. That was her way out. Beyond that, she would be safe, lost within the screaming hordes. She crossed the open area. To her right, she spotted the medical tent. Security guards saw her half-running towards them and she slowed down. She placed a hand on her belly and made eye contact with the guards. They stepped aside and she passed through the turnstiles, ready to seek refuge in the crowd, metres away.

She heard running behind her. Alan arrived at the turnstiles but stayed behind them. He nursed his hand. She was safe. She spun around to lose herself in the crowd, but someone blocked her path.

Adolpha grabbed Christy's forearm and lifted it in the air with the force of three women. She twisted Christy's wrist and plucked the box of mementos from her. Christy yelped.

'Is that a little Jay or a Jane you're carrying?' Adolpha asked, lifting the lid of the box.

With her free hand, Christy served Adolpha the hardest punch in the face she could muster. This brought two guards over to them.

'Leave us,' Adolpha said to the men. She pushed Christy away and removed the fob from the box. 'You're wondering why Harriet died with this on her.'

Puffing, Christy shook her head. She didn't care. She had to get out of the gates.

'Let's make a deal. I keep this,' Adolpha said. She pocketed the fob and thrust the box violently into Christy's chest.

'What do I keep?' Christy asked.

'Breathing.'

85

Harriet stood in the doorway of a derelict gift store, its recessed shopfront blocking the wind. From the shadows, she flicked the butt of her rollie into a puddle. Light from the streetlamps confirmed the shower had stopped. She debated her next move. Going home with so much cash on her was risky. Her housemates were the snooping kind. There was the option of asking Jay to let her stay. But he'd want to know what was up, and Christy would be there.

Out of nowhere, a man stepped under the shopfront cover and said something about a lighter. He was agitated, eyes darting under a cap pulled low on his forehead. His small steps back and forth had her trapped.

She tucked the money in her pocket and went to pull out her lighter.

He struck. The knife entered her chest twice before she managed to respond. He paused, waiting for her reaction. Dropping what was in her hands, she grabbed his sleeve. This seemed to spark a frenzy in him, like a switch had gone off. He yanked her towards him to serve blow after blow. His cap fell to the ground. In his fury, the chain he had around his neck came out from under his shirt.

Her splayed fingers caught it and broke it. She felt herself falling. She hit the ground, an object in her grip.

*

Sniffling, Alan scooped up his bloodied cap. He would need to destroy it. He ran to the waiting car, where Adolpha held out a green bin liner and a towel. He placed the knife in the bin liner and cleaned his hands and face with the towel.

'Is she dead?' Adolpha asked, starting the engine. 'She has to die.' Looking straight ahead, Alan nodded and stifled tears. 'Good,' she said. 'Let's get you cleaned up.'

In the quiet, Alan noticed his hearing was muffled. He only heard the rhythmic click of the car's indicator. It blended with his booming heart.

Click, *boom*.

Click, *boom*.

Click, *boom*.

Adolpha made a U-turn. They slowed to a crawl as they passed the shop, where a man was leaning over Harriet. He looked their way, but Adolpha accelerated.

Her expression was steadfast.

'Welcome to Scot Free Six, Jay Marsden.'

86

Hours after the season ended, Alan stood smoking on the fire escape. Five floors below, the rigs for the screens were coming down, and beyond the studio gates the crowds had all but dispersed. Little sound travelled up to him and a steady wind stole his grey smoke. In his left hand, bandaged and sore, he cradled his phone. Bow's exit interview was replaying.

Asked by the presenter if she had a message for her fellow inmates at Barton, Bow nodded and stared down the camera. Her voice floated from Alan's mobile. 'Superintendent Carlisle, you may never replace me. It's all pot luck.'

Alan heard Adolpha before he saw her. He tucked his phone away. She was talking on hers. The fire exit door opened and hit the wall, and she stepped onto the balcony, her heels clattering on the metal. Alan took a last drag of his cigarette and threw it over the edge.

She had no good reason to join him. She despised cigarettes. She despised him.

'Sup – Superintendent Carlisle, this is standard. I'll do nothing of the sort.' Her voice was infused with irritation. 'I am going home now to have a celebratory drink and watch the repeat. As season winner, Bow is entitled to her prize. And that includes freedom and –' Adolpha passed the phone between her hands as she let Superintendent Carlisle interrupt her. 'No, you listen. Bow, your prisoner, failed the drug screening before the season started. We don't ever need to speak about the test result, but if you –' Her look confirmed Carlisle had hung up. She clicked her tongue. 'He got there in the end.'

Grabbing the rail, she nudged closer to Alan and took in her surroundings. 'Ooh, this is nice. Your own little place away from it all. I feel like I'm stepping into your office. Are you going to make me feel welcome?'

'Welcome.' He lit another cigarette and blew smoke out vertically.

She retreated. Her heels seemed to rattle the entire fire escape. 'I nearly twisted my ankles racing down these stairs to get that blasted woman.' She watched the crew dismantle the rig. 'I normally don't like to see the screens packed up. It's sad. But we're finishing on such a high. We've broadcast arguably the best scenes in SF history. In Australian television history. We'll get even more seasons out of tonight. We should be very proud. And two more murders than the sponsors thought they were getting. They're beside themselves.'

'That's how we want it,' Alan said.

'Good things come to an end and we say goodbye.' Alan went to puff his cigarette but stopped. She held out her hand and stepped to him. 'I believe this is yours.' Without looking, he extended his arm and opened his palm. He knew what she had. His old fob. 'Forever tidying up after you. It's not good, Alan. It will be a miracle if Jay's girlfriend doesn't go to the police. A pregnant woman broke into the building carrying your security pass, which you dropped that night. She's strong-willed.'

Adolpha fell silent. Muffled clanks and dings from the crew working below sounded like an orchestra that was dying.

Alan blew smoke upwards and waited. Adolpha clearly had a plan. He wasn't going to make it easy for her. She played with her phone.

'There'll need to be an accident. It can't be suicide. That would ruin us.' She leant over the balcony and pulled her head back sharply. 'That is some drop.'

'Do we need to act right now?'

'I have the show to think of. I can't keep saving you, Alan. Jay's dead. Christy won't let that go, knowing what she knows about his sister's death.'

'Why did you let her walk free?' He stepped towards Adolpha. She backed away from the edge.

'She's pregnant. There were witnesses.'

'There must be another way. We scored the television hit of the decade tonight.' He blew more smoke.

She waved the fumes away and headed to the door. 'Smoking while you plead for your life. Pathetic.'

'Wait.' He stepped closer. 'Why did you save me after season three? You had your chance to get rid of me when the massacre ended that run.'

Adolpha looked up at the stars, as though it pained her to say it. 'Because, most of the time, you work well.' She opened the door and turned back. 'Up here is good. Someone could easily fall from where you're standing.' She stepped inside the building. Before the fire exit door fully closed, she poked her head out. 'And Alan' – she waited to catch his eye – 'don't screw this up.'

Part 7

Show off

87

Close to midnight, Alan was alone in the building, except for the ground floor porters. He moved through the office. His emergency bottle of Absolut, normally hidden in his desk, swung in his hand. His wound was hurting more. He could see the skin starting to bruise under the bandage. From a cupboard, he took one of the season's unused weapons. A cutthroat razor. Adolpha had rejected it early on because it hadn't looked menacing enough onscreen. 'We might as well send in a paperclip,' she'd said. Alan slid the razor into his pocket.

He took the lift down to the main production suite. At the control desk, he fiddled with an array of buttons and adjusted the scheduling. Footage from the grand finale that was currently airing on the Scot Free channel would end in fifteen minutes. Then a live broadcast from inside the house would start. He piped classical music through the house and raised the lights.

Everyone watching at home would witness Alan's special screening.

Carrying the razor, the vodka and his cigarettes, he entered the house through the garden. The night air was still warm and carried the fragrance of gardenias. He passed through the sliding doors and sat on the edge of the hot tub, which he had refilled a little earlier. Cleaners had already removed the bodies of Jay and Taran, and the place was ready for the next season that would never come.

He opened the razor blade and laid it on the ledge. He drank half of the vodka and savoured the burn in his throat, the familiar throb in his body. There was time for two cigarettes. The first one was soothing. Over the chorus of violins, he heard the fizzle of the butt hitting the water. Beautiful. Adolpha would hate that.

His phone alarm sounded. The broadcast was about to go live.

One final scene to go to air.

He rolled up his sleeves. Time for the second cigarette, which he smoked slowly. Smoke rings became his final creation. He destroyed one with his finger but let the others go free. One more drag and he drove the butt into the soft flesh of his wrist. He sucked in air through gritted teeth. His cigarette went out and he tossed the butt in the water. Burning skin.

After removing his shoes and socks, and checking his hair in the window, he climbed into the water. The ideal temperature. With the warmth intensifying the sting, his burnt wrist and wounded hand were the only submerged parts of his body that he could feel.

He found the best spot in the tub. Where the dark eyes of the cameras stared down. His head rolled to the swooping violins. He patted around the tiles behind him for the razor blade. The steel was cold, hard. He peered into the camera. One eye stared back. Adolpha was watching at home, for sure.

'Goodbye seasons seven, eight, nine. Time to make this place Scot free.' He chuckled to himself.

Vodka coursed through his blood and a symphony swirled through the house. He brought his forearm out of the water. No longer his limb, it was a violin itching to be played. His other hand gripped the gleaming metal bow. He was set for the performance of a lifetime. A pause in the music was his invitation to begin. He squeezed his lips in concentration and played. With vigour. With passion.

Part 8

After show

88

A year later

Christy squeezed knitted boots onto her daughter's wriggling feet.

Eyes wide, the baby stared up. A smile was about to break out on her face.

'There you go, precious. Don't you look heavenly?' She placed her hand behind the baby's head, which sported a mane of black hair. Christy lifted her up as if she were made of glass. She settled the baby on her shoulder.

'Promise me you won't be sick. Aunty Teddy will be here soon.'

*

The courier rang the doorbell. She held a cake box up high so that her face was obscured. A young man in a party hat opened the door.

'Package for Saoirse.'

'It's my birthday. I'll take it.'

'She needs to sign.'

He walked off, leaving the door wide open. 'Mum. It's for you.'

Moments later, Saoirse appeared. Hair styled, a little make-up, new dress. Her attention went to the package.

'Who sent this? We've got one for him. Well, we had one. We're halfway through it.' Only when the courier stepped inside the house did Saoirse's gaze lift from the cake.

The courier brought a finger to her lips, revealing tattooed knuckles. *HARD*. Saoirse gasped and fell back to the wall.

'Nicky.' Saoirse's voice broke. Tears came straight away.

Trembling, Nicky handed over the cake. 'Shush,' she said. 'They might be watching the house.' They squeezed hands for a few seconds. 'I have to go.' She gave Saoirse a wink. 'Please read the card, Madam.'

*

The doctor laid the baby on his back and brought his chubby legs together. The baby's mother jiggled a toy lobster as a distraction.

'I thought I'd bring him in. To check, you know. I … worry.'

'He's a healthy boy. You've nothing to worry about. With his legs, it's hard to say at this age. Babies often have a bit of a bow. They're all curves, aren't they? We can tell better in a year or so.' He relaxed his hold on the baby's legs and brought them together again. 'But if he has it, it won't be pronounced.'

'Mine was visible early on. Apparently.'

'That happens sometimes. You must have a more pronounced form of it. If he's lucky, he takes after his father.' He handed the baby over to his mother.

'His father had good genes, strong bones.' She zipped her jacket up and settled the cloth carrier across her chest. Her baby fought, but finally slipped between the tartan folds. She put a woolly hat on him. 'What he didn't have was longevity.' An image of Sonny with a bag over his head sprung into her mind. She pushed it away.

The doctor accompanied her outside the small building, which was perched on the western edge of the settlement. South Atlantic gusts lapped them instantly and her hand came up to shield the baby's face. Tristan da Cunha felt like the end of the world and the start of a new life. Brooding sea for three hundred and sixty degrees. Above, white clouds and blue sky.

'It takes my breath away to watch the ocean roll past. It's unnerving at times,' she said.

'Are you sure you should be on an island?' the doctor asked, with a half-smile. He watched her free strands of hair from her mouth. 'You'll get used to it.'

'How long have you been on the island?' she asked.

'I came from Argentina two years ago.'

'Ah. You speak Spanish.'

He nodded. 'Do you?'

'No,' she said. 'No other languages.' She kept her gaze on the rolling waves.

'Why Tristan?' he asked, moments later.

'An old boss had a picture of it above his desk. He'd summon me to his office. For years, I'd stare at that photo and dream of living here.'

'Summon you? He sounds like a bit of a tyrant.'

She patted the baby's back through the carrier. 'That's why I had to escape.'

'That's exactly what this place is,' he said. 'An escape.'

ACKNOWLEDGEMENTS

My immense thanks go to:

Toni Jordan, my incredible mentor. Whoever would have thought I'd get to this point after our paths crossed that day in the café. You were a godsend, and you helped me see beyond the words on the page to who my characters truly were. Thank you for your stellar commitment to this project. It is an experience I will forever treasure.

My wonderful test readers. Your feedback was vital as I shaped the story and curbed (most of) the excesses of creativity. You told me when I'd crossed a line or hadn't even assembled one. I owe so much to the international writers group I belong to, with special mention going to Beth Buechler and Patricia Jablonski. I must also thank local readers Bronwyn and Barry Guy. Please give Tilly a hug for me.

Christina Roscoe. I asked a key question about knitting and you delivered! Next time I'm in Hobart, dinner's on me.

Brian Radam at The British Lawnmower Museum and Eddie Batchelor. Thank you for your machinery know-how. You helped me bring life to some pivotal scenes.

Simon Dunne. Thanks for your invaluable insight into construction zones.

Jeremy Barbouttis. I am indebted to you for your work on visualisation. It seems that you saw the screen in my head clearer than I did.

Victoria Cook, Katie Kearns, Claire Smith of BookSmith Design and Kerry Cooke of eggplant communications – the editing and design experts who made my words sparkle. I am so grateful for your skill and creativity.

Dr Neil James, Dr Peta Spear and the team at Plain English Foundation. How lucky we are to work in an environment where we practise writing every day. The techniques I've learned with you all have truly served as a foundation for my crime fiction path.

The Australian Society of Authors. Thank you for your outstanding work in supporting independent authors and the local book industry.

And finally, my family and friends, especially Dympna, Ella, Jacintha, Matthew, Nadine, Sophie and Stephen. You kept me motivated when it felt like I too might become trapped in the Scot Free house. And you let me test wild ideas out on you when you could never be sure where my fiendish mind would lead. Your support is more valuable than you know.